"YOU'RE MINE NOW...
AND EVERYONE IN THIS
CITY KNOWS NOT TO
TOUCH WHAT'S MINE."

BEHIND CLOSED DOORS

ALSO BY SHAIN ROSE

**STONEWOOD BILLIONAIRE
STANDALONE ROMANCES**

Inevitable
Reverie
Thrive

**NEW REIGN
MAFIA DUET**

Heart of a Monster
Love of a Queen

**TARNISHED EMPIRE
STANDALONE MAFIA ROMANCES**

Shattered Vows
Fractured Freedom
Corrupted Chaos

**HARDY BILLIONAIRE
STANDALONE ROMANCES**

Between Commitment and Betrayal
Between Love and Loathing
Between Never and Forever
Between Desire and Denial

BEHIND CLOSED DOORS

SHAIN ROSE

kensingtonbooks.com

KENSINGTON BOOKS are published by:

Kensington Publishing Corp.
900 Third Avenue
New York, NY 10022

kensingtonbooks.com

All Kensington titles, imprints, and distributed lines are available at special quantity discounts for bulk purchases for sales promotions, premiums, fundraising, educational, or institutional use.

Special book excerpts or customized printings can also be created to fit specific needs. For details, write or phone the office of the Kensington sales manager: Kensington Publishing Corp., 900 Third Avenue, New York, NY 10022, attn: Sales Department; phone 1-800-221-2647.

The K with book logo Reg US Pat. & TM Off.

First Kensington Trade Paperback Printing: March 2026

ISBN 978-1-4967-5817-0 (trade paperback)

10 9 8 7 6 5 4 3 2 1

Printed in China

Electronic edition: ISBN 978-1-4967-5818-7 (ebook)

The authorized representative in the EU for product safety and compliance
is eucomply OU, Parnu mnt 139b-14, Apt 123
Tallinn, Berlin 11317, hello@eucompliancepartner.com

Dear reader,

Thank you for taking a chance on reading Jameson and Mia's story. I know that I am a reader who loves surprises, and so I enjoy going into each book without any spoilers or content warnings. Yet, this is your experience now, not mine. So, I want to give you the opportunity to know what sensitive content may be in my books. You will find the list here:

shainrose.com/content-warnings

BEHIND CLOSED DOORS

1

Mia

"HE'LL BE HERE SOON. He's never late." Franny's dark curls whipped in the wind, hitting my favorite patchwork dress as she stood beside me looking out over the horizon. Her tiny fingers threaded through mine almost instinctively.

Squeezing them gently, I reassured her. "Of course he will. Your father probably called the phone inside and I didn't hear it while we were out for recess."

She nodded solemnly and mimicked my tone. "Yes, of course."

She stood as tall as she could and smiled tightly. I sighed. "You sure you don't want to go play on the swings for a bit?"

Her blue eyes stayed glued to the lush green rolling hills. Franny, at the age of seven, was an old soul who was not willing to engage in frivolousness when she thought something might be wrong.

"My mommy didn't pick me up from school one day," she shared. Her concern became more evident when she continued, "Then she never came back."

It wasn't my job to pry into the child's homelife. Summer school was all I could provide—or rather, all I was *told* to provide. Despite that, I responded with, "But I bet your dad probably came instead, right? He always comes."

She didn't even hesitate. "Yup."

"Then there is nothing to worry about," I said confidently, but doubt crept in. No cars were in sight down that road. So, I pointed over to the swings. "Look, I put some extra flowers above your swing this morning. Why don't you tell me what scents you're smelling over there?" I'd threaded lavender into the bouquet last night and tied crystal beads in, too, hoping it would give the children a calming effect.

Each of my five students for the summer were always wound tight. There most likely was a study out there that stated it would make them successful in the future, somehow. They were products of high-achieving parents, ones that sent nannies to get them from school or were on phones as they drove in daily for pickup.

Franny's father, Jameson, was always present without his phone though. Every day, he would get out of a black SUV and kneel to catch Franny as she ran into his arms.

He was prompt, never late. And never dawdled to talk about much with me either.

"I'm not super interested in swinging with flowers right now, Ms. Darling."

"I know, Franny. Would you feel better if Xavier went to go call him inside?" I pointed behind us toward the ornate building where one of the armed guards stood.

Blackstone Academy was an imposing, secluded, stately structure. The first time I saw it, I almost resigned. Surely, they didn't want me, a woman in her twenties with only a few years of teaching experience, to be the supervisor of this entire school for the summer. It had to be hundreds of years old, all stone angles with a Gothic central tower that reminded me of medieval times. It was clear it had been built for many students, and during the school year, it housed some of the most elite college kids from around the world. Yet, I'd been informed I would be making it a welcoming classroom for just five second graders for the summer with only the help of armed guards.

"Well, someone should call him." She huffed like she was the teacher.

It was probably that time. Twenty minutes had passed since the last student had been picked up. Normally, I didn't call. I'd been hired at this private academy as a last-minute addition and didn't want to ruffle feathers by overstepping. This was unprecedented though. "Xavier." I turned back to one of the armed guards. He wore black and didn't so much as look at me unless I asked him to. "Could you call Franny's father and see if he's headed this way?"

His small shake of the head signaled all I needed to know. Something was amiss. He glanced at his partner on the other side of the porch and then murmured into his headset. "We're calling."

I heard the rumble of engines just as Xavier's partner started talking to someone. The scramble of guards overtook the serenity of Blackstone Academy and Franny tapped my leg. "Who's that driving to see us?"

I watched the cars speed around the winding road, moving so quickly, I could see smoke as they turned the corners. It was almost picturesque, the way they shined in the sunlight, such a juxtaposition to the surrounding nature.

"Ms. Darling." Xavier's voice was close now and much more commanding. "You both need to go inside with Archer immediately."

"Inside?" The question tumbled from my mouth as Archer jogged over and tried to take Franny's hand. I gripped it more tightly and pulled her close. If my children's parents weren't present, I was their guardian. I stayed by their sides. I kept them safe. It might not have been what I was told, but I felt it all the same. So much so that I'd overstepped at my last job and almost been fired.

And still I would do it again in a heartbeat.

Archer narrowed his dark eyes at me, his brows slamming down. "We've got a safe space inside. Out here, you're exposed and . . ." He glanced down at Franny, who was listening intently.

"Okay." My voice shook, but I tried to keep calm even though their stances suddenly seemed on edge. "Franny, we're going to play inside for a bit. Mr. Archer here will show us where to go. We'll play a fun little game of hide-and-seek for a bit, right, Archer?"

I shoved my loose chestnut waves away from my face while I shuffled Franny ahead of me, keeping hold of her while Archer hustled us in from behind. He explained, "Yes, hide-and-seek is my favorite game, Franny. And there's a secret spot I want to show you. You're going to be very quiet in there, okay? Because we only want your daddy to find you and no bad guys."

"That's weird." Franny wasn't convinced. "Daddy doesn't like games. He likes to get home so we can have dinner."

"Oh, today, he will love this game," I said with conviction, even though I had no idea. Jameson Knight, although beautiful and open with his daughter, was a locked box with me. I'd only gathered he was a creature of regimented habit by observing he was always on time to pick her up. He also wore a different version of the same suit every day. I guessed that he owned dozens of that specific style. They were impeccably tailored for him, too, draping flawlessly over his massive shoulders and hitting his wrists at precisely the correct length while tapering nicely down his torso. Plus, someone must have advised him on the color selection as well with how each suit always complemented the deep ocean-blue hue of his eyes.

Not that I was looking.

I was simply his daughter's teacher. I didn't care about how his powerful jaw flexed every time he glanced at me or how those blue eyes seemed to hold judgment. Instead, I was happy he smiled genuinely at his daughter every single day and said in a clipped tone, "Always a pleasure, Ms. Darling."

Truly, I didn't believe it was a pleasure for him to see me at all. And from those chilling glances, I would guess he'd hate any sort of game.

"He also doesn't like bad guys," Franny continued. She was right about that. With the love he showed his daughter, he'd despise any bad guys coming her way.

"It's just a game we planned, Franny."

"He didn't tell me about it. I would have brought my binoculars," she pouted. It was the one game Franny really enjoyed like a kid. She'd pretend to be a spy, observing things in the distance with her binoculars some days.

"Well, today, he's the spy. He knows to find you right away, okay?" Archer said in a soft voice he used only for the kids.

I'd gotten to know the guards this summer, saw how they played with the children and how they talked with the parents. They were sweet and trustworthy, but when I glanced behind me one last time, I saw Xavier pulling an enormous gun from behind his back. I knew they always carried them but didn't pay much attention after the first day because things didn't go wrong here. This couldn't really be happening.

The first bullet whizzed by, precise and powerful in the air, like a knife cutting through the wind. One of the arched windows shattered just a room over as my heart rate skyrocketed.

Darting into the great hall, Archer slammed the door behind us right as Franny cried out, "What was that?"

He was speaking in his comms while pointing across the room. I felt my breath coming faster and my body starting to shake. But Franny's hand squeezed mine tighter. I knew she'd see panic if I didn't contain myself. I took a breath again and said, "Part of the bad guys coming in the game. They're just trying to scare us. Ready to hide? There will be a prize later if you win!"

"This way. Let's hustle. Your dad is almost here, Franny," Archer said, giving me a small nod as I glanced back at him. He motioned us to the right, where we ended up in the formal living room that boasted wood floors, cathedral ceilings, and paintings over the fireplace that I knew were expensive. With the vast amount of space, I'd always felt overwhelmed with how to utilize it. Now, all I could do was seek out where to hide.

Every day, I'd bring students in here to read to them while they sat on the ornate Persian rug, drinking homemade lemonade. There was a grand piano and a fireplace, but nowhere to hide. Not until Archer rushed forward and yanked the rug back. He knelt and dragged his hand across the wood, where he found a groove. When he pulled at it, the boards swung up together like a small door, but the underside of them had a lining of pure, thick metal. It was a sort of small panic room.

Never had they shown me this feature of the academy. Shouldn't I have been trained for this, given a warning about the likelihood of it happening while I was teaching, or maybe tipped off that my children's lives were at stake? I would have prepared. Or at least tried to.

When I took the job, they had glossed over emergency procedures. I was only told that there would always be guards as a precaution and that they would be up to date on all mandatory protocols. I could rely on them in case of an emergency. With a substantial salary and their protection, I didn't ask questions and reassured myself that we were safe, that nothing life-threatening would actually happen, even when the children made comments about their parents doing extremely secretive things.

He waved us in. "Fun, right, Franny?"

The small room was lined with metal, and nice oak chairs along with a table were set up a ways in. Six chairs, like they'd planned for me and five children specifically. There were also tablets with headphones and snacks. He pointed. "Want to watch your favorite show while you wait for your dad?"

She hesitated and looked to me. "Heart-in-pinkie promise it's all okay?"

There are pivotal moments where a person has to make life-altering decisions. They're made after analyzing every single aspect or in a split second, based solely on a gut reaction. Right then and there, I knew Franny was a kid who could read a situation better than most, and she didn't trust easily.

Throughout this month, we'd built a bond deeper than I had with the other students. It may have been partly because she stuck by my side most of the day, but also, she'd told me once that promises were easily broken, so she didn't believe in them. When I told her I put my whole heart into promises when I kissed my pinkie and she could count on that, she didn't seem to believe at first.

Yet, trust is built one promise at a time. And every heart-in-pinkie promise I made her, I kept.

Promise by promise, our bond was formed, and I wouldn't break it now.

My gut made the decision for me then. "Heart-in-pinkie promise, Franny. It's all okay." I would have to make sure of it, even if it literally killed me.

My little student was all smiles as Archer put her headphones on and pressed a few buttons. Once she was situated, he pointed to the wall of monitors. "Watch these. There's a lock on the door. When I swing it shut, turn it and don't move it for anyone but Jameson. You understand?"

"Should we call the police or . . .? What if Jameson doesn't make it?" It was the only thing I could think of.

The popping of bullets flying sounded nearby. Not just one, but so many this time. Hundreds over and over so fast, like my beating heart. "He'll make it. Just stay here." He was backing away.

"But you're leaving? You can't stay in here with us?" I said fast, sounding pathetic as I glanced between him and Franny. How could I protect her by myself? I didn't have a weapon or even know how to use one. I was a teacher, not a trained assassin.

"I have to get outside to hold them off. Jameson and his crew are five minutes out." He was looking at Franny and then I was looking at her, too. She was smiling at the show, completely unfazed.

"Five minutes?" I squeaked. That felt like a lifetime. But I could do it. Would have to do it.

His face was grim. "You'll be okay. Reinforcements are coming."

I cleared my throat and tried to take one breath slowly so that I didn't scream accusations at him. I smoothed the worn fabric of my dress and nodded. "Right. We'll be fine. Just hurry."

Another round of gunshots rained overhead, and Archer scrambled out quickly. The last I heard from him was, "Five minutes, Ms. Darling. If I don't hold them, you better."

2

Mia

I SHOVED THE LOCK as hard as I could right as Archer closed the floorboards over us. The clicking of metal seemed so secure and final, but the sound of guns firing didn't leave me with much reassurance.

Hurrying over, I sat down by Franny, who was already deep into a show. She glanced up at me as I folded my hands in my lap. They were shaking uncontrollably, and I didn't want her to see.

Still, she leaned in and grabbed one before she spoke loudly over her headphones. "Don't worry, Ms. Darling. Daddy will find us. Right? He doesn't like games, but he's great at hide-and-seek."

I nodded while she kept rambling on like any seven-year-old would, wanting to share all the information.

"Did you know my daddy's a doctor? He always saves good guys. The bad guys are the *only* ones that should be worried."

"Of course, of course," I agreed while I patted her little hand. I wasn't going to disagree with a second grader right then, but there was no way her dad was a doctor. Unless it was for the cartel or something.

Jesus. What if he was in the cartel?

I took a deep breath and pointed to her tablet, trying to get her to focus on that. She was the child, I was the adult. I had to shield her from whatever this was. Her gaze shifted, and I was able to look behind her at the security camera feeds.

I'll admit, for the past few years, I was voluntarily sheltered. Maybe even abnormally so. My parents were still married, living their best life in the small town I grew up in. Not that I wanted to go back there or that I would talk to them if I did. My older sister knew why I left and why I couldn't come back.

Her and my parents. But my parents had stopped listening a long time ago, and even still, I tried to make them proud by Bubble Wrapping my life and living out my days watering my plants with not even a pet to commit to and a career that was a safe and noble profession. At least that was what my advisor told me.

Kids couldn't be monsters, right? Yet, I forgot that parents could be and would be. It was really the only reason I took this job. The public schools weren't going to have me back any time soon after what had happened.

This job may have been a little different with the abundance of background checks done before I started. Yet, the summer salary was good, good enough that maybe I'd have enough to tide me over for a year and even help my sister out if she ever chose to leave her mess of a husband.

It was supposed to be an easy summer job.

Instead, I was committing to a heart-in-pinkie promise, locked away in a panic room while I watched security feeds, hoping no bad guys would come for us.

One camera showed the horizon we'd been looking at out front. The driveway now had more SUVs flying down it. I squinted and hoped they were Jameson's. Even if they were, I didn't know if they'd be fast enough for the yelling I heard above us.

There was thumping of footsteps before I saw one man fly into view, weapon raised as if he were ready to shoot at anything.

His boots sounded heavy and large, like he could crush our little panic room below.

Then, Franny giggled at her show. I swung my gaze to a small air vent and then the screen. My breath caught as I winced at him stopping suddenly. And my heart jumped into my throat when his boot thumped one step toward us. As quietly as I could, I tapped her shoulder and put my finger to her mouth, signaling to be quiet.

She shrugged and looked back at the cartoon while I stared at the monitor, stared at that large man with a mask on. I was still staring when I heard a small, almost soft *thwack*, then his whole body crumpled to the ground.

I frowned at the screen and saw that behind a couch, Archer had hidden. He now looked like a man trained to kill rather than talk sweetly to a child. He didn't move an inch as he waited for the second and third men to enter the room.

None of them he had to touch. He dropped them with the same precise aim. The blood splattering onto the camera lens only looked a dark gray, the black-and-white screen shielding me from the brutal scene.

Archer didn't drop the fourth man as quickly. He waited, like he didn't want to kill him immediately. The popping of bullets sounded in the distance, but Archer wasn't using his gun now. He waited and waited until the fourth masked man walked near his couch, and then he lunged for his weapon. They both fell to the floor, grappling right above our heads.

I glanced at Franny, but those headphones must have been the best soundproof, noise-cancelling kind since she was still smiling.

And just as that masked man was disarmed, Jameson Knight walked into the camera's view.

I heard his muffled voice talking to Archer and the man as he unbuttoned his navy suit jacket. He placed his jacket on the couch before he took his time folding up each cuff of his white collared shirt, one fold perfectly bending into place before he started on the next. "Who do you work for?" he asked the man.

The man shook his head even with Archer holding a gun to him. Jameson motioned for Archer to lower his weapon, and as he did, Jameson pulled a knife from his pocket at the same time.

"This is my *daughter's* school. The only person I care about. You get that?" He stepped close to the man and pulled the mask from his face. "Did you come for her?" he asked.

The man's eyes widened, but he didn't admit to anything.

Jameson was professional and cold, but I knew how he was genuinely kind to his daughter. There was no way he would hurt this man, I told myself.

Yet, he murmured one more sentence I couldn't make out before he shoved the knife into the man's stomach and then wrenched it up toward his throat so hard there was no time for the man to reply. He dropped to the floor with another loud thud.

Then, Jameson's cold gaze turned directly toward a security camera like he was peering into my soul as he unrolled his sleeves and put his navy suit jacket back on. He was covering up the speckles of blood on that white shirt and was careful as he stepped over the bodies. He walked over to the rug and pulled it up. "Unlock the door, Ms. Darling," I heard from above.

I shouldn't have hesitated, although my body froze for a second. I was either opening the door to killers or I was staying locked inside.

"Ms. Darling?" I heard again.

All it took was a flick of my wrist to move that metal and for Jameson to lift the floorboards.

Light shone in as he opened the hatch, and Franny peered up, her blue eyes filled with happiness as she said, "Daddy! You found us. Told you he would, Ms. Darling."

He walked down the steps and knelt at her side, his arms open wide and that smile just for his daughter back on his face. When he looked at me over her shoulder, though, his gaze was cold. "I'm taking Franny outside to her grandma. Archer will escort you out."

With that, he scooped up Franny and told her to keep watching her tablet. I heard her laugh fading away while I stared at Archer. "I don't think I should go up there."

"Just keep your eyes forward, and we'll get you out of here, okay?"

"No thank you." I shook my head, but I didn't have much of a choice as he reached in and grabbed my elbow to yank me up the stairs. I hated that my first instinct was to squeeze my eyes shut, that I didn't want to see in full color what I'd only seen in black-and-white on a screen.

"Hey, it's okay. Just . . ." Archer had that sweet voice again, like he was talking to one of the students. "Focus on what's outside the window, okay?"

He turned my body toward it and told me I could open my eyes. When I did, I saw a car toppled over in the distance but, more importantly, I saw Franny standing stoically beside an older woman. She wore a black dress, pearls, and sunglasses. Her dark hair was done up in a smooth bun, and she smiled wide at Franny like this was a beautiful day filled with rainbows and sunshine.

"She's safe and happy, Ms. Darling. You did great. Do you have any belongings upstairs?"

Safe. Happy. Great. Words that couldn't describe the day at all. "Belongings?" I said as I frowned, not comprehending exactly what he meant. "I mean I have my clothes and a dresser full of things. I have my plants. Ms. Prim needs to be watered daily, and my bonsai finally has decided it likes me." I stopped myself from going into detail about my plant care routine.

"Do you need to take them all with you?"

"Take with? I'm . . . no." I stepped back, glancing around the room. "No. I'm not going anywhere. I need to clean—"

"What's going on?" Jameson cut me off as he walked back in and frowned.

"She needs a minute."

Jameson's jaw popped before he nodded at me. "Do you have important belongings you need upstairs? You don't have time to dillydally, Ms. Darling. Unless you intend for Franny to witness something she can't come back from."

"Can't come back from?" I said in a high-pitched tone as my eyes jumped around the room, taking in the destruction. "Mr. Knight, I would never intentionally harm Franny." I breathed out, feeling dizzy all of a sudden.

"I know." He pinched the bridge of his nose. "Just . . . We can discuss everything later, okay? We have about eight minutes until four more SUVs come flying up the road. So, I'm trying to be understanding, but we don't have time for you to go into shock right now. We need to get you out of here."

I glanced at Archer, and my question sounded shaky even to me. "What if I don't want to go with you?" He rubbed at that strong jawline of his in irritation. "I have a car. I'll just go my own way."

Now, Jameson closed his eyes for a brief moment, like he was actually annoyed with my antics. "You have nowhere to go, Ms. Darling. I know that because you wouldn't be teaching my daughter if you did. You're coming with us." He looked at Archer then and said, "Get her in the vehicle while I grab her things."

Jameson turned his back on me for a second, and that's when instinct kicked in. I moved to run away, but Xavier walked in right then, clocked me, and was faster. He raised his gun and pointed directly at me. "Don't make me shoot you, Darling."

I gasped and Jameson spun around. "What the fuck are you doing?" He paced toward Xavier, moving directly in front of his gun and pointing his own at the man's temple. "Don't threaten my daughter's favorite fucking teacher. She's the reason Franny smiles every damn day. You cause her trauma, and I'm gonna kill you. Understand?"

"Jesus Christ. We don't have time for this," Archer grumbled, stomping toward the stairs and leaving Xavier and Jameson in a stare-off.

Suddenly Jameson's hand gripped Xavier's wrist and twisted. The man yelped while his gun fell to the floor. "Stand down, dumbass."

"Fuck, Jameson," Xavier bellowed, the grown man kneeling to the floor to alleviate the awkward position of his wrist before Jameson let him go.

"My men think before they pull their weapon. Or I blow their brains out. Understood?"

Xavier winced and nodded immediately. The man was using brute force and everyone was just going to listen to him?

"Search the house and pack up her essentials," Jameson told him, and I saw Archer pick up the pace as he rounded the corner to go upstairs with Xavier following.

I tried to counter Jameson loudly, though. "Don't get my things. I'm not going."

Jameson lifted a dark brow as he turned to face me. "You can't go off on your own or stay here, Ms. Darling."

"Actually, I can." My tone was shaky, but I crossed my arms over my chest, trying to seem confident. "I'm your daughter's teacher. Nothing to you, nothing to anyone else. Whoever came here doesn't care about me. He—" I pointed and glanced over at the man lying on the ground. Blood was still spreading across the wood floor, that thick red liquid seeping into the cracks, staining the ground where my students had played just hours before. I whispered, "Oh, God. Should we help him? Aren't you a doctor of some sort?"

"He's dead." He said it with finality, but he also stepped into my line of sight, blocking my view so I couldn't focus on it longer. "We need to go."

I closed my eyes, trying to erase the scene from my memory. "They don't know me. Just let me go, and you'll never see me again."

I felt his hand on my cheek, a thumb brushing across my skin. I opened my eyes to see how close he was, to see that his gaze looked concerned rather than annoyed with me now. "That's the point, Ms. Darling. My daughter and I *want* to see you again. So you are coming with us."

I licked my lips to keep them from trembling as I breathed out. "And if I don't, Mr. Knight?"

He sighed, his jaw ticking as he stepped back, breaking our connection. "You either come willingly or I drag you *unwillingly*. You understand?"

My eyes were drawn back to the pool of blood as he stepped away. They were stuck on the fact that he'd done that, that my class and summer were now tainted.

I couldn't go with a man like that. I wouldn't be forced to stain the sheltered life I'd made for myself.

My body reacted before my brain. I lunged for the back door, ready to sprint to my keys and my car. I wasn't exactly a runner, but I could move quick enough if my life depended on it. I had a fighting chance, but I only made it three paces before Jameson's hand was around my neck and he slammed me into the wall.

He'd gone for the most vulnerable part of my body, where he had me at his complete mercy. He moved closer. So close that I had to look up at him, but I could also feel his strong body against mine. "Don't make me use force, Ms. Darling. It's something I enjoy too much."

My breath came fast now, adrenaline going. I watched him glance down, tracked how his gaze lingered on my lips, and wondered if he felt my pulse racing under his hand.

"Seems you might enjoy it too. And this isn't the place or the time for it."

He had some audacity to insinuate that right then. "Are you kidding me? I'd never— Let go of me," I seethed. At that moment, I didn't care if he killed me, I was so mad. I slapped at his wrist and then said, "I knew you were all corrupt. I should have never taken this job."

"Too damn bad." He shrugged like this was a normal conversation, like his hand wasn't still tight around my windpipe. "Franny loves you. You make her happy, which in turn makes me happy. Know what that means?"

"What?"

"I'm taking you with me, whether you like it or not."

I narrowed my eyes now, ready to fight. "Want to bet?"

With that, he threw me over his shoulder, literally kicking and screaming. I clawed at his back and fought the whole way. He didn't falter one step. It was like I was fighting a damn brick wall.

They had me in an SUV to his hometown within minutes.

He'd told me to act right or he'd drug me.

So, I was drugged.

And when I woke in the most beautiful bedroom I'd ever seen, handcuffed to a bed, I screamed like a banshee into the night.

But then Jameson came to the room and leaned against the doorframe. "I'm going to make you an offer you can't refuse, Mia Darling. Still, if you do, I promise I'll let you go. But be aware, they *will* kill you without my protection."

3

Jameson

The promise was empty, and Mia Darling wasn't an idiot either. She had to know I wasn't letting her go. She was an intelligent woman who'd fallen victim to the brutality that was my life.

Or she'd chosen that.

She wasn't an innocent bystander. The children of the academy, the salary, and the contract she signed when she started made it quite clear she hadn't just taken a job at a normal school. There were NDAs, protocols, rules she had to agree to.

All completely necessary considering that now, she was a witness. A pretty, sweet witness who I'd tried my best not to notice all summer.

Had I known she was going to give me this much hell, I might have reconsidered bringing her here.

She yanked her wrists against the bed with a lot more force than someone should have had after a drugging. "Who's *they*? I might be better off with them than with you."

"Doubtful." O'Connor's men would have disposed of her almost immediately. We'd already pinned the incident on him. O'Connor was the head of the Irish mob out East and I knew they were frustrated with how I'd continued to push them into turmoil, but it was bigger than just them. They'd all pay for it in the end.

"You drugged me and expect me to just comply? Like an idiot?" She yanked again. "Let me out of these cuffs this instant, you freaking asshole."

"Asshole?" Okay, I wouldn't have reconsidered. Her surprising need to fight me at every turn since the incident should have pissed me off, but it intrigued me all the same. She'd been an outstanding teacher to Franny. Kind and compassionate. Never missed a day. Provided daily reports. And was utterly professional.

Until now. I found myself smiling at the fact that she wasn't scared of me and had a colorful way of showing it. "I've been called much worse by people with much more power. You'll have to do a bit better than that."

"Fine. Entitled piece of shit. Kidnapper. *And* asshole." Her warm brown eyes burned and sparkled with fury and emotion I'd never seen her exhibit. I had her file, knew most everything I needed to about her, that she was as clean as they came and that she didn't cause trouble.

Except for one complaint where she stood down another teacher and parent to protect a student. That complaint made me want her working for me even more. I hadn't held it against her but instead hired her because of it.

Her small frame and soft demeanor had always seemed to emanate a sort of wholesome goodness, but there must have been fire there if she'd step in the line of fire for her students. Even still, my men provided updates about the sweet teacher. "A true darling," some of my guys had mumbled here and there.

Not to me, it seemed.

"Well, calling me an asshole isn't going to get you anywhere." I walked over to the dresser at the side of her room near her en-suite bathroom. We'd placed her in one of the spare rooms on a quiet wing of my estate that overlooked a lush tree line. The bedding was cashmere, the walls a soft cream, and the curtains sheer. It was supposed to suit her. Or at least the version of her that existed when she wasn't warring with me.

Lined up across the top of the white dresser were her two plants. They were green, bright, and wildly full of life. One had compact hot-pink blooms and another dark leaves with tiny clustered flowers much too delicate for the things to have survived us transporting them.

Then again, my men had glared at me like I'd lost my mind when I told them to keep them intact. Touching one of the leaves, I added, "Especially after I made the effort of bringing these plants here."

"I don't care about plants while I'm being treated like a prisoner." She exhaled sharply, but then she glanced at her plants like she might need to apologize later to them. "I'll be happy to call you *Mr. Knight* if you uncuff me."

"Jameson." She'd been around my daughter long enough that we could be on a first-name basis. "You know I can't uncuff you until you settle down."

Her eyes widened, not in fear but in wild fury, like her desire to fight was overtaking her. She wasn't scared, and my respect for her grew just a little. Another note to make.

"You entitled piece of—" She stopped short of another swear, looking down at her clothes. "Did you undress me?"

"You were groggy when we got here. You may not remember, but Rosy helped you change. Took you to the bathroom. Got you cleaned up. She's our estate manager." We'd treated her exceptionally well. Rosy had even expedited some clothing for her, although the getup she was wearing wasn't a part of that. Rosy insisted she'd be more comfortable in her own attire, so now cartoon plants dotted her ass.

"Oh, well. How sweet. Should I thank her?" She sneered the question and wasn't at all appreciative.

Her small pajama shorts were all rumpled, along with the button-down shirt that matched. With all the consideration we'd taken in such extreme circumstances, I actually thought I might have received a thank-you. Sure, maybe I should have taken better care of welcoming her, been ready when she woke up, and allowed for her to be free of any restraints. But after the struggle we'd had in the SUV, she'd earned this.

She challenged me further when she curled her body and legs up, as if to get as much leverage as possible, before kicking out directly into the bedpost. She hit the wood so hard, I jumped.

And then she did it again. Over and over as she ground out, "You can't just kidnap someone and get away with it."

"I'd hardly say it was a kidnapping. I saved your life." I figured she would tire within ten seconds, but when the pounding of her kicks continued past that, I knew I had to stop it. "Mia, the wood of that bedpost is near a foot thick. You're going to hurt yourself."

"Or I'm going to break your ridiculous bed." She grunted, kicking it again—hard. I saw how her wrist twisted in the steel of the handcuff, and then how she yanked even harder, the skin not standing a chance.

She didn't wince or even hesitate as blood dripped down her arm. She recoiled her leg and slammed her foot into the post again, gritting her teeth. "Who even has bedposts this thick?"

"*Fuck.* Stop," I grumbled, hurrying toward her, but she was like dealing with a rabid animal by this point. Even as I wrapped my forearm around her waist, she struggled in my arms, elbowing me in the gut before she fought harder.

"I want out of here now, *Jameson.*" She hissed my first name like vitriol, her voice frantic.

"Don't make me drug you again," I threatened.

"You'll have to keep me drugged the whole time I'm here if you don't uncuff me right this second. And soon I'm going to start screaming—that will really annoy you."

"Do not." I lost my patience and the command flew out loud with authority. "You'll upset Franny, and she's already been through enough."

Finally, she froze. And her eyes melted from fury to honey in an instant. She whispered, "Franny." And turned to look over her shoulder at me, her brows dipping in concern. "Is she okay?"

"I think so." My voice softened too. "She needs peace right now, though."

She chewed on the inside of her cheek, and her plump lips pursed for a few seconds before I felt her body relax under my arm. "I won't scream or run, but you need to uncuff me. I won't be held anywhere against my will."

She was talking to me like I was her freaking student, like she had a leg to stand on when I could have done anything to her at that moment.

I assessed the situation and almost laughed. Glancing at the cuffs, I leaned in close to Mia and murmured against her cheek, "You realize you're in no position to make demands, right?"

She didn't move away but breathed out slowly and matched my tone. "You realize I'm your daughter's favorite teacher, and I've calmed her down more than once. I'm guessing you need me, or I'd already have been disposed of."

Not that I was going to share, but my daughter had been happier this month, more willing to open up, more of a kid. Franny was quiet when her mother left but we'd always had a bond, one I was scared we were losing with how much work I had.

My daughter asked for Ms. Darling to stay. And I wasn't going to tell her no. Especially not after I'd informed her that Ms. Darling was just sleeping on the way back to the estate.

She'd narrowed her blue eyes at me, fierce in a way that mirrored my own, before saying, "She didn't even want to come with us, Dad. What did you say in there to her? You scared her with those men, and if my teacher ends up not liking me, I *won't* forgive you."

Ruthless. And direct. If her words hadn't landed like a punch to my gut, I'd have been impressed.

"What men?" I'd asked her, because I thought she'd been watching her tablet.

"I heard *bullets* flying past us, Daddy." She rolled her eyes like my treating her as a child was ridiculous. "It wasn't a game. I want Ms. Darling here. *Safe*. And I don't want her to leave like Momma did. Please make sure of it." She patted my hand, and that was it.

That thought had me pulling away from the woman even if I didn't want to. Even if I wanted to choke her into submission again. To breed some damn fear where she should have had it.

The sooner I got Ms. Darling to cooperate, the sooner I'd be able to soothe my daughter, to right this situation.

I stood and looked down at her as I pulled the key from my pocket. "I'm going to let you go, but like I said, this is the place you're safe. I'm protecting you, not holding you against your will."

"I'll be the judge of that once I'm out of handcuffs."

Nodding, I stuck the key in the lock and removed the cuff from her wrist. I left it hanging on the bedpost as she pulled her wrist away and rubbed a short, green-manicured nail over the bloodied gash there. "I'll have a first aid kit brought to you for that."

Her nose wrinkled at me as she stared in what looked like disgust. "Well how nice. After today, could you send a psychiatrist and a whole police crew also, Mr. Knight?"

"Yesterday," I corrected her.

Her pretty lips plumped in confusion. "I've been out a full day?"

"Give or take a few hours, yes. No police will get involved, but if you'd like to talk to them, fine. As for a psychiatrist, they'll explain that you have PTSD, that you should take care of yourself, and potentially have therapy. I'm happy to schedule you an appointment with mine, if you'd like, over the next few weeks."

"I don't want an appointment. I want a plane ticket home."

"I told you you'd die if you left."

She studied me, as if she were trying to figure out a math problem or an impossible equation. "I think I might just take my chances."

"Afraid of me, Ms. Darling?" I asked the question because I wanted her to be. It held power, and I'd embrace wielding it over her or anybody if it got me what I wanted.

"No." One word that challenged me, taunted me, and made me more intrigued with her than I normally would ever be with a woman. It was especially true now because I heard the tremor in her voice, caught how she'd wanted to say the word with conviction but faltered just at the end.

"So you're choosing to be reckless and stupid with your own life," I summarized, straight to the point.

Her eyes widened. "How dare you—"

"I'm not a teacher and you're not a child. I'm not going to coddle you."

"Is that what you think I do all day?"

That came out wrong, but I wasn't going to admit it. Dragging a hand down my face, I tried my best with a different angle. "I don't have time for bickering, but you're staying . . . For your safety. And for my daughter's well-being." The latter was mostly what I cared about, what I needed her for.

"And how long will I have to stay for that?"

For as long as my daughter needed. Mia's needs weren't my concern. But my daughter's love for her was. With me working overtime to ruin everyone who'd threatened my child, she would need stability.

And the idea that Franny was being targeted as leverage meant my relationship with my daughter had to change too.

Everything had to change, but not at the detriment of Franny if I could help it. If Mia could help it.

I'd keep the nuisance here as long as necessary. Instead I answered, "At least until the end of the summer."

She spun around, as if looking to grab anything of hers she might be leaving behind. My crew had packed most of her belongings, and she hurried over to her purse and a duffel. "I think leaving today is better."

"You're not leaving, Ms. Darling." I waited a beat. "You've signed a contract that commits you to providing services to the children of the academy for the summer. Do you recall?"

"That . . . was a job offer." Her hands fisted together enough that her tan knuckles whitened. "Look, let's be frank. If you're keeping me here because of what I saw, honestly, I barely talk to my older sister, and definitely not my parents. I . . . don't have many friends. I won't tell anyone—"

"You could tell the whole world, Darling. No one would do a thing. You're here because Franny will need you this summer."

She pinched her lips together before murmuring, "Someone *shot* at your daughter and me. We had to hide in a crawl space. I should have been made aware that there was a possibility I would actually have to use such a thing."

Fuck, did she want an apology? I wasn't born a gentleman or a businessman. I'd grown up with a father that wasn't and a mother that could endure the most brutal shit in the world. Kindness was only a tool where fear and power were threaded behind it as a base.

Still, Mia Darling was a necessity, because I had a daughter that I didn't want raised in the same type of world I was raised in. I hated admitting fault, but I appreciated that she'd included my daughter in her worry, nonetheless. "I should have had better control of that situation, Ms. Darling."

That's all she would get from me.

She raised a dark eyebrow and crossed her arms as if she wanted more. "I agree. And then your response was to kill them and choke me. Can you at least control your response in the future?"

What the actual fuck? Was she now reprimanding me like I was the child here? "You're using the word *choke* very loosely. If I'd choked you, you'd be dead."

"*That's* what you want to argue about?" she almost screeched as she threw up her hands. After snatching her purse up, she shoved it over her shoulder. "You know what? You have a beautiful home from what I can tell. And an absolutely perfect daughter. I don't know what type of life you're living here, but I know I want no part of it because it must not be legal."

"Jump to a conclusion like that, you'll find yourself in a hole you can't crawl out of."

"It doesn't really feel like *I'm* the one in a hole here. I mean, were those people there for you yesterday, or for your daughter?" I opened my mouth to answer, but she continued. "Actually, don't even tell me. I don't want to know. That way, I can wash my hands of this more easily."

It was actually best she didn't learn more about my life. She only needed to be involved in my daughter's. "So easily? So you don't care about my daughter at all then?"

"What?" Her stance snapped upright, and those pretty brown eyes ignited with a blaze that was wild. "Don't twist my words when it comes to my students."

"You'd leave her?"

She frowned, and I knew I had her. She'd need to stay, but I could warp her perception if that's what it took. She gripped her purse so tightly I saw the whites of her knuckles as she fought with herself on what to do.

"My daughter still needs a teacher."

"Teachers don't live with families—"

"A nanny that teaches, then. Franny would be devastated if you left. Surely you can adjust to a new environment for one of your students."

As if on cue, my innocent little girl came barreling into the room. "Ms. Darling!" she cried, and the woman's face changed from fury to pure, unfiltered joy.

"Franny! Oh, my sweet Franny."

I might as well have not been in the room in that moment. My daughter flew at this woman like a chick finding comfort in a mother hen.

And Mia Darling welcomed her by dropping to the ground to catch and curl around her like she could protect my daughter from the world—and from me. Her eyes filled with tears instead of anger as she soothed Franny, who was now sniffling in her arms. Mia didn't look at me but focused solely on calming my child.

She must have surmised that I was abominable as a father, a man who'd hurt my own baby.

My jaw worked up and down. It was an accurate assumption, honestly. Even if I hadn't meant for my world to bleed into my daughter's life, it had. For a child, she bottled her emotions exceptionally well. I figured she mustn't have been aware of the gravity of the situation, but even still, I'd brought in the best child psychologist to talk with her yesterday.

Valerie was a trusted employee and had been a stand-in for a nanny for quite some time. She'd assured me that my daughter didn't have signs of trauma, that she'd seen almost nothing and was okay.

Franny sniffling was not "okay" behavior, though.

I considered whether I wasn't observant enough, hadn't

parented well enough, and had overlooked my most important priority.

"I thought you were hurt," Franny whispered, but then her eyes widened as she took in Mia's scraped wrist that was, of course, bleeding now. "Oh, you are!"

"No. No." Mia hurried to cover her wrist with the white sheet and wrapped it around her shoulders. "Those are just some scrapes from . . ." She glanced up at me. "A terrible bracelet I had on."

"Ms. Darling, my grandma always says if jewelry hurts, it's not good enough. I had earrings once that weren't for sensitive skin. They made my ears bleed too. You'll need a Band-Aid for your wrist." Franny frowned and then looked at me. "Daddy, make sure you fix her wrist, okay?"

I nodded slowly and considered my daughter's concern, considered how her eyes softened when she peered up at her teacher and murmured, "No one told me anything after how mad you were on the way home. Then Grandma said we had to leave you. I didn't want to. The hide-and-seek game wasn't very fun for you, was it?"

"I'm not sure I love hide-and-seek," Ms. Darling whispered as if they were sharing a secret.

"I didn't like that game either." Franny wrinkled her nose and glanced at me like we all knew the secret of the game. Then I heard it, the genuine laugh that fell from my daughter's lips. Pure. Real. Rare. I hadn't heard it since yesterday, and the more I worked, the less I heard it. I was sure I'd do just about anything as a parent to continue to hear it.

Even if it was keeping Ms. Darling.

"Probably there was too much blood for you, Ms. Darling." Franny's small hand smoothed over her teacher's cheek. "Daddy says some people are afraid of blood. I'm sorry."

Seems Valerie missed these concerns. Franny hadn't let

on—to me or the trained psychologist—that she'd stopped watching her tablet long enough to take *in* the scene.

The only person she opened up and gave that information to was a teacher I didn't know at all, that I shouldn't want to know, but that I was going to find out everything I could about.

"Oh, Franny. None of this is your fault. Don't apologize to me." Mia's gaze held mine over my daughter's shoulder, and her look held disgust and contempt now.

"Were you scared?"

Mia combed her fingers through my daughter's hair and whispered, "A little. Just a little. But you're fine. And I'm fine."

"I was a bit scared too. It's better we're home and safe with Daddy," my daughter admitted to her, and I slid my hands into the pockets of my slacks so I could clench my fists and hold back my fury.

Someone had tainted the life I'd built for my daughter.

Someone had tarnished her joy, her innocence, her perception of safety.

Someone would pay dearly.

I collected each and every one of these realizations as ammunition for how much I would torture them.

"That's right, Franny. We're here now."

My daughter didn't look at me. Instead, she pulled back to look at Mia directly and combed her hair, and the woman didn't stop her. She just let a small smile slip like those two had secrets between them. "You'll stay, right? Daddy said he'd ask you to teach me here instead of the bad place."

"The bad place?"

"I don't think it's a good idea to go back to school. You can't go either." Franny shook her head solemnly. "Okay?"

"Oh, Franny." Mia continued, "Your dad is here and—"

"He can't teach me like you do, and he's very busy. He's a doctor who helps lots of people, you know?"

"A doctor? Is that what you call it now?" She narrowed her eyes at me.

It was technically true. I wasn't exactly practicing, but I'd become a surgeon at a private institution overseas—one of the youngest in my class. I thrived in that environment. The structure, the silence, the adrenaline rush of that razor-thin line between life and death. Put me in an ER at a hospital and I'd relish in the control and precision under tight timelines. The pressure. The thrill. Saving a life or watching someone die out was a rush.

"A doctor among other things, Ms. Darling." Right out of med school, I contemplated if it would be enough. A fresh clean slate, a wife that strengthened the syndicate's ties, and a newborn.

But my wife had left Franny and me.

Then, the order of Paradise Grove was disrupted. Of the syndicate I'd been raised and bred in.

I was a Diamond always in the end. A part of an elite society hidden behind country clubs and contracts. Billionaire ties and businesses. Men and women who controlled policy with the same ease they controlled people. They sat at the table with governors, rewrote city maps, buried bodies with clean hands, and decided which businesses rose and which burned.

The Diamond Syndicate didn't run just Paradise Grove—we shaped the country from behind silk curtains and blood-soaked ledgers that we deemed necessary.

When my father disrupted my home and my paradise, he put my daughter's life in danger, and in turn, I took his.

I didn't ask for power, but I took it if need be.

Ruthlessly. Coldly. And without remorse.

"Please say you'll stay. Just for a bit." That little girl knew how to get what she wanted.

Mia looked at me, and that's when I saw her hate for me but

love for my daughter. "Your father and I will have to discuss some things, but—"

"But you'll stay?" Franny smiled big and patted Mia's hand before turning to me with a look of victory. My child negotiated Ms. Darling perfectly into her assembled trap.

"Of course I'll stay . . ."

"Heart-in-pinkie promise?" my daughter asked as if it meant something.

They both puckered their lips and kissed their pinkies before hooking them. "Heart-in-pinkie promise. I'll stay, Franny." She glanced at me in resignation. "But just for a little while."

My daughter's face lit up, and that's when I knew: Ms. Darling would be staying with us for much longer than she thought.

4

Jameson

"So, we're keeping her?" Hades's voice cut through the soft music playing as I stepped into my study. He didn't even look up from the ice he was swirling in his drink, having no opinion one way or the other. His cool gray eyes were focused on the whiskey, unreadable like always.

Across from him, my brother Callahan lounged like he owned the damn place even though his estate was further south in Paradise Grove. One arm was draped across the back of my leather couch and the other tossed a stress ball in the air. His polished wing-tipped shoes rested on my hand-carved coffee table. "Of course we have to keep her. She witnessed a shoot-out."

"Not the end of the world. She's under an NDA and contract," Archer reminded him, like he wanted to give her a way out. *Fucker.*

Hades took a sip of his drink before murmuring, "Could have just done the same to her as you did most everyone else." He knew it was the cleanest of scenarios.

Archer glared at him. "She's been the teacher to Fran Bran all month."

"What's a month?" Cal scoffed.

"Fran likes her," Archer threw back, and I couldn't argue with that. None of these guys could. Fran was our one and only princess between all of us. She'd weaseled her way into all of their hearts with none of them having kids yet.

Cal sighed and squeezed the ball in his fist, assessing the situation. "You really don't think she'll talk?"

Archer's dark brows were furrowed in concern as he swirled his own tumbler, leaning against the fireplace. "Don't think so. She's sweet on the kids, doesn't want to cause any harm."

"Doesn't mean shit when she's offered a mint to give a story." Cal shook his head, throwing the stress ball up again. Leave it to my brother to be concerned about our image. "Plus, I saw her. Mia Darling in a sundress on the top of academy hill, her pretty brown curls blowing in the wind telling her story to the news? Yeah, she's the kind of beautiful people sit up and listen to."

Cal was right. I saw the way Archer looked at her. How every one of the men at the academy had eyed her up at least once, their features softening for the girl.

Mia Darling was flawless. Her skin color was warm and tan, her curls that grew past her shoulders were loose just enough that I could thread them around my fingers. Her lips were pink and plump and her eyes the color of whiskey that warmed a man's stomach. And that's where I tried to keep my gaze rather than letting it travel down the curves of her body.

"What in God's name are you worried about the news for? Not one outlet is going to push a narrative of our syndicate being painted in a bad light anyway." I swiped Cal's feet off my table.

My brother chuckled and set his elbows on his knees, his blue eyes the same color as mine as he looked over at me. "You got the Irish and Paolo's cartel pissed at our syndicate, Jameson. You think they wouldn't pay to sway the public?"

"The Irish are dead men walking after what happened at

Franny's school. Those were his men. You and I both know it." Every one of the guys in that room knew that if I'd decided their fate, it was already done. I had names on lists now, phones tapped, routes traced, and deals made. "And I'm considering Paolo's involvement—"

"Agreed on O'Connor and his men. The world will be better for it too," Cal started, but then pissed me off by saying, "Why not meet with Paolo though? Even if it's quiet and unofficial."

"For what, exactly?" I asked, looking over a paper on my desk and trying to appear unbothered. I knew Paolo's cartel was crumbling. They'd misstepped and made one too many wrong moves over the years. Begging for our help or leniency under the guise of diplomacy wasn't something I had time to listen to right now. They needed us more than we needed them.

"The senator was close with Paolo's father. It's a courtesy and smart business to hear him out. He's saying he wasn't involved."

Cal might have cared about courtesy, but I didn't give a fuck. "Paolo can *wait* while I decide how involved he may or may not be." They knew I meant it, as my tone was as razor sharp as a blade now, ruthless and unforgiving. "Plus, I'm not leaving Franny right now to pacify his ass . . . or the mayor's."

Cal sucked on his teeth, holding my gaze. My brother ventured to the East Coast more, had stronger ties there, and stronger feelings about it than I did. "Fine. I get it," he conceded, only for now. He had as much fight in him as I did. "We'll adjust schedules. I'm just keeping up appearances. You know as well as I do it's good to keep a senator happy, bro."

"Which is why we buried that little mess he had with the union funds last year and ran cleanup for the 'accident' he had with his deputy."

"If anything, Senator Panwell can keep up appearances by making sure the mess we're making over this academy shooting isn't in the headlines," Archer grumbled.

"Wouldn't be a problem if you hadn't killed half the town in front of the teacher and then kept her alive to tell the story." Cal jabbed at my men like they were novices. Archer was highly trained and one of my best. Couldn't speak for my other hire, Xavier, who had almost got his head blown off after I saw him pull his gun on Mia, but he'd been reprimanded.

"Would you shut up, Cal?" Archer rolled his eyes and then threw back more whiskey.

"Yeah? Why? He can't really let her go back home like nothing happened now. You've made a mess—"

"It doesn't matter." I summarized, "Franny confides in her. Likes her."

"Exactly. No one's touching Mia," Archer ground out before his gaze hit me hard and mean. "Right, Knight? Because she would still be teaching at some regular old school had you not hired an inexperienced random girl who you then proceeded to manhandle."

"Manhandle?" My brother's dark eyebrow raised with interest.

Archer was quick with his response because his ass wanted the heat off himself. "Jameson choked her."

My brother whistled like I'd stabbed her when she was fine. I pulled at the collar of my shirt. "Hardly choking. She was wasting time I didn't have. Quite frankly, she's a waste of time now, too, other than the fact that Franny is comfortable with her."

Franny even thanked me and told me I was a good dad on the way out of Mia's room. She didn't see that I locked her teacher in there and told her to keep quiet or else.

"Franny's comfortable with Ma and Valerie."

"Is she? When's the last time she asked you to play a game?" I pinned him with a look. "We had lunch last week with Ma, and what did they discuss?"

"I don't know. They chat about nothing for hours."

"Ma talks. Franny listens. With her teacher, she *learns*." I took a breath before I admitted the rest. "She also told Mia she saw the bodies at her school. She didn't tell Val that."

"Shit," Cal swore, and Hades whistled low.

"I took Ms. Darling's phone. She doesn't have much family. And I've informed her of what will happen if she leaves. So, let's accept that Franny needs her friendly face and move the fuck on."

My brother hated complications. "I'm friendly," he replied gruffly as he cracked his tattooed knuckles. "And so are you. Why can't she confide in us?"

Hades, Archer, and I had dumped more bodies in the last twenty-four hours than I cared to count.

"Your face has never screamed friendly, dumbass." I dropped into my leather chaise to contemplate our next move. "The school have evidence for us, Archer?"

"What evidence do we need?" Hades answered for him, now looking at his phone, only giving us half his attention. "O'Connor's leading the charge. Those were his men and we know why, that's obvious—"

I hummed to cut him off. "You don't attempt to kidnap my child over a few legislative quarrels. There's more to it than that. The East Coast is most likely coming together against us." Hades tried to argue, but I held up my hand. "I don't give a fuck who is. All of it will come to light in the end. We start with O'Connor. He's going to pay the ultimate price with his fucking life."

"You think Paolo's involved too?" Hades said what we were all thinking.

Paolo Ruiz and I had a history no one liked to bring up or talk about. Dropping his name alone tightened the room with tension. He used to run most of the East Coast cartel activity with dirty money from his father and was able to leverage ports, launder through shell corps, and buy off power. But his global reach had withered in recent years, and we all knew it was because of us.

"I know he's bitter." I also knew I didn't really care.

"Your relationship is strained at best after you endorsed a clean pharm company over the ones he wanted," Hades agreed.

"Not my problem. He should have known going legal was the smart move. I can't help if his shipments have been cut in half over the past few years." I could have probably done more to tip him off, but we weren't allies or friends. I owed him nothing.

Less than nothing.

"They know those businesses we endorsed have been making money hand over fist after legislation passed to tighten import inspections and limit unregistered chemical imports." Cal chuckled and then set the stress ball down to meet my gaze head-on. "That was a big fuck you to them and we all know it. They were bound to retaliate."

I rubbed a hand over my jaw. "Not by involving my daughter. It crossed a line. And I'm not calling a damn meeting or a full table for permission to answer that retaliation."

"The Diamond Syndicate has been quiet now for years, Jameson. We should enjoy that. Enjoy your daughter. Disrupting it isn't my idea of a fun summer."

My brother was playing the pacifist. Trying to be an ally to everyone. He was the gentleman I pretended to be. I'd slipped though. Time and time again over the last couple years. That's what happened when you took over, when you had to step in after your father had made a mess of everything.

"I'll enjoy my daughter when she isn't plagued by the memory of dead bodies around her."

"Your anger will get the best of you." Cal shook his head like somehow he'd contained all his anger even though I knew that wasn't the case either. I saw how his jaw ticked about Franny and knew he'd become just as unhinged as I was when the time was right. His anger lurked in the shadows while mine had already been unleashed.

To many, the Diamond Syndicate was a secret society that most knew of as peaceful dealmakers. We were talked of in whispered reverence behind closed doors. We operated quietly and politely with more money and ties throughout the United States than most had in the world. Families from generation to generation were born into it, and we expanded through marriage and partnerships that were exceptionally lucrative for us. Most thought that we prided ourselves on logic, not emotion. To many, we wanted peace, not destruction.

As for me, I'd learned to kill a man quietly and unapologetically for posing any sort of threat.

"When it comes to Franny?" I stared him down, provoking him. "My *daughter*? Should I care?"

Hades had no problem stepping in. "Franny is first always."

"Exactly. She woke up screaming, which isn't like her."

Cal's brows slammed down now, and he combed a hand through his dark hair cut just a little longer than mine. "She had a nightmare?"

Oh, *now* he gave a shit? "Last night."

He adjusted his cuff links like he could somehow manage his attitude, and then he threw his stress ball all the way across the room. "Fuck it," he grumbled. "I tried to be nice. I get at least one of them to kill."

I took a sip of the amber liquid as Hades finally sighed and looked up from his phone. "We should call the Stonewoods and Armanellis for sure. Hardys too." He started listing off our partners. "They need to be aware. You'll want them to agree to what is essentially a mob war, Jameson."

I slid my phone out and called the most unhinged man I

knew. "Bane, your syndicate hear of infiltration at my daughter's school?"

"You're late. I texted you *hours* ago." His tone was cool, calm. Collected. Bane didn't get mad. He got even. "Of course I heard. Hades had to tell me she was okay. My wife isn't happy you kept us waiting."

"So, you and Hades have already discussed?" I glared at my right-hand man and watched a small smile spread across his lips.

"What's there to discuss?" He seemed bored. "The Irish and cartel need a reminder that even if some of you are soft, I'm not. The blood running through my veins isn't going to rest for very long, Knight."

Nor would my blood. "She cried over it, Bane. I want every man brought to me personally."

"Good. Finally." His sigh of relief was the only emotion I got from him. "Everything's in motion then. You need to meet with a few families. We can take them one by one quietly or cause a disturbance. You know what I prefer."

"My daughter's summer has already been ruined. Quietly for now."

"Let me handle it until then."

"No way in hell, Bane." He'd already disrupted enough on his own. It was my turn. "I may live in Paradise, but I'm not going to relax in it until everyone pays. To me discreetly. One by one."

It was the principle of the matter. They'd fucked with my utopia.

"Paradise with that woman there too?" Bane chuckled. "I hear she's giving you hell?"

I glared at Hades. "Yeah, the teacher isn't as sweet as I'd been informed," I growled, staring out of the doorway.

"Well, that one isn't my problem unless you want her to disappear."

"She's holding Franny together."

"I'll assume that you should be nice then, Jameson."

"I am nice."

He sighed. "Probably nicer than me, I guess. Want me to send Pink there to keep her company?"

"No. Nobody wants Pink here. She's more of a menace than both of us."

Franny called my name from the doorway, and I turned to see her standing with her dog, Malek. Why she picked the meanest looking Doberman out of the litter a year ago was beyond me, but I loved how he stood next to her—and me when she wasn't around—most of the day like he knew his job. Protect us at all costs.

"If Pink wants to come visit, I would like that, Daddy."

Bane's laugh was almost evil. "Well, Franny has spoken. The women will be filtering through to vet this Mia woman anyway. Make sure she's an ally rather than an enemy."

"No, I don't want—" He hung up.

Then Franny sighed, resting her head on Malek's forehead. "You're always on the phone, Daddy."

"Franny, honey, I have to work."

"Uncle Bane is work?" Franny had about a billion uncles in her mind. They were like family even if they weren't blood.

Bane Black ran the West Coast territory of the syndicate out of his Black Diamond Resort and Casino. And although his territory was a lot dirtier than mine and embroiled in money laundering, murder, and much more scandal, he was family. Most of our alliances were.

"Uncle Bane is sometimes work for me, but he's always just your uncle, okay?"

"Okay." She sighed and twisted the tulle from a black dress she always wore when she was feeling particularly blue. The syndicate had done this. My job, my position, my duty.

It didn't negate that I had another duty to her now as the only parent in her life. She needed me to do more than just be a dad.

I got down on her level, kneeling before her, and brushed a curl from her shoulder. "How was the movie?" Rosy had taken her to the theater room with candy and popcorn about an hour ago.

"I think the cat was about to die, so I made Rosy turn it off. I don't want to die. Ms. Darling doesn't either. She screamed when we brought her here. Do you think she thinks this place is going to kill her?"

The child asked the most morbid questions some days. "Franny, no. What would make you think that?"

She hummed. "I don't know, but maybe you could get her a Band-Aid. She told me her ouchie didn't hurt, but there was lots of blood."

"Right." I closed my eyes in frustration. "Hades, can you take Franny to her room? I'll get Mia a first aid kit."

Franny shrugged at Hades but reiterated to me again, "Be nice to her, Daddy. Her wrist hurts."

And that's how I ended up right back in her room with bandages like I was a dumbass doctor there to fix her.

Fixing her attitude, though, was going to take a lot more than a bandage.

5

Mia

HE RETURNED WITH BANDAGES, a first aid kit, and a look of remorse. Jameson Knight was only supposed to be the drop-dead gorgeous dad who never talked to me but who I got to stare at from afar every day.

He was not supposed to be a man I had to live with. A man who drugged me, locked me in a room, and then offered to take care of me.

"Let me see your wrist," he said like I was just supposed to listen.

"Where's my phone?" I'd tried to leave the room but found the door locked after Jameson left. So, I rummaged in my purse, trying to keep calm, ready to make my own calls and maybe even book a taxi out of here, but my credit cards and cell had been taken.

That's when I had to start breathing exercises to calm down.

"I'll replace the phone. We don't need anyone tracking your location." When a man offered an explanation so readily, I knew it wasn't real. "Now, wrist."

"You locked me in this room."

"Mia . . . it's for your own protection while—"

"Don't ever do it again," I blurted out, my breathing starting to get erratic again.

"Interesting that you think I'll take on your demands." And truly I think he was somewhat puzzled by it, like he wasn't used to grown women telling him anything. His eyes narrowed and he tilted his head. "Tell me why you don't like being held against your will."

No, really? "Does anyone?" If he thought I was going to confide in him, he was grossly mistaken. My response was normal, or at least much better than it would have been three years ago.

"You're especially opposed to it," he pointed out, way more perceptive than I wanted him to be. "So much so that you'll stupidly hurt yourself. Why?"

Stupidly? Did he hear himself? "It's not stupid. You could have killed me. It was self-defense. And I'm opposed to being held against my will, like any woman should be, because a man who thought he had power over me tried to exert it by locking me in a room the same way you did." I was breathing hard, not realizing how much I'd disclosed until after I finished my sentence.

I shut my eyes, irritated with myself. What Jameson had done was not *exactly* the same. He hadn't taken advantage of me. He hadn't built my trust from childhood to adulthood and then preyed upon it in a locker room as my coach had back in college.

No one had taken advantage of me like that since then.

And I would make sure no one ever would again.

"Who?" Jameson demanded quietly, and when I opened my eyes to meet his, that blue color was dark and cold in some sort of restrained anger.

"Well . . . that's not really important." I frowned, shaking my head.

He cracked a tattooed knuckle as he walked over. "I want a name."

He also probably wanted the whole story, but too bad. A growl bubbled up from inside me. "None of your business."

The glare that he shot my way was lethal. My heart jumped in my throat, but I reminded myself I'd already be dead if he wanted me to be. Something stopped the man from actually hurting me, most likely Franny. "Most everything in my house is my business."

"Not me." I couldn't keep from snapping at him to save my life, so I was happy my relationship with Franny was doing that for me. In my defense, this wasn't exactly a teacher-parent relationship where I was to show him respect. And it was clear from my last year in academia that I didn't have much respect for parents overall anyway. Not after I found out that Maisy's dad had hired the same coach and that he wouldn't believe her claims. "Just leave the first aid kit *and* the door open on your way out."

He let out a long sigh. "Don't be difficult, Mia. It's your right wrist. Fixing a bandage with your nondominant hand is going to be annoying."

"I could be left-handed."

He rolled his eyes at me. "You're not."

"Well, I'm more than capable." I lifted my chin even though I was sitting on the plush bed and had cradled my wrist into my lap. Knowing my luck, at this point, it was probably broken.

"I didn't ask if you were capable, Mia." His tone suddenly was as crisp as the sound of a whip as he walked over and sat down right against my body, his side touching mine like we didn't need any personal space whatsoever.

I couldn't hold in my gasp at feeling him so close, but he ignored it to softly grip my forearm, looking at the damage.

He hummed and frowned at the dark spots under my skin. I'd gone a little overboard trying to get free from the bedpost.

"It's not broken. Might be lightly sprained, though." He waited a beat. "And bruised because of your outburst."

"Oh, like you'd know," I snapped. Frustration bubbled inside my veins at my lack of control with him.

"My daughter wasn't lying when she said I was a doctor. So, yes, I would know." He slid his hand into my palm and then threaded his fingers through mine enough that he could move my wrist with his up and down. "Movement is fine. No pain?"

"Not much," I whispered, staring at our hands. His were so massive, they dwarfed mine enough that I knew with just a little pressure he could probably snap my fingers quite easily. It should have sent fear through my body, but instead it sent heat between my thighs.

What was wrong with me? Of course he was good looking, and his hands felt strong enough that I'd have enjoyed them in a completely different context. This feeling, though—after he'd handcuffed me to a bed against my will—was totally wrong.

He smoothed a thumb over a darkened spot, softly. "No fast movements. It's definitely swollen after what you did to it."

"Or what *you* did to it since they were your cuffs." I glanced over at them still hanging from the bed.

He appeared inquisitive as his gaze swept over me. "What is it you really want here? Would a 'sorry' curb your attitude?"

I snatched my hand away to cradle my wrist in my lap again. "This is hardly an attitude."

"Really?" Did the corner of his mouth twitch as he asked that? "So you're holding back the attitude?"

Narrowing my eyes, I tried to figure him out while he did the same with me. Did he also feel the electricity building as he continued that slow rub on my skin, or was he just one to subconsciously touch a woman? "Obviously, I'm holding back." It was a lie. I wasn't one to snap and stand up for myself . . . until provoked.

"I'm inclined to believe that even though my men said you were a darling to work with. A darling of the school, actually."

"It's just a punch line because of my last name. That's all."

"I don't think so, darling Mia. I think you've been nice to all of them but me."

"You want kindness after all this?" I shouldn't have asked the question, but words seemed to tumble from my lips as he watched me, as he talked to me like he had every right to even though he was practically holding me hostage.

His lips thinned. "Let me clean up that cut as an apology."

"I said I can do this myself. You don't listen well, do you?"

"No need to when you're in my house. While you're here, I will make the demands."

"I'm not here for you." I shook my head at him. "I'm here for your daughter . . . and only until she feels more secure."

"No. *Until* I say so. Your safety is at risk also."

His control grated on my every nerve. It took everything in me to be professional, but his efficient attitude felt dismissive. "I'm not concerned."

"I am," he threw back. His gaze flicked to me, sharp with irritation.

I looked toward the ceiling. "I should have never decided to accept this position."

"Probably true." He shrugged like it was the most obvious answer in the world. He pointed to my wrist. "This isn't a difficult decision though. Just let me clean your wrist."

I sighed and conceded by extending my arm for him to take into his hand as I murmured, "Honestly, the job wasn't supposed to be difficult either."

"It's just June to September, Mia. The academy's living quarters weren't much different from here. You'll even have access to most of Paradise Grove—to a whole town full of amenities for you to take advantage of." He waved a hand behind him. From the high ceilings to the comfortable bed and overly sturdy headboard, I could tell the rest of the house would be extravagant.

"We moved in here a couple years ago from down the block for more space. So you'll have ample room here too."

"Well, I have family and friends . . ." I felt my control of the situation slipping and his grip tightening on it instead. The rush of blood through my veins was thick and heavy, moving to my heart that beat so loudly, I wondered if he could hear it.

"I'm sure they expected you to be gone for the summer when you accepted this position, no?"

"Yes, the job with a simple application and extremely good benefits . . . which I'm going to continue to get as long as I'm here?" I asked him because that salary was going to tide me over from going back to the town I didn't belong in anymore. I needed this position after what happened with Maisy's dad, especially considering my sister said she'd heard about me attacking a parent from the grocery clerk in town. "Guess the Darlings aren't so darling with that one" was supposedly the phrase she'd used.

Which was quite unfair. I'd been held back by the principal and hadn't even scratched the smug look off the face of the father who was willing to put his daughter at risk just for a sport.

So, I stood by the fact that he deserved it, but I also knew I had to fight for this job because no public school was going to have me back . . . not after I told the principal I wouldn't be apologizing.

"You think you should?" Mr. Knight raised an eyebrow as he brought a wrapper to his lips to tear with his perfect teeth before pulling the alcohol wipe from it.

I watched in fascination how he maneuvered the wrapper quickly to the first aid kit and then unfolded the wipe with one hand like he'd done this a million times.

"Of course. You actually *should* compensate me a lifetime salary after putting my whole existence at risk."

"A *whole* lifetime's worth of your salary?" There was a smirk there, like he thought I was ludicrous.

"Why yes, Mr. Knight. Teachers are underpaid in general." I lined my tone with snark, annoyed that he probably thought otherwise. A teacher's love and devotion couldn't really be covered, not when we were providing the basics of a human's intelligence.

He shrugged. "You accepted that measly salary, Ms. Darling. You can only blame yourself."

"I accepted what was offered because I needed the money." And I needed out of that godforsaken town. "Maybe I shouldn't accept anything at all now and leave." It was an empty threat since I'd already told Franny I would stay, but he didn't need to be reminded that he could pay me peanuts considering I was basically in witness protection.

He chuckled and pressed the alcohol wipe on my cut. It was more painful than I anticipated, and the pain burned through me fast before he removed the cloth just as quickly to blow on my skin.

The cool air somehow warmed every atom of my blood, lit me on fire, and I felt how my whole body blushed, how my thighs clenched at having his breath on me, over me, and brushing against me.

"Mia, you'll stay because you love Franny. I think we both know that. Even still, I'll compensate you with a lifetime's salary of your silly paycheck for the summer if that means you'll drop the attitude." He didn't smile or even blink at his offer.

"What?" I almost gasped the word. "I'm taunting you in anger, not actually negotiating," I blurted out like an idiot.

"A small salary is nothing for me to pay for your life and my daughter's."

"It's not small," I whispered, our eyes locked on one another.

"What are you, twenty-five? Forty-five grand for thirty-five years? Round up if you teach and nanny here? Two mil for the comfort of my daughter and your life?" It was the first time he smiled directly at me. He wanted to prove a point, and the point was he had ridiculous amounts of money and could control me all he wanted. "Fine. The comfort of my daughter is priceless."

I took note that he didn't say my comfort was. Still, the money was unfathomable. Life-changing. Life*saving*. I should have just accepted it right then and there, but instead, I blurted out, "I was joking."

"I'm not," he said pointedly. "Drop the attitude and do your job well. I'll wire you two million by the end of summer. Earlier if you need the cash."

I touched my wrist where my sister and I had gotten tattoos the year my parents stopped talking to me. She told me she'd be there for me always, and I told her the same. That money would allow me to do that, would allow me to start anew too. "No strings attached?"

"Every single string is attached, Ms. Darling. You'll follow my rules for the summer."

After that, he bandaged my arm in thirty seconds and stood up quickly, like being near me was burning him. With that, he told me to wash up, that clothing would be delivered, and anything else I needed, I could text him for.

He even slid a new phone out of his pocket and placed it on the dresser. So easily, he reorganized my life. "You should get some rest. And my team will keep you updated on your stay. We're investigating the situation, but weekends off are fine, and as long as you take one of my guys with you around town, feel free to go wherever you need to go on your off-hours. Franny stays on the premises."

"Like a bodyguard? That seems like overkill."

"And yet I just killed a man who was willing to gut you, Mia Darling." He said the words so casually, and it reminded me of the enigma that he was to me. I knew nothing about him, and that should have scared me a lot more than it did.

"They don't care about me. They obviously wanted . . ." I couldn't even say Franny's name. I'd bonded deeply with that little girl. Out of all the kids I'd been teaching, she was closest to me. She didn't play well with others, and I think that was based on her being around adults most of the time, but that was a topic for another day.

"They didn't get either of you."

"I'm so happy no other kids were there. What about them? Who will teach—"

"We've got it covered." I knew he meant I had been replaced, and I didn't want to think about how that would affect the kids.

"Kids need structure."

"Which is why you're here with Franny."

"The others need it too, Mr. Knight."

"They'll get it. All of us parents are resourceful enough."

"Money doesn't buy everything," I grumbled.

"No. I never said it does. Resources aren't only monetary, Ms. Darling. But they do help." He nodded tersely before sliding a credit card from his pocket and placing it on my nightstand. "Utilize this for anything you may need. If you can't order something, my number is on your phone to request it. Other than that, you're to teach my daughter during normal school hours. Are you comfortable nannying after schooltime?"

"At my salary, I guess I should be comfortable with anything," I grumbled.

"Great. I can send a list of tasks to your new phone." He smiled like we were all set. "Also, you can join us for meals if you'd like."

"You going to give me a tour now, or am I to just stay in this room?"

It was like he couldn't leave my room fast enough. "I'll send someone to do that with you. Please don't leave until then. Our dog isn't exactly welcoming."

"How kind of you." My tone was so sarcastic I almost cringed. "Anyone else in the house I should be afraid of?"

He glanced at the wedding ring on his finger, and a jolt ran through my heart at remembering what Franny had told me—one day, her mother didn't come to pick her up. Had he remarried? And why did my stomach tighten at the thought?

He cleared his throat once before saying, "Well, my late wife was formidable. But she's gone. She's been gone for four years now."

"I . . . I'm so sorry," I whispered. I couldn't be snippy with an admission like that. I'd lost communication with both parents when they disowned me, but I couldn't imagine losing a partner. "I know it's not easy losing someone." That was the only way I could relate.

"Yes, well, we've managed." He shrugged, and I saw how the emotion shuttered out of him. Jameson wasn't a man who wanted to be figured out. "When suffering a loss, you either fall apart or move on."

I frowned. I wanted to tell him there were a million steps in between and that you could do both. My parents hadn't died, but they were dead to me, and I went through every stage of grief. Denial, anger, bargaining, depression, and then acceptance to move on. I'd fallen apart over and over again.

"You have something you want to add?"

"No," I rushed to answer. It wasn't my place to tell him how he should handle the loss of his wife. I wanted to ask more questions, pry in a way his daughter's teacher shouldn't, but I didn't.

"Then, Hades will give you a tour in the morning." He was about to swing the door closed.

"Hades?" As in the god of death? Might as well have sent me to hell right then and there.

"Yes. He'll also be security to make sure you and Franny are safe. He'll be at your door at eight a.m. tomorrow."

"And let me guess. I should stay behind this door until then?"

"I wouldn't want you getting lost, Ms. Darling . . . and wouldn't want you talking to anyone unnecessarily, which is why I'm going to have to ask you to refrain from calling anyone other than me at this time."

I jumped up and blurted out, "I won't just stay locked in here all summer without communicating with anyone. I won't cope well with that."

His strong jaw tensed. "I don't expect you to. All of Paradise Grove will be accessible to you in time. There're tennis courts, restaurants, golf courses, and clubhouses. This is a luxury enclave. Everything you could want will be at your fingertips."

I crossed my arms over my chest. How did anyone feel comfortable living like this? Always looking over their shoulder. "What exactly is it that you do for a living?"

"I graduated at the top of my class as a surgeon."

"So that's what you do? You're a doctor at which hospital?"

He smiled. "Why don't you get some rest?"

"Because I've been sleeping for a day supposedly." My stomach rolled at the thought, and then I realized I was actually queasy. I abruptly sat down.

His jaw worked up and down. "You may feel a bit dizzy for a few hours."

"Right." I rolled my eyes. "Of course I will."

There was more awkward silence between us, and I wasn't sure if I needed to fill it. Was that my job too now? To make my boss comfortable so that he wouldn't fire me or let me out of here to supposedly be killed?

"If I'm to stay here, I'd like to make a few requests."

"Of course you would." He flicked his gaze down the hall.

"You think I shouldn't ask for anything?"

"I think you're smart to continue negotiating."

"And that's all I'm doing?" I placed a hand on my hip. "Negotiating a business deal?"

He stared at me like I was dense.

"I have to live with a stranger who—"

"Drugged you and choked you, right?"

"No. Well, that too." I shook my head because I didn't like him finishing my sentences or putting words in my mouth. "But I don't even know where I am."

"Paradise Grove. It's not a secret. Name your requests, Mia. Quickly."

It made sense that, like most parents I'd encountered at Blackstone, he was rushing me. They were intelligent, successful, and thought they knew exactly what was best for their children. He must certainly think he knows best regarding everyone under his roof too.

"I'd like Archer to be here."

"Archer?" His eyebrows shot up in surprise.

"Yes. He was with me at the school," I pointed out. They must trust him, and he must have known Jameson, because he seemed to have a direct line to him. "I think he's capable. Does he know your house?"

"Yes, but—"

"I'd like *him* to give me the tour then, if possible. Instead of this man Hades—who I don't know—ushering me around, I think Archer's capable of continuing to keep me safe."

"Over my recommendation and over me?" Suddenly Mr. Knight looked appalled. "He works with Xavier on a daily basis—and Xavier pointed a gun at you."

"Archer wouldn't have let him shoot me."

"Mia Darling, *I* didn't let anyone shoot you." His words trickled down my spine and were laced with a sort of venom.

"I trust him," I repeated, trying to stand my ground even

though Jameson's gaze was now wild with something more. "Honestly, it was Archer's job to keep me safe over the past month. He succeeded in that."

"I disarmed Xavier in literally a second and could do the same with Archer, Mia."

Did he think this was some sort of competition? "Well, I think Archer could take you. And maybe Xavier was giving you the upper hand because you pay the bills and all."

"Even if that were the case, which it's not," he made sure to clarify, "you shouldn't want a man that's willing to give you up for his paycheck as your last line of defense."

"He's *not* my last line." I crossed my arms. "I, myself, am my last line of defense."

"Are you trained in combat?"

"No, but I'd like to be. I want classes if I'm to stay here. Or at least someone to take me to a range of some sort."

His smile was completely pretend as he said, "That's not necessary."

"That wasn't an inquiry. These are my *conditions*. You can take them or leave them." And if he was anxious to leave, I'd be fast to push him out. "That's all. You can go."

Instead, he grumbled under his breath, "You're so concerned about having Archer here, you're not even thinking of food? You haven't eaten in over a day."

The thought of eating anything made me queasy. I wrinkled my nose. "I'm not sure I can eat."

"Well, you need to try," he commanded, his blue eyes snapping up at me in authority. Then he sighed and offered, "If you don't get food in you, the side effects will be worse. How about soup?"

I think my face probably turned green.

"Bread? It's fresh from this morning," he tried again.

"I can just eat something in the morning."

His jaw was clenched enough to cut steel. I heard him swear under his breath before he glanced at his watch. "Ms. Darling, if you don't give me an idea, I'll have everything from steak and fries to ice cream brought up here."

Brought to me? As if I was a prisoner here. "Whatever, then. Send bread. I'll try to eat some, I guess."

"Right." He straightened his cuff links. "Be gentle on your wrist tonight. I'll check it tomorrow. And make sure to eat something once it's brought."

He left me in the perfect room of a perfect estate with the perfect view.

Steak, fries, five different flavors of ice cream, and bread were brought to my door within an hour.

I didn't eat any of it.

6

Mia

THE NIGHTMARES WEREN'T THE worst part of sleeping at Jameson Knight's estate that evening. For me, it was the unknown.

While sleeping, I couldn't control what thoughts raced through my mind, but when I was awake, I wondered about the man who'd dragged me here. Was he keeping me here to protect himself or me? Was he actually a good dad and man? He couldn't be when he'd killed others.

And that's where my nightmares took me. To the killing. To the blood. To the school.

I woke to my own screams and a swift knock at my door.

I glanced at the clock and grumbled about it being only seven in the morning. If it was Archer, he was a whole hour early. So, I wasn't feeling great about answering the door in pajamas, which I'd found in the dresser—in my size. They were black silk and not at all what I would normally wear, and so I'd dug in my duffel for my tried-and-true cactus pajamas.

Padding over to the door, I cracked it open. And there stood Archer with Franny, her grandmother, and another man. I remembered her haughty stare and how she'd looked completely put together even in the midst of an attack on the school. Now, she looked down her nose at me, her wool suit pressed perfectly and her makeup not a touch out of place.

"Ms. Darling? Are you okay?" Franny wrung her hands while she stared at me with worried eyes.

Grandmother Knight added, "You were screaming." Her tone wasn't at all concerned like her granddaughter's, but rather annoyed.

"Oh, of course." I patted Franny's shoulder as I assessed the man next to them. He was tall like Jameson but had almost completely black hair, so dark it was almost a hue of blue. His eyes were all shadows, an onyx color as he stood there with his arms crossed like he was perturbed with my presence already. "I was having a bad dream is all."

"I get those too." Franny nodded as if this were all completely normal. "I can check your room though." She lifted pink little binoculars from her neck and ran in to look out the window. "Sometimes I can see if there's a threat from afar."

"No threats, Franny," the formidable man responded immediately. "I'm here to make sure of it."

She dropped the binoculars and smiled over her shoulder, her curls swaying wildly. "Hades, I had to double check the perimeter just in case. It's all clear." She smoothed her maroon dress with a black bow down before she got to the next matter she felt needed to be discussed. "Now, Ms. Darling, have you met Hades and Grandma? Archer gets to play with us all day, too, he said."

I smiled at Archer, and he winked at me. "Seems I've been called to duty."

"Thank goodness. Mr. Bos and Ms. Prim were missing you already." I pointed behind me at the foliage on my dresser.

The sigh that fell from his lips was like an old melody to my ears. "Those flowers don't care one iota about anything."

"Then why is their color off today, Archer?"

He took a second to narrow his eyes at them. He'd see the environmental change affected them. It was so completely obvious. "They look the same, Ms. Darling."

Botany wasn't Archer's strong suit. "I'll show you what's different later." I waved away his frown, and then I folded my hands together as I turned to the others, not sure how to approach any of them.

I tried not to shrink under their assessment, but I was still in my pajamas and my hair probably looked like a bird had made a nest of it.

"I'm only Grandma to Franny. To everyone else, I'm Mrs. Knight." The older woman smoothed the tight dark bun on her head and pointed to Hades. "Hades is head of security and is trained in combat. He will protect Franny at all costs."

"He would have been very good at protecting us at the school with Archer, Ms. Darling. Hades is even better than my daddy at hide-and-seek."

Franny's tone was grave, and I saw how her grandmother's facade broke for just a moment. The one line between her brows deepened as she patted Franny on the shoulder. "You're always protected, Fran."

"I know, Grandma." The little girl sighed. "But Ms. Darling was scared. So, we have to make sure she understands how good Hades is at his job." Although the man's gray eyes didn't seem to change at all, I saw how one corner of his mouth lifted. "And where is Malek? He should be watching over Ms. Darling's door if she's having nightmares. Malek!"

In just a few short moments, a Doberman more than half my size came bounding into my room. Mrs. Knight scoffed, but Hades stepped aside like he knew the dog was on a mission. It halted right in front of Franny and sat, tongue hanging out.

"Good boy," Franny praised. "Now, make sure you watch over Ms. Darling too. Do you see her there?" She pointed to me and then motioned as if aggravated with my hesitation to come over. "He doesn't bite, Ms. Darling. At least not the people I don't want him to. Put your hand out and let him get to know you."

Franny was always confident in her commands and impressed me with how she acted well above her age. Even still, I wasn't too sure about the dog. He stood only a couple inches shorter than her and sat at her side as if he were guarding his favorite treasure.

A wrong move with a powerful animal like that could be disastrous.

"Ms. Darling, heart-in-pinkie promise." Her eyes held mine, and that's when I stepped forward without a second thought.

"Franny, honestly, the dog in bedrooms is uncouth."

"Grandma," she said, mimicking her tone, "don't get crabby over a house pet who only wants to protect us."

Both the girl and the woman stared one another down, but the younger generation had the advantage. She must have learned from the best and then studied to become better than the best. Her grandmother tsked and then waved them on. "Are you seeing me out before I leave?"

I pet the dog, not sure the question was directed at me. Instead, I was finding comfort in how he leaned into my touch and didn't bite me, because I wasn't sure if Hades or the grandmother would.

"Are you ready for a tour, Ms. Darling? Daddy said you need one."

"Yes, well, it's quite early." I glanced at Hades and Archer. "Are you both normally up this early?"

Hades shrugged. "I'm up at five every day. Franny wakes at around six thirty for breakfast with her father and Mrs. Knight."

So, she was here every morning completely done up? And I stood there in cartoon pajamas. Great.

"Okay." I dragged out the word because I wasn't sure what to do next. "Well, we should start lessons earlier then. I can be ready at seven tomorrow."

"You can come to breakfast too," Franny offered.

Her grandmother was quick to jump in, though. "Franny, Ms. Darling obviously needs extra rest. She can eat with Rosy later."

The tension in my shoulders unwound with the out she gave me. "Right. I'll just eat with Rosy." Away from this woman and her cold son. I didn't belong at that table, not at all.

"Should we get on with the tour now?" I glanced at the imposing man standing in a black suit, and then at Archer. There was no way he'd gotten dressed like that for a tour. "You must have other things to do today."

Mrs. Knight gave me a thin smile and nodded. "Well, I do, and I don't need a tour of my son's home. It was quite nice to meet you, even if you were much too loud for waking hours this morning. I intend to have Franny for tea with our friend, Valerie, on Wednesdays and Fridays at four p.m. Please make note of that in your schedule."

She gave Franny a hug and told her she'd be there for breakfast again in the morning. Then she turned to Hades and murmured, "Leash that dog outside, would you?"

"No, ma'am," he said back, and she walked off with a *tsk* like she dealt with Hades's insubordination all the time.

She disappeared down the hall without so much as a goodbye to me. "You *must* be trained in combat because I would never tell that woman no," I muttered, breathing out a sigh of relief now that she had disappeared.

The corner of his lips raised at my comment, but that was all. Like a British soldier standing guard, he wasn't giving much away. "If you're ready, we can make the kitchen the first stop on the tour so you can grab something to eat." He spun on a heel and started down the hall so quickly that I stumbled to keep up with him.

"You two know each other?" I fell into step with Archer, and he nodded.

"Well enough. Jameson brought a lot more of us on when everything changed."

I hummed, trying to remember that it wasn't my place to ask questions, that I was a teacher and a nanny, not anything more. Even still, the question bubbled up. "What changed?"

"We moved here after Grandpa died," Franny announced, and then she sprinted all the way down the hall, her pink binoculars bouncing over her shoulder the whole way.

Her words took a second to digest as I pieced together the timeline of her losing her mom and then her grandpa, Jameson losing his wife and then his father.

Moving on might have been survival for him after two pillars of his life disappeared suddenly. His statement made more sense now, made my heart ache for him.

"My room is over here," Franny yelled in excitement, but the hallway seemed to go on forever with doors on each side before opening to large wood banisters that overlooked a beautiful living area. There were expansive windows on one side with a view of a lush forest area, and on the other side of the walkway, there was a foyer of sorts with a large crystal chandelier.

Hades didn't say a word about the closed doors or the living spaces down below, nor did Archer. Instead, Archer hinted at the fact that I should avoid them. "Jameson doesn't talk about his father. We don't either. Franny's the exception." I met his gaze and saw the warning there.

When he got to the end of the hallway, which honestly felt like the length of a football field, he pointed to Franny's doorway.

"This is her room," Hades informed me with what I was finding was his signature monotone voice.

In it was a beautiful, ornate table with teacups and a bed that looked like Cinderella's carriage. The lush pillows inside it were all pinks and whites, like she was sleeping on the comfiest setup ever known to man. I took in how they'd also built thin stairs against the wall up toward the cathedral ceiling to a small second story that had a play area filled with toys.

The space was probably bigger than the whole apartment I had back home before I'd taken this job. "This is amazing, Franny," I told her.

She jumped on the bed and told me all about how her carriage bed lit up at night with sparkling lights. I saw how they intertwined around the bed frame. "They're like a night-light."

I smiled at how happy the little girl was. Here, I had to admit that Jameson had spent his money well. She appreciated every part of it, walking me around and pointing out all the toys. "Ms. Rosy sometimes has tea with me, and she even makes me fruity tea sometimes."

Hades nodded in the doorway. "Ms. Rosy cooks for the family, helps with Franny at off-hours, and lives in the guesthouse."

"How many staff exactly are here?"

Hades looked at Archer like he was considering it for a couple of seconds. "About ten of us. You'll meet everyone."

"We used to have more people here, but they didn't listen," Franny offered. "Ms. Valerie liked Daddy too much. She cried and cried when Daddy said she couldn't stay or work here every day anymore."

I glanced at Hades, but his thin-lipped grimace told me all I needed to know as Archer chuckled at Franny's observation. Jameson probably had many women he'd slept with, and Valerie wasn't one that got to stick around. "Well, I'm sure Ms. Rosy is going to stay around much longer," I said.

What else could I say to a seven-year-old?

"You too. Ms. Valerie wanted to babysit Daddy, not me. That's what I heard him saying to her. He wasn't very nice." Franny pouted as she grabbed one of her stuffed animals and set it on her bed.

"Your father was just protecting you, Franny," Hades reminded her, but it was like he was talking to me.

"So, ten staffers." I shrugged, trying to change the subject because I didn't want to think of Jameson paying attention to Valerie instead of Franny either. "How big is this estate, exactly?"

"Over twenty thousand square feet. And we're on about five acres."

"So, not very neighborly?"

"You'd be surprised. Although the driveway is long, most neighbors know Jameson quite well. He grew up in Paradise Grove and everyone is . . . neighborly. His mother is only a few minutes away too." He wasn't offering the information to be nice. It was used as a warning. "His mom and friends come around. It's a small town."

"Town?"

"Community," Hades corrected himself and then tilted his head. "You'll find everything you need within these few miles, I can assure you. Paradise Grove is an exclusive, luxurious enclave. We're all very happy to be within it."

The line was scripted, but it sounded like Hades believed it too.

"Did you both grow up here?"

"Hades moved here when we moved into this house. Daddy knows him from college. Archer knows Daddy because of Hades. Right, Hades?"

His jaw flexed, and he motioned us both out of Franny's room. "We can continue down the staircase this way." We walked past

Franny's room and around a corner, which had me turning back toward my room. "There's more than one staircase?" We'd passed one that led to the foyer.

"Of course."

We wove down a curved staircase and through another living area with cathedral ceilings and windows that stretched all the way up to them. Curtains that seemed at least fifteen feet long framed each window, and the room connected to an expansive kitchen with a dining area. "Rosy's kitchen is behind this one." Hades pointed at a doorway to the side of the cabinets without directing me back there.

Before he turned to go the other way, though, I told him, "I think I should see what Rosy's kitchen area looks like too. I also need to meet her." I was over not actually learning anything. I was a teacher, after all.

Hades frowned. "She's busy."

Franny sighed, grabbing my hand to lead me around the granite countertop toward Rosy's door. "She's not. Daddy and Hades always say she's busy, but every time I go in there, she gives me candy."

"That's . . ." Hades wiped a hand over his face. "She shouldn't be giving you sweets."

And right before we could walk through the arched white door, it swung open. And there stood a tall, beautiful brunette with red lipstick and a black and white apron on. Her smile was measured as Franny ran to her side and hugged her waist. "Hello, Hades." She didn't even wait for him to answer before turning to give Archer a hug, and then she swung her gaze over to me. "And you must be Ms. Darling?"

"I am. Just got up and am not dressed at all for the day, though. If you see me in my pajamas, I'm just Mia." I wasn't sure if I should have shrunk under her assessment. The woman didn't look like she'd just rolled out of bed like I had.

"Is that rule for all of us?" A voice rolled smoothly through the room, so deep and in control that Archer, Hades, and Ms. Rosy straightened right away.

I whipped around to find Jameson staring at my legs . . . or my pajamas. I wasn't sure which. I thought I caught a hint of fire in his eye before it was gone as he blinked once to look up at me. "Getting started early, then?"

"Daddy!" Franny ran over to him excitedly. "We checked Mia's room for bad guys. I can call you Mia now too since we're not in school, right?"

I smiled at her and nodded.

She carried on talking to her father, "I cleared the perimeter while she talked with Grandma and met Malek."

"Malek . . . my mother was in your room?" Jameson asked me as he casually scooped his daughter up. Somehow, a man in a business suit holding a little girl made my ovaries ache like they shouldn't, especially when I saw tattoos on his wrist, like he wanted his dark side hidden but it crept out anyway.

"Franny wanted them to meet me, I guess."

"Guess that's what I get for taking a work call rather than seeing my mother out. Well, seems the tour is well on its way even earlier than we anticipated." I didn't know if he was chastising us for not keeping to the schedule, but he kept his expression unreadable.

Rosy must have felt the tension because she cut in, "Makes sense since Franny rises with the sun and had your mother all to herself while you made a call after breakfast. I'll have pancakes ready for you in just a minute, and what would you like to drink?"

"Oh, I can help myself. I don't eat much in the mornings." I tried to be strict with my diet and didn't want her going out of her way to learn it when I was more than used to waiting on myself.

"Rosy cooks for all of us, and a hearty breakfast is the most important meal of the day," Jameson said as he walked over to a table and pulled a chair out, lifting a brow as if he expected me to take his cues. Arguing with my boss shouldn't have been on my agenda, but I found myself staying right where I was as I turned to Archer.

"Do you eat what Rosy cooks, Archer?"

He smirked at me and rubbed his jaw before answering. "I eat at home, Darling."

"Oh, well, I'm sure you make your own food there. I can cook for myself here too." I winked at Rosy, who took it upon herself to smile before she ushered Franny into her hidden kitchen for what I'm sure was another treat. Hades followed with a frown on his face.

"What cupboard are the cups in?" My question was mostly directed at Archer. I trusted that he'd answer me even if Jameson wouldn't. He pointed to the cupboard next to him, but when I opened it, I saw most of the shelves had wineglasses and cocktail glasses. The only logical cup I would have wanted to drink from was high up on a shelf I could barely reach.

I stretched and even went up on my tiptoes for the closest glass, but thankfully Archer was close enough to grab it for me.

His suit was a breath away from brushing against me before I heard his name rumble out low from across the room. "Archer, go check to see if Rosy has given Hades and Franny more sugar than the daily limit. I'll need a minute to discuss the schedule with Ms. Darling."

Archer stepped back without handing me the cup but murmured, "Good luck" before he did.

Rosy's kitchen door swung closed behind him, leaving me alone with Jameson. His gaze burned into my back. I could feel how it singed each part of my body. And then I heard his footsteps, slow and casual, as if he had nothing else to do with his day. Shouldn't he have been at work rather than dressed in a suit at seven fifteen stalking his nanny?

I wouldn't turn around, because it felt like that's what he wanted, felt like he was willing me to focus on him when he wasn't the focus of my job at all. Instead, I reached up for the glass again and stretched as far as I could, my shirt rising up enough that when his suit brushed against my back and when he reached past me to grab it effortlessly, I felt the material against my bare skin.

"All the drinking glassware is in Rosy's kitchen because she enjoys serving everyone. She takes pride in her job. As I'm sure you do too."

He held the glass in front of my face, not backing up at all, but rather caging me in and waiting for me to respond. He smelled of sandalwood and leather and luxury all wrapped into one perfect specimen.

I breathed him in before I murmured, "Thanks." Grabbing the cup with my eyes shut, not wanting to turn around and face him while he was this close, I tried for a quiet *thank you* but the words that bubbled out instead were, "But I can reach my own cups in the future."

"Really?" His breath was near my ear, so close I could feel it on my cheek. "Because you were about to let Archer grab it for you without a problem."

"Yes, well, Archer and I are friendly."

Jameson's hand came down hard on the counter, so loud and abrupt that I jumped, but his other large hand immediately drifted over my midsection as if to soothe my concern. "Define friendly, Mia."

The command was soft in my ear like his touch was over my stomach, his thumb brushing just under my pajama shirt in a way it shouldn't. In a way that had me shivering.

"I'm used to Archer's help, Mr. Knight." It was a silly excuse.

Really, I was used to not reacting to Archer being close to me. We had a professional relationship that felt friendly. Nothing more.

With Jameson, my body almost ached when I looked at him, when he touched me. It was probably how all women felt around him. He was classically handsome, but his stare was lethally intriguing while his body was huge, like he could dominate a woman in all the right ways.

Or wrong ones, I reminded myself. He'd almost choked me.

And even with that reminder, my thighs clenched together, as if to argue that he hadn't choked me though, and he should be rewarded for that.

I was losing it, I swear.

"You live here now. It's Jameson."

"A live-in nanny still has a boss, and there are still boundaries." I looked over my shoulder at him. Because without boundaries between us, I think I would find myself hopping on the counter and spreading my legs for him.

A rumble came from deep in his chest before he nodded against my cheek. "True, Ms. Darling. True." He stepped back then, and I immediately missed his warmth but knew it was for the best. "You'd do well to dress in appropriate attire then at all times and not let my guys stare at your perfect ass as you reach for things in my kitchen."

My ass was perfect in these pajamas? I almost smiled before I caught myself.

Unprofessional, Ms. Darling, I chided myself. Two freaking million and I'd better find a way to keep it together.

I whipped around to find him staring at my legs again. This time, I saw the fire for the desire it was and lashed out at him instead of myself. "Seems your guys aren't the ones with the staring problem."

"Fair." He didn't even try to hide it, nor did he stop. His eyes licked over every inch of my thighs and calves. Goose bumps rose on every single centimeter his gaze touched. "I assess everything in my house from the very top to the very bottom." And that's when I watched his gaze drag up my whole body before locking on mine. "Especially when they look out of place."

My stomach plummeted at how cold his gaze turned. *Screw him.* "Maybe you shouldn't have things or people who look out of place in it then, Mr. Knight."

That large hand of his that had just been on me rubbed over the scruff of his five-o'clock shadow as if the fact that I emphasized his last name again was pushing his irritation to the brink. Through clenched teeth, he responded, "Or maybe those people should try blending in better when they're working."

"I was woken up early and didn't have time to change." I threw my hand up and felt the grip on the glass tighten. It wasn't even eight yet, and I was already considering throwing dishes at him.

"I'll let my guys know to give you more time." His jaw popped.

"That's not what I'm getting at." I set the glass down on the counter harder than intended. He immediately stepped close to me again, and I gasped when his body brushed against mine. I swear I caught his mouth tipping up. "I'm just tired. I have to adjust to being here and feel comfortable to do my job."

"Are you not comfortable?" He didn't attempt to give me any sort of space for comfort. Instead, he frowned and pushed a loose curl from my cheek. Then, he glanced toward my bedroom. "Did you not sleep well?"

"No. I slept fine." Biting my lip, I slowly gripped his wrist and pushed it away. I couldn't have him being nice or I wouldn't stand a chance keeping whatever it was between us professional. And complaining on my first day was out of the question. I wasn't going to tell him about the nightmares or that I liked flannel sheets rather than cotton. They blasted the air conditioning like it was a hundred degrees outside, and I always ran a bit colder. Plus, I'd normally open a window to feel a breeze, but I swore there were men or something out in those woods. I was paranoid, I knew it. The incident at the school had made me jumpy and skittish. "I'm just not used to men watching my door or knowing I'm sleeping under the same roof as the parent of my students."

His eyes narrowed and darkened like he didn't like the idea of any of this either. "Archer watched the premises at the academy through the night."

"Only him. I'm fine with him watching me sleep," I summarized. "Not Hades or whoever else is here."

"You want him watching you sleep?" His eyes sizzled with a look I didn't understand.

"Watching my door. You know what I mean." I waved off his question.

"They watch the house. And the premises from now on. For your safety, Mia."

My safety. Or theirs. I wasn't exactly sure. It didn't matter, I reminded myself. Two million. Two million for a summer.

He chuckled and stepped back, letting his hand fall away. It snapped my attention back to him. "You're right. Two million for a summer, Ms. Darling."

Crap, I must have mumbled that out loud.

"What could go wrong, right?"

So many things. The fact that I was staring at his lips as he said it, that I was considering how wrong it would be if I leaned just a foot closer to him to smell a hint of sandalwood and leather on him again. I couldn't bring myself to respond to him at that moment.

Instead, we both let the silence stretch between us as we heard everyone in the kitchen approaching the door again.

It's as if he took that as his cue to back away from me. "Dress appropriately around my men from now on, Mia."

"Or what? I'll pay the consequences?"

The corner of his mouth kicked up before he warned, "They will, darling Mia. Not you."

7

Mia

JAMESON DIDN'T STAY FOR the tour, but he was more than happy to iron out everyone's schedules as he called them all back into the room before he left.

Throughout the week, Rosy would relieve me of nannying at four on Tuesdays and Thursdays, as she taught piano and foreign language to Franny before Jameson had dinner with his daughter at six o'clock. My meals, I insisted, would be brought to my room unless I needed to venture around Paradise Grove for a particular craving. In that case, Archer would escort me.

That morning, Jameson instructed Rosy to take Franny while Archer drove me to pick up materials for the study area we would set up. There, I would find a laptop and tablet ready for me.

He excused himself to work in his office but not before he informed me that after my tour with Hades, I could go over lesson plans with him if I needed to, but it would have to be quick.

"I can email them if you don't have time to meet," I offered.

"Probably for the best," he agreed as if his time were so valuable. And maybe that's how they all felt, because we only got through about half of the estate before Hades summarized that we didn't need to look over the rest that day and I was pawned off on Archer. I agreed we didn't have time to meander about, considering I was now worried I'd have to prep an area for learning and order teaching materials all in one day.

Yet, Paradise Grove supposedly had a hub that corporations would ship quickly to if residents couldn't find what they needed. Same-day shipping on steroids.

I'd heard of this enclave but couldn't have imagined the beauty and architecture as Archer drove me around and pointed out the tennis courts, gardens, country club, salons, and boutiques available. I was able to find some teaching materials in a department store I'd never heard of. For the rest, Archer supposedly put in an order.

Then, we worked to set up the study next to Jameson's office as a classroom, and by the end of the day, I had to smile. Plants were basking in the sun by the floor-to-ceiling windows with a calendar on the wall that I'd picked out for Franny to stick different Velcro items on for specials for the day. I had a learning rug where we'd read and a desk where we could practice writing together. I even found some lavender to place in a vase by the window. It was perfect—except for my boss.

The first day of teaching should have started smoothly, but I woke to a knock at my door at *six* in the morning this time. "You're whimpering in your sleep, Ms. Darling," Archer informed me.

I rubbed at the sand in my eyes. "I set my alarm for six fifteen in an effort to make sure no one heard me."

"It's only me." He shrugged and I patted his shoulder to let him know I was thankful.

"*Psh*, the only person I trust around here."

"Don't forget Franny," he pointed out.

"Her too. But I only get to tell you my thoughts on it."

"I don't want your thoughts, Ms. Darling." Archer almost groaned. We'd built a sort of camaraderie over the month and I was happy to see that it was still there.

"Not even about how to keep your plants alive?" I faked a look of horror.

"I don't have any plants." He harrumphed.

"I told you to get one weeks ago. I'm disappointed. They're good for your health." I glanced over at mine in the room. "Although, I have to make sure these survive first."

His blank stare told me he wasn't at all interested in their well-being. Instead, he moved on to his priorities. "I'll knock if I hear you in the morning so as not to disturb anyone else . . . and you can water your plants when you wake up."

I smiled. "There's the spirit. Don't let me or Ms. Prim and Mr. Bos down. We need you. Plus, I can't have my boss hearing me screaming."

I saw the corner of his mouth lift a little, and I was happy about it. Normally, Archer was pretty laid-back, but he'd been wound tight since we arrived in Paradise Grove. He even pointed to my attire. "I can bring breakfast up for you, but you were also invited to eat with the Knights. What would you like?"

"Is there a third option?"

Being sequestered to this room again wasn't ideal. I sat in it for hours in silence, not sure who was listening or watching. My mind ran away with the possibilities, and I hated it. Hated feeling trapped and like I was in witness protection.

Or prison.

The nice room didn't change the fact that I would go insane if they tried to keep me in it.

Archer's face wrinkled in distaste, but I held his gaze, not willing to waver in my request. "No. So, get dressed." He pointed at my pajamas. "If he sees, Mr. Knight won't like those."

I popped a hip and looked him up and down. "What? He complained about my pj's yesterday, didn't he?"

Archer chose to plead the fifth.

I scoffed and pointed to the red flowers on my shirt. "Tulips should bring everybody joy." That got me a chuckle. I smiled back. "Ah, there's the Archer I know. I thought I might have lost you to the cold clutches of Paradise Grove."

"Yeah, yeah. It's not that bad."

"Really?" I walked over to grab attire from my dresser. "So, you just decided to come check on me rather than eating with the Knights downstairs?"

He glanced away. "My job is your safety, Ms. Darling. Plus, no one really enjoys eating with them but Valerie and Hades when Mrs. Knight is here. Breakfast is . . ." He hesitated on the word.

"Frigid?" I couldn't help myself.

And then we were both laughing before Archer informed me, "You were invited, like I said."

"Probably by Franny."

He shrugged, and therefore I knew she was the one asking for my company. "If she asks, we tell her meals are for time with her grandma and dad. Got it? I don't want her feelings hurt." I shook my head and waved at my pajamas. "Instead, I'll get ready quick so I can help Rosy." I hated the thought of her alone in that kitchen dishing out meal after meal for everyone.

"You saw that woman. She likes cooking for everyone and running this house."

"How about we sneak around to the back entrance of Rosy's kitchen to help her and munch there until they're done?"

"Eat here or with the Knights, Mia. Those are our options."

I frowned. "According to who?"

"Your employer?"

I hummed without so much as an argument and went to

the bathroom to change into a green flowy dress that reminded me of my plants in their better days. I walked over to them and told Archer, "I think they're dying because I've locked them into this stuffy room. What do you think? The air in this place is somewhat uncomfortable and suspicious. I'll need to maybe sage it too. Do you think Jameson would mind if we did that to the halls I've seen so far?"

He groaned. "I'm not doing that with you again." He had walked the halls of the academy with me after I'd heard a few noises one night.

"It helped last time. Just admit it." The place had felt so much lighter after we'd done it, but he just shook his head at me like I was a little too off the beaten path for his taste. I patted his shoulder as I walked past him out of the room. "Come on. Let's go eat where *we* want to, Archer. Maybe today we'll see the rest of the estate?"

"I think we will when Hades and Jameson find the time," Archer grumbled, resigned to the fact that we wouldn't be spending the morning in my room.

We walked quietly down another hallway and made it into the kitchen without disturbing the Knights, who were chatting quietly in the dining room.

Rosy shook her head at both Archer and me right when we arrived. She was in that signature black-and-white apron with her red lipstick in place. "Let me guess. You just can't let me make breakfast for you and you'd rather help."

"I really can't." I shrugged and grabbed a spoon.

"Or you really can't sit with them, right?" She looked to Archer instead of me, as if he would be honest and I wouldn't.

"In my defense"—I held up a finger—"Archer said no one ever eats with them. Plus, it's true, I like making my own food."

"You realize I get paid very well to wait on this family and manage the house. And that includes their guests."

"And you do a fantastic job of it. I'm simply used to helping myself. Plus, I'm more of an employee than a guest."

She nodded like she understood before pointing to a plate that was covered. "Just eat the pancake I made you and wash your plate yourself then. They're just finishing up eating out there, and I believe Mrs. Knight is on her way out."

I picked up the cover, and rich yeast laced with cinnamon wafted my way. "This smells amazing." I almost moaned, realizing that my appetite finally was back.

She set warm maple syrup down next to my plate and handed me a fork before turning to Archer and pointing to his plate. "I don't normally let people eat in here."

"Just us from now until the end of time, right?" I said as I moaned into the food, taking my first bite. "What did you put in these pancakes?"

"Secrets, great and small, Ms. Darling."

"Mia," I corrected her. And when she frowned, I added, "Please. It's always awkward when adults call me what children do all day."

"Makes sense," she agreed as she buzzed around picking up utensils.

"How early was breakfast for them today?" I asked, trying to gauge how much time I had.

"Franny rises with the sun." Rosy shrugged and chuckled as she turned to put away some spices. "And I'm convinced we all orbit around her schedule."

"Is it good to orbit?" Franny frowned as she walked in with Malek prancing by her side. The dog looked completely out of place with his thick black leather collar, but he came to sit in front of me as if expecting something.

I took a step back from the animal, pulling my plate toward me, but he stepped closer and started panting. I glanced at Franny. "Um . . . orbiting is great. It means we all have our attention on you, missy." I shifted my gaze back to the dog, not sure if I should trust him today. "Does your dog want something?"

"Your food," Archer said, glancing toward the door now, as if ready for our boss to walk through.

Rosy laughed and pointed to the cupboard behind me. "He wants his treat, and Franny wants her chocolate. Means grandma is gone, huh?"

Franny smiled big. "She didn't even let me put chocolate chips on the pancakes today. So, I need double the chocolate now, Ms. Darling."

I wasn't so sure. "Your father and Hades don't seem to be too keen on sweets. So don't tell—"

And as if he were conjured from my saying his name, Hades walked in. "She won't tell anyone, but I will," he said as he glared at Rosy like this was all her fault.

"You would tell," she scoffed, tension snapping between them, and turned to go back to her skillet. "If you don't want sweets handed out, probably should stay out of my kitchen."

"See"—Hades looked down at Franny as if she'd gotten him in trouble—"I told you we had to stay out there while she cleaned up."

"She wants you out, not me." Franny rolled her eyes so dramatically, her dark curls swung as she eyed me expectantly. "The chocolates are by the dog treats in that cabinet."

Hades glared and Rosy raised an eyebrow. A test to see which side I was on. Maybe it was because I'd always yearned for a friendship I'd never had or because I wanted to shove it to Jameson and his team any way I could, but I reached up and grabbed the chocolate jar and dog treats. Franny smiled while Malek's tail wagged.

The winning moment was when Rosy's face relaxed like she knew she could trust me as I handed both the biscuit and chocolate out.

"Unbelievable," Hades grumbled, but I think I saw his shoulders ease, too, as if he were relieved to know I had a backbone. "Jameson won't be happy."

"Don't pout, Uncle Hades. It's *uncouth.* Daddy will be just fine if we stay on schedule. He has other things to worry about." Franny explained, "Being a doctor is hard." She grabbed Hades's hand as she turned him toward the door, having gotten all she needed from us. "So, maybe keep this trip to the kitchen to yourself. Daddy has so many calls and meetings today that he can't worry about this. You understand?"

Her tone was so haughty and mature that each of us started laughing while Hades attempted to frown at her like he'd been outwitted.

"What's so funny?" Jameson's voice rolled smoothly through the kitchen but still made everyone straighten up as he walked in with his suit pressed perfectly. His expression was almost relaxed until he saw me. Then his stride faltered just a fraction, though enough that I clocked it.

The laughter on my lips died along with the comfort in the room. Instead, unease twisted its way in and held us all captive. His blue eyes found mine and pierced straight into my soul. "Well, this is interesting," he said with a scowl. "I see there's a party in the kitchen this morning." His voice was cold and low, as if such a thing was against the estate policy.

Was there an estate policy? A handbook of some sort?

"I felt it was better to eat here with Ms. Darling on her first official day than disturb your breakfast," Archer offered quietly.

"I don't believe I asked you to make decisions based on how you felt, Archer. Ms. Darling was to either dine with us or be brought to Franny and me after she ate in her room."

Jameson didn't even glance Archer's way. The way he held his power over Archer without even looking at him had my feathers ruffling and my hackles raised. I'd requested his presence because he'd shown me loyalty and compassion. Archer was a good egg, and I wouldn't have him take the fall for me. So, I let Jameson's stare dig into mine, and at his intimidation tactics, I lifted my chin. "It wasn't Archer's decision. It was mine. He's not going to physically restrain me . . . unless you've given him permission to?"

Rocking back on his heels, Jameson pulled at the back of his neck. "It's too early for this, Mia," he grumbled under his breath and then said, "No. No one is going to bodily restrain you to a specific location to eat."

"Oh, well good then." I clapped my hands together and smiled brightly. "I wanted to eat here and help Rosy clean up."

"You'd rather eat standing up instead of sitting down in your room or being brought to have a meal with me? You could have eaten in the dining room with us."

"No thanks." I wrinkled my nose at the thought. And then, when I realized how rude that sounded, I tried to follow up with, "I'm not really— I don't belong at that table."

"Everyone here belongs at that table and has been invited to eat breakfast with us in the morning."

"And yet no one does," I pointed out.

The silence was so thick, a drip from the faucet practically echoed like a damn countdown. Jameson obviously didn't get that no one would be sitting with him at that table anytime soon.

Or so I thought. But then he skimmed his thumb over his bottom lip slowly and asked, "And why do you think that is?"

I wasn't going to be the one to tell him. "An employee-boss boundary, Mr. Knight?"

He stared at me like he was reading every part of my face before he chuckled and murmured, "Rosy, is that the reason?"

"I think you know it's because your mother is ridiculous."

"She was even worse this morning," Hades added, and my jaw dropped.

"She's stressed about the situation but also completely intolerable. You're right." Jameson took his time reaching behind me to grab a chocolate from the cupboard. He leaned so close I felt his breath across my cheek as he whispered only to me, "Might be time for you to rethink that employee-boss boundary. I like my staff honest; no need to sugarcoat the truth for my benefit." His gaze sparked and ignited with mine, clashing and wrestling my confidence away from me.

"I'm not sugarcoating anything," I argued, immediately offended.

"I think you're used to everything that comes out of your mouth being sugarcoated," he said with an undertone that mocked me, and I wasn't sure how to even respond. People pleasing had been a part of my job and maybe a part of my life for a long time too. He smiled at how tongue-tied I was and whispered, "That is . . . unless we're in private. You seem to have a mouth that bites then. Have a good day, darling Mia."

And then he was gone, leaving Hades to say he was going to walk with Archer and Franny to the study so I could finish up breakfast with Rosy. Once they walked out, Rosy smiled. "Oh, you're so screwed."

"What are you talking about?" Fifty-fifty chance she'd buy my faux innocence.

"Don't play dumb with me. I'm even better at catching a lie than Jameson, although he's gotten quite good at it over the last few years." She saw the questions on the tip of my tongue. "Ask me anything you want, and I'll answer what I can. The rest will be met with silence, because I hate dishonesty."

"Why would a doctor need to catch people in a lie?" I blurted out.

"I think you know the answer to that one." She leaned a hip on the counter and pointed to the pancake I had yet to finish. "Multitask so you won't be hungry later."

"The only answer I can come up with is that he's not a doctor." I took a bite before asking, "So what does he do if that's the case?"

"He *was* a full-time surgeon at one point."

"But a full-time surgeon doesn't wear a business suit all the time. Or spend whole days in meetings or on calls."

"Well, you're an observant teacher." Her plump lips curved into a smile like she was proud of me. "Have you asked him what he does for a living?"

"He said it's best I don't know."

"And he's probably right." She waited a beat before saying, "But it might be best for *you* to decide that over time. Sometimes a person holds the truth back not to hurt you but to protect you."

Paradise Grove was well known. Everyone had heard how rich the residents were. And the whispers that came with that luxury weren't exactly respectable.

These people were dangerous. I knew money like he had was laced with some sort of corruption. "I've taken extra precautions to avoid secrets in my life and things that are too good to be true."

"Isn't that what the summer school job was?"

"Yes and no." I hadn't made the decision lightly. I'd built a life in a way no one could take from me, or so I thought. I'd abandoned my parents' hopes and dreams for me, following my passion for helping children into a reputable teaching position. But I'd acted out, done what society deemed wrong.

Again. It put me in a position where I had to flounder, where I had to make one questionable move in order to right the ship again. "Blackstone Academy is renowned." In some circles. "A job offer from them is a coup. Accepting it isn't out of the ordinary."

"I'd assume a teaching job with armed guards is, though."

"You know a lot about Franny's institution then?"

"Not because of Jameson or Hades." She waved away the men like they were ridiculous. "Franny tells me things she doesn't care to share with them or her grandmother. Or Valerie, at that." She wrinkled her nose at the woman's name. "She'll be here this evening, by the way. Avoid the shrink at all costs."

I wrung my hands. "Really? She that bad?"

"She doesn't like other women around." Rosy shrugged. "She'll be territorial with you."

"Why me?"

"Because you're sweet and pretty and, although you're not his normal type, he's made an exception with you."

"An exception how?"

"He didn't kill you."

Shouldn't that have scared me? Turned me off? Made me want to run rather than stay and find out more about him? I knew the answer, knew I shouldn't be lusting after him, but still, I bit my lip to hide my response to her statement. "Well, I'll stay out of their way then. I planned to anyway, but I appreciate the warning."

She nodded. "I'm honest if I can be, like I said." Then she pushed her hip off the counter to add butter to the skillet, which hissed as it melted. "And my honest opinion is that you should ask him for details on his life. Demand them if you're ready to be a part of it. Don't if you're not."

"Oh, I'm not," I clarified hurriedly. "I'm only here for the summer."

She hummed and nodded, as if absentmindedly pushing the butter around the pan. "I thought the same." Her eyes only moved from the pan to the door when she heard Hades chuckle from the other side of it. A small sigh escaped her cherry-red lips. "Sometimes the heart and mind don't agree. I saw you and Jameson yesterday out there."

"Saw what?"

A smile so big and perfectly framed by her crimson lip stain whipped across her face as she put her hands on her hips. "I saw how you were looking at him . . . like you wanted him to throw you over the counter and fuck you senseless, Mia."

My jaw dropped at how easily she said the words when she stood there so properly in her black-and-white apron.

"Oh, close your mouth. We're going to be friends right? And I said I would be honest when I could, didn't I?"

"Not that honest!"

"So you *were* looking at him like that." She caught me. "Thought so."

"Oh my God. We're working here, not—"

"Hey. Speak for yourself. Just because I dress professionally and take my job seriously doesn't mean I don't get mine with Hades."

"Rosy, that's . . . Well, he's . . ." How did I even respond to this? I cleared my throat. "I hope you're both happy."

"I think so. Probably." She shrugged. "Everyone is hiding something behind closed doors. For most of us in Paradise Grove, it's because we don't need to share it with the world. For others, it's because they're ashamed. I hope it's the former rather than the latter with him and me. As for you, decide what hiding something for Jameson will be before you ask him to clarify what he does and who he is, Mia."

The rest of the workday flew by in a flash.

It was only in the evening, when I'd been brought to my room, that I considered what she had said. And I only considered it because the vent to my room kept humming in a way that it shouldn't, the metal rattling against the wall, almost making a buzzing sound behind my nightstand. Once the nightstand was moved over and I shoved a piece of paper between the metal of the vent and wall, the noise stopped.

But then the voices started.

Softly, I heard them. The murmuring. I sat on the edge of my bed, right by that vent, leaned in, and then I heard that smooth, deep voice.

Jameson Knight spoke harshly to another person. "Your service isn't needed."

"You can't mean that." There was a shrillness to her voice, and I immediately realized this vent must have been connected directly to Jameson's office, where he was ending a discussion with Valerie.

"I appreciate you eating dinner with us and spending time with Franny, but—"

"Of course I would be here. I've told you I will be here any day you need me to be."

"*I* don't need you here at all, Valerie. We've been transitioning you out. I've made that quite clear, but Franny enjoys your company . . . whether she's telling you everything or not."

"So that's what this is about? I told you Franny only told her teacher about the blood she saw back at the academy because they experienced that trauma together. I've explained to you if I was here more frequently, I could get more—"

"That's not necessary."

"What is necessary then, Jameson? You want me to leave?" The woman sounded hurt.

"If there's nothing else, then it's best you do."

"Well there *is* something else." Her words were breathy as she replied, "You're stressed. You had such a hard weekend. It stressed me out too. Look at me. Do you really want me to leave like this? Wouldn't you hate that?"

Moments of silence stretched on and on, and I wasn't proud to say I literally held my breath while waiting for his next move.

I knew he was a man that would have women around. I just didn't think I'd be able to hear every moment of it, didn't think I would want to succumb to listening to it, or that my body would actually tremble with anticipation.

"Please," she almost whimpered. Desperation laced her voice, and I understood because I was on the verge of something, too, tiptoeing toward an edge I would fall down if he gave in to her.

When I heard, "Turn around then, and be quiet," my breath caught. My heart lurched. My mind tried to scramble for sanity, but my body responded too fast. His voice shot straight to my core, lighting a flame so hot, I was burning and aching for whatever release I could chase to extinguish the intensity of it. Then I heard the gasping start. Her moaning was loud, her begging more and more intense.

With each minute that passed, my breathing turned shallower, my body grew tighter.

The fact that I clenched my thighs, that I bit my lip and considered snaking my hand down to my center, was absolutely ridiculous.

He was making love to another woman.

Roughly.

I heard her mostly, imagined that he was attending to her every need, how he probably had slipped his large hands into her clothes, pulled them off her, how rough his touch would feel while the scent of him encased her. The rumble in his chest would vibrate through me like it was doing to her right now, their skin would be hot to the touch, damp with passion.

She pleaded for more and then chanted his name louder and louder until something muffled it. He chastised her for not staying in control.

"This is a release. Not a show. Shut up."

So vicious, and yet she still whimpered, "I can't. It's so good. Jameson, you make me feel so good. Right there." She sounded almost frantic, like a fiend who would do anything for him, and I should have gotten up and not listened to the rest, but my nipples puckered at the thought of what he might be doing to her. Of how he might be touching her, of how his eyes must get dark or light when on the brink.

I heard how he breathed harder too, and something was wrong with me, because even as they finished, I went to the shower and imagined him all over again. Never was I into getting myself off like I was then. Never did I touch myself twice or three times in a night thinking of the same man.

Yet, I did for Jameson Knight. For a man I couldn't have. For a man I shouldn't want.

He had secrets, and they were his to keep. But my secrets were mine to keep too, and so I muffled my own screams in the night, calling out his name.

It was like I'd been told . . .

We all had things we hid behind closed doors.

8

Mia

For the next week, a routine was established. Every morning, Archer would walk me to Rosy's kitchen and then wander off . . . to do routine checks, I was guessing. My schedule became that I'd give Franny her chocolate and Malek his treat when they walked in like clockwork too.

I taught throughout the day, and I kept the boundaries between Jameson and I strictly professional like I knew I should.

"You know, boundaries are meant to be broken," Rosy singsonged as I sprinkled a tablespoon of cinnamon into a waffle batter she was having me stir that morning.

"No. They're in place for a reason."

"Or we bet on who will overstep the boundary first. I'm betting him."

"Why would he when he has . . . other women?"

"Like who?" She lifted a brow. Rosy, I found, sniffed out gossip like a shark finding blood.

"He's a good-looking man. I'm sure he's used to women throwing themselves at him."

"So you think he's good looking?" She winked at me.

I didn't answer. For all I knew, Jameson would be walking in at any moment. He was always behind Franny and Malek, never to start a conversation.

It was like we'd fallen into the nanny-teacher schedule perfectly, except I never got an update on who had attacked the school. Or if they'd been taken care of. Or what "taken care of" might have meant.

Instead, I engrossed myself in teaching Franny all I could, and on the weekend, Franny went off to her grandmother's and then I was alone . . . so alone I tried to occupy myself with reading on the phone I was given but would end up staring out my window, imagining that I saw things I didn't.

No one was out there in the gardens or forest. No one cared that much about us . . . I hoped.

Another week passed, and the routine became my norm. I ate with Rosy every morning, exchanging a simple hello any time Jameson came into the kitchen after his daughter.

Jameson never reached for another sweet again. Instead, he chatted with everyone else and then murmured, "Have a good morning, Mia Darling."

My name sounded almost sinful rather than cordial on his lips, and I shivered every time I heard him say it. That alone had me emailing Franny's educational lesson plans and progress rather than scheduling a meeting with him.

At five, I retired to my bedroom, where Rosy had made note of my favorite dishes and sent them up. Archer would keep me company and tell me that we needed to go out and have dinner in Paradise Grove sometime soon instead of hiding away while the Knights ate downstairs.

By seven, though, I'd tell Archer that I wanted to read because the Knights operated like clockwork. I knew Jameson would have had dinner with Franny and put her to bed. By eight, he would be back in his office and wouldn't expect to hear a single thing from my vent.

So, I was quiet. And completely still. A pathetic mouse tiptoeing around as I listened.

Every other weekday, though, him and Valerie weren't.

All the staff neglected to tell me that on those days, Valerie stayed much later to *talk* with Jameson. But she actually stayed to have Jameson do anything but talk with her.

Although I still didn't know what she looked like, Valerie's voice was soft, raspy, and sounded laced with sexuality. The second time I heard it, I tried my best to avoid it, even vigorously cleaned and watered my plants.

But listening and enjoying it became a part of my routine too. And every night I hated myself for finding pleasure in that man's voice. It was his fault I was sitting here bored and wound tight anyway.

Emailing him Franny's progress felt ridiculous too when his email responses were succinct and short with a brief "Thanks for the update" line. Didn't he realize she was bored as a kid too?

That night, I decided to push his boundaries—not for myself, but for Franny.

Maybe I should have kept it short and practiced efficiency like he did with me, but Franny's education was at stake. I saw how she squirmed in that study, like she couldn't stand being home all day. I couldn't either.

He didn't even want us going outside.

It was practically a dungeon. Not just for me, but for her too.

So I wrote my daily email quickly, trying to avoid the discomfort I felt asking him for something. I'd been good about not using the card he'd laid out for me the first night. I was thankful for the borrowed phone and laptop too, making sure to tell him as much in my progress reports. Tonight though, my email was different.

From: Mia Darling<Miadarling07132001@gmail.com>
To: Jameson Knight<DrJamesonMD@KnightInc.com>

Dear Mr. Knight,

Franny is progressing quite nicely. I've uploaded some baseline scores to a drive folder I created that you can look over. We'll be working on multiplication and division tables soon. I've attached suggested curriculum. Please review and let me know if you have any concerns.

I do have a small request. Franny enjoys being outside. Recess was a time she bonded with other students and really expressed herself. Do you think we could incorporate daily walks and gardening around the estate? I think outside communication would be good for her.

Thanks,

Mia

Immediately, I got a response.

From: Jameson Knight<DrJamesonMD@KnightInc.com>
To: Mia Darling<Miadarling07132001@gmail.com>

Mia,

Thanks for the update. The curriculum works. Franny

goes with me places and to her grandmother's on weekends. It is safest indoors.

Jameson

Under normal circumstances, I would have left it alone. Yet, Franny was always staring out her binoculars at the trees and sighing half the time. I recognized longing on a child's face even if Jameson was choosing to ignore it.

Protecting ourselves didn't always mean avoiding all the risks.

From: Mia Darling<Miadarling07132001@gmail.com>
To: Jameson Knight<DrJamesonMD@KnightInc.com>

Mr. Knight,

I really would like you to reconsider, as she has spent most hours inside with me this week. She's antsy and restless. I realize you might be protecting her from a world I don't understand, but that doesn't always mean avoiding all the risks.

I'd like our schedule to include two outdoor activities, rain or shine. I'm sure Archer would be fine walking with us and being outside for an hour each day. I'll tell him you approve?

Thanks,

Mia

From: Jameson Knight<DrJamesonMD@KnightInc.com>
To: Mia Darling<Miadarling07132001@gmail.com>

Mia,

You will not. I do not approve. That's my decision.

Jameson

What an ass. Didn't he care? Didn't he want to discuss it at all?

From: Mia Darling<Miadarling07132001@gmail.com>
To: Jameson Knight<DrJamesonMD@KnightInc.com>

She needs outdoor stimuli and novel experiences. She wants adventure and discovery. I really hope you reconsider.

He didn't. He freaking ignored me even though his little icon showed he and his stuffy suit avatar picture were active online.

I went to bed furious that night and acted out the next day after Archer roused me from yet another nightmare.

"Franny, we deserve an outing for a bit today, huh?" I whispered to her while she stared out the study window. "Want to go for a walk or maybe to the Paradise Grove club?"

She dropped the binoculars and practically vibrated in the plush chaise. "Heart-in-pinkie you're not fooling me?"

I held up my pinkie and linked it with hers. "Nope. I even made a picnic."

Not only that, I'd dressed in a bright fuchsia tank and jean shorts after seeing how sunny it was outside, because I was on a mission.

She jumped up and squealed while I laughed at her excitement. Archer would be at the front door, and Hades somewhere down the hall. I'd have to fight them, but I knew it was doable. Rosy had helped me pack up a basket. I was on a mission to breathe summer air no matter what anyone said. We deserved an outing, and I would take it whether Jameson Knight liked it or not.

"Mia." Archer's voice sounded alarmed when the front door opened. Two men were standing with him outside.

Armed.

"Archer." I nodded and held up a basket. "We're having a picnic later, but first we'd like to go to the country club to . . ."

I wasn't sure what Franny enjoyed doing at that stuffy place.

"To play tennis and eat chicken fingers." Franny nodded next to me.

"That's not authorized, Mia," he said softly, glancing at his guys. One of them walked off, mumbling into what I was sure was his earpiece.

Great. This wasn't going well.

"Will you drive us, or shall we walk?"

"Woman, are you trying to get me in trouble?" Archer crossed his arms, and I shrugged.

"We haven't even saged this place yet. If we had, it might help you be in less trouble, you know? Maybe we can stop at a store on the way home?"

"What's *sage* mean?" Franny tilted her head curiously.

"Can you both go back inside?" Archer took a step forward and so did his men, as if to corral us.

I wasn't a sheep.

I would not be herded.

"We'd like to be outside today, Archer."

His shoulders were getting tenser and tenser. "It's not safe out here, Mia."

Franny stiffened at that, which had me glaring at him. Didn't he realize she needed this as much as I did?

I lifted my chin in defiance. It was obvious Jameson had given him orders, and if I was going to be the only one to be considerate of her needs, so be it.

I grabbed Franny's hand and stomped forward off the porch steps. "We will walk, then."

"No. You. Will. Not." Jameson Knight's voice sliced through the whole front yard. He stood at the top of the stairs, his fury palpable.

Maybe it wasn't smart to be willfully ignorant of what this man did for a living or be unconcerned with my own self-preservation in that moment. But I didn't care.

I was getting my way for Franny, come hell or high water. So, I smiled broadly at him and dared him to say no again. "Oh, so you're driving us then, *Jameson*? Great. Of course I know it might be a bit of a bother for you to take your daughter and her nanny out, but we'd appreciate it. Which car of yours should we take?"

9

Jameson

A BIT OF A bother? Mia Darling's mouth didn't seem to know the half of it. The idea of her in my head didn't seem to get the memo about that, because it ran like a fucking unhinged animal through my thoughts all day long even though I'd purposely avoided her for two weeks straight.

She'd avoided me too.

I'd see her in the hall, and she'd turn the other way. The only time she graced me with her presence was if Franny needed something, but my daughter was all smiles and barely asked for me.

I should have been getting work done. The syndicate would be having another meeting soon, and I would be sitting at the head of the table.

Yet, when Archer, Hades, and Cal met me earlier that week, Hades had to elbow me to get my attention. I found my mind wandering to what she was doing, to how her wrist was healing, to what her life was like before I dragged her here.

Mia Darling was a menace to my focus, and I couldn't keep having her be that.

Case in point, every male within a fifty-foot radius was watching her smile in the sun at me in her tiny pink tank and shorts. Her lack of fear shined bright too, which was, frankly, impressive, especially after she revealed to me that a man in her past had tried to exert power over her. I wanted to know who. And why. Just for the record, nothing more.

Although, I'd admit, the idea that any man other than me had tried to hold her against her will didn't sit well with me.

Even knowing all that, she still wasn't cowering. She just kept pushing for her way, and I wondered how much it would take for her to wise up.

So far, she hadn't.

And she needed to, considering she was a part of my daughter's life now. My number one priority. And my little girl hadn't even run to greet me with a smile today. She'd stayed by Mia's side. That was a problem, since I was considering ending that nanny's life because of the sheer fact that she showed no remorse or guilt about disobeying my specific direction.

Instead, she put her hands on her hips and waited for my response. Just stood there in that loose tank so thin that when the wind blew the fabric, it outlined her every delicious curve. "Well?" She lifted a brow as if I were wasting everyone's time.

So, that's how she wanted to die, her chin held high, and fiery hate for me in her eyes?

Yeah. I was going to kill her.

Or if I let her walk away now to go have their picnic, someone was going to snatch her and my daughter, and then I'd have to kill them *before* I killed her.

Either way, she was dying.

I'd be the one to do it.

She didn't seem to care though. She spun on a heel as if she'd won and stomped toward my row of cars on the brick driveway, making a big scene about which one to choose. "Franny, do you like shiny black or matte black or, hmm, not a lot of color options. Maybe this one? It looks very fast."

"I know. I always wanted a pink car but instead they're

all black. Fuchsia is your favorite color too, right?" Of course it was.

"Yes. I love that it's almost purple but still pink," Mia answered, like she wasn't concerned with me and my men waiting for her to move her sweet ass inside.

"We should tell Daddy to get one. But right now, if I could pick to ride on one thing, it would be—"

"Franny," I cut her off, "go back inside."

My daughter turned toward me, and I saw the devastation on her face. Not only was Mia directing her anger at me, my daughter was directing her sadness and disappointment. "We're not going, Daddy?"

"Franny, it's—"

"Just for an hour? Please?" Mia asked, saying *please* like she hated the taste of it on her lips but was willing to sacrifice her pride for my daughter.

It was reckless, idiotic, and completely troublesome that I even considered giving in when I'd just made another of O'Connor's men disappear. I was picking them apart piece by piece after the incident that we knew they orchestrated now.

Everyone was waiting for a response from me. But both Mia's pleading eyes and my daughter's weighed me down. "One hour in town. The clubhouse, Franny. That's it," I bit out, but I don't think anyone heard anything past my time constraint because both Mia and Franny squealed before Franny finally ran toward me.

Her smile was real, her excitement palpable, and for a moment, I felt like I'd done something right with her.

Was it because I'd kept Mia here, or that I'd given in to this one demand? I wasn't sure, but that woman smiled at me and my freaking chest warmed too. The sun or her brightness. Something was blinding, and that couldn't be a good thing. Blind spots were weaknesses.

I couldn't figure out what the feeling was either. It wasn't one I'd ever felt, and that was dangerous, risky, and somewhat adrenaline inducing. I shouldn't have enjoyed it.

We got into the Rolls-Royce Phantom because Franny pointed and said, "Shiny black one, please." I nodded at Hades, so he knew to have some men follow us.

If I was going to be an idiot, we'd need to be well protected. I opened the car door for my daughter, and she jumped in the back seat, but I held Mia's door closed so she couldn't open it until I shut Franny's.

I turned to her. "You're not following my orders, Ms. Darling."

We searched one another's gaze. I searched hers for fear or submission or maybe some sort of contrition. A fire of defiance sparked there—and maybe something more—before she blinked and looked away.

"I appreciate you overlooking that this once for Franny's sake," she murmured quietly and tried to open her door again.

"For her need for outdoor stimuli?"

"Yes, and I can give you a list of reasons and show you the research on why being outdoors and discovering new things is beneficial if need be in the daily report today."

"How about you give me a list of things that will make you follow directions? I'd like that instead."

She scoffed and pulled at the handle. My hand held it closed still.

"So I'll take that as another rejection to my request. I'm going to have to discover it myself?"

She caught my innuendo loud and clear, because those lashes fluttered closed and then her gaze snapped to mine. Nothing was sparking now. Her gaze was alight with bold, daring emotion. "Remove your hand from the door, Mr. Knight."

"Jameson," I corrected her, and then, "If you're going to defy me in my own home with the most precious part of my life, might as well be on a first-name basis, right?"

She took a deep breath, like I was the irritating one, and then said through clenched teeth, "Fine. *Jameson,* please remove your hand from my door so I can get in it."

Christ, even her gritting her teeth while she said my first name sounded good.

"Darling Mia, don't you know a gentleman never lets a lady open her own door?" I said, stepping close. She backed away from me fast. She felt it too, the sizzle when we touched, and now I knew she was afraid of it, trying to avoid it, trying to avoid *me.*

She straightened as I swung open the door and waved her in. "I don't need the gentlemanly act, Mr. Knight. I just need you to be my boss." She brushed past me, slipping gracefully into the Phantom's passenger seat. When she reached for the handle to swing the door closed, effectively snapping me out of the spell she had me under, I winced at the harsh sound and took to stomping around the car and slamming my own door after her display.

If she didn't want chivalry, I wouldn't give it to her.

She was right that we were just boss and employee. Never mind that I'd saved her life or given her a good salary or allowed her to stay in my home, which I never did with women.

No other woman had even spent the night in this house.

And I didn't give a flying fuck if her residence here was against her will at first. She should have been grateful.

I revved the engine and pulled away from my house. Down the winding brick driveway we went. Usually I appreciated the beautiful overgrown trees bordering the drive, but today they felt suffocating as we sat in silence, tension rolling around between us and bouncing off the windows.

Her eyes were on the ironclad gate as we finally got to the entrance of my estate, and she watched how it opened for us.

Her mouth opened slightly as if she were letting out a breath. “Thank you,” she breathed softly. Two words murmured so quietly I barely heard them.

And just like that . . . The anger at her uncoiled and released an emotion much scarier. I was happy for her appreciation, and that was not at all what I needed to feel.

Not with my daughter’s teacher.

Not at all.

Fuck. Today was going to be hell. She wasn’t a damn darling. She was my devil in disguise.

10

Mia

How the iron of that gate curled and coiled around in a beautiful pattern probably had so many people fooled with the type of luxury this estate held. It had to be twenty feet tall and opened slowly, smoothly. It was easy to forget that this grand entrance was a barrier that kept unwanted solicitors out . . . and kept people in.

What happened behind all these gates? Behind all the doors? Behind the places people built up so that no one could see inside? Did these fancy gates and wealth hold on to their happiness the way they wanted?

Was the beauty of a fortress enough to distract someone who was locked away?

It wasn't for me.

It couldn't have been for Franny either, and that's why I thanked him. Even if we were only getting an hour, the imaginary ropes that bound me to this property loosened a little bit. I felt like I could pull a little bit more oxygen into my lungs, could see a little clearer. Even the feel of the wind on my skin as I rolled down the window was different.

"I know I'm not making this as easy as you would like," I

told him while he inched the expensive car out of the driveway and onto the road.

"You're not making it easy at all," Jameson clarified in that grumpy voice of his.

"Oh, Daddy. At least we didn't go without you." Franny bounced in the back seat. "Now you can play tennis or swim or play golf with us! Mia, what's your favorite sport? We can do any of them at the club."

Of course they could do any of them. It only took us another few minutes to arrive at the country club. We didn't have to leave the gated community of Paradise Grove, even. Instead, we pulled up to more iron gates that immediately opened for Jameson's car.

"Remind me to get you a watch so you'll have access to everything in Paradise Grove."

"If there's a cost, I can—"

"The cost isn't a concern of mine." He threw me a look with those cold blue eyes.

I wasn't going to worry about what could happen though. Instead I was taking in what was supposed to be their little country club.

Sprawling across hill after hill was a pristinely manicured golf course, an Olympic-size pool on one side, a large building in the middle—presumably the clubhouse—and courts for tennis and basketball in the distance. The circular drive had a fountain in the middle, and Jameson drove right up, not even looking for parking.

"It doesn't cost anything, Ms. Darling." Franny giggled. That girl didn't have any idea how much it would cost to be a member here. To live here. "I like tennis best. Daddy taught me."

"I can teach Ms. Darling, too, if she wants," he said, like he was going to try to be nice and do me a favor. I almost laughed at the gesture, especially knowing he'd never be able to teach me anything when it came to that sport.

"We can play tennis." I shrugged. Here, playing would mean nothing even though it meant everything in high school and college. To my parents and to my town.

I halted immediately as I got out of the car and realized every single person was dressed a certain way. Of course they were. This was an exclusive country club. I should have known that, should have anticipated it. Tennis clothes, polos, skirts, pastels. Most of them scanned a watch as they walked in.

"Maybe I should actually wait in the car?" I glanced at Jameson in concern, but he was handing off the keys to the valet. "I'm not exactly dressed appropriately."

He looked me up and down and then frowned. "Should have thought about that before you decided you wanted an outing. You wanted to come, Mia. So, here we are. You won't be waiting in the car." His tone was final.

What an ass. "Suit yourself. I'm only trying to save you secondhand embarrassment considering you're about to be seen with me in this ritzy place." I was being childish as I walked past him to catch up with Franny, who was already sprinting in, excited.

He grabbed my elbow to halt me. "I don't care what other people think. You'd do well not to worry about them either." He held my stare for a moment, as if he wanted that to sink in. "There's a clothing store inside if you'd like tennis attire. I have an open tab."

"I can pay—"

"Don't start." He rolled his eyes and waved Franny over. "Let's go change and then go to the courts, Fran. Ms. Darling needs to grab some clothes and will meet us there."

I nodded and looked at Franny's flushed face. She was

so excited she could barely contain it. "I'll be there in a few minutes."

"This is going to be the *best*, Ms. Darling. Sometimes other kids are there to play too."

I nodded and waved to them. Grabbing clothes from the store should have gone quickly, but when I threw a white skirt and collared shirt on and told the saleslady it would be going on Jameson's tab, she questioned who I was.

"I'm sorry, you said Mr. Knight? As in Jameson?" She smoothed her straight blonde hair. "What's your name again? I will see if he's approved you."

"That's not necessary. Ring up the items," I heard from behind me, and Archer appeared out of nowhere.

"Oh, hi, Archer." The lady blushed and immediately started typing away on the register, not meeting my eyes again. "You're all set. Have a great day," she said softly, but as I left the store, I heard her whispering to the other saleswoman. They weren't subtle about questioning why he'd bring help with him to the club.

"Ignore them and every woman you meet today," Archer told me as he pointed me in the direction of the courts.

"Dare I ask why?"

"Because most of them have tried to be a nanny, and more, in Jameson's life."

And as I glanced around, I saw woman after woman whispering.

Even some that were with husbands and other men. I tried to keep my head down, because I didn't need to make small talk with Paradise Grove's elite. I just needed to play tennis with Franny.

By the time I caught back up to her, Franny's sneakers were already eating up the clay court as she chased the ball around, completely out of breath. Jameson had arranged for a private attendant to fetch Franny's balls. Her eyes lit up when I grabbed a racket.

"Fran, you have to swing once your eye is on that ball," Jameson told her as he lobbed another one her way. He'd changed into white tennis shoes and a short-sleeved polo that had my eyes glued to the tattoos on his forearms that I'd never noticed.

Then he smiled as Franny swung with all her might and made contact with the ball, squealing in delight. "Good job!" He clapped and then started laughing as she danced around in pride. That moment ruined me. His laugh with hers on a sunny day, casually enjoying each other, was picture perfect. It's what a father-daughter relationship should be, and they both looked so effortless in it.

So in their own world.

And then a woman chirped in from the sidelines, "Nice hit, Franny. Jameson, so good to see you both here." She walked over as Franny missed Jameson's last soft serve toward her, and then the private attendant stepped in to help Franny get the ball while Jameson talked.

"Good to see you too, Becky." He didn't ask her any questions or try to further the conversation, but she stood by expectantly nonetheless.

"How's the estate coming? We should have coffee sometime with the kids." She was inviting herself over. Not subtle at all.

"Things are good. Just busy right now." He smiled while speaking to her like a charmer even as he made eye contact with me and motioned me over. "Our new teacher and nanny, Ms. Darling, just started. We're going to work on tennis today. Isn't that right?"

"I guess so." I shrugged, but instead of going to his side for the lesson, I went over to Franny's side and whispered, "Ready for me to show your daddy who really knows how to play tennis?"

She giggled. "Are we about to win a game against him?"

"Yup." I swung my racket around, being silly with her, and she giggled.

"Heart-in-pinkie promise we will win? Daddy hates to lose."

"Heart-in-pinkie promise, Fran. Because I hate to lose too."

He smiled at us while that lady talked his ear off, and the smile he sent me wasn't nearly as friendly as the one he gave her before he said, "Just keep your eye on the ball and try to swing after one bounce on your side, Mia. It takes a minute to get the hang of it."

I hummed because it was just like a guy to mansplain without asking me if I knew what I was doing.

He lobbed it my way, and I winked at Franny before moving in and smashing it back to his side.

It whizzed past him, and the woman jumped back with a yelp.

"Whoops, sorry about that!" I offered her. "Don't have great aim all the time."

Now, I got his real smile, one that I thought might have only been reserved for people he genuinely enjoyed, but his eyes danced with delight or competitiveness, I wasn't sure which.

He lobbed the next ball to Franny once and said to me, "You play tennis."

"I wanted to be Serena Williams but fell a little short." It was a half-truth.

"Interesting."

And then he served to me. Hard.

Rough.

With no mercy.

I was rusty, and my leg still hurt some days, but I wasn't one to give up a serve. I lunged for and hit that ball over, pulling back at the last second so he'd have to run for it.

He didn't get there in time, and I smirked down at Franny. "Do people beat your dad at tennis a lot?"

"No." She stared at him breathing hard on the other side of the net. "Normally Daddy's good, so you must be a superstar. Is that who Serena Williams is?"

"For tennis, yes. Superstar material for sure," I informed her. "And if you practice, bet you can be just like her."

"Okay." She pushed her fingers into the netting of her racket like I did mine, and it made me smile at how quickly she picked up on this. "I want to be just as ready as you when the ball comes."

"Good job. Then you want your racket in front of you like this." I showed her my stance and said, "And get your knees bent a little so you're prepared to move when the ball comes. Then, like your dad said, keep your eye on the ball." I turned to Jameson, who was assessing us quietly. "Want to toss the ball her way again?"

For a moment longer, he held my gaze and then looked down at his daughter. Her face was scrunched with determination.

"You're doing great, Franny," he murmured, but he was saying it to me. He gave me one nod, and I knew it was him recognizing how good this was for her. He agreed, finally. She had needed this, and I couldn't help but let a smile slip.

He lobbed the ball her way and then said to me, "You're next, and I won't be as easy on your serve."

I let out a *ha* and got ready for it.

We played back and forth every other time, keeping Franny involved but letting our competitiveness fuel the one-on-one volleys. At one point, another little girl came to watch and asked Franny to bounce balls at the court next to us. I saw Jameson motion behind him, and there were Hades and Archer, moving in to make sure Franny was well watched.

From that point on, I was merciless on that court. We played for real, and Jameson didn't go easy on me. It felt good to push myself and shut down everything else. We didn't talk at all other than a swear from him here and there, but on the second to last point to win the match, he screwed me on a fake-out. I stormed toward the net and growled, "What a cheap, lazy shot."

"What?" He actually laughed.

"Well it was!" I laughed too at how rude I was being.

But then he rubbed his jaw and pointed his racket at me. "You'd have taken that exact same swing if you had the chance, Darling," he threw back, his hand resting on his hip.

"Oh, bullshit." I smiled, but when I realized what I had said, the laughter on my lips died as my eyes widened.

I didn't swear at work nor at my boss. I'd forgotten my place and let it slip.

His gaze didn't turn cold though, instead it danced with fire as one side of his mouth kicked up. "A little bit of devil in that darling, I see."

"Sorry."

I shook my head and started to step back, but he caught a finger in my collar and leaned close. "Don't apologize to me for this. I'd rather get the real you over the buttoned-up version any day."

I bit my lip, trying to hold back a smile because it felt like a compliment when I shouldn't be seeking one from him. Somehow, in playing this game against one another, we'd gained mutual respect. I appreciated that he didn't hold back, that he met me with his best, and that he let Franny play beside us, allowing her to be a kid while we were adults equal to one another.

When he held me by the collar a second longer, I felt the spark, and there was no denying the dip in my stomach. I shouldn't read into what he said or question him about exactly how much of the *real me* he wanted. So I glanced at his lips and licked mine, backing away.

He let me go that time, his eyes glued on the spot where my tongue darted out as he backed away too. "Last serve, Mia.

Should we make it count?" He held my gaze, and I swear the air crackled with tension. It was palpable, tangible and impossible to ignore.

I was competitive, had been all through high school and college. And this was something more than competition. This was attraction, deeply rooted and profound for me in a way I'd never felt before.

Yet before he served it, a woman with dark red hair that coiled around her shoulders and down her back walked toward him. "Jameson, you're out and about today."

His jaw ticked, his whole body tensing. Maybe it was that I was there, or maybe he just didn't want to deal with her, but I knew that voice and had a hard time focusing on him when my mind raced quickly at seeing her.

It was like a bucket of ice water doused me.

Valerie the psychiatrist was gorgeous. Tall. Toned. And full in all the right places. He probably was taking her in like I was, because he was a man. How could he not? Plus, he knew her with clothes on and without.

And it seemed she was also a member of the country club, and when she smiled at me and said, "Introduce me to your friend," I felt like I was absolutely not.

Of course she'd look this good after playing tennis, whereas I was drenched in sweat and felt my curls blowing wildly in the wind. "She's Franny's nanny, Val. We're just finishing up here."

"Oh." Her eyebrow raised because she knew he was dismissing her. "Well, then. Good to meet you, Ms. Darling. I've heard great things. Take care of Jameson and Franny for me until tomorrow. I'll see you at the usual time?" She communicated so much with those few words.

He nodded like he just wanted her to leave. I did too. Suddenly, the bubble around our match had broken, and we were exposed again.

I was down one, and when he served, I let loose something coiled in me.

Sports were about controlling your emotions, and my control was slipping.

Seeing how he talked with these women, how he'd kissed Valerie on the cheek and murmured something in her ear before she left, how he told her he'd see her tomorrow. How he was almost gentle with all of them and yet so cold with me.

My smash was too hard. It flew out of bounds and Jameson watched, not even going for it.

There went my emotion. And there he stood, cold and detached, letting it fly by.

It was a demonstration to me that I didn't belong here.

"Game, set, match, Mia," he said softly, extending his hand out over the net like I should shake it.

I knew everyone was looking on. Probably Franny too. So, I swallowed my pride and gritted out, "Good game, Mr. Knight," as I walked up to him and shook it.

The electricity in our touch was still there, the way my blood pumped with a heat I shouldn't have, and the sizzle I shouldn't feel on my skin was almost too intense. I tried to pull my hand away, but he held me there for a second longer.

"That last hit was in fury." He searched my face.

"What?" I whispered.

"You heard me. Tell me why."

"I don't know what you're talking about." I shook my head. Was he asking if I was jealous? If I didn't want to see him with other women? I would never admit to that. "We should get Franny out of the sun."

"You used to play. Why did you stop?"

"Injury."

"You don't seem the type to just quit." He still held my hand hostage, trying to find out more about me than I would ever tell him. My quitting shifted my whole life and my whole makeup. It wasn't something I would share with just anyone.

"Maybe I just wanted to."

"You're not good at lying, Mia," he murmured.

"Good game, Daddy." Franny bounded up to us. "You'll win next time, Ms. Darling. Are you guys ready for chicken tenders? They have some on the menu today. My friend told me."

I nodded, and Jameson let me go to put an arm around Franny.

As we walked through the clubhouse, I reminded myself that Paradise Grove was paradise to everyone except me. I was still getting odd looks and knew these women were making it a point to show I didn't belong. They flocked to Jameson as we ate and openly glared at me as they did.

I paid them no attention, showing Franny how she could mix ranch and ketchup instead, and we giggled over her adding more ketchup for the perfect pink color.

Jameson Knight, though, here at the clubhouse, was a man in his own element. It was obvious he knew when to smile at all the right times and how to charm each and every person that approached him. The broody personality he had with me never came out.

The way they fawned over him should have been a turnoff, but I saw Jameson more relaxed, like he knew the environment and controlled it well. His eyes flicked toward the door every now and then though, like he was still on guard and mindful to keep Franny safe as she ate her chicken tenders.

When another woman finally walked away, Franny sighed and rolled her eyes. "Daddy is very popular. Our neighbor Olive said all the girls know him *very well*." She emphasized that, and I immediately lifted a brow at him.

"Is that what Ms. Olive says now? What's *very well* mean, Mr. Knight?"

He didn't seem to want to answer that, and he didn't have to. I shouldn't have even asked. Instead, he pointed to my plate. "Eat."

"I'm not really hungry." The women flirting and smiling and trying so hard had turned my stomach. The fact that I couldn't control my last smash on the court irked me too. I should be able to control my feelings with him and remain passive. That's all I had to do.

"Eat now, or I'll make sure to come to your room later and serve you a meal privately, Mia." There was that broody, cold tone.

I picked up a chicken tender and pointedly took a bite. "Happy?"

"Good girl," he said, and I almost choked on my food.

What the hell?

He patted my back like we were just having normal conversation, and I glared at him but stiffened as I saw a man walking toward us. Both Hades and Archer stepped in his path. Jameson saw it too and was quick to tell us, "Time to go."

The man shoved a letter into Hades's chest and said, "Well, he shouldn't be here then. Make sure he gets it."

When we were safely in the car, Hades handed Jameson the note through the window, and I caught a glimpse of a symbol on the front.

Jameson didn't give me much time to stare, though, as he hid it immediately in his coat pocket before I could make out anything else. "Doctor business is alive and well?"

He sighed. "Yes, Mia. That's exactly why we don't go out and about. Because the doctor business is going *so* well."

"He didn't seem dangerous—"

"He could have been, and you would have never known." He was white knuckling the steering wheel. "I pay you to do a job. Do it and don't do mine."

"What exactly is that job?"

"To keep my daughter safe and you safe."

"You don't have to keep me safe." I wanted to take away some of his anger or maybe some of his responsibility, because it seemed he was carrying the weight of the world there in that car. I felt guilty because he looked so troubled with it.

"But I'm going to, Mia. I'm going to."

Thankfully, Archer's familiar knock roused me from my scream. "Mia, wake up or you'll wake the house up."

"I'm up. I'm up," I grumbled and threw my blankets off in frustration. I'd fallen asleep fighting my mind and body, trying to resist the dreams of Jameson Knight. But not thankfully, I had nightmares instead.

And then I groaned remembering what day it was. Friday. The day Valerie was coming to see Franny and Jameson.

Would I honestly be able to endure this all summer for two million? I had to find a way to stop myself from listening this time.

I even gave myself a pep talk while I slid on a black skirt and buttoned up my white blouse to my neck. I pulled my dark waves into a bun and rubbed moisturizer on my face. When I dragged lip gloss over my bottom lip, I wondered if he bit hers while she was in the study, and then I slammed the gloss down on the counter.

My secret obsession had gone too far, and I knew it. So, I did what I didn't want to do. I called my sister, knowing she'd put me in my place.

"Hello?" her husband's voice growled over the phone after two rings.

"Hey, Felix. It's Mia. I got a new phone." My words were measured, knowing that man seemed to steal some more of my sister's spirit every time I talked with her. "Is Marian with you?"

"Mia." He sighed my name like it was a relief to know I was the one calling from an unknown number. "You should text us if you're changing your number."

"I know. I've been busy. Sorry." My neck muscles were already tightening at how I succumbed to apologizing immediately to him. "Is she there?"

"She's still asleep. We had a long night, and you know how she is." His tone was patronizing, and his words circled the real reason for her not talking with me.

I considered my options. "I got a new job and really wanted to tell her about it."

"Did you now?" That piqued his interest. "Where?"

"A private residence. Better money than the academy, you know?" I dangled the only information I knew he'd bite on. I could see him licking his chops the way he used to when we were younger.

"Better than the academy?" I held my breath for his response. "That's good news. Hold on. I'll see if I can get her up."

After a few moments of rustling, she came on the phone, her voice bright. Too bright. "Mia, your phone has been dead. I've been worried."

"I know. I know. My other phone got lost in the shuffle of moving because I got a new job."

"New?" Immediately, her tone changed. "The public school was stable, Mia."

"Yeah, but they're not going to have me back there and you know it."

"Mom and Dad think that maybe if you apologized—"

"I won't," I cut her off. "They supported hiring on my coach,

Marian. They supported him and didn't stand up for their daughter when she said something."

She sighed and whispered, "I know." Marian wouldn't argue that. She knew the pain he caused, knew I was right even if every damn person in that town thought I was wrong. "Where's the new job?"

I waited a moment and then murmured what I knew would send her into a tailspin. "In Paradise Grove."

"Paradise Grove?" Felix blurted out, and I reminded myself he was always listening, always keeping tabs on her so I couldn't tell her the whole truth or my whole plan. He whistled over the phone. "He better pay you well."

"Paradise Grove is . . . Mia, you need to be careful. People there are very connected."

"Yeah, for the better," Felix seemed to growl at her. "She's finally doing something right. Don't patronize her. We're happy for you, Mia. You should have us there, and maybe we could meet some people."

"Right." That was never happening. "Or maybe at the end of the summer, I can come visit?"

"I don't know—"

"Of course you're always welcome here, Mia," Felix purred, and I recognized that voice all too well.

"Good," I said because I would be coming one way or another. "Hey, how's the weather there?"

She sighed, and to most people it would have seemed like she was assessing the clouds, but it'd been our code for a long time. "Summer's always hot, but it'll get better." *Life was shit, but it'll get better.*

"And the baby?" I asked, because she hadn't offered and that had me more concerned with Felix hovering over her.

"Pregnancy is going great. Baby's healthy. How do you like the new job?"

"It's fine. With this job, I think we'll be able to enjoy that better weather together soon."

"Oh, Mia. Don't keep a job just for that."

The way she whispered the words before we got off the call was all the motivation I needed to remind myself that I didn't care what Jameson was doing with his life—with or without Valerie.

His secrets were his to keep, I told myself. I didn't need to know any more about him or why he kept his women at arm's length but employees so close they could be honest with him.

I wasn't permanent here and didn't need to follow in their footsteps.

I went through my morning routine, and when I saw a couple tech giants walk past the study doors while teaching Franny, I didn't listen. When I saw a man dragged past the study, I made sure Franny was focused on her work too and had Archer close the door.

"I think we should have snack time with Rosy in her kitchen," Franny announced at her desk as she finished her writing assignment and petted Malek, who was constantly by her side.

"I don't think your dad wants you snacking around the house," Hades said from the corner of the room. Archer didn't even respond, just rolled his eyes at what a stickler Hades was.

"Hades doesn't know, Ms. Darling. He lies a lot. I'm not sure why Daddy doesn't fire him for lying," she said matter-of-factly.

"What?" Hades almost gasped, as if completely offended with her statement, but she was already standing to hand me her assignment. "All done. Can we go?"

I shrugged and waved her forward while Hades glared at us, including Archer. "I don't approve of this," he grumbled to him.

"Well, all the more reason for you to accompany them.

Xavier, Bane, and Cal want me to go over a few . . ." Archer glanced at me before he finished, "issues."

"Right." Hades waved Archer away, and Archer motioned to his ear at me.

"Call if you need me."

I found that Archer wasn't necessarily at my side every moment of every day, but he was watching the perimeter of the house with Hades or checking security and rooms that Franny and I went into. Maybe it was overkill, but mostly it made me feel safe.

Even if Hades grumbled about our insubordination the whole way to the kitchen, when we got there, I found his glare was directed more at Rosy than us. Still, she smiled at Franny and pulled her in for a hug. "Did you come to visit?"

"Yes, but Hades didn't want to."

"That's not true. I just said—"

"See, you *are* a liar," Franny pointed out. Rosy glanced at Hades before starting to laugh.

The room snapped with tension when Hades made eye contact with Rosy, though. "You'd be wise not to laugh at Franny's jokes."

"It's not a joke, Hades." Franny lifted her chin and pointedly repeated, "You are a liar."

His mouth dropped open, and Rosy stared straight at him, her gaze unwavering. "You're right, Franny. I think he is a liar."

"We came for snacks." Franny batted her long eyelashes at Rosy, and Rosy immediately threaded her fingers through the child's hand to walk her around the kitchen, picking out strawberries and grapes and cookies and chocolate.

Rosy arranged it all on a platter and pointed to the dining room for us to go sit.

Once there, Franny looked up from her massive pile of food

to say, "Well, this was a great idea. Ridiculous to think Dad would be mad about this."

Although she didn't directly call him out, Hades blinked a few times before his bottom lip almost pouted. "Franny, you've called me a liar, and now ridiculous? I don't try to lie to you, and I'm not ridiculous."

"Oh, Hades." She sounded like she was the adult consoling the child. Then she lifted her binoculars to look through them at Hades as if gathering more evidence. She sighed and lowered them to say, "I think my daddy makes you lie. It's okay, but I don't like it, and we should be honest with Ms. Darling. Honesty is best, right?"

"Well, yes, but—"

"She's living here now, Hades. You and Daddy said you're my uncle because you live with us and now you're family, right? She's going to be family too."

Hades glanced at me and then back at Franny like he'd been broken, like she'd crushed the heart that obviously belonged to the seven-year-old. "Franny, not everyone who lives here can be family."

She tsked. "Of course not, but Ms. Darling is. And she doesn't want to be lied to, right, Ms. Darling?"

Were we still talking about a snack? What else could I say other than "Right."

"So anyway . . ." The little girl popped a strawberry in her mouth and chewed before she said, "I think you should go talk to Rosy before she gets really mad at you, because she said you're a liar too. We'll just eat snacks here."

Hades's frown got deeper, like his whole world was falling apart in front of him. "Are you okay for five minutes?" he asked me.

"Of course." We'd be fine eating together for a few minutes, but as soon as Hades walked into the back kitchen again, Franny jumped up.

"I think today is the day you should probably see where Daddy works."

"Franny, why don't we eat and wait for Hades to get back?"

Curling her lip in disgust, she bolted down to the other side of the room. "Don't be ridiculous like Hades, Ms. Darling. I'll show you *why* Hades is a liar."

"Who's a liar?" Two women that were drop-dead gorgeous, one with a pink bob and the other with brown hair curlier than my own, stood in the doorway of the kitchen.

"Auntie Pink! Olive!" Franny squealed before she leapt into the first woman's arms, then the other's. She whispered to them before announcing, "I knew something was happening today. I was just about to take Ms. Darling to the basement. She's my new nanny."

"Yes, I heard." Pink's gaze was on me, assessing, before she nodded. She had high cheekbones and skin just a bit lighter than mine. Her features were almost fairylike, but her stare was vicious. "You look nicer than I pictured."

"She's very nice." Franny giggled and waved us forward. "Let's go."

Both the women eyed me expectantly, as if they were waiting on me to make the decision to leave Hades behind.

I glanced back and forth before stepping forward to follow the little girl in my care. I shouldn't have. I'd told myself his life was his and a complete secret. I'd made sure to instill that today with a call to my sister. My focus was going to be on rebuilding my life with this salary . . . and maybe hers.

Still, I had to follow Franny. To make sure she was safe and all that.

"Good choice," Olive murmured as we walked down the hall. Pink laughed at Olive and elbowed her.

"Don't reinforce with positivity yet. The girl has to deal with whatever mood Jameson's going to be in down there."

"Who cares?" Olive shrugged and glanced at me. I didn't find myself around other women much, probably because I'd learned the hard way that they could be cruel, but Olive's eyes seemed warm and kind. And full of mischief. "He hasn't even invited me over to meet Ms. Darling."

"Oh, it's Mia. And I'm sure he had intentions of introducing me to . . ." I hesitated, looking over the women. Neither of them looked related to Jameson or Franny. "To family."

Pink seemed happy with the conclusion I'd come to, because she smiled wide before hooking an arm in mine and rounding another corner. "His ass had no intentions, Mia. It's why we're here—to rattle his cage a little. See if we can get the real Jameson to come out."

The real Jameson. Was that the one who took Valerie in the study, or the one who put his hand on my throat to get me to listen with bullets flying outside?

"Has Jameson told you what he does for a living?" Olive inquired, her eyes dancing as we made our way down some stairs and came to a stop in front of double doors.

"He said he was a doctor."

Pink chuckled, and Franny bounced on her toes. "He is. He helps people."

Olive swiped her watch over a small pad to the left of the entry.

The doors unlocked.

That's when I heard a man scream.

11

Jameson

"Fucking Christ, Knight. That burns." Jacques deserved more pain than me scrubbing his road rash clean.

"Should have gone to a hospital, then."

"Can't you give me some drugs? You're killing me," he practically cried.

"So you can go back to rehab?" He knew better, and his eyes danced with mischief I didn't have time for. "I should actually shoot you up with something so you have to endure the withdrawals again."

"That's fucked up." His dark brows slammed down before he started laughing. "I like it. That's the Jameson we're used to."

I poured disinfectant in his wound. Mostly because I wanted to hear his scream. "Franny's here today. A hospital would be better suited for your—"

"Jesus, you fucker." He shoved my hand away that held the liquid. "What do you want me to tell them? Xavier stabbed me after we raced down the highway?"

"I want you to consider the repercussions of your choices."

"You sound like your father."

"My father's in the ground, Jacques, and maybe I sound like *your* dad, but definitely not mine. Mine never considered the repercussions of his actions either. I agonize over every single one." Then I poured more disinfectant on the wound for good measure. Another scream. I should have recorded this to hold over his head.

"You're an asshole. You know that? You were the least careful of all of us before Franny. And now you're even more twisted. I heard what you did to Paolo's men. You got one here now, don't you?"

"I don't know what you're talking about." I wasn't answering any of his questions because I didn't have to. They all answered to me. Not the other way around. "Whatever it is you or the other Heathens think I did, I can do much worse if you keep stumbling in here, bleeding out every week." It was a warning to him and his motorcycle club as I started to close the wound with a sutured needle. It would only take seven stitches, but I intended to make each one hurt.

He winced at the pressure. "What else you got this room for if not to help us?"

The last-minute addition three years ago had served our community well, actually. I'd perfected surgeries, treated gun wounds, saved lives, made allies.

And made enemies.

"Not to deal with you and Xavier's spats. You're two stupid cats from the same litter clawing at each other. I don't have time for it."

"Cats?" He looked affronted as he jumped off the metal operating table, holding his side that was now bandaged. Immediately, two of my guys started cleaning the area. "I'm a pit bull of a fighter."

"You're choosing to argue about that?"

"I'm not a damn cat."

I walked to the sink to clean up. "Get out of my house, Jacques. My daughter is home, and I have a new nanny who's skittish. I don't have time for this."

"If you want the Heathens to run down any of the guys left who came to her school . . ." He clapped me on the shoulder, his voice sincere.

Being allies with his club afforded us a certain amount of protection, but I didn't need favors. "I'll be handling all of them."

"The Diamonds okay with that?"

As I washed away the blood from my hands, red ribbons threaded through the water and swirled down the stainless-steel sink. Mixing and tinging the water pink, just like my ties to the Heathens, to clubs, to societies—we warped and changed each other's existence. Since my father was gone, I led the Diamonds. They didn't lead me.

"Daddy?" My daughter's voice singsonged through the basement walls, and I narrowed my eyes at Jacques as I finished the last of my cleanup.

Two of my men continued cleaning the operating table, and another folded up the stained clothing I'd cut from Jacques.

"Franny, we're back here," he yelled out, because not one of the men I dealt with missed a chance to see my daughter. I would have let it be had I thought Franny was only with Hades, considering it wasn't the first time she'd stumbled upon me while operating.

Not the first time I'd worked on Jacques either. He was reckless on a motorcycle, and with his life. Faulting him for it would have been hypocritical after what he'd said—we both knew I enjoyed tempting death before my daughter.

My problem now wasn't Franny. It was with Mia. Pretty, sweet, naïve Mia, who followed my daughter in with Pink and Olive flanking her.

Two women who weren't sweet or naïve.

Olive lived down the street and had grown up with me. She was sharp, strategic, and always three steps ahead of anyone who dared to cross us. Plus, she was married to Dimitri, who owned part of HEAT, one of the largest tech and real estate businesses in the world.

Then there was Pink, Bane's girl—a player in her own right, one who had a seat at the table of the highest syndicate discussions. Her involvement went far beyond being a companion—she was a mastermind, known for navigating our world in a way that left our enemies scrambling.

They always had a seat at our table when large decisions were made and always would. I trusted them both with my life and with the syndicate.

Trusting them with Mia was a whole other situation, though.

My daughter flew at Jacques and abruptly stopped right before she hugged him, her brows slamming down. "You're hurt again, Jacques? You have to drive safe and stop at all the red lights!"

Jacques whispered placations to her as I took in that Hades was nowhere to be found but Mia stood there almost frozen. Her eyes were wide, her tiny fingers wringing themselves into oblivion, and the rapid rise and fall of her white blouse told me she was uncomfortable. Her cheeks were flushed and she took breaths in through her nose, out through her mouth, like she was trying not to faint.

Glancing behind me, I knew what it looked like: A crazy surgeon had built his own little hospital. Glass walls stood around an operating table with lights that were state of the art, as were all of my tools. I could rip someone apart and put them back together on it easily. I'd done it time and time again.

I'd designed my space with some of the best engineers in the country. I took pride in it but also knew how it looked to an outsider.

And that's what she was.

"Ms. Darling, you're supposed to be teaching," I ground out.

"Franny wanted a snack," she murmured as she took a step forward, but then, like she thought better of it, she took one back as she glanced at the blood seeping through Jacques's chest bandage.

"In the basement?" I ground out. I didn't wait for her answer as I glared at the other women. Both of them were meddlers, and both served our society well. I had utter respect for them in that regard and no respect for them when it came to snooping. "You two have anything else to do with your lives?"

"Nope," they said together. Olive pulled me in for a hug and continued, "My husband has Baby Grayson at work today, and I was bored as ever, but then Pink showed up at my door wanting to come visit you. You're welcome for not bringing all the nosy neighbors too."

"Can you imagine?" Pink snickered.

They both chatted on and on, but I watched how Mia's hands shook at her sides. "You should be upstairs, not down here," I said.

"You're not a real surgeon. This isn't . . . The liability of—"

"You're right. He's a half-assed surgeon, for sure." Jacques laughed as he scooped Franny up with a wince and held her on his good side. He walked over to Mia and held out a hand. "But I can guarantee you I'm not worried about any liabilities. Ms. Darling, is it?"

I shoved his hand away. "We don't need introductions. You need to leave, and Franny needs to go upstairs with Mia."

My daughter frowned at me. "You used to let me come down here." Her tone was hurt, and I didn't know what to say. Yesterday, I'd seen a glimpse of the old Fran, carefree while she swung that racket with us at tennis, but we couldn't be that way always.

Jacques wasn't deterred; he leaned around me, and Franny started giggling. "Of course Ms. Darling needs to know my name is Jacques. I'm here all the time. Right, Olive?" He continued on like he was going to tell Mia everything about our lives. "Olive comes over way too much too, but I guess that's what happens when you grow up neighbors. Old habits die hard."

"He does get hurt a lot, Daddy," Franny reasoned with me quietly while Olive rolled her eyes and brushed a curl from her face.

Then Olive walked around me like no one had any respect for my concern. My daughter shouldn't be exposed to any of this. It'd bled into her life too much already, figuratively and literally. Olive pulled Jacques in for a hug to tell him, "You're making this worse for Jameson. We already had planned to surprise Ms. Darling. Now she got two surprises."

"But who doesn't like surprises?" Jacques scanned Mia head to toe, and his smirk hid nothing. I didn't like the hunger in his eyes. I didn't need complications with someone who was employed in my home.

"She doesn't." I shoved him toward the back door. "Go home, and don't come back here."

"I'm waiting for a ride. My bike got laid out and I'm injured, remember? Unless you want to lend me that Ducati?"

"Fuck off. You're fine. Wait outside, and don't come here for stitches again. If you and Xavier want to spar like children, my doors aren't open to you."

That's when Hades walked in, nostrils flaring like he'd sprinted down here.

After five minutes of Franny and Mia being unattended, his hustle didn't matter.

"You take a wrong turn?" I lifted a brow at him.

"Rosy and I were discussing the week. Ms. Darling and Franny were supposed to stay put," he pointedly said at Mia, but then his gaze fell to Pink and Olive. "Figures you two were behind this."

"Oh no, Hades. I wanted Daddy. I knew he would be down here. I was using my spy eyes and binoculars this morning. I saw Jacques, and you lied about it." Franny pouted as she leaned into Jacques. "Jacques, when you come to get fixed up, I want to visit."

"Of course you do, Fran Bran, but you were learning, right? School blows, but you gotta do it."

"Actually, school doesn't blow," Mia piped up, crossing her arms. "And although I'm not sure this is the routine learning space"—she cleared her throat and looked between my daughter and me—"Franny obviously enjoys new, *outside* experiences."

I tried not to growl in annoyance at Mia. Her pushing me continually still wasn't warranted. That email was out of line. Her insisting on being at the club was out of line. And her being down here was too. She'd caused another bloody crime scene with her actions, because I'd been done with checking over my damn shoulder at the club after yesterday. She'd be happy to know we'd neutralized the threat late last night. My men dragged O'Connor to one of our warehouses, and I had personally pulled information from him piece by piece before taking his life. We were all wound tight because of it, but I'd acted quickly after seeing my daughter at the country club. Seeing her smile outside, under the sunshine, made the decision quite easy.

Maybe seeing Mia in a different element had made it easier to act quickly too. She'd met me swing for swing on the tennis courts and opened up to me in a way I didn't expect. I wanted that more from her.

For Franny.

"I do like outside experiences." Franny nodded vigorously. "I even want to ride Daddy's motorcycle bike, too, but he won't let me. Probably because Jacques keeps falling off."

"A motorcycle?" Mia's wide eyes ping-ponged everywhere.

I pinched the bridge of my nose. I didn't need this girl

knowing any more about me or my family than she already did. I turned to Hades. "Are you capable of escorting her back to the study?"

"I don't know. Maybe you should, since you want me to continue to be the prick," Hades threw back at me. He was running on about an hour of sleep, but I didn't give a fuck.

"Don't make me fire you today."

"We can't fire Uncle Hades, Daddy. He's family."

"Yeah. I'm family." He chuckled and patted her head like the happiest man in the world. Franny had him wrapped around her finger. "Anyway, I'm guessing Franny actually needs a snack since she barely ate any of the food on the table after calling me a liar."

Franny huffed. "You said nothing was going on today, but you *knew* Jacques was here. I know it." She wiggled away from Jacques to stomp her little foot.

"I'll make it up to you, kid. We can go beg Rosy for more food, huh?" Hades said, his voice full of remorse as they started walking toward the door.

"Oh, I want a snack, too, I think," Olive announced while Pink considered her options.

"Really? I wouldn't mind seeing this play out." She smiled between Mia and me like she knew we were about to bite each other's heads off.

Mia needed to know her place around here, and the conversation would have to be direct. She couldn't wander around unattended or follow Franny wherever she wanted to go. She needed to be the disciplinarian along with being the nanny.

"Just get out of my operating room, Pink."

"Fine. Fine." Didn't they know they should fear me just a little?

When Hades hesitated, I told him, "I'll show Mia back to the study after we have a discussion."

"Maybe on the way, you can show me the rest of the house, too, since I never saw this part on the tour," Mia said.

"Yeah," Hades said with a chuckle. "Show her the *rest* of it." His statement was pointed now, poking at the one place I didn't want him to, and he knew it. I kept one other room sectioned off from all the staff. Mia would be no different. "*Every* single room."

"Get the fuck out of my sight." Or maybe she was already so different that I didn't want her seeing that room at all. Not after the way her eyes widened at seeing the basement.

Hades walked by me and leaned in. "Lay ground rules for the teacher. She's already completely bulldozed through the norm."

He was right.

And I wasn't sure if I cared, because I was about to bulldoze through every single professional rule I had as soon as they left.

12

Mia

EVERYONE LEFT . . . ABANDONING ME with Jameson Knight.

With the boss I never wanted.

With the man who meticulously sewed people back together in his basement while dissecting me piece by piece. He didn't look at all concerned or flustered by the fact that a man had been bleeding on his basement floor.

Rather, he looked only irritated with me in the lower level of his home that seemed to essentially be a small hospital. A place he practiced medicine on men who obviously were hiding their dealings.

And not one person who'd come down here with me acted at all disturbed. Instead, they were comfortable with him. This was a man in his element, perched on his throne, confident in his power with people he trusted by his side.

I might have watched Jameson charm people at the clubhouse yesterday, and they might personify the wealth and luxury of this exclusive enclave, but this Jameson was the king of Paradise Grove. A man of power and precision.

Calculated and commanding.

In control.

I'd known he was part of something sinister all along, but his confidence told me he ruled it. He managed it. He structured it. I'd been a fool to think otherwise.

And not even his daughter appeared surprised.

Instead, she'd looked hurt he'd left her out. Which was a whole other issue. Their relationship was strained. She loved her daddy, but I saw her little glances and pouts over the last week when he didn't stop by the study to say hi, when he didn't include her in whatever he was working on. Something had changed between them, and she didn't understand it. She was seven. How could she?

"Mia Darling, time to lay more ground rules, it seems."

Oh, please. I wasn't about to carve out more stipulations and rules on the imaginary wall between us when the secret waters would just seep through the cracks and flood it. "Or we have a real conversation," I blurted out, but my body shook with adrenaline at confronting him.

Who was I? A teacher he could get rid of in an instant. Not many would really miss me. My parents would probably sigh and finally speak of me just so they could put on my tombstone, "She got what she deserved." My mom always believed it was better to stay quiet, and my dying for speaking up would have proved her right.

She'd thought that with my coach. But I spoke up. She thought that with my job, but I spoke up, and then with my sister too. Silence could be perceived as acceptance more often than it should. But I wouldn't allow it anymore when I needed to be heard.

"What is a *real* conversation to you?" he asked as if I were dense.

Fine. He probably thought being a teacher made me somehow inferior to him, and I could see it in his judgmental eyes. But I could be judgmental too. "Same as there are dirty cops, I guess there are dirty surgeons too . . . Are you 'helping' criminals down here daily?" I whispered. "God, I knew it would be bad, but he's a part of a motorcycle gang. That wasn't just a scrape. I saw the blood. He was *stabbed.* And no one—not even your daughter—cares."

"Well, let's be clear. Franny thinks it's a bike accident. And everyone else is used to it, Mia." Jameson leaned casually against the table Jacques had been sitting on while I paced back and forth.

I combed my hands through my hair, feeling the bile swirl in my stomach. "Am I aiding and abetting? I'm just as bad if I stay here being your stupid freaking nanny! I'm teaching her math while you . . . what? Sew up felons?"

He didn't deny it. He just let me pace back and forth, back and forth.

"And the motorcycle gang will keep seeing my face, and you told them my name, so I'm practically *in* now."

"You're not in a motorcycle gang." Did he sound freaking bored? "It's not a gang. It's a club."

"Same thing! Next thing I know, I'll hear you're selling drugs."

He blinked slowly, no denial leaving his lips.

"Oh my God. You're a drug dealer in a motorcycle club, and I'm helping you. I'm trying to get out of one mess and stepping into another." How could I save my sister if I couldn't even save myself?

"What mess?" His blue eyes were laser focused on me now. Jameson Knight thought he knew everything about me, but he didn't know what drove me to take that summer school job in the first place.

I'd known it wasn't stable, wasn't smart, was too good to be true. I'd dealt with all those things before. That's exactly what Felix was in our lives. "Not your concern. Your salary offer will fix my problems."

"You don't have debt." His eyes narrowed on me, searching for answers I wasn't going to give him.

"Well, we all have secrets, Jameson." I crossed my arms over my chest, and his eyes flicked down. Oh great. Now we were dealing with my attraction to him too.

"You say my first name only in anger, Mia."

I scoffed. "I really shouldn't be saying your first name at all."

He rubbed a hand across his jaw, a tell I was starting to learn was him trying to wipe away an emotion. "True, and yet I continue to find myself interested in what it will sound like coming from your mouth in a different tone."

Trying to squelch the heat I felt at him staring at my lips, I murmured, "Maybe try not being in a gang then."

There was that half smile of his, like I was ridiculous. "Mia, I'm *not* in the Heathens motorcycle club."

"You have a bike." I pointed toward the door, getting angrier at the secrets because I knew I shouldn't care about him, but I was finding that I did. I told myself it was just that he'd saved my life at the school, or that he was Franny's dad and I wanted what was best for her. I'd have to focus on that. "Your daughter said you ride when she's not around. It's dangerous."

"Yes, a Ducati can be dangerous, and when she's not around, I'm on it."

"Right. And you helped Jacques, who is—"

"In a motorcycle club." He sighed like he didn't want me to put two and two together. "And I'm there when the club needs me, but I'm not a part of it. Don't make assumptions."

"So, you just help anyone who pays?" That wasn't it. It couldn't be. He held too much authority, and even if he didn't want me to, I could put two and two together.

"It's complicated."

"Or it's not. You're secretly in a gang and probably are the head of that gang because they all listen to you. To lead a gang like that . . . it's not complicated. It's *dangerous*." I couldn't help but take a shaky breath as I paced over to the sink and then turned to him to lean against it.

"*If* that was the case, Mia, that I was in a sort of gang, would you be nervous for me?"

Was he for real?

"For *Franny*," I corrected him fast, "and myself."

He took a step toward me, and I leaned back. "It would be no more danger than you were already in when you took the academy job. Less, actually, with me and my men here."

"It's true then? You lead them?"

"Are you asking even when I told you it's best you not know?"

The room was probably holding its breath waiting for my answer as I looked into his blue eyes. "I'm asking what was in that envelope you took at the country club, what club you're in exactly, and what you do for a living, Jameson. Yes, I'm asking."

"A lot of questions."

"And I want all the answers."

He nodded. "I *lead* something with a few others, yes."

"And Franny?" I couldn't stop myself from whispering because that girl was just a child, just an innocent little thing who deserved the world.

"And Franny has . . . been born into it. I promise I'm keeping you and Franny safe."

His words felt so sincere, laced with such sweet poison, I almost crumbled and folded right there, but my hand gripped the side of the sink to steady myself and slipped.

Red stain smeared across my palm. I saw how it painted my skin crimson and jolted away from it.

Immediately, Jameson steadied me by putting an arm around my waist and gripping my wrist softly.

"You can't promise anything. There's blood. His blood is

everywhere." I wheezed, and suddenly my breath caught like it didn't want to enter my lungs. Blood—like at the school, like in my nightmares—filled my eyes. That red would not wash away no matter how hard I tried.

"Mia." His voice was steady, strong, solid. "*Darling* Mia," he murmured again, and I felt the tone of it, like I was too sweet, too naïve, like I couldn't handle this.

"I saw you kill a man, and now I've seen you piecing another one back together. That's what a life like this is. Destruction and then piecing it back together as if it can be whole again. You realize that, right? Whatever you're in can't just be fixed."

He nodded like he agreed that it was complicated, that my emotions were relevant, that I wasn't spiraling into the panic attack that I was. "I like to think I can fix most anything."

My brain tried to catch up with what was happening. I clawed through my memories and hoped to find more clues, things I'd missed, evidence in this estate. "The letter and the emblem on the seal—"

"You can't go back to the life you lived, Mia, if you find out about this one. I'm trying to—"

"I'm already here. I already can't go back. Because none of this is normal." I gasped for air, but he didn't let me get lost in my feelings or emotions.

"It's normal *here*. Where you live. Now." He yanked me into his chest, body to body, and let go of my wrist for a moment to turn on the water. Then he gripped it again to put my hand under the faucet.

When he splashed it over my hands, the ice-cold water jolted me, but he held me steady, firm, and with care as he rubbed at the red on my hand.

"Paradise Grove? A paradise in hell?"

"Maybe." He took a breath. "Isn't it normal to help a friend though? It was a minor procedure. I'm a doctor, he's a patient. You saw him up and talking. His blood is being washed away."

Washing away the stain didn't mean that I forgot it had been there, that I wouldn't be traumatized from this now too. "Everyone is just okay with this. How are you all okay with it?"

Jameson's jaw worked up and down before he responded. "Time allows for adaptation. And we've all had time. I realize this is hard for you. If you need someone to help you teach Franny until you're ready—"

The panic screeched to a halt as his words hit me straight in the chest. "I don't need help with teaching." There was a difference between doing my job and not being comfortable with what he did, with adapting to a new environment.

Franny was thriving because I treated her like a child rather than an adult all the time. She trusted me. Yesterday she'd had her father, not just stuffy Mr. Knight, at the clubhouse. I saw how the light glittered in her eyes, how her smile reached higher than it normally did. "I'm good at what I do, and your daughter trusts me."

Was he trying to dispose of me now after holding me here against my will? And after I cared for his daughter in a way that others weren't? Nobody else saw her. They weren't paying attention to how reserved she'd become.

He narrowed his eyes. "I wasn't insulting your work ethic or skill, Mia."

I tried to pull away, but he held me there. "I. Don't. Need. Help." Maybe I was stubborn, but I found myself holding firm on this. I'd put Franny's needs first. Always.

Could he say that about someone else he'd bring in?

"Okay," he said slowly, "but if you need more time to acclimate. Her psychiatrist—"

"Valerie?" That woman definitely wouldn't put Franny's

needs before Jameson's or her own. Was he kidding me? "The woman at the country club yesterday?"

"She knows Franny. And maybe a little time and patience with this change would help, Ms. Darling." I was starting to realize he used my formal title when he pushed me professionally, when he wanted his way and thought he could get it with a stern hand.

I lifted my chin so that we were just a breath away from one another, his thumb still rubbing away whatever was left on my hand. "If that's the case, why did you already *let* Valerie leave? And why on earth would you bring someone back who didn't work in the first place?"

He tilted his head as if considering, "How do you know?"

"Franny told me," I blurted out.

He hummed, his voice vibrating between both of us.

"I'm guessing she was fine with all this as well? Is she a part of it?" I glanced at the blood washing away in the sink.

He pulled my hand from the water and grabbed a napkin from a dispenser on the wall. He wiped droplets from me instead of letting me do it myself. "I had her step away from full-time nannying because she wanted more than what was available to her."

He evaded the real reason, and I found myself digging in deeper. "Wanted more from her job, from whatever group you're in, or from you?"

He threw the napkin past me, where there must have been a garbage can, and looked down at me for a moment. I swear his mouth curled a tiny bit on one side, like I was amusing him. "You can't help but ask questions, can you?"

"I think at this point it's best to get as much of the whole picture as possible." I took a deep breath, my words echoing through the room. Why did I need knowledge about my elusive boss when really I just needed to keep this position long enough to get paid and live through it?

Because I wanted it.

Because I thought about him constantly, couldn't take my mind off him or what was happening in his office. With Valerie and without her.

Still, Jameson contemplated how much he wanted to tell me. His arm was still around my waist, and mindlessly, he rubbed my back. The man was obviously comfortable around women—from the way he held me to the way he'd handled my anxiety to even how he maintained my eye contact.

He wasn't what I was used to. So confident that he could command the room, control emotions of everybody in it.

"Valerie needed a clear line of what our relationship was and what it wasn't. She's here now only to provide therapy to Franny and to visit. She was relieved of any further duties unless—"

"I can do my job *by myself*." My words were final and almost rabid. I was protective now, ready to pounce if he insinuated I couldn't. "Unless you want Valerie here for your own . . ." I looked away, stopping myself.

"My own what?"

"Never mind." I shook my head.

He leaned in though, and I felt his breath on my cheek. "Does it help your whole picture to know who I am and am not sleeping with, Mia?"

I jerked back and caught his stare. "Of course not. I don't care about your personal life. I agreed to stay here for my protection and for a salary. To be an employee."

"Yet, you're asking about my sex life. Are you not?"

"You're accusing me of that when you're holding my waist right up against you, Jameson? Not very professional," I pointed out.

The smile that whipped across his face was fast. I'd never been on the receiving end of it like that. Franny normally was the one who got his genuine smiles. Taking it in and reveling in its brilliance wasn't something I had time for. I was sparring with the man, for God's sake, but I wanted a picture of it, a framed painted portrait to remember it by.

"Do you think I care about professionalism, Ms. Darling?"

"You must, to some extent, with the secrets you keep. Why sneak around risking Franny's safety and not tell the police that someone is after you if you're not doing anything wrong?"

"Because I know I can control and take care of what the police can't." He leaned in and whispered, "I don't keep secrets because I want them hidden, I keep them because people can't handle knowing them. Can you?"

I looked him up and down. Had it been three weeks ago at the academy, I would have laughed nervously and backed down. I would have skittered around the question and acted like I didn't hear it. I'd been taught to not ruffle feathers and to be thankful for everything I got.

Maybe the push was small and maybe my voice shook when I answered, but I still quietly answered, "Yes."

"You want the whole picture—tell me what you think could possibly be worse than a motorcycle club."

"The mob. Part of the Armanelli Family." They'd been infamous for years. Most of Chicago knew of them, and they were revered nationwide.

"Try again," he told me, and my breath caught.

The murmurs when I was young had been around. People had conspiracy theories about everything and everyone.

Still, saying the name felt silly when it probably wasn't true.

"A Diamond?"

He didn't answer yes or no, but he stepped back, letting his hands drop to his sides. The silence spoke volumes, and a tiny ringing started in my ears, like a siren or an alarm. It echoed over and over around me and sank into my skin, my veins, my bones.

"No." I shook my head once. "That's impossible. The Diamonds are of myths and legends."

"Or citizens of Paradise Grove."

"Everyone here?" My voice came out a squeak.

"No. We don't share that privilege with everyone, but most are eager to be a part of it if they know."

"Why?"

"*Adamantem infractum manet.* You and I both know what that means." A diamond remains unbroken. The saying that meant they were indestructible, all powerful. Most of the nation had heard the statement. People knew of the secret society and how much power it held, knew of the saying. I nodded as he dragged a finger over my collarbone. "You're trembling."

I gulped and looked away, not sure I could respond without my voice shaking too, but I had to try. "I'm digesting the information."

"You finally fear me, darling Mia? Have I cracked that resolve all of a sudden?"

"All of a sudden?"

"You've held your own this long. Nothing should change now. A secret society can't possibly be worse than what you were imagining I was part of."

I wasn't sure about that. "What's your role? Do you lead it?"

"I'm a Knight, Mia. And my father used to hold most of the power."

"And so now you do." He didn't have to say another word. "What happened to your father, Jameson?" His eyes held mine. "And your wife?" I didn't miss how they hardened at that question.

"I think you've asked enough questions for the day." He locked down his secrets so fast, like he couldn't trust a single soul, like those barriers were permanently in place, keeping everyone out.

"Have I?" I blurted out. There was no use fearing him now. I was too far in. And didn't I deserve the answers when I'd been made to stay here?

"My wife never showed to pick Franny up from school, and later she was found dead. I won't have the same happen to Franny . . . or to you."

I pieced together what must have happened, how he had to tell Franny that her mom was never coming home.

And my heart broke for not only the man who lost his wife and his partner but also the daughter who lost her mother. "Jameson, it must have been hard for you and Franny to—"

"Franny only thinks her mom *left*. We don't discuss anything else. You won't either." He stood there stiff with authority, so disconnected that I wondered if it was a defense mechanism.

"You know you could just ask me to rather than demand it," I pointed out.

He clenched his jaw down like there was a struggle, a struggle to trust me, to see me as an ally when it came to his daughter and his life rather than an obstacle. "I could, but then there would be the risk that—"

"That I respect you rather than fear you, Mr. Knight?"

His brows slammed down in agitation.

"I'm here for the best interest of Franny. You know that by now. So, work with me and try to trust me."

"Trust is a weakness."

"Do you think that with your friends? With Archer? With Hades and—"

"They're different."

"Your wife would have wanted—"

"Me to trust no one because I couldn't trust her either, Mia." He swallowed and sucked on his teeth before saying quietly, "We knew she abandoned us before her accident." He didn't say why. "It was hard enough to explain to my daughter that Lex didn't care to come home. We don't see a need to tell Fran she died a year later, or have her mourn a mother I couldn't trust enough to stay." His words were harsh, but as I digested all that information, I found myself hurting for him. For his loss. And for the resilience he had to have.

Yet, I tried my best not to feel bad for him now. He didn't want the pity. "I understand. But you *can* trust me. I'll prove that with Franny. I want what's best for her only, and I won't tell you how to parent, but . . ."

"But you want to?"

"I think at some point, you should consider telling her the news about her mother as she gets older."

"Of course you think that." He scoffed. I knew I was overstepping, but I couldn't help myself.

"Kids are tougher than you think."

He hummed. "That why you want to go on adventures with her off the estate?"

"Well, honestly . . ." I couldn't stop myself from throwing my hands into the air. "What's the endgame if we can't even go outside, which is what's best for *her*. When will the Diamonds be protected enough for that, or can't you guarantee our safety?"

"Watch yourself," he warned, eyes darkening and turning cold. The pride that man had was a weapon I'd use against him and all of the Diamonds if it meant I got outside.

"No. You're concerned that your daughter's life is at risk, but quite frankly, this is putting her mental health at risk when she can't even go outside these walls!" Didn't he get that locking her up like Rapunzel wouldn't work?

"You think I don't know that?" he bellowed back, his control slipping too. Good. I probably should have cowered at the volume, knowing now who he was, but I didn't care. "You think I'm unaware that this isn't the ideal life for a child? I saw her at the country club yesterday. I know she needs to get out and be a kid. I'm working on it."

"Yeah, well, work faster," I threw back. I couldn't believe myself. He was going to throw me out on my ass and let whatever rival mob or secret society have me.

His eyes widened before he let out a low chuckle, rubbing one large hand behind his neck before it snapped out and gripped mine, hard enough for me to get nervous, not so hard that he took my breath away. "No one talks to me like that."

"Well, I do," I murmured, holding his gaze, ready to fight if he wanted to.

"I can't believe I haven't strangled you yet."

The ringing in my ears got louder, and along with it, my blood pumped faster. But also my nipples tightened, and my core clenched. It was embarrassing that I found myself wanting to see if I could make him completely lose it, to see how far this man would go, and to see how much I already desired it. I was supposed to be the responsible one here.

"You'll have to if you expect me to just roll over, *Mr. Knight*," I retorted, holding his gaze.

"Careful, Mia."

"Or what?" I asked, leaning into his grip. I knew what he was a part of now, and maybe I was this unhinged because I was in some sort of shock. Maybe I always had it in me to fight back when I needed to, and maybe I wasn't going to stop now.

That high-pitched sound in my ears became a roar, drowning out every other worry of mine as his jaw flexed like he was trying to hold back.

"Or. What?" I asked again.

"Or you'll find I'll lose control . . . and you might just like it."

"Like it?" He didn't know what I was feeling. He couldn't. I didn't even know fully what was going on with *my own body* around him. "There's nothing about you that I like."

That was the truth too. Sure, his hands burned into my neck and lit my soul afire, but he was still a member of a secret society, still a danger to my life, still the boss I'd grown to hate.

"You say that with such confidence, and yet I distract you. Your eyes wander. Much like my mind has wandered to you in my house these past few days."

"You're mistaken." I hurried to correct him as my heart beat faster, like I was guilty, like I could lose control, like I wasn't as morally sound as I was making myself out to be. "In any case, if you have such a problem with me, I promise not to distract you in this operating room. I'll make sure to stay out of your way."

"You in my house is distracting enough," he grumbled, his thumb rubbing over my pulse. Then he pulled his hand back.

"Seriously?" I blurted out, almost as irritated with myself for missing his touch immediately as I was with him for complaining about my presence. Why did I always have to be the bigger person? The one who made sure everyone stayed in line. My next words flew out like an angry bird aiming to knock down some of his confidence. "You were the one who wanted to force me to stay here. Don't forget. And please tell me you're capable of avoiding me in this massive house of yours if I annoy you so much."

His hand twitched like he was reconsidering choking me out. "Every woman is annoying. God knows you're the worst of them. But when you watch me with those big eyes filled with fiery attraction that completely contradicts your contempt, I'm *distracted.* Not annoyed. When you look at my lips and lick yours, I'm *definitely* distracted, Mia. And that's a problem."

"Excuse m-me?" I stuttered. "I don't look at you like that."

"So, this is still *just* the job, us arguing?"

He moved closer, and I tried to control my rapid breathing. "Of course."

"Really? Because I'd hate to think you're distracted when

taking care of my daughter. Quite frankly, your comfort here is of the utmost importance too. It's the only thing that matters for your job." He tilted his head as if gauging my reaction to him. "Can you be comfortable in the presence of a Diamond who disgusts you but who's paying your bills?"

I lifted my chin.

Fucker.

"Yes. I'll be fine with it." I'd just curse him every time I walked out of the room.

"If you're distracted while teaching and caring for my daughter, you're not giving her your best. I expect it."

"Oh, well, then. Good. Because I'm fine."

He pushed his chest into me, and his hand came to my neck to feel me taking a gulp at our proximity. "The blush on your cheeks, the biting of that lip, and your rapid breathing say you're not."

"You're fucking delusional."

"A filthy mouth too. I guess you got a little devil in the darling then, huh? I'd say I like the Devilish Darling, but I don't like you lying and it's what you're doing now. You know I'm not delusional." He dragged a finger across my jaw and then down my neck to my collarbone. He watched how I swallowed and shivered against his touch, so soft and yet so in control that it couldn't be ignored.

"Your ego is huge if you think you're affecting me, Mr. Knight. This is unprofessional."

"Actually, it's the most professional thing I can think to do. That way, you don't keep thinking about what it'd feel like to have my lips on you, and I'm not thinking of you spreading your legs for me twenty-four seven."

"I don't think about that."

"*Darling* Mia." He said my name as a chastisement. "I saw the way you looked at my mouth."

"How?" I whispered.

His eyes dropped to my lips, where his gaze practically burned my flesh, searing into my body and straight to my core. Suddenly, his cold stare melted away and he held nothing back. I felt his hunger and unrelenting need in the air.

I fell into it and couldn't climb out. Down, down, down I went. I wondered what it would be like for him to take me after looking at me like that, what his lips would feel like, if his touch would be rough or soft.

When he leaned in a centimeter, I grabbed his shirt and murmured, "Jameson."

He didn't come closer, even as I pulled him toward me and slid to the side of the sink so I could lean against the steel counter behind me. His jaw flexed as he let out a low growl. "I might enjoy my name on your lips like *that* a bit too much, Mia," he said, his gaze snapping back up to mine. The hunger was gone, almost like I'd imagined it. "Anyway, now you understand."

"Understand?"

"How it feels when you look at me."

"You're kidding?" I practically seethed, but then his hand was at my hip, fingers sliding into the waistband of my skirt.

"You want me like I want you." He wasn't asking. Just stating a fact. "If not, tell me to stop before I touch you."

My skin lit up, ignited from his calloused hands digging into that sensitive spot at my inner hip, at his thumb swiping down lower toward my core. He did it slowly. I could have grabbed him, I could have shifted away, but instead I held the edge of the counter behind me, my body practically begging for him to go further. "You don't want this. I'm your daughter's teacher."

It was all I could get out. I didn't say *stop*, and he knew it. He leaned in, breathed in my scent at the base of my neck. "I've wanted this since the first day I saw you. Pretty dark hair blowing in the wind, your voice as sweet as a melody when my daughter ran up to you. Now, you're in my house and it's all I think about . . . how you'll sound when you moan for me. I don't practice resistance because it breeds longing and weakness. I'd rather find out how you taste and indulge in the fantasy so I don't have it again. Wouldn't you?"

That brought me back to what he truly was. Meticulous. Calculated. Cold Jameson Knight. He wanted resolution to his feelings—he wanted to get rid of them.

"If that helps you draw a professional line, Mr. Knight." I lifted my chin, because if he was drawing a line, so was I. He wanted to get me out of his system, well, I wasn't going to even let him in mine.

"'Mr. Knight' again, huh?" His smile was slow and vicious. "I guess it's imperative that I prove it to you."

"Prove it?"

"Prove how you're going to be soaked for me and dripping from this counter, begging for me to fuck you."

I was so worked up I just blurted out the truth. "That's nearly impossible. No man has ever made me want to beg. Quite frankly, I don't even get that wet for myself."

"Yourself?" He searched my eyes for more information, and I immediately regretted what I'd said.

"Probably forget I said that."

"Share with the class, Ms. Darling." He smirked, and I hated how much I loved it. "How wet do you get when you touch yourself?"

"That's not what I meant." I shoveled lies onto my truth, hoping to hide it.

"I'm going to enjoy making you tell me. You'll tell me everything I want, and you know why?"

"Why?" I asked, because I was a weak woman giving in to a

freaking gorgeous man that probably would never stand in front of me like this again.

He yanked my skirt down in one swift movement, then grabbed the backs of my thighs to shove me onto the counter, spreading my legs wide so I sat there exposed in front of him with just my panties on. "Because we Diamonds might disgust you, but we also get everything we want. Now take your shirt off."

I lifted my chin even though I was so turned on I knew I was giving myself away—my panties couldn't hide my arousal. They were wet already. "You get what you want because you take it rather than anyone giving you it willingly."

His voice rumbled out deep, threaded in irritation. "What if I told you that from now on, you can take Franny anywhere in Paradise Grove that you want, Mia?"

"What?" Was he bribing me? Negotiating?

"Untie your blouse and you can."

Jesus, that was hotter than I wanted it to be. I bit my lip before bringing my hands to the tie at my side. His blue eyes were there, watching with piercing intensity. "And you show me the rest of the house?"

"Fine. Take. It. Off."

I undid the material. I gave in. I handed him my naked body on a platter, and as I dropped the fabric over my shoulders, I wondered if I ever really stood a chance at all.

13

Jameson

SHIT.

Shit. Shit. Shit.

The devil of the darling in front of me was that I couldn't resist her. And she didn't even try to resist me either. I'd clocked how her eyes flashed with recognition when I told her I was a part of the Diamonds. Still, she hadn't left.

It wasn't common knowledge that a secret society was laced throughout Paradise Grove, but it wasn't a huge secret either. People talked, rumors spread, and people either believed it or they didn't.

The thing about the news nowadays was that most people were so self-absorbed they barely even blinked when aliens were proven to be real. No one cared about a secret society . . . unless, of course, they could benefit from it or lose everything to it.

Ours was the most beneficial, the most influential, and the most powerful in the world. We could hand someone diamonds, or we could hand them the dagger that would end their life. Once people were close enough, they realized that and begged.

Begged for their life. Begged for wealth. Begged for their hopes and their dreams.

They squirmed for most everything. All of them.

But not Mia. Mia Darling had the audacity to turn her nose up to me and look physically ill. Maybe it was the fact that she wasn't starstruck, that she didn't bend to my will immediately, that she didn't fawn over me when most women did. Or maybe it was the fact that she was so uptight and innocent that I wanted to peel back every part of her personality.

She was professional at every turn until it came to taking care of my daughter. Then she pushed and broke every rule. She was sweet to everyone, but when she talked to me, she was rude and disobedient. It fucked with my head enough that I'd avoided her for weeks. Avoidance only went so far when she pushed me in ways I couldn't ignore, though. Coming into my basement was the last fucking straw.

Indulging in this would deter her and set us straight again. We get a fix and flush it out of our systems. I needed it after the night I'd had. What I didn't tell her was that I'd already sent my men on a rampage, and that's why Jacques was here bleeding out. I wouldn't have us cowering inside my walls a second longer, not when I'd seen how happy Mia and Franny were outside of them.

Mia shouldn't have been in that equation.

And I shouldn't have used it as a negotiating tool to get her naked.

Yet, I was a Diamond and a Knight. I'd do anything for the upper hand. Or what I thought was the upper hand, because as that blouse fell from her shoulders, I almost lost my balance.

All the blood flowing straight to my cock must have caused it. And that was a problem for a man who had a million enemies . . . and one in particular who wasn't admitting to attacking his daughter's school. I couldn't be distracted or have my attention elsewhere. She needed to be swept out of my thoughts and put back in a place where I didn't give a damn about her.

Yet, her skin was smooth, supple, not a tattoo in sight other than a small one on her wrist as I dragged an inked knuckle over one breast. I was interested in why she hadn't marked up her body more and wanted to ask, to see if her answer would be as judgmental as her comment about the Diamonds. Everything about the woman had become interesting to me. Why she liked fuchsia, even. The fact that I remembered such small things about her was getting to be ridiculous.

I hooked an arm around her to pull her closer to the edge of the counter and sighed, letting my gaze slowly creep over her. "You had to be even more flawless without clothes on, didn't you?"

"Hardly flawless." Her voice was gentle, like she was suddenly shy even though she'd not stopped my perusal. She let me stare, and I did. The top of her breasts filled her bra enough that they were almost spilling out, her arms sported goose bumps, and her hands were gripping the counter's edge like she was trying to keep from moving. I stared, probably could have all day, but she chewed on her lip and finally said, "You get your fill?"

"No. Do you rush all men?"

"Men I'm with don't stare."

"Men you *were* with," I corrected immediately, as if I had some claim on her.

She pursed her lips but didn't argue. Instead, she bit the corner of her lip as if she were trying not to smile and murmured, "Done now?"

"Not even close." I brushed my thumb close to the end of her bra, and her lips parted enough that I could bring my other thumb to that bottom lip and slide it onto her tongue. "I'm memorizing every part of you, darling Mia. Taking in perfection shouldn't be rushed."

That pull between us coiled tighter as I turned my hand over her breast and cupped it while my thumb pad pushed further into her mouth, seeking that wet tongue of hers. We were dancing on the edges of her boundaries, I knew it, but I chose to overstep as I leaned in and murmured in her ear, "Suck it, darling devil. Give me an image I couldn't forget if I tried."

The blush on her cheeks heated her face either in embarrassment or desire. I curled my thumb over the lace of her bra and brushed her nipple as I whispered, "Please."

Maybe it was my hand in her bra and how I touched her nipple, or maybe it was me being at her mercy and begging, but instead of biting my damn thumb off, her tongue slid up and around me. She closed her eyes as if too shy to hold my gaze while her lips wrapped around me and, then I felt it. The pull of her suction as her cheeks hollowed.

It shot straight through my body and almost had me losing control. Instead, I gripped her jaw just to hold her there and take it all in before I let the swear rumble out of me, "Fuuuck. You want to ruin my mind, don't you?"

Her eyelids fluttered open, and I took my time pulling my thumb from her mouth. Slowly. Deliberately. I wiped it across that bottom lip of hers, the one that drove me mad every time I saw her bite it. I wanted to see her pretty mouth glistening like it was ready for me to put something much bigger in it now.

Then, I moved my hand down her back to pop the clasp of her bra, letting her breasts spill out. My hands were on them immediately, massaging and molding them to my grip before I moved to touch her everywhere. I couldn't get my fill, from her tits to the slope of her waist and how it flared wider into her hips. I gripped her there, took hold of her, pressed harder than I should have in hopes it would leave marks. Her curves were ones she kept hidden under flowy dresses and blouses. And even though I was used to women flaunting their figures, I was mesmerized by the fact that she hadn't and I got to explore what felt like a hidden treasure for the first time. I memorized the feel of her being within my grasp and catalogued it so I wouldn't need to come back.

That was the goal. It had to be.

She squirmed under me, her body either wanting more or less. I had to give her an out before we went too far. "You can say you're done and want to go back to your room, Ms. Darling. I told you all you have to say is *stop*."

This was the responsible thing to do. I was ready to take way more advantage of her than I had originally intended. I was already way the fuck over the line, but now I'd lost control. She'd need to be the one to exercise it if she wanted this to end. I wanted her pussy on my mouth, her arousal on my tongue, and her moaning my name.

Just once.

"You said you needed to eliminate the distraction," she murmured. "If it hasn't been eliminated, I'm not done and neither are you, right?"

I nodded, even though I shouldn't have agreed. When I moved my hands to her knees and slowly slid them up that silky skin on her inner thigh, she gasped. She wasn't made for this, I could already tell. She was the darling, the sweet teacher, the woman who thought she couldn't even get aroused enough to drip down my counter.

One time. This was an indulgence and distraction we were going to get out of our systems.

"You need it too. Don't lie to yourself. If you're telling me no one can get you wet, I have to show you that you're wrong, darling Mia."

"It's not possible," she whispered defiantly and boldly, her tone pointed in the confidence of what her body lacked. Yet, her hands tightened on the edges of the counter like I gripped her lower thighs. Maybe it was our sanity that we were trying to hold on to at that point, or our dignity, but I'd lost that a long time ago. Didn't give a fuck now what anyone thought of me when I'd built my own path and way.

I knew her squirming and wiggling her hips on the stainless steel was evidence enough that she'd come all over it if I did this just right.

My hands slid up her thighs farther and farther, her tan skin so perfect under my rough grip that I wanted to mar it somehow. It was disturbing how much I wanted to disrupt every part of her. Would it glisten if I worked her pussy enough? Redden if I gave it a slap or two? And would she moan my first or last name while I did?

My vision was tunneling around this woman, and it shouldn't have been. I knelt before her on my tailored slacks and watched as her breath caught while mine brushed against her panty line. I wanted to know her thoughts, wanted her to share every single feeling she had instead of rolling her lips between her teeth and clamping down on what she wanted to say.

She gripped that counter with the same force she'd used to erect that professional wall she'd created between us. I brushed my thumb right over the wet lace covering her pussy. A feather of a touch, just to see how sensitive she'd be to it, how firm of a grasp she had on the edge, and she hissed. That hold was slipping so easily I almost groaned.

Mia Darling wasn't supposed to be such an intrusion on my life that I struggled to see past her smile with my daughter. I couldn't spout off at my men and tell them to go on a killing spree just so I could see the smile again.

I pulled her panties down so I could watch drops of her arousal build and coat my stainless-steel counter. I wanted a whole damn puddle of evidence that I was affecting her as much as she was me. I spread her legs further apart and, with a hand around her waist, pulled her closer.

"Look at that. Seems possible this pussy does get wet for me now." I felt her trying to lean back, but I held her waist there. Then I traced my other hand along her panty line and shoved it over so I could massage her clit.

She shuddered and chastised us both. "We shouldn't be doing this."

Catching some of her arousal with my thumb, I pinched her bundle of nerves, then rolled it while I yanked her waist closer. "Want me to stop?"

She was so small, I could've wrapped my mouth around her tits easily. They rose and fell right in front of me with her rapid breathing, but no denial came from her lips. Instead, her nipples puckered, tinging a pink that would be burned into my memory forever. I wanted to consume the color, drink it in, taste it. I dragged my tongue over her skin there and then bit the point. I sucked away the pain it caused immediately and rubbed her to the rhythm of my tongue so I could hear her moan.

Still, her hands held the counter. And it became my mission to make her let go. I wanted all of whatever she was holding back.

Her arousal on my counter grew, but it wasn't good enough. I pulled her closer, sucking harder, dragging my teeth over one nipple and then the other before making my way up her neck, where one of my hands slid to tangle in her hair. She smelled like lavender and cherries, but I wanted her to smell like me instead.

This was my house, my place of work, my domain.

When I got close enough to her ear, I whispered, "Yeah, I don't think you want to stop, Mia. I think you want me to keep going."

Her pretty eyes were misted over, her lips parted as I rubbed between her legs, back and forth, faster and faster.

She was close, so close that I would get to see her unravel and fuck her completely uninhibited.

I wanted to hear her say it. She was stubborn, though, with her gritted teeth and her knuckles whitened.

"My darling Mia, say it. Say you want this."

Her breath came faster. I watched her skin change to that pretty pink blush I knew meant she was right there.

"Say it, baby, or I won't let you come."

Her eyes whipped to mine in fury. So I slowed the pace against her pussy. I hadn't even slid my finger into her yet, and she was going to come. She was like a live wire, ready to snap and catch fire. "Jameson Knight, if you don't let me come, I promise you'll never have me."

That mouth. I needed to remind her who was in charge, so I stood straight, my hand still at her center. She gulped, her eyes following me to my full height. "Want to repeat that?"

"Let me come or don't have me. I think you heard me fine the first time."

My other hand was at her throat again, but it flew without my control now. I'd been unleashed and didn't care. She taunted me because it was what she wanted. She wanted whatever was in me that had never been pretty. I normally never let it out because women liked a good-looking man who made love to them, not fucked them.

Her back slammed into the metal counter hard. Her hands finally flew off that edge to clutch my shoulders. Or to push me away. Who knew at this point. I pinned her there and took her lips in mine with no pretense of romance. My teeth scraped at her lips and my tongue laid claim to every part of her mouth. She whimpered into it like maybe she'd hoped for a kiss, but this wasn't at all what she expected.

Good.

It was inevitable that at some point she'd end up fearing me anyway. I didn't need to be obsessed with her much longer either. If I gave her this uncontrolled version of myself, she'd back away.

She'd learn.

I stepped between her legs, shoving my cock right below my hand at her clit. She gasped at feeling me against her there even if my slacks separated us. "I could fuck you here with no repercussions whether you liked it or not, Mia." I thrust up against her just to prove my point.

"And yet you'd still not have me at all," she responded.

My mind scrambled. My body roared. And my dick hardened further. She didn't realize she was waving red in front of a bull, releasing a venom in my veins that could only be cured by finding a way to consume every part of her being. I don't think I knew it then either, even if my body subconsciously did, because I dropped to my knees and lifted her thighs to place her feet on my shoulders. Instead of taking her, I lowered my mouth to that pussy of hers before she had time to reconsider.

I was going to *devour* her orgasm.

Make her scream my name—and it'd be my whole fucking name, not first or last.

She'd give me every part of herself whether she wanted to or not.

Her hands finally flew to the back of my head as she moaned and arched off the metal, and now that death grip was in my hair, pushing me farther into her scent.

And, fuck, I wanted to die being smothered by it so much that my grip became bruising.

Somehow, just like her smell, she tasted of sweet cherries too. Addictive and all-consuming.

Maybe I was tasting my unraveling, because I knew then if I

had died right at that moment, I would have went to hell, where I would have met my darling devil.

My darling demise.

My darling Mia.

And I'd have been happier than if I'd gone to heaven.

14

Mia

He didn't just eat me out. He ravaged and savored me in a way I'd never experienced. From him humming against my folds, to him murmuring sweet nothings between thrusting his tongue deep into me.

He told me how good I tasted, how much he thought about me, how he didn't think he'd ever get enough of me. I reminded myself that the words were empty and hollow, ones I knew he probably didn't mean.

But I was only human, and my body listened and responded like I was a prized possession. I clung to his hair for dear life, wanting it to never end but also not sure how much sensation I could endure.

No man had made me feel fear and excitement so quickly. I was on the edge of death with his threats but more alive than I'd ever been. The roller coaster of emotions was fast, dangerous, and addicting. No person should have been exposed to that type of thrill, because I was sure afterward I'd struggle to come back from it.

Closing my legs and leaving wasn't an option though. Jameson Knight would get what he wanted from me because my body was ready to give him everything. The way his tongue swept through me built a pressure that needed to be relieved, that twisted a desire so powerful that I was ready to scream for the orgasm I so desperately needed.

"Please," I whispered, pulling at his dark hair.

He brushed his fingers over me so he could pull back and stare at me with those cool, blue eyes. "What are you begging for now, Darling? Am I not giving you exactly what you need?"

I bit my lip, because asking him for his cock wasn't something I was used to. Asking for *anything,* really, wasn't something I did.

When I hesitated, he stopped touching me, as if it were punishment for not answering. "If you need something, you say it."

"I need it all. You," I blurted as I rolled my hips down on his fingers. He met my movements perfectly with his own, like a damn reward. "Please. Just screw me, Jameson. I'm not used to playing games in the bedroom."

His stare became inquisitive as he worked me at a steady pace. Round and round his fingers went on my clit, with just enough pressure to excite me but not make me lose my mind. "Has no one played with your pussy like me, Mia?"

I gasped when he thrust a finger in and curled it against a sensitive part. The sensation left me with no filter. "No one. Oh my God. That feels good."

"How good? Ride my hand and show me how you like it." Those blue eyes swept down my body like an ocean rolling over the sand and moved me to listen. I was malleable under his touch and wanted to obey his every command, because I was rewarded when I did. I rolled my hips, and he licked his lips like he was hungry for me. I rode his fingers harder, and his gaze darkened while his jawline clenched. I was affecting him the way he affected me, and the sheer idea of it had me on the brink.

"Look at how wet you get for me, Mia. These pretty thighs against my counter glistening and getting the metal all wet. You told me it was impossible. What else are you lying about? Did the men you've been with really actually play with your pussy? You leading me on?"

"They didn't," I reassured him as I panted, my hands gripping my thighs now as I rode him faster and faster. "Honestly, the men I get with just get what they want before ever worrying about me getting mine."

He hummed, pulling his hand back a little, but my hips chased his fingers best they could. I was so close, but he wanted to drag this out. "They were selfish and stupid men then."

"I don't know," I whined, frustrated he wasn't unbuttoning his slacks, but then he slid another finger in me, and I whimpered. "Just give me more. I don't care about the others. I want this right now. I'll turn around. You can take me from behind, do what you want, anything."

I'd lost control and said the last bit as a bargaining chip. He didn't know I knew that's the way he liked it, that that was the way he did it with Valerie.

Something shifted in his stance and his gaze, even in the way his hand moved in me. Those blue eyes pierced sharper, that touch felt predatory, and his muscles bulked as his hand stilled. "You intend to not look at me when I fuck you?" His tone was dark, flattening into a voice that was almost primal. "Do you want to forget it's me?"

"No." I shook my head fast, realizing that's what he must have been doing with Valerie. "Of course not. I just want to get off. What are you waiting for?"

He chuckled, but there was an edge to it. "Mia, I'm meticulous if nothing else. Your body needs to be ready."

"I am ready. If you're not capable of finishing the job, then let's just stop." The snark flew out of my mouth.

"Capable?" He smirked. "I'm going to watch your pussy *soak* my hand for that. Slowly and surely."

"I don't get wet like that, Jameson. I'm telling you, I never have!"

"Let's see then. I want these nipples puckering for me. Your body shaking. You moaning. And let's see if this pussy weeps for me, because when I fuck you, Mia"—his thumb was tracing my clit now, deliberately and possessively, as he bent over me—"I'm going to watch and memorize every inch of you . . . of how you look when you scream my name over and over."

I moaned, pulling him closer so I could move onto his fingers faster, getting the friction I wanted. I didn't care what he wanted anymore—I'd do all of it just to hit my orgasm.

"That's it, pretty darling. Ride it just like that," he encouraged me. "Tell me who you're riding."

"Mr. Knight."

He smacked my thigh with his other hand and pinched my clit. I gasped at the pain zinging through my body, but he immediately massaged both areas as he commanded, "My whole name, Mia. Who's going to make you come all over and leave a mess?"

"Jameson Knight."

"Whose household do you teach within?"

"Jameson Knight's."

"Whose rules do you follow?"

I bit my tongue now. The man knew I needed this. I could hear my own arousal from him sliding his finger in and out, and still he slowed the rhythm. "Jameson, I'm going to act more unprofessional than ever if you don't let me finish."

"Say it then. Whose rules do you follow, baby?"

I was going to go wild in a second, I was so close. "Yours, you *ass*."

He hummed in fucking delight, and then he smiled wide. "Such a little pretty brat when you could just submit for a second. I'm not an ass. I'm Jameson Knight, your boss, and you should show me some respect. Tell me you'll listen, Mia. Moan it for me out of that snarky mouth. Then I'll let you feel it, that high you want so bad."

I dug my nails into my thighs. "Jameson Knight, your rules are ridiculous half the time." He started to take his hand away, and I grabbed for his wrist like a fiend. "But I'll listen. I'll listen, okay? Please. I'll listen, Jameson Knight."

I was rewarded by his fingers sliding back in and curling right into the sweet spot I needed. "That's it. You feel how soaked this pussy is now?" My eyes drifted shut as the heat built at my center, but he growled, "Eyes on me, Mia. I want your eyes locked on mine with you this wet. I won't blink, nor do I intend to miss a second of you wild, riding me."

He said it with promise rather than condescension, like he was seriously considering getting dry eye just to watch every millisecond.

I didn't understand it. How could I? He never had Valerie look at him. "I'm just a distraction you're getting rid of," I whispered, trying to find my way back to sanity, to this meaning nothing, to this being only for pleasure.

He chewed on the corner of his lip like he was holding back more that he had to say and then knelt again. "Yeah, don't I wish," I thought I heard him say, but I probably imagined it.

Not that it mattered. His mouth descended between my legs again, and he sucked hard on my clit this time. No more games were being played. When I looked down, he was looking up, meeting my gaze with hunger and intensity that fueled my libido, that fed the girl in me who wanted to be desired, that pushed me over the edge.

I bared down on his face, writhing against him as I got lost in the blue ocean of that stare. I drowned in it and didn't care about coming up for air because the deep sea of pleasure overtook me, wave after wave. I hit a high I couldn't control as I screamed out and rode his face for minutes or hours. He let me, too. Like he was some sort of gentleman. The complete opposite of what I'd made him out to be in my head.

And he followed that up with holding me there while he took a napkin from the dispenser near his sink and wet it to gently brush over me. His movements were still meticulous and measured but with care rather than authority.

"Jameson, what are you doing?" I frowned at him. He was holding me open even while I tried to close my legs.

"Cleaning you up," he said, like it was normal.

"But what about you?" I pointed to the tent in his slacks. "We didn't even—"

"We're not going to." His tone was sharp. "A man doesn't always need to get his after you, Mia. Sometimes all it takes is for a woman to get there."

"So, we're done?"

His blue eyes snapped and clashed with mine. "Are you still distracted?"

I stuttered, not sure how to answer. "No. That was great, but—"

"Then you'll be able to finish your work duties for the day and give Franny your full attention."

He walked over to the trash can and stepped on a lever to open the lid. He threw the napkin and what felt like our whole connection away in that bin. I jumped with the sound of the can snapping closed.

The tension in the room was back. The darkness, the authority he held over me as my boss. Jameson didn't want complications, and I was one, that was obvious. So, I moved quickly to snatch up my clothes and slid my panties and skirt on. "I would have been able to finish my duties just fine before all this had I simply been informed of every aspect of this job."

"You were informed enough," he said gruffly, looking the other way.

I walked right into his line of sight though. "Oh really?" I wrapped my blouse back around my waist. "Seems you left out a few things, like you being an elusive ass of the Diamond Syndicate while moonlighting as a surgeon for criminals downstairs half the time."

Shock flickered over his features followed by amusement, which pissed me off more. He crossed his arms. "And the other half?"

Oh, he wanted me to continue. *Fine.* "The other half of the time I might get a bonus of you sticking your fingers between my legs, it seems. Or was that a one-off and I'll have to go find help with that elsewhere the rest of the summer?"

The growl he let out was low, and it sent shivers over my skin. But he worked his jaw up and down a few times before he announced, "Well, like I promised, you're free to go anywhere in Paradise Grove from now on if you need *help* elsewhere, although I don't recommend it."

"Why not?"

"Because they'll have to deal with me after, Mia," he said, and he held my gaze, making sure I knew exactly what that meant. "Anyway, I'd like one of the guys to accompany you if you leave with Franny. I should have taken the well-being of you two exploring outside into consideration earlier."

What could I say to that? Now, not only was he a member of the syndicate, but he was being considerate too.

It left us in unknown territory where I couldn't argue with him about professionalism but didn't have my legs wrapped around his head either. I worked my hands in consternation. "I'll keep you updated on Franny's progress with exploration. I should get back to her and—"

"I'll walk you upstairs." He pointed to a back door, and I hesitated. "It's the other staircase."

"I haven't seen that part of the estate."

He nodded, and his voice cooled slightly. "It's my wing."

I wasn't sure if that was a boundary he was putting up or an offer for a future invitation. The hall to the stairs was dim as we moved through it. Gone was the clean smell of the house, and in its place was that leather and clove that reminded me of him. Jameson motioned me to take the stairs, and he walked behind me. The staircase curved up, narrow but elegant.

Each step creaked like he took these more than others, like whoever had lived here utilized this path regularly.

We made it to the ground level, and he pointed to double doors. "My room is there, and if you turn here, we'll be back at the study."

Yet, my eyes weren't looking down the hall that led to the bright normalcy I was used to at his estate now. They were on the door that was next to his, that had a handle that shined with gold elegancy and a keyhole that was shaped like something from a storybook.

This door was substantial, and I was sure it would be heavier. Carved with wood vines and ivy, it was unlike all the others.

"What's in there?" I murmured almost to myself. "It looks like it belongs in another time."

"It does," he grumbled. "That door is completely off-limits. Some parts of this house don't need to be explored by my daughter's teacher, and some doors are better left closed. Do you understand, Ms. Darling?" His whole demeanor shut down, his tone shifted. The barrier was back up between us. I was Ms. Darling again. Not the woman he'd just had relations with.

Not someone he cared to trust his secrets with.

Just a woman he'd removed as a distraction. Just an

elementary school teacher he'd lusted over, but now he'd cut the cord between us.

I felt the knife to my gut as he said it, as he shuttered closed the window into his thoughts.

He'd put me back in my place, and I had to push myself to remember it. I took a step back from him and nodded. "Understood, Mr. Knight. I'm a professional, after all. As the *nanny*, I know exactly where I should and should not go now."

With that, I turned and went back to the study all on my own.

He didn't come after me.

Why would he? After all, we were just boss and employee.

15

Jameson

Keeping my distance from Mia was harder than I'd originally envisioned it to be. She meddled and snooped and asked questions in ways I wasn't used to. She pried like she genuinely cared rather than as if she were using me as a means to an end. I wasn't used to people who were real rather than strategic, innocent rather than ruthless, and honest rather than calculating.

Maybe that's why I gave the fucker, Paolo, a chance for a meeting. Or maybe I just wanted to further justify my actions to the syndicate. Either way, I needed answers.

I knew Paolo's history, that he was a snake and a liar, but everyone else needed to see it too. He'd slithered in and out of my life for years. His cartel on the East Coast had global reach for a time, money laundering pipelines through shell corporations with heavy influence in South American ports. He even controlled several international pharm transport routes years ago.

My father turned a blind eye to it, and my late wife, Lex, wanted direct partnership with it when her family's company, Wilshire & Co., were found in a scandal they'd hidden from all of us.

She saw it as a way to save them, but I saw it as a cheap, easy way to make money.

I'd been right and most likely would be right again after this meeting.

I stared out the floor-to-ceiling windows in an office atop the Stonewood Tower, overlooking the calm but deceptively deep waters of Lake Michigan. That lake hid secrets just like I did. "You asked for a face to face, Paolo. You got it for the next twenty minutes."

I looked over my shoulder to see Paolo appearing anxious today in a gray suit that clung a little more loosely than in the past to his tall, thin frame. He'd always had distinctly high cheekbones, but his skin seemed to sag more under his dark, beady eyes now. He was sitting at the table with his brother at his left and his niece right behind him. She had a calm, cobalt gray gaze that was locked on the man beside me.

Cal held her stare in his black on black tailored suit, his silhouette sharp against that Chicago skyline. My brother was always diplomatic but also more alert than me, his training embedded in him. He'd watch Paolo's men and women because he knew to trust me, knew to have my back even when he wanted peace.

"I appreciate you finally seeing me even if it's under these circumstances. I shared my frustration with Cal about the school shooting, although I had nothing to do with it . . ."

My brother didn't speak, move, or confirm Paolo's words. He just watched, and as I looked Paolo over, I saw how my brother's silence made him squirm more. He'd expected an ally in my brother, but my brother was truly only ever loyal to me.

"And yet you've worked closely with O'Connor for years." I lifted a brow and walked to sit across from him at the large table. This game of chess was one I'd been playing for a long time, and I wouldn't be outmaneuvered. "You might not have been at the scene, Paolo, but are you saying you didn't know O'Connor's plans? That you let someone that close to you do something so stupid?"

His eyes flashed with a bit of fear. It was the first crack in his breakdown. I might have been the only one to catch it, but it was all I needed to see. I fed off finding the cracks in someone's armor. He swallowed. "It would have never served me well to go after your daughter. O'Connor knew better. I told him not to use any sort of force to get his way—"

"You told him, did you?" I locked eyes with him.

He glanced away. "Look, I . . . I'm not here to waste time with small talk, and I know you aren't either."

"Is my daughter small talk to you, Paolo?"

"No, n-no . . . Of course not," he stuttered. "I just wasn't at all a part of what happened. You understand? I want this time between us to be mutually beneficial and . . ." He leaned forward, folding his worn hands together and clearing his throat. "I've wanted to discuss a merger. I help you and you help me. All I need is port access again. The updated international pharma-trade legislation has limited us."

"That's not my problem," I stated flatly, shrugging because I didn't care.

He bristled. "You helped push it through."

"My partners at Stonewood Enterprises have always been clean. They invest in by-the-books pharma companies. We do what's best for them."

"Fine, but you know how strong we once were. If legislation had grandfathered in older import-export lanes or could revise their stance—"

"Not happening."

He scoffed. "Then give us a clearance window or two through one of your bonded warehouses so that we can move synthesis-grade precursor chemicals. One or two shipments a month, no questions asked. With your warehouses having medical classification clearance and my cargo routed through as a biotech subsidiary, we could move millions, and I'd give you a fifty-fifty cut."

I waited to hear if he wanted to add any additional benefit and, of course, he didn't disappoint.

"I realize it's somewhat of a risk, but . . ." He cleared his throat. "It'd help Lex's family's company."

There it was.

"Wilshire & Co.?" I asked, more to confirm he had the gall and audacity to bring up my late wife, confirming my suspicions.

"Well, you know how Lex was." He smiled like we both had shared memories of her. "Your wife always wanted them to do well, you know? I tried my best to keep her dream alive after she . . . passed. A gesture of sorts."

"A gesture for who?" Listening to a man with an ego talk normally always led to more than they wanted to say. So, I pried, keeping my tone even rather than correcting his statement. Paolo kept her dream alive because he'd fallen victim to loving and blindly investing in whatever she wanted.

My late wife had loved him and the idea of partnering with him. I knew that. She'd had relations with him before our marriage and probably after. I didn't really care one way or the other. Her family had the pharma company us Diamonds wanted access to. They were tied to the FDA and politically valuable. My marriage was arranged, and it was a power move for both parties.

Even still, we enjoyed one another at first. Enough that she got pregnant, enough that I wanted what was best for her and my daughter.

When scandal around her family's pharma company hit, though, we pulled back. The fact that she had never confided in me that they were distributing contaminated meds along with falsified trial data for cancer patients meant I couldn't see a benefit to having her as a partner either, except with Franny.

My daughter was in love with her mother. And I was in love with having a perfect family for my child. Those were the only two reasons I afforded her a chance to be faithful to me and to Franny. Instead, I saw how she changed, how the strategy in her bled out, how she desperately tried to outmaneuver everyone to keep her family's company alive.

I didn't give in to the demands of aiding her family, of partnering with Paolo, who had bigger ties to the FDA at the time.

"Look, all that investment in Wilshire & Co. I did for her family," he said quickly and then tried to seek out my pity or guilt and prey upon it. "They were mourning, Jameson. I know their missteps led to her accident, but someone had to do something."

"Are you insinuating that I should have done more?" I chuckled. "I let you and my wife live even after she ran off with you, Paolo. That was more grace than either of you deserved, especially with how she didn't show up to pick Fran up from school." I would never forgive her for the way she left Franny, for not saying goodbye, for abandoning her at school one day just so I had to pick up the pieces.

What Paolo didn't understand was I didn't care about Lex's family or their company. My wife had been a strategist who held love like a tool against my daughter and me. She hadn't understood that had she confided in me before that scandal of Wilshire hit, I would have saved her company easily. Instead, I worked day in and day out to make sure the Diamonds partnered with Stonewood Enterprises and solidified our influence within the FDA.

I knew it was only a matter of time before Paolo's influence crumbled and his investors got frustrated and got even. I heard the whispers of them targeting the heiress of Wilshire & Co. and wanting revenge by taking her life.

I didn't intervene. I knew that made me more of a monster than even her. I didn't care.

I was given the autopsy report of her being so badly burned they were only able to identify her through her teeth. I didn't mourn her loss, only considered all the angles. An accident is how everyone classified it. Supposedly her car blew up. Maybe an angry party was involved and cut a wire.

Or maybe something else.

I knew more and more every day that it was the latter, because Paolo tried for more meetings after that. He thought that was how he would get his foot in the door with me, but I always declined. Even the new senator wouldn't have swayed my decision to see him.

Yet, his insistence for meetings grew, and so did my suspicions. I only called the meeting now because of the feeling in my gut. Something was amiss with my daughter's school shooting, and Paolo had to have been behind it.

"Of course she shouldn't have left you like that. Lex was ruthless sometimes."

"Indeed. So ruthless that she left her family because we weren't of use to her anymore. You were supposed to be the useful one. Don't forget: Lex didn't want a damn thing to do with the Diamonds when she left."

"Right." Paolo rubbed his eyes, his fatigue from playing the game he wasn't going to win showing now. "But she's gone now. Has been for years. And honestly, I still think it's the right thing to do to help her family, especially when it benefits us both."

"Tell me then, Paolo, is Wilshire beneficial to us both while they continue to fuck up?" I leaned back and draped my arm along the back of my chair as I waited.

"What are you talking about?"

"They're still using their medications for unapproved conditions. Off-label uses. And not well enough that the FDA isn't sniffing around." One move closer to checkmate. "I get updates from my men at the FDA every month. You think I didn't know? They're flagged."

He tried to recover with a smile, but it didn't reach his eyes at all. "They've been under pressure, but all businesses are right now." He hurried on, "And once I have port access, it'll be a fifty-fifty deal between us. Everything legal on paper, and your name stays clean."

I didn't need to respond. I just lifted a brow and let him talk.

"You know the ingredients go straight into generic production and how fast they move. Painkillers, supplements . . ."

"Cancer meds?" Of course it would still be beneficial to Lex's company.

"Yes. The product will move fast." He tried so hard to pretend this was just business, but I saw through it. And then he said what I knew he would. "You know, Wilshire does have the distribution already set up. They might be struggling, but they're known in this world. We could use them and also prop them back up along the way. If Lex was here . . . she would have wanted this."

He said it like he could make us all believe it even though she wanted nothing to do with the Diamonds. She thought Paolo had it all. His statement was just another nail in his coffin. "Lex always had unrealistic ideas and goals, Paolo. And those unrealistic goals are what killed her."

"No. No . . . Lex wasn't unrealistic. If she were here today, I bet she'd be excited." He hurried along, scrambling to give me something to be enticed with. "A diamond remains unbroken right? I mean . . . I could be a part of that. A diamond remains unbroken, and the Ruiz cartels are there to take care of the cracks."

He said it fast and smiled like it was a good line.

What he didn't realize is he'd just shown his hand. Our game of chess had just elevated. It fed my gut instinct.

As I stared at him, I was beginning to think he was just a pawn. "She used to say that to me," I told him and watched his every movement.

He glanced away, but I saw how his jaw ticked just once. He had cracks that I was chipping away at to show either that he'd loved my wife so much that he couldn't really want to partner with me, or he was hiding a deeper secret, one I was going to find out. He grumbled, "Oh, really? Well, no matter." He wiped a hand over his face. "Wish she could be here today."

"I bet you do." I narrowed my eyes at him.

"Even still, her dream could live on with Wilshire & Co., Jameson."

"Is that your sell, Paolo? To play into the goodness of my heart for my *dead* wife's legacy?"

"If not for Lex, then maybe for the legacy she wants to leave behind. I'm just saying . . . she'd have wanted us to try at least for Fran—"

"Paolo . . ." I stood abruptly. "You know that you were supposed to be Lex's solution. She was wrong then . . . and now. You can't rewrite history. You bought into Wilshire & Co. thinking you could save her family's company and bury their hardship. You didn't. You think I want to be a part of that?"

He glanced around as if flabbergasted and offended. He was down to only a few guarding his king . . . or his queen in our chess match. "Look, in the grand scheme of things, the company doesn't matter much." He waved away my intel, but he was sweating now, trying to weasel his way into another tunnel to feed off me.

"Why bring it up then?"

"Because I thought that you—"

"That I might feel indebted to you for funding *your* lover's family business?" I tapped my fingers on the table and tsked. "I don't give a fuck what you do with your money, Paolo. This meeting is over."

"Wait." Paolo stood too, his frown deepening and his brow now sweating. "Don't you get that her family will suffer?"

"Just them? Or you too?"

He threw up his hands, looking around like he needed someone to back him up. His brother next to him didn't say a damn thing. "She might not be the love of your life, but she is mine."

The man was panicking and showing all the moves he planned to make without making them. "She wasn't, no." I said that with finality.

"But she was still the mother of your—"

"Yes, she was. But now, with her gone, that's over. And so is this meeting."

"Have you no mercy?" the woman who stood behind Paolo blurted out.

A scoff left my brother's lips before I could answer her. I glanced at him and saw the look he shot her way, so cold we all felt the temperature drop. He didn't look away from her for even a second as he said, "We never promised mercy, Jasmina."

She grumbled something under her breath, and normally Cal would have let that go. He was the diplomat, after all, but he taunted her instead. "I'm sorry, we didn't hear that, Jasmina. Want to speak up, or are you scared to in a room full of men?"

Whoever that woman was, it was clear they'd brought her because she was trained to kill, and even I was impressed at how fast her knife flew across the table toward him.

My brother was trained in combat though. We all were. And still, he barely dodged the blade. Paolo bellowed her name, standing over her as if he were going to beat the shit out of her.

"Everyone, stop." Callahan kept his eyes on her while Paolo's men backed off in surrounding her. "Jasmina has never been to one of our meetings before. I might not have mercy, but I do have grace to give sometimes. She's fine."

"We meant no disrespect. Right, Jasmina?"

My brother didn't even wait for her to answer. "Oh, she meant every ounce of disrespect she could muster in that throw, but I don't mind a fight."

And as we walked out, I heard him as he passed her by, "Next time, try not to miss, baby."

When we got back into the SUV, I laid my head on the seat rest and closed my eyes. "Do I want to know what the fuck is going on between you and Paolo's niece?"

"Nope." But the corner of his mouth lifted like he knew it was going to be a whole lot of trouble. "Do *I* want to know what the fuck *you're* thinking happened back there with Paolo?"

"Nope," I said right back. Then I sighed, shaking my head. "Not until I'm sure, brother, not until I'm sure."

16

Mia

He'd been gone most of the very next day, and when he passed me in the hall later that evening, he only murmured a "good evening, Ms. Darling" that was tight with tension and formality. I went to my room and tried to just listen to the quiet as I tended to my plants.

"Ms. Prim, I'm quite sure that if you die, I'm dying too. So, you better buck the hell up," I told my cape primrose. Her flowers were wilting rather than blooming, and I hated to see it.

Then, I turned to my azalea bonsai. "Mr. Bos, you could try a little harder too. I told Franny I'd read her *The Nightmare Before Christmas* again for the third time today even though I didn't want to. She enjoys the page that talks about things hiding under her bed. You think I enjoy that?"

I tsked and poured a cup of water slowly into the fertilizer. I checked that the dampness was perfect and sighed. If Mr. Bos didn't make it, I would be giving Jameson a freaking mouthful. I'd nursed this plant for months to make sure he was vibrant and green. With the color seeping out of him, I was getting nervous.

Nervous about that and nervous about how attached I'd gotten to this home, to Franny, to Rosy, who'd given me the side-eye and mouthed that we needed to talk earlier that day. She'd become a friend with her figuring out my crush on Jameson, and now I would probably have to try not to ask her about that stupid door.

The beautiful, whimsical door that Jameson didn't care to share with me.

I sighed and chose to curl up in another pair of pajamas—a tank and pants long enough that they whispered around my ankles as I made my way over to the sitting area by the window. There, I listened to the vent the whole evening, hoping to hear his voice.

Nothing.

There was no movement from the office, and I wasn't sure why, but I was relieved. The night air called to me here as a summer breeze blew in through the curtains. Sometimes fresh air cleared a head, eased a mind, and soothed a soul.

After Jameson's tense good evening in the hall, I needed something of the sort. I reached for my phone and found myself dialing for my older sister, like she had the time or mental space to deal with me.

"It's late, Mia," she answered on the first ring.

"Crap, sorry," I grumbled. "It's been a long day."

"Tell me about it." She sighed right as I did, and then we both chuckled.

"How's my niece or nephew doing?"

"Okay, I think. Wondering if I should figure out the gender soon. Felix is on a work trip, so we're on our own for a couple more days." Relief always washed over me when she got time to herself. Felix never really updated her on his schedule because he didn't want her to plan on his going anywhere, but on those days, she sounded lighter and freer without him there.

"So weather's great then? Why didn't you call?" There was the all too familiar knot that was tightening in my chest.

I heard the soft smile in her voice. "Weather's great, and I just . . . I don't know." She hesitated. "He's been okay. Things are good."

There was the dreaded line I hated to hear. He'd been "okay," as if *okay* were a reason to stay, as if it took away all the turmoil, the abuse, the pain.

"Okay." My response was practiced as I kept my voice soft, pressing my lips together and trying my best not to push her. "How is he with the pregnancy?"

"He's trying . . . I think."

"Right, and how are you holding up?"

She exhaled as if my agreement was a weight off her shoulders. "I'm tired. Felix has been good about letting me rest."

"You're growing a baby. You should be tired, shouldn't you? That's nice he's letting you rest." My complimentary tone felt forced, and we both knew it.

"Yeah, maybe," she murmured. Then I heard a sniffle before her voice cracked. "You're supposed to fight me on how he's not nice and I should leave again, so I can push back and hang up on you and stay, Mia."

It would have been the easy way out. I'd done that before, and she hadn't spoken to me for months. "I'm here for you either way." My heart broke admitting that, because I didn't want to support her staying there, didn't want to support her holding on to a man who didn't deserve her.

She chuckled. "Wish I could say the same for Mom and Dad."

It was true. My sister was the shining star my parents now showed off around town ever since she'd married Felix and had a wedding they could all remember. His parents were local celebrities with that liquor company they owned and with the money they put back into that town. Marian divorcing him would have been the equivalent of what I'd done with my coach, and my sister saw how that had worked out.

"Yeah, Mom and Dad are probably hoping I find a life exactly like yours in the next year or two. Maybe then they'll forgive me." And forgiveness felt wrong, jaded, twisted. Still, as a daughter, I wanted to smooth things over and make the connection with them strong again. But families were complicated. Sometimes a family was meant to break and you had to learn to choose yourself over them—or find the people who that would accept you for who you truly were and call them family instead.

"I wouldn't ever wish this life on you," she blurted out.

I heard her take a shaky breath before silence stretched between us. Maybe I was waiting for her to admit what was really going on, because there was always more. He got angry, he drank, he hit her, he lashed out. There was always, always more.

Or maybe she was waiting for me to reassure her that everything would be okay, but I couldn't do that. The silence over the line felt fearful, sad, and weighed down by expectations that might never come true.

I tried to wait it out, letting the wind from the window talk to me instead of my sister while she mulled over how to move forward. Instead of the wind, though, a snap at the edge of the estate's forest drew my attention.

A flicker in the trees had my heart jumping. I stood abruptly and blinked to get a better look, but it was gone. I tried to remind myself that I was living on a huge property with staff and people who watched over me and it was probably just them, but paranoia bled in, making me think that strangers might be watching too.

I hated the feeling of being watched, because I'd only really felt it with my coach and then when I'd stayed with my sister and Felix.

She was five years older than me and newly married when I graduated from college. I hadn't gotten my first teaching job yet, and she must have known my parents wouldn't offer me a place to stay after the fallout with my coach.

So she did. It only took two weeks for me to find a job and only two weeks of her husband watching me at night, his stare becoming heavier and heavier, for him to come on to me. "If you're going to stay here, I hope you'll let me stay in this bed with you sometimes," he'd whispered to me in the doorway of the spare room where I slept.

I'd told him to get the hell out. My sister didn't know. And she never would, because in the time I was there, I'd also witnessed his abuse and how accepting she'd become to it. Her faith in him made it so her trust in anyone else had dwindled. I could only tiptoe around the subject.

Instead, I moved out the next day and called my mother. She always answered but either hung up on me or explained I'd have to make things right with my coach before she would feel like my mother again. This call was only different in that she wanted me to make things right with Felix. Her response still festered in my heart. *"What were you doing that night? Did you leave your door open for him as an invitation? My God. You're in another woman's home—your sister's, Mia. And his family just gave your father a great job. Just say sorry and move on. I raised you girls not to make a scene. Be a Darling."*

Be a Darling. *I* hung up on her then.

I pulled the curtains closed hard on the view and on the memory. Since that day, I'd started saving and dropping money into an account for my sister. "Marian, you just have to get on a flight if you're unhappy. I can help with the rest." My sister might not have known about me and Felix, but I knew about her. She'd called me the first time he'd forced himself on her, and then she'd begged me not to say anything.

"I'll think about it." She wouldn't. "The savings account I started doesn't have nearly enough, Mia. It takes time. He's got so many connections. And I don't know . . . We're going to have a baby together, and I don't work. He provides for me, you know?"

"I know." It was the line she always gave me, but when I dropped money into that account this summer, it was going to be enough that she wouldn't need to worry about the financial side of it anymore. "As long as you're safe and think you'll be safe when your baby comes . . ."

"I love the baby so much already." She sighed, like the thought of her love hurt. And I wanted to sigh with her, because what did you do when a man trapped you with a tiny little human that you already loved? I couldn't fault her for wanting to stay. She continued, "If I'm honest, the weather's been absolute shit lately. It'll be a hurricane if I leave. Mom and Dad will—"

"They'll get over it. They'll get over it because they'll have a grandkid and their daughter to protect."

"What if they don't though?" she whispered. "What if they never forgive me? Their reputations will be ruined."

"The alternative is you'll be ruined," I threw back, my anger starting to snowball even as I tried to roll it back up the hill. My sister couldn't handle that right now. "Who cares about reputation? They should move from that godforsaken town, quite frankly."

"They'll never move." She sounded so dejected.

"Okay. And that's fine . . . But you will. You just need to get here, and I'll help with everything else. I'll be the freaking sunniest day ever."

"I might need you to fly with me," she whispered the confession, as if ashamed, but it was the first time she asked, the first time she went that far in contemplation. "I don't know if I can do it alone."

I jumped onto the hope and rode it quickly forward. "Oh, Mare, I'll come. Just let me know the day. I promise."

I hung up with a heavy heart, though it held some tiny sliver of optimism. She was considering leaving, and that was the first step.

Maybe I was too preoccupied yesterday and with the phone call today, or maybe I subconsciously just didn't want to email him after how our interaction ended the day before, but I turned in without emailing Jameson and woke when a message came through hours later.

I expect a report daily regarding my daughter's studies.

I stared at that screen like my eyes had laser beams that could melt the phone.

It's 2 a.m.

Oh good. You're awake. Then you can give me that report for yesterday and today now.

Wow. Or he could fuck right off.

I should have texted that back to him. Instead, every person in the world including my parents would be proud to know that I responded just as a Darling should.

Apologies. Franny had unexpected visitors yesterday that she was able to interact with in the morning, as you know. She loves seeing you every chance she gets. Today was a fun reading day where she made huge strides in reading to Malek and me.

There. Professional. We'd gotten rid of the distractions yesterday like he wanted. So there we were, acting like boss and employee. I laid there for two whole minutes before I kicked the plush sheet off and went to splash water on my face, hoping it would cool me down. I looked at myself in the mirror. My hair was sprouting curls every which way while steam practically shot out of my ears with how red my cheeks were with anger.

I hated being a Darling. I hated suppressing everything I was feeling. I hated that it was expected of me.

I considered changing out of my pajamas with the low-cut tank, but screw him and his rules.

I left my room needing a glass of water because if I didn't distract myself, I'd probably text him something I'd regret.

Now, did I sort of hope Jameson got an alert that I left my room and looked to find me flipping off the security camera in the corner of the hall, sure. And maybe I'd regret that too later.

I mean, obviously, I needed my salary. It's what was going to help Marian and me later this year, and I actually enjoyed teaching Franny every day. Something about that girl holding my hand and asking for a heart-in-pinkie promise got to me.

I was being stupid acting out, but hopefully Jameson's guards were the only ones watching the cameras now considering they didn't sit outside my door anymore. Plus, Jameson barely did anything himself when it came to his estate anyway, the prick. He wanted to text me about his daughter when he could have been spending quality time with her throughout the day. Franny yearned for more interaction with him. She had talked about him incessantly all afternoon and told me how great of a doctor he was.

Even still, I shouldn't have given him the power to rile me. Not when so much was on the line.

A Darling I would be.

Even if it killed me.

And how was the afternoon?

Great. Franny did well.

I just needed the conversation to end so I didn't dig myself a hole by telling him the afternoon was sprinkled with me thinking of his hands on me even though he was a Diamond. He was a dangerous murderer, and yet I had the audacity to encourage my sister to get out of an abusive relationship? I was so ridiculous.

Tomorrow I'd reset and be able to handle him.

A teacher should elaborate.

I growled in frustration.

In the afternoon, she picked a state to learn about. She was delighted to hear that you can see snow and the beach in the same day in California.

No mention of the academy incident?

I think having you to talk about instead made her forget that for a day.

And you?

And me what?

Did it make you forget about the academy for the day?

I froze in the middle of the kitchen. Had Archer told him about my nightmares? I didn't want to explain if he didn't know. But if he did know, I needed to explain. Maybe he was gearing up to find a reason to fire me. To let me go and get rid of whatever complication I was creating.

Not only was I the teacher that saw something I shouldn't have at the academy, now I was mixing business with pleasure.

Of course he'd be having regrets and want to get me out of here.

I mentally kicked myself and combed a hand through my curls before replying vaguely.

I'm fine. If I can't sleep, I just get a glass of water and read for a bit. It usually helps.

I set the phone down and opened the cabinet to reach for a glass, but each one of them were now at eye level.

The lowest shelf.

So I didn't have to reach.

17

Jameson

"So you can't sleep then?" The little devil of a darling jumped at hearing my voice.

Good.

It was better if she thought she had something to fear, although I had men and security in every part of this house to the point of overkill. Cal had given me an earful about it twice today, but I didn't give a fuck.

I was watching her and Franny's rooms constantly too. It's how I knew she'd walked down here, and that was after I saw her give the hallway camera a one-finger salute. She was containing the fire and anger behind her composure, her formalities, and her professionalism.

Fuck, I was sick of it. It was starting to fester and infect and rot under my skin how much I was sick of her composure. I'd texted her tonight hoping she'd explode, but she hadn't. All I got was a secret fuck-you gesture she didn't think I'd ever see.

It was good enough for me to leave my bedroom, where I was up thinking about my meeting with Paolo anyway. I *needed* a distraction now. I needed *her* as my distraction, because she was the only one who could provide it. No one else got my attention the way she did.

When she turned finally, I almost groaned at seeing her low-cut top and soft pajama pants that stretched over her hips perfectly. But she sucked in a gasp and backed up against the counter as her eyes widened. "What are you wearing?"

I crossed my bare arms, shrugging. "What I wear to bed, Darling."

"But . . . it's not a suit. You don't even have a shirt on." Her eyes dragged down and then up my body, and I saw how she licked her lips.

She looked positively confused about it, and I held back a smile. "And sometimes I sleep without pants too."

"You have tattoos everywhere," she whispered, mostly to herself. Her gaze was hungry across my chest, and I let her look. Fuck, I *wanted* her to look.

"I like ink." I leaned against the island, watching how her hands gripped the counter across from me. "Seems like you like it too."

Finally, her brown eyes met mine quickly and widened. "Sorry. I just don't normally see so much of it. It's . . . good art." She cleared her throat as I let her stutter around checking me out. But then she pointed behind her to where I'd rearranged the glasses. "Did you do this?"

No point in denying it. "Can't have you trying to climb on the counter just because you can't reach."

She lifted a brow. "That the only reason?"

I should have lied, but we were already in this deep.

"No. I don't want another man leaning over you to help you reach it either, Mia." I knew my jaw was ticking.

"That part of protecting me too?" She mirrored my stance, crossing her arms as she leaned against her side of the counter.

"Among other things."

"Like what? Archer is harmless."

The trust she had in that man was infuriating. "Well, for one, it might not be Archer in the kitchen with you all the time, and you in those pajamas are—"

"If someone can't handle my pajamas, that's on them," she snapped, her tone full of anger. Fierce. Real.

Fragile. Like she might have been hiding an emotion much more vulnerable under her lashing out.

"It is," I answered in a measured tone. "And although I shouldn't admit it, I'm oddly protective enough of you that they'll pay dearly for their eyes wandering. I figured you'd want to save them from going blind, but in all honesty, it'd be their fault."

Her mouth dropped open a little, and I got to see that pink tongue before she rolled her eyes and smirked a tiny bit. "Jameson, you wouldn't—"

"Mia, I would," I corrected her as I walked over and then caged her in with both hands on the sides of her hips, gripping the counter so I didn't press my fingers into her waist again. Restraining myself after yesterday was near impossible.

What we had done was supposed to curb my enthusiasm to fuck her, but instead it had amplified it. The way she moaned my name, the way she spread her legs, the way her pussy dripped for me.

Fuck.

"No man is going to look at you like they want to fuck you in my house."

"You can't control a look." She bit her lip. "Plus, I'm fine. I can take care of myself if I want to."

"Does that mean you might not want to?"

"Depends." One small shoulder lifted in a shrug, her answer quiet, honest.

My blood quickly turned from a simmer to a boil at thinking she'd let a man take advantage of her. "On what, exactly?"

Her eyes held fire and fight. She was mad about something,

but I couldn't figure out what. "On if I want the guy looking or not. You don't get to make all the rules for me just because I'm living here, you know? Just because you're my boss doesn't mean you get to tell me how to dress or act in the middle of the night."

"This about my text?"

"No. It's . . . You made it clear where the line is, Mr. Knight. Not me. We relieved our distractions, but I'm still a girl. Could be a girl who wants a guy looking at her for the summer too." She lifted a brow. "A man to look at me more than once when I grab a glass. And if you don't like it, I've been made aware that you have more than one guesthouse on this property for me to stay—"

"You're staying here." I swear to God, she was going to kill me with her logical train of thought. "It's where I have the most security and where I can keep an eye on you so you don't run off."

"Yeah, because I'm just going to up and leave Franny behind." She scoffed. So easily, she dropped my daughter as a reason rather than the salary I promised her.

I closed my eyes at how it affected me. Her blind loyalty to my daughter was dangerous and naïve, but damn if I didn't love it. It wasn't my cock this time that was attracted to her, but something else. Something shifted in my mind, in my heart. Something I couldn't control. I didn't want to have to scramble to find a fucking fault in this woman in front of me. She was supposed to mostly care about the money, and it was supposed to give me a reason to keep her at arm's length.

"Well, I can't be too careful after the show you gave me on the way here." I reminded her and myself that she secretly was lashing out at me.

"The show?" She frowned. She thought I wasn't watching.

I grasped her wrist and unfolded her middle finger from the fist she made, tracing it with my forefinger and thumb.

"I watch the cameras, Mia. If you wanted to say fuck you, you could have called or texted."

"That— It— I meant that for Archer."

"Archer's harmless," I mimicked her earlier phrase. "Were you mad I texted so late?"

"No." Her eyes were now watching how I dragged my fingers up and down hers. Why did I need her to tell me so badly?

"Were you mad I inquired about your teaching?"

"No."

"What, then?"

"It was nothing."

"Distracted on the job isn't an option. Answer my question."

Her eyes snapped up and held mine for a moment, ready to fight, but then she looked away as if conceding. I hated the disconnect.

"I'm just tired. It's not every day your boss admits to being a Diamond, Jameson. And my sister is being . . . difficult. I do have a life outside of this, even if it appears to be a small, irrelevant one to you." She chuckled, but it was forced.

I took a calming breath. Then another before I let go of her finger and dragged the back of my knuckles over her cheek. Maybe it was my touch or that she was so tired, but her emotions brimmed on the edge of her eyes, tears glistening and ready to spill over. My gut twisted. "Want to fly out to see her over the weekend? We can take the jet. Franny's at her grandma's like always."

She frowned at me as if I confused her. As if my offer was out of character. It was. She was a fucking employee, not my damn girlfriend or wife.

"No, but thank you. She'd kill me if I showed up unannounced. I just need the weekend to process everything. It will be fine."

I reached behind her head and grabbed a glass for her.

"You're exactly right. Diamond or not, it changes nothing for you, Darling. You're still teaching Franny, same as you always were, and I'm handling everything else."

"But handled in what way?"

"Ask only questions you want answers to."

She winced and glanced away like she wasn't sure she liked imagining what that might mean. She hesitated and then sighed before saying, "I guess I'm retracting the question then."

Her hesitation and the way she wouldn't meet my eyes in that moment had me reconsidering if I wanted her fear. If her fear was good like I'd first thought walking into that kitchen. Of course I wanted her aware of dangers, but did she know she didn't have to fear me? I probably should have wanted her to, but did I really?

"Are you scared of me now that you know I'm a Diamond?"

She didn't want to admit it, but I saw the hesitation, how her eyes danced away from mine as she muttered, "No."

I slammed the glass down next to her, and she jumped against my body.

My heart fucking stuttered as she did. It gave me the answer to my question.

I should have relished in her fear. I'd been wanting it from the very beginning because I knew exactly what it meant. People listened to fear, and it gave me a power over her.

It was an easy way to control, to manage, and to direct a situation in the way I wanted it.

And yet, for the first time in a long time, I feared the fear I could instill.

"Fuck, baby." I shook my head. "I won't hurt you."

"Right." She rolled her lips between her teeth as she closed her eyes. "I know. I actually really believe that even though I probably shouldn't, Jameson. Still, you belong in a world that you *can* do just that without repercussions, it seems. And I don't think you'd even feel bad about it."

"Feel bad about hurting you? I'd be fucking gutted, Mia." I blurted it out without even thinking, but it was the truth. "Now, hurt someone for them coming after you or my daughter . . . I'd *revel* in that."

"Maybe I'm scared for the others around us that piss you off, then."

I nodded over and over again, trying not to care and shut off whatever I was feeling for her. "Right. As you should be."

"Well, then . . ." She picked up the glass, accepting that wall I kept erecting between us, and turned to fill the cup before taking a long sip, letting me watch her swallow every drop of it. Then she patted my chest. "Time for us to go to bed, I think. Franny is going to be up bright and early and will probably want to go on an adventure if that's now allowed."

"Come to the country club with me tomorrow," I blurted out. "We can do tennis and lunch again."

"Um." She frowned. Yep. I'd ripped the fucking wall back down myself. I couldn't make up my damn mind. She frowned but begrudgingly said, "Of course. She likes to have you around if you can fit us into your schedule. She told me you used to go with her all the time."

Suddenly, the need to explain bubbled out of me. "It's not good for Franny to have me around much anymore. I'm the only parent she has left, so I have to do what's right even when it's hard."

"Staying away from her is right?" She tilted her head, setting the glass down on the counter carefully, like she was thinking.

"You just reminded me that I can kill men, Mia."

"And you argued that it was for your daughter."

"Doesn't make it right."

"Maybe, but a daughter always needs her father to be there for her. You even more so since her mom isn't." Her voice almost shook as she said it. "Don't step back and just blend in with the scenery, Jameson."

"That's not what I'm trying to do . . . If something happens to me, I'm creating a space for her to be fine in. She won't even miss me if—"

"She misses you now!" She shoved both hands into my chest. "She's practically begging for time with you. The poor girl talked about you all day because she was happy you were finally *there*. And you're what? Being a good martyr by keeping your distance in case someone tries to blow your head off?"

She waited for an answer, not at all scared now. Instead, disgust with me was etched in her features as I struggled to find the right answer.

"Oh, get a grip and man up. You've got security on every damn side of this house. Are you that weak?"

"Diamonds aren't weak. *Adamantem infractum manet.*"

"Great. Exactly." She rolled her eyes as if the whole society, the most powerful one in the fucking world, was stupid too. "Then teach your daughter that. For as long as you're here. Whether it's you dying tomorrow—"

"I won't." Did she think I was incompetent?

She threw up her hands. "Or in fifty years. Because a daughter needs her father. And I'll be damned if while I'm working here, that little girl doesn't get everything she needs."

With that, she stomped away from me without a backward glance while I stared at her retreating the whole way.

I had a feeling she wouldn't be damned, because she was going to get everything for Franny come hell or high water.

As for me, I was damned either way.

Because Mia Darling standing up to me even while scared but for my daughter was the prettiest thing I'd ever seen.

18

Mia

I ADMIT I AVOIDED everyone the next day, telling Archer that I'd eat breakfast in my room after his daily tap on my door. Plus Ms. Prim and Mr. Bos needed me in their pathetic state. Misery loved company, right? Their wilting leaves matched my state of mind. I was a mess, my heart jumbled, and my emotions unchecked. I even kept Franny away from Rosy for snacks because I didn't want to discuss anything.

Somehow, I felt like she'd ask or pry and be a friend.

What could I say without being embarrassed? That I screwed around with our boss, agreed it was a distraction I didn't care about, and then yelled at him for not parenting correctly? Also, could you please divulge what's in that pretty door near his room and why he won't let me in?

I was a freaking mess . . . so, yeah, avoiding felt easier.

Not only that, but it was Friday, and we all knew what that meant: Valerie would be here in the evening for her glorious show with Jameson. But not before he casually interrupted the teaching for the day to tell us we were going to play tennis.

How could I object after yelling at him last night? I was only the teacher who had a schedule for his daughter. The library could wait, especially when she jumped up and screamed in joy.

So, I went with them to the country club and endured the torture that it was.

And it *was* torture for me. Jameson being completely appropriate and fatherlike in his perfect tailored suit in the car. Then, he changed into a polo and shorts to play tennis with his daughter while I opted to sit out this time. Franny having quality time with her dad was more important. I told myself that same thing when he promised her tennis time every other day of the week. He hugged her and mouthed a "thank you" to me as she squealed.

Damn it, did he have to be an actual good dad underneath the tough exterior? My stomach flipped, and my mind cursed him. He couldn't be great *while also* being elusive and an ass. It wasn't fair. And it made me volatile. I went from wanting to act out and yell at him to wanting to jump his bones to thinking having a professional relationship was best.

Screaming at him to stop being the perfect father while teaching Franny how to hold the tennis racket seemed unfair. Although, my ovaries were screaming at me the whole time that banging him and having his children might be okay.

That wasn't at all what I needed in my life.

But the bastard laid it on thick when he asked for a locker room key for me specifically like I'd be there longer than the summer.

And then I had to deal with the female attendants bending over backward to accommodate him. They knew his favorite drink and Franny's too, and I'd never seen women sprint so fast to get him a freaking towel.

Each woman's eyes were on us—or mostly him. He could be in a pressed suit or dripping sweat in a polo from a match, and they buzzed toward him like honeybees searching out pollen. Maybe they were obsessed with his single dad parenting skills, or maybe they were all obsessed with his Diamond emblem, which I now saw everywhere. I tried to ignore both their advances and that little symbol I would catch glinting on a bracelet or a ring or sometimes embroidered on a shirt. They all had them, and now I knew what it must mean.

They all belonged, but I didn't.

Hurrying to my bedroom after saying bye to Franny was for the best. I wrote a fast report and emailed it off to Jameson before I laid in bed considering what expenses I could put on the card Jameson had given me.

I'd need earplugs to get me through this summer. I glared over at the vent now. Somehow, it had become my nemesis in the last day or two. I had been staring at it for the last hour, contemplating if I should close it somehow—cover it with a pillow and run the shower for hours while Valerie visited.

What Jameson and I had done in his basement shouldn't have mattered after what we agreed upon, but somehow it did. Him offering to fly me out to see my sister and then also taking Franny to the country club mattered too.

The knock at the door stopped me from buying a thing. "Yes?"

"We're taking you out." Rosy burst into my room without any food. It was near dinnertime, and I expected Archer to come bother me soon about a meal, but not her.

Or Pink or Olive, who followed her in.

"Out?"

"Yes. We're bored, and the boys want to talk business." Pink waltzed in with a duffel, plopped it on my bed, and started unzipping it immediately.

"What's that?" I pointed to the bag and then frowned. "What boys and what business?"

"Our outfits, plus accessories." She threw off her top as she smirked at me. "Rosy has options for you too. And *our* boys. Bane, Dimitri—Olive's husband—and I'm sure Archer and

Hades are there. Who knows who else? They should have a—" She stopped herself.

Rosy jumped in to cover up whatever she was about to say. "Please don't say no. You've been avoiding me, and I can't take it." Rosy walked over to my bed with an armful of dresses. "We're the women of the house, and we need each other."

"You are . . . I'm just here for the summer," I grumbled.

"Maybe, but for the summer, we're a team. And when the house manager decides, it must be done." She winked at me.

I bit my lip because I couldn't help but wonder . . . "How did you get this job, Rosy?"

She pointed at the dress, ignoring my question. "I'm wearing the red, but you can pick whichever other one you want."

Then both her and Pink started changing immediately. Olive shut my door for them and shrugged. "I'm keeping this on if you don't want to dress up." Her skinny jeans and crop top made all my clothes look less than average. "Why are you avoiding Rosy?"

"I'm not. I'm just . . . processing some things." I hesitated, questioning whether any of these women knew what was really going on.

"Right. Processing the syndicate?" Rosy lifted a brow as she pulled her dress on and then sashayed over to me.

I opened my mouth but wasn't sure what to say, so I shut it and waited. I guess she knew that I knew.

She chuckled. "I got this job because I was born into it . . . and the syndicate. My mom took care of his mom's life, and Jameson needed more taking care of than anyone else in his family now. Plus, he's easy to manage. Jameson's all rough around the edges, but he means well. He told me you knew. Thank God, because I was over keeping that secret."

"He's talking about me to you?"

"To all of us . . . And only when he's trying not to." Olive rolled her eyes. "He's literally the worst at expressing his emotions."

"Anyway, I have dinner all ready for them, so we don't need to be here." Rosy rearranged the dresses on the bed. "What do you want to wear?"

All three of them stood there looking at me expectantly, as if waiting for my response to that rather than the freaking ginormous elephant in the room. "So you all know he's a part of the syndicate? That it's completely dangerous? And you're okay with it? Was he—"

Rosy held her hand up. "Let's get this over with. No, we don't care. Why? Because we're all a part of it too. Sure, it's a bit dangerous. Yes, we're willing to take our chances. Most people are. And to get in, well, you're either born in, work your way in, or marry in." Rosy shrugged, not really explaining herself as she straightened a fuchsia dress on my bed. Pink and Olive held up shoes.

Or you stay out of it. "But why try to be a part of that?" I asked instead, shaking my head as I stood there, frowning at the heels Pink threw on the bed.

Rosy pointed to the dresses. "You realize that most people are a part of *something*. Why not be part of a protected society that has maintained an elite status for centuries?"

"Might be a little weird for you, but I'm just happy he told you about it. Would have been awkward if I'd been the one to have to tell you while out drinking," Pink said as she turned, presenting her friend with the back of the dress she'd wiggled into. "Zip me, Olive."

For some reason, this was more surprising than anything else they'd said. "You all *really* would have told me?" I asked as I walked over to my favorite color dress. Fuchsia would have to work even though I wasn't sure if I'd be able to squeeze into the one they'd brought.

"Of course. I let you into my kitchen every day. We're friends," Rosy answered simply.

My heart twisted at her words. *Friends*. Did she really find it so easy to put her trust into someone? Like people didn't put themselves first and sweep others' emotions under the rug.

Maybe I was still raw after the conversation with my sister, after thinking of my mother's response to Felix coming on to me. My throat tightened looking at these women. They'd come purposely to get me ready for a night out instead of stuffing me into a corner when I didn't even belong in their society.

Pink cleared her throat. "And by the end of the night, you're going to be friends with Olive and me too. Probably best friends if you drink tequila straight."

When I turned to smile at that comment of hers, my mouth dropped. The black leather bodycon zipped up was lethal. Her pink hair and pink shoes popped perfectly, and I immediately realized: "I don't think I can go out with you guys. I'll look like a doormat."

"Please." Pink waved me off and pointed to the dress I was running my hand over. "Wear that dress with those heels and you'll outdo us all. Plus, I want to see Jameson's face when we tell him we're going out."

"He won't care. It's Friday, which means . . ." I glanced at the stupid vent and then stopped myself. "It's the weekend. I can do whatever since Franny is going to her grandmother's."

"Right. He won't care," Olive mimicked as she looked at her lip gloss in the mirror over the dresser and fluffed her perfect curls.

"Dimitri will be mad too," Rosy informed Olive as if she were unaware, but the girl was smiling like she knew exactly what was about to happen. "And, honestly, Bane's not letting you go out with that dress on, Pink."

Pink did a little shimmy in the mirror. "My husband can get

fucked if he thinks he's stopping me from shaking my ass in this dress. It's too perfect to not."

I chuckled and chewed on my cheek, considering my options. I could stay in and let my mind wander about the syndicate, or go out and learn about it with new friends.

And bonus: I didn't have to listen to whatever Valerie and Jameson might end up doing later. I sighed as I grabbed my dress and walked toward the bathroom, but before I did, voices were heard from the vent.

It couldn't be.

Jameson didn't go into his office ever before dinner. It was a time he spent with Franny and his mother.

But I heard deep voices, ones belonging to men that must have been the husbands. I hurried over to the vent, but it was too late.

Pink stepped in the way, and her smile was wicked as the murmur coming through the vents grew louder and each of the women's eyes shifted fast directly to where my nightstand had been moved.

"Oh shit," Pink whispered. "Yeah, I think you just got promoted to best friend status without the tequila."

19

Mia

It was obvious now why we were all whispering while I got ready. I applied the lipstick that matched the fuchsia dress and let Olive work some cream into my hair. "It's not what you guys think," I whisper-yelled.

"You're in here every night, which means you're listening to anything and *everything* that happens in that office, Mia," Rosy pointed out, her tone accusatory but also sympathetic.

"Oh, what happens in there?" Pink inquired, and I held up a finger.

"Don't say it, Rosy."

She obviously didn't care to censor herself. "Valerie and Jameson bang every time she comes over!"

"Oh my God," Olive said louder than she should have, and we all shushed her. "And you listen?!"

"It's not like that!" I whined, but it totally was. I groaned. "At first it was a fun little outlet, okay?"

"*Fun*? I'd probably rip my own ears off, but to each their own," Rosy said and completely meant it. I wanted to hug her.

"And now?" Olive inquired.

"Well, now . . . and before . . . it's a complete invasion of privacy, and I'm stopping," I concluded, lifting my chin. They didn't need to know I was turning into a jealous shell of a woman when I didn't even have a relationship with him.

"Bull," Pink spit out. "Now, you're going to make him stop that shit because no one likes her. *He* doesn't even like her. That man can't take his eyes off you. I saw it in the basement. She probably is shaking in her boots that you're here. She wants that Knight name after hers."

"Well, she can have it." I applied some blush to my tan cheeks and then started with a heavy eyeliner. I probably went a little overboard since jealousy had started to creep into my veins. I didn't want to be the professional, nice, darling teacher now. I wanted to send a statement that I wasn't—that I wasn't on the job, that I was something more than just a nanny.

And that I was available. Just like he was. He could fuck someone else, and so could I. No strings had been attached to our little rendezvous.

Olive scoffed. "Don't be ridiculous. Can you imagine her as Franny's stepmom?"

I'd hardly spoken to the woman, but . . . "No one's good enough to be Franny's mom," I said, and meant every word.

Rosy laughed. "You need extra shots tonight. We can stay out way late so you don't have to be here to listen."

"I really don't listen every time." I blushed.

"Oh please. I would listen too. It wouldn't be fun though. I'd be enraged."

"Yeah." Glancing at these three women, I saw actual compassion on their faces and realized I could be real with them, so I admitted, "I might be at that point, unfortunately. I've been staring at that vent all day, dreading it. You think she's coming even with your husbands here?" It was a hopeful whisper that sounded stupid and desperate.

Rosy patted my shoulder in pity, because who was I kidding?

These women knew something was happening between Jameson and I even if I denied it.

"She's already here with Mrs. Knight," Olive said softly.

I sighed as I stood and took one last look in the mirror. My hair cascaded in soft waves down my back and over my bare shoulders. The sweetheart cut and tight, short dress had me feeling exposed but also single and available.

Like I was.

Very exposed and very available.

I nodded once and murmured, "Let's go."

Pink smiled and threw an arm around my shoulder like she'd be there to prop me up. I hoped so. I needed girlfriends, needed an outlet, need a distraction from the fact that Valerie and Mrs. Knight were here, that Valerie had his mother's attention and was bound to have his later that night.

This was the normal sequence of events every Friday. I knew it was happening. And I'd actually had fun with it before.

Before the basement.

Before talking with Jameson.

Before starting to have feelings for my boss.

"I truly don't know if Jameson will let her go out in this," Rosy snickered as we made our way downstairs. "You all see how he looks at her. And now she's a freaking smoke show."

"Those boys aren't *letting* us do shit," Pink reminded us, and we all agreed in solidarity.

"Remember, we stand our ground. Even if Hades makes heart eyes at you, Rosy," Pink told her as we rounded a corner. "And I'm going into Chicago. They can get fucked if they want us to stay in Paradise Grove."

"Oh, Lord," Olive groaned.

"What?" Pink shrugged. "If he wants to send security to watch Mia so she doesn't run off, they can, but no one is staying locked inside this community all summer."

"Excuse me?" I halted. "I would not run off on Franny."

"Or us," Rosy added just to be clear that she was a part of the equation.

"Right, or you. Or Archer. Jameson knows this. So it should be fine." All of them stared at me. And it dawned on me in that hallway that I wasn't privy to the whole story. I hated feeling like someone hadn't told me something. "What?"

Pink smirked like she had a brilliant idea. "You know what, let's go tell him."

I stumbled, not at all sure I wanted to barge into that office, but I mean, I was a big girl. I stood up for myself. Even if the man behind that door was also a killer.

And when we opened the door, I was sure his friends were too.

The faces of those men, all dressed in dark suits, were murderous.

"Bane Black," Pink singsonged as she sauntered in with her hand tightly gripping mine. "I'm leaving your ass to go dance tonight with these lovely ladies."

Each of the men halted their conversation to look our way. I could tell who belonged to who immediately by the way their eyes drifted over their significant other. Bane was a beast of a man, eyes so cold they could make you feel like you were in Antarctica, but he kept his stare on Pink. Jameson and another man sat on the leather sofa, but Jameson's eyes didn't look up from the paperwork he had in his lap, as if he were completely unaffected by my presence. He did shift enough to pet Malek by his side, but that was it. Instead, the man next to him glanced up at me and smirked, while Hades acted like the grim reaper in the room, a cloud of darkness shifting between Rosy and him, although he didn't speak first.

He left that to Bane. "Mrs. Black, you sure you don't want *me* to come dance with you?"

"Negative." She looked at her fingernails as if completely unaffected, but I saw the blush on her cheeks. "It's ladies' night."

"It's your night every night. So, do what you want, but I'll be watching and tracking you the whole time."

"Don't trust me?" She lifted a brow.

"Don't trust men around your pretty pink—"

"Shut your mouth, Bane," she told him as he walked over to her and kissed her full on the mouth. The girl was still holding my hand and didn't even let go as he gave her a kiss to make even my knees weak. She shoved him back after a second and murmured, "Love you."

He didn't hesitate to say it back as Olive's husband leaned against the desk and stared her down. "Why do you have to go without me?"

"Because girls need time away."

"From the love of your life, honeybee?" He sounded like a dejected baby, but when he moved in to kiss her, he grabbed her ass and proved he was very much all man.

Olive rolled her eyes and kissed him two more times before pulling back. "You'll be fine, Dimitri. Be a good daddy tonight and put our little one to bed."

The man next to Jameson tsked at them. "I'd tell you all you've gone soft, but I think you know that already."

His voice was a lot like Jameson's, and his eyes just as cold. Their jawline and bone structure were very much the same, and it occurred to me that Jameson had a brother he'd never told me about.

Maybe more than one.

I honestly didn't know anything about him, and he probably wanted it that way.

He wanted me disconnected, and so I would be. How dare he even act as though he cared enough to offer a flight to see my sister, when now he couldn't even be bothered with my presence?

I didn't know what infuriated me more: his lack of attention, or the fact that I knew he would be giving it to another woman that night. A woman who knew much more about him and his family.

His brother was quick to cover for him, though, during the awkward silence of him not acknowledging anyone's presence. "You must be Franny's nanny?"

"I am." I nodded, and the title was a good reminder. That's where I fit in with all these people.

He stood to his full height, and I was shocked at how his walk was even like Jameson's. So easily they could be mistaken for one another, which meant they must have been close in age. "Want a guy friend along on your girls' night?" he offered. "I'm Callahan. The nice Knight. I'm lots of fun."

"No," Pink interrupted. "Girls' night only."

Then she elbowed me as if it were my turn. Why were my knees suddenly wobbly and my palms starting to sweat? "So, I haven't been outside of Paradise Grove since I've started working here, and Pink mentioned a nightclub in Chicago, which would be great considering—"

"Chicago?" Jameson's head snapped up. I got his acknowledgment finally, but only because we were disobeying him. The deep timbre of his voice held a tight edge, and I had come to know that I didn't want to push him over that edge.

"Chicago's a good time." Callahan must have known too, because he immediately tried diffusing the situation.

"No." Jameson's voice was loud and clear. "Mia isn't allowed out of Paradise Grove."

"Bro." Callahan gave him a look. "Allowed?" Something unspoken passed between them. "She's an employee, not a prisoner." Then he turned to me. "We Diamonds have always been accommodating, but we're also overly cautious. Unless my brother has another reason for you not going into the city . . .?"

The tension was thick in the room as we waited for Jameson to answer. A part of me wanted him to say that he cared, that I *wasn't* just an employee, that maybe some of his feelings might have been involved, but there was no indication of it as he waved us away, his emotions shut completely down in the blink of an eye. "As long as security goes with—"

"Which we always make sure they do." Callahan lifted a brow like he was waiting for more of an excuse.

There was a moment of long silence before Jameson seemed to concede. "Hades can go, then."

Hades shook his head while keeping his stare on Rosy. It was deadly. "I think that's a bad idea. Archer can."

Another jaw tick from Jameson, but he didn't look up. "Fine. Him and a team."

"Great. Tell them to stay back," Olive concluded, starting to back out of the room like we needed to keep our eyes on them.

Hooking an arm in mine, Pink led me to the door, and we were almost through it when I heard, "Ms. Darling, a word with you first."

"Shit," Pink grumbled, "almost made it."

He got up to walk past me, and his arm brushed mine as he said, "In the study. Now."

I guess that meant I had to follow him. Freaking jerk. If we'd been alone, I'd have sat my behind down on the couch and waited for him to realize I wasn't a dog who was told what to do.

And when Malek didn't even follow him, I lifted my chin. "Mr. Knight, even my students know how to ask nicely."

Callahan, I swear, covered his laugh with a cough as his brother turned around, shoulders tense and eyes with murder in them. "Please, Ms. Darling, get your ass in the study before I drag you to it."

I scoffed, literally scoffed in his face, and I think the whole room tensed. I didn't care. Just because I taught good manners to my students didn't mean I had to have them all the time. I didn't want to make a scene in front of everyone, but I did take it upon myself to stomp my way loudly down the hall. I only paused when we passed the living area and laid eyes on Mrs. Knight laughing with Valerie and Franny.

Both of them glanced over at me while Franny continued to laugh and draw on a sheet of paper.

"Ms. Darling, good to see you. You look . . . nice." Valerie's eyes swept over me, and I instantly wanted to shrink away from the doorway. My dress was probably too short and way too tight for Mrs. Knight to be assessing. And Valerie was in a pressed polo, all pastels and proper etiquette aesthetic. Her hair was in a soft bun, and the blonde highlights were perfectly blended like she had all the time in the world to make herself look the part. "You off for the weekend? You must have plans somewhere."

"I do," I answered cautiously, not sure what to say to her or Mrs. Knight. Both of their eyes held judgment that I wasn't ready for.

Franny glanced up and gasped in delight. "You're wearing your favorite color, Ms. Darling. You look like a princess. Right, Daddy? Are you taking out a princess tonight? You could dance with her until midnight like Cinderella does with her prince."

Jameson cleared his throat and looked physically pained. He wanted nothing to do with this moment, and neither did I. Still, he answered. "I wish I was taking her out, Fran." His stare felt heavy as he met mine. "She's going to dance with her friends. But no prince better dance with our princess, right?"

Franny chuckled and nodded, going back to drawing. Mrs. Knight's eyes stared inquisitively at me, but Valerie's were daggers. "Franny?" Valerie's tone was sharp. "You know that dress's color is quite bold, a bit bright for around here." Her insult hit right where it needed to as she raised her eyebrows at me and her lips curved condescendingly. "Sorry. I know you're probably going into the city dressed like that, right? I just want Franny to understand the community *here*. It's quite a respectable neighborhood."

She crossed her arms, and I saw that emblem flash, reminding me that somehow she was part of the Diamond Syndicate. Whether it was generational grace or she worked for all of them, I didn't know. All I knew was that I wasn't a part of it. I was in a borrowed dress and on borrowed time here.

Yet, I saw how Franny chewed her cheek, absorbing the divisive comment and information. Valerie was constructing a box that Franny thought she'd have to fit perfectly into, but I wasn't about to make her feel that way.

Maybe if it was just me, I would have shrunk back. But not for that sweet girl. "Probably time for Paradise Grove to respect more than outward appearances though, right? It takes more than an outfit to make a princess, right, Franny?"

She smiled. "Heart-in-pinkie promise?"

"Of course, and remember that when someone makes you feel less than, Franny. Friends love you for who you are, not for what you dress up to be."

I turned and walked off before anyone could say another word, because I wouldn't act out in front of Franny no matter how bad I wanted to.

I heard Jameson behind me as he closed the door to his study. When I turned to meet his eyes, they were cold and unreadable. I didn't care. "She had way worse coming, and you know it."

He pinched the bridge of his nose. "You know what I'm going to say, Mia."

"What? I'm out of line? Not to talk to your girlfriend that way?"

His eyes snapped open to hold mine under their glare. "She's not my girlfriend."

"Oh. Then maybe future fiancée? From how she's sitting with your mother?"

He clenched his teeth. "She's my child's psychiatrist. You're her nanny and teacher. You two should be getting along."

I scoffed at that. He didn't know I'd heard them banging, so I couldn't throw it in his face even if I wanted to. "Come on, *Mr. Knight*. She seems quite cozy in your house and with your mother and your child to be only that. But if that's the story we're going with, fine. I don't really care about anything else she might be to you anyway." It was a petulant thing to say, but I felt petulant. I crossed my arms to try to hold onto my jealousy.

"Bullshit, Darling. I think you *do* care. Want to admit it now, or will I have to make you confess later?"

The fact that he thought he could was disrespectful enough for me to tell him, "Neither. I care about your *daughter*, Jameson. And she's being fed a crock of shit by her psychiatrist, so I hope you're considering that."

"Now you're definitely out of line," he practically roared, probably because that hit too close to home for him. Because I was onto something.

"*I'm* out of line?" I stepped up to him and let him look down at me. I'd meet him bellow for bellow if necessary. "You just swore at me in front of your family, friends, and staff, then proceeded to threaten to drag me down the hall!"

"Swore?" He looked flabbergasted. "You should be happy it was only words. I'm the leader of arguably the most powerful syndicate in the world, Mia. I swear all the goddamn time!"

"Well, I don't like when it's directed toward me," I told him. I was trying to not swear, and he could too. "So *fucking* quit it."

"You're unbelievable."

"And you're rude! God forbid I want to look a certain way while going out."

"I didn't say anything about how you looked—"

"Exactly. You didn't. You stood there and let another woman tear me down in your daughter's presence. So, I had to be the boss, I guess, and put another one of your employees in her place so that your daughter doesn't take up being a mean girl."

His hands slid into his pockets as if he needed them there. Maybe he wanted to strangle me at this point, but instead, he tried to take the higher road. "Valerie's just prickly when—"

The low road was clearly where I was comfortable with him at this point. I was so annoyed as I thought more about how disrespectful that woman had been and how he hadn't done a thing about it. "When she's off the clock and being herself? Or when she feels threatened? Either way, she's instilling values in Franny that make your daughter uncomfortable. Are you a father, or a fucking people pleaser?"

"Jesus, Mia," he whispered, but it whipped through the room with a vengeance. "Do you want me to lose my mind and control with you? I swear you do. I swear you enjoy lashing out at me."

"I do what I have to for your daughter."

He shook his head. "Valerie's right that Paradise Grove is a certain way with women."

"What women, exactly? Because Pink and Olive—"

"Live a different lifestyle," he finished, his eyes blazing angrily toward me. "One I don't want for my daughter."

"Because they're a part of the syndicate?"

"They've taken an active, dangerous role in it, and now you're going out with them." Jameson looked toward the ceiling and started pacing the study.

"And what? You'd rather me stay home and twiddle my thumbs like Valerie, listening to your every demand?" I wrinkled my nose and scoffed, realizing that was who my parents wanted me to be, my old town wanted me to be, and who I definitely wasn't. "No thanks. I don't think I'm that type of girl. I tried that for the first few weeks I was here, Jameson. It's not who I am . . . not who your daughter is either."

He seemed to breathe out a sigh like he was expressing his demons. "You have no understanding of how dangerous Chicago can be."

"So is that what you wanted to discuss with me when you so rudely commanded me in here? You're upset that I'm going out because it's dangerous?"

"Of course."

"That's *it*?" I asked, wanting him to care more about me, about what I was doing, about who I'd be doing it with.

His jaw went up and down for almost a minute, and then his voice rumbled out, "What else would I be pissed off at, huh? Enlighten me."

"Nothing." I ground my teeth together, because if he didn't want to admit I was more than a distraction, so be it. "You have a great security team, Jameson. We'll be just fine. *Adamantem infractum manet*, right?" I blurted out, and even *my* eyes widened at my boldness.

"*Adamantem infractum manet*," he reiterated quietly, like the words tasted bitter in his mouth. "Be careful, and have a good night."

"Great." I started to walk past him, but he caught my arm at the last second.

His voice was dangerously low as he said, "Don't do anything stupid in that pretty little dress of yours."

Some sort of understanding passed between us then. He looked remorseful and concerned, whereas I felt uneasy that we were bickering like much more than boss and employee.

I looked down at the dress and rolled my lips between my

teeth before realizing that even if we were bickering, I wanted his real opinion. "Be honest, is it too much?"

"Mia Darling"—he groaned my name, his guard finally down for a moment—"you're killing me, baby. It's murder waiting to happen."

"What do you mean?" My eyes flew up to him.

"The dress you have on would make me murder men who look at you wrong. And they will. So, do me a favor and listen to what I told Franny."

"What's that?"

"Don't let any princes dance with you, my darling princess."

"Jameson . . ." My heart beat faster, my mind falling victim to his words. I took a step closer to him, like I wanted to be by his side. Yet, he stepped back right away and dropped his hand from my elbow.

"Go. Now. Because in about one second, I won't let you. And if you're not home by midnight, I'm coming to find you."

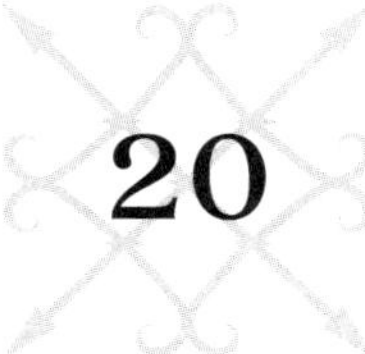

20

Jameson

Never was she actually darling Mia when I wanted her to be. Instead, the devil darling came out and the sweet, vulnerable side of her fucked with my head when I didn't want it to.

Was her dress too much? Of course that shit was. She looked flawless in it though, and her little pout made me want to drag her over to the desk and spank her ass so she really had something to pout about.

And she was a menace to me in front of my guys, who all gave me shit after they left.

"She always talk to you like that?" Bane asked once we all settled in my office after I sent my mother, Franny, and Valerie off. I could barely look at her, let alone fuck her, tonight anyway. Sitting with my men instead was probably for the best.

"Pink always talk to *you* like that?" I retorted.

"My *wife* can say anything she wants to me. I'm surprised you allow your nanny the same leniency."

Maybe it wasn't for the best. "She doesn't understand the dynamics," I explained, pouring myself a finger of whiskey. Truth was, I didn't care if Mia spit in my face while she talked to me as long as she kept on talking.

"Well, there was a woman in the next room who does," Cal

reminded me with a damn twinkle in his eye. “Valerie is always ready to get on her knees for you right when Ma leaves with Franny. How’s that going by the way?”

“Fuck off,” I grumbled, because I didn’t want to talk about it. The woman had been around for as long as my ex hadn’t been, and she’d made it known that she’d happily take the place of a Diamond wife in my household if given the chance. Not that I’d ever give it to her after her display tonight. I told her to go home and we’d talk later. Tonight wasn’t the time with my mother there or the guys. “You were all used as my excuse for her to leave, by the way, in case she asks.”

And she would, because Valerie had a way of getting the truth every single time she dug for it. My mother loved her, Franny tolerated her, and she was a constant in Diamond circles. That alone gave her way too much access to me.

Valerie had been convenient for a time, but she wasn’t anymore. I only fucked around with women who didn’t cause me problems.

Except for Mia.

“You used us as cockblockers? Interesting.” Bane tilted his head and smirked.

“She wasn’t getting the hint.”

“Oh, she gets the hint, she just doesn’t want to take it.” Hades leaned against my desk and pet Malek. The dog looked dejected, like he missed a certain someone, and it made me realize he was starting to follow Mia around more than he did Franny or me now. “Valerie told Rosy she’d fuck you until you saw the light and it didn’t matter who else you dabbled with in between.”

“Probably because she dabbled as much as I did when we were screwing around.” I shrugged.

“Were? She know that’s past tense?” My brother wiggled his eyebrows like I wasn’t getting off the hook that easily. I would, though. Our relationship had been one of only convenience, but not anymore. Not when I couldn't see anyone else in my mind but Mia. "Supposedly she hasn't looked twice at another guy for a while, according to Ma. Even heard she cut that dumbass, Trent, off too."

"As she should. Trent's going nowhere fast. He's been flipping loyalties, right?" Bane added.

I nodded, but didn't waste time going over it. Trent wasn't high enough up that I'd have to worry. He'd be taken care of over time for leaking information to O'Connor's men. "Either way, it doesn't matter who Val sleeps with or doesn't. She's lost sight of the big picture. She's been around my daughter far too long, and she got comfortable giving her unsolicited advice." It hadn't been the first time either. Tonight, though, was a violation that was way the hell out of line, an overstep that Mia pointed out. I wouldn't tolerate it any longer even if Franny had known her a long time.

"Isn't her job to give you and Franny advice?"

"Do you have to question everything I do, Cal?" I threw back at him. "How about you worry about you and Paolo's niece."

"Niece?" Bane frowned. "Don't tell me you're getting mixed up with Jasmina."

Cal was quick to respond. "If we're discussing our sex lives . . . Jameson can tell us about the nanny instead. You with her officially, or can I take a shot at her?"

"You better shut the fuck up." I took a step toward him, and he held up his hands as Bane stepped between us.

"I flew in for updates. Not to watch you two bloody your knuckles."

"He'd deserve it," I grumbled but spun away from them and grabbed cigars from my drawer. We each took one and sat to discuss the business Bane was talking about.

We pulled up figures on a drop-down screen and discussed

new numbers and legislation. When the topic of our pharm partnerships came up, I told them, "I'm not opening any warehouses to Paolo. Not ever going to be an option when we work as closely as we do with the Stonewoods."

"Agreed," Bane confirmed in a measured tone.

Cal was the one to speak on what everyone wanted to, though. "We're not making friends on the East Coast by dumping O'Connor's body and passing on this partnership with Paolo."

"Do we need more friends, Cal?"

"No." He paused. "Our casinos there give us enough pull, but that's just stating the obvious."

"Well, you *obviously* have some connections over there." I hinted at him and Jasmina's spat. "So, you can go make more friends if need be."

The room was charged with tension and anxiety. Could have been from what we were discussing, could have been that things were too quiet after what I'd done to the Irish. Could have been a lot of things, but I knew that Dimitri, Hades, Bane, and I all felt the same thing. Something I shouldn't have felt considering I wasn't even attached to Mia in the way the other men were attached to their partners.

Yet, it wasn't long after Archer alerted us that Rosy, Mia, Pink, and Olive arrived at the dance club that we all decided we needed to switch from business on the screen to security in case something went wrong.

"In case something goes wrong?" My brother laughed. "Who the fuck do you think you're kidding? You all look ready to call in every one of our made men to guard that place for no other reason than because they're in there."

"This isn't real time," Bane told us as he ignored Cal. He glared at the screens before pulling his phone out to call someone.

I swore while Dimitri asked, "How far behind?"

"At least a minute. Pink just texted me that she was in the bathroom." And then we watched her on the monitor whisper to the ladies before heading off to the bathroom.

"Fuck." Dimitri looked concerned suddenly.

I didn't feel much better. Pink and Olive were accustomed to our lifestyle, but Mia wasn't. She couldn't and didn't understand the gravity of it. Yet, they weren't going to come home just because we didn't want them out.

I passed more cigars around. "Archer's there with his team." I tried to be a voice of reason, but fear and unease snaked through me. "We've issued a warning. Plus, we're here. If someone wanted to fuck with us, they'd come for us."

"Or they'd come for what we care about," Bane grumbled. He had his phone to his ear and growled, "Get the cameras up to speed, or I'll be there to do it myself."

And the relief for someone other than my daughter sank into me stronger than I would have imagined.

Mia was becoming a weakness. More than a distraction. And more than someone I could ignore.

Mia Darling was becoming mine.

Instead of dwelling on it, we discussed business. We made plans for next quarter and mapped out territories we could expand into.

I was happy to say I'd distracted myself until past midnight, but we still had the cameras on in the background, and we all still watched them dancing while we lit more cigars and drank away our concerns.

Cal threw up his hands when there was a lull in conversation. "Are we just going to watch them all night? It's a complete invasion of privacy." He just wanted to fucking goad me.

"Go home then," I growled.

"Why did you all let them go if you can't handle it?" he asked us collectively.

"I don't *let* her do anything." But I wished that was the way it was.

Daily report?

I sent you one.

Not for my daughter. For you.

Why are you texting me? Aren't you busy on your Friday night?

No. Instead, I'm worried on my Friday night about one of my employees.

It's well past my curfew, Darling.

Funny. I don't recall having a curfew. I'm staying out. Chicago is alive at this time of night.

Then give me an update. How's the club?

How do you know it's a club and not a bar?

Because I've got eyes everywhere.

Do I even want to know what that means?

Do you?

She didn't answer, but I saw her looking around and making eye contact with a few of the security cameras before narrowing her eyes. Then, she flipped off a camera, and Pink frowned at her. She pointed to all of them, and I saw Pink nodding.

She knows as well as I do, Darling, you guys are going nowhere without being watched. Now . . . Provide me an update. Dance with anyone yet?

I saw her shake her head and then try not to smile down at her phone like she was avoiding the inevitable. It wasn't one that she let me see easily, and it had me smirking too.

This is too over the top. I don't need a stalker, Jameson.

And yet you have one while out.

Well then you know, there's been no princes to dance with yet. How long have you been watching me?

The whole time. Make sure you keep it that way.

You know you don't get to tell me what to do with my weekends. I'm off the clock.

How about I hire you for overtime and tell you everything to do all weekend? Like that better?

Probably out of your price range considering my salary already.

I'll bet that whole salary it's not out of my price range, Darling Devil.

Oh stop. Let me have my fun. I'm sure you have yours. A prince or two or maybe even a knight would be nice for a dance or a few tonight.

Don't make me come there to stop you.

She rolled her eyes and sent me another middle finger before I saw her get pulled onto the dance floor with Rosy.

"That must be for you?" Bane chuckled.

I shook my head and didn't answer him. I was in too much of a trance as I watched her swaying and moving through the crowd like she belonged there, like the beat of the music moved through her body perfectly. Mia was coordinated and athletic, which I'd clocked when she played tennis, but on that dance floor she was also languid, sexy, and knew how to draw attention.

Her dancing with the girls wasn't a problem, but after one song, they made it a problem when Rosy pulled Pink onto the dance floor but Mia grabbed Archer's hand too.

My security.

The guy who wasn't supposed to look twice at her shook his head once, then gave in. He moved close and wrapped his arm around her waist.

I stood abruptly, but my brother's hand clamped on to my shoulder. "Calm down. It's Archer, bro."

He liked to goad me, but he also knew he didn't need Archer's blood on our hands. He wouldn't incite me to kill one of our most loyal men if it wasn't necessary.

"Fuck off. He's not doing his job," I growled.

But it was clear he was scanning the environment even while he danced with her. Even while he dipped his fucking head and whispered in her ear.

I was going to kill him. "I'm going to the club."

"Jesus Christ," Cal mumbled.

The guys knew it was inevitable and got up to follow me.

"You're all following, no questions asked?" Cal sounded disgusted.

What questions were there to ask at this point? Were we watching a security feed to a club we had access to? Yes. Were we acting like possessive bastards? Yes. Did I have a right? No. She was my employee, not my wife.

Did I give a damn? Also, no. Because she was still mine.

21

Mia

"Come on! One dance," I yelled at Archer, because he was the only guy I trusted in the whole club.

"You're trying to get me killed," he grumbled, but I didn't care. The strobing lights kept the beat of the music, the alcohol pumped in my veins, and the laughter of my new friends fueled me to loosen up more.

Screw the man who didn't want me to enjoy my night off. He surely was enjoying his. I needed to forget about the pull he had on me and focus on something else.

Or someone else. I couldn't live in Paradise Grove all summer without an outlet. Not after the way Jameson and I were so close to combusting.

And that someone was Archer, who was finally stepping onto the dance floor with me. He was stiff and didn't move at all at first. But I laughed at him rolling his eyes and spun around before dropping low to the beat and whipping my curls to the side. "Having a little fun sometimes isn't going to get you killed."

"You don't know Jameson," he told me, scanning the place like his boss was going to be there any second.

Doubt it. Then again, the thrill that he was watching, that

he'd chose to do that rather than Valerie tonight, had me shimmying closer to Archer. I needed out of Jameson's orbit and to be pulled into someone else's.

"No, but I know you haven't had a night out for a while, considering you've eaten with me every night. So, before the Knights take over our lives, let's live a little."

The man was tempted. I saw it in the way he pulled at the back of his neck before he finally ground out, "One dance." And then he pulled me close and rocked to the music with me. "I'll take the risk tonight only, Ms. Darling."

I glanced up at him and tried to feel something for his chocolate eyes and warm smile. It was comfortable, but not intoxicating. Nice, but not lethal.

Holding back the sigh I wanted to let out, I moved my hips against his and let the song play out, searching for some spark of chemistry.

There wasn't much there, but we laughed and danced. As the alcohol flowed through my veins to the rhythm of the bass, I threw my head back and let go of my worries.

"I needed this," I shouted to everyone in our dance circle as the song ended. We walked back to the bar and chatted more. I got a glass of water this time, watching people dance around us as Archer scanned the club. "You know you probably need to loosen up more than I do."

He harrumphed, and so I sipped my water as Olive told us about how nice it was to be out. "Lucille across the street keeps talking to me about a bush we planted because I'm somehow not nurturing them right."

"Archer sometimes talks to my plants for me and it helps them to grow." I winked at Archer. His eyes widened and he stepped back like he wanted nothing to do with our conversation.

Pink eyed him up and down. "You only nurturing her *plants*?"

Archer groaned and I frowned at him and shrugged. "You want air instead of talking here?" I pointed to the elevators to go up to the balcony. He gave me a look, but I completely ignored it as I pulled his arm and told the girls we'd be right back. He let one of the guys know we were going out there, and of course half of them followed us onto the elevator.

"We need this security all the time?" I leaned against the metal rail to question him.

"It's a privilege to have it, Ms. Darling. You should be thankful." He pulled at his black shirt and then ushered me out of the elevator so that I could walk through another room full of people dancing that led to the balcony doors. I pushed through them and let the cool air embrace my glistening skin as we walked out.

"Well, thanks for the security and for the dance, Arch."

"It's Jameson's security. And as for the dance . . . you're aware of the boundaries you're pushing, I assume," he warned me as I breathed in the night breeze. "He's more than a little uncomfortable."

"With me? Doubt it." I hadn't received another text from Jameson, and it shouldn't have mattered if Valerie was there to keep him company anyway.

He shook his head and sighed. "*Only* with you. He isn't this way with anyone else, not even Valerie . . . even if you hear them." My gaze whipped up to his as a gust of wind blew my hair back. I hated that my eyes watered, and I blamed the wind, but we both knew that wasn't it. I was embarrassed Archer saw my weakness and looked away immediately. Then he said softly, "I know why you ask me to leave your room after dinner, Darling."

"Oh God," I whispered and ducked my head as I shivered at the idea. Archer mistook it for being cold and immediately unbuttoned his suit jacket to drape it over my shoulders. I pulled it closed and murmured a thanks. It was handy that I could tuck my face into it and hide my shame. "Did you tell him?"

"Fuck no, I'm not telling him you're listening to him and Valerie," Archer swore, and I knew he wouldn't. He'd been a friend when I didn't have one, and someone who sat with me through dinners when he didn't have to. We laughed together, watched shows together, took care of those kids together at the academy. "I'm not telling him shit. I'm just telling *you*. He's got his demons, and he protects those he cares about. He's starting to care more about you than most women. It scares him."

"Because . . ."

"Because . . . it's his story to tell." Archer sighed. "Just trust me when I say if you keep pushing those boundaries, they're bound to break, and you should be ready."

"For what?"

We didn't get to finish our conversation. It was only two or three songs that we'd been standing out in that cool breeze on the roof. I heard the bass hit like a warning. Or maybe it was the feeling of being watched by him that erupted over my skin.

Predatory. Invading. And dangerous. Jameson stood at the entrance of the balcony in all black, leather stretching over his shoulders instead of a tailored suit.

His hair looked ruffled, and his jaw was set in that sharp way I was used to seeing. He'd arrived in a hurry, probably to yell at all of us. His men flanked either side of him, and they all looked lethal, ready to stand behind him in whatever he did.

A syndicate that was powerful. *Adamantem infractum manet.* I saw it in that moment more than I ever had before.

The music around me died, the lights seemed to shine only on him, and the world faded out.

He was the only thing there for me as tension whipped

between us. I felt Archer step back. "If you can't find me tomorrow, Mia, I'm at the bottom of a damn lake."

I opened my mouth to reassure him, but Jameson's murderous blue gaze stopped me from saying a word. He had Archer in his sights, and I knew keeping him here wasn't worth it. I waved him away quickly, but he stood his ground even as Jameson walked out the door someone on his security opened for him.

I heard people inside as he did: "Get out of his way. He's a Knight," and then, "Is that Bane Black with Dimitri from the HEAT empire?"

Even I realized how people had moved for him and how people were looking through the window now.

Jameson didn't stop for any of them. He was on a damn mission to meet us at the railing of that balcony and confront us.

People pretended not to stare, but I knew they were, knew that if I didn't de-escalate the situation, Archer might have to stand toe to toe with him.

I wasn't quick enough though. Jameson acted faster than I could move and plowed a fist into Archer's face right over my head.

His guys flanking behind him meant to block the scene from others, but people inside screamed, and I lunged for Archer. Not before Jameson's arm wrapped around my waist and pulled me up against him, though, gripping my hip hard enough to prove a point. I shoved at his grip, digging my nails in and probably drawing blood, but it was no use. "You asshole. You know I dragged Archer out onto the dance floor. Let him be."

He ignored me. Didn't even look my way. Archer was the one he wanted, and he made that clear when his tone rolled out, so pointed and matter-of-fact as he told him, "You're dead to me and the Diamonds, Archer."

I had to give Archer credit. He didn't cower or bow to

Jameson. He spit blood onto the cement and then licked the split lip. "You saying I'm not officially a part of the syndicate?"

"No. That's not what he's saying," Hades interrupted, combing a hand through his hair as he glared at Jameson. "What the fuck? He's my guy and yours."

"He could be my brother, and I still would have made him bleed for touching her," Jameson growled, and then he looked at Pink and Olive, who were shaking their heads. He eased me away from him and told them, "Keep her on the balcony."

"I'm not staying anywhere if you take Arch—"

"He's going to the bathroom with us," Jameson said, eyeing Archer with pointed authority.

"Don't go," I told Archer, but he was already wiping his face and walking forward like he had a death sentence but intended to take it with pride. He even nodded at me and gave me a wink, which I tried to take as a signal that everything would be okay.

I didn't have much of a choice either, because four huge men blocked the balcony entrance after Jameson and the guys walked through it.

I was being held against my will again.

"He won't kill him, right?" I asked the girls quietly.

Pink glanced at Olive and Rosy, who both shrugged. She then tilted her hands up and down like it was a fifty-fifty before she answered, "No . . . well, I don't think so."

22

Jameson

"You want to fight me for her?" Archer asked me even though he was on his knees now in the guys' bathroom on piss-stained tiles about to beg for his life. We'd caused a damn scene that Cal would have to clean up tomorrow, but he was good for cleaning up messes anyway. If there was footage of Diamonds acting out in the news, he got rid of it before it saw social media outlets.

I wasn't concerned about that.

I was concerned about my own men turning against me for my pretty little teacher.

"Fight me and you lose, Archer, every fucking time." I had my damn pistol out, and I wanted to use it. My finger itched to pull the trigger on him because I hated men who weren't loyal to a fault.

Didn't anyone get that? How could they not after what I'd done to my father?

"That's the problem with you, dumbass. *I* won't fight you. I'm on your side. But you can't trust a fucking soul."

I didn't need a lecture; I needed him to shut up. The gun was at his temple as fast as my fist had connected with his mouth earlier. Through clenched teeth, I told him, "You knew better than to dance with her."

"Calm the fuck down," Cal yelled from behind me, but he didn't step in my way. This was my choice, and he knew it. No one was saving Archer but Archer himself.

And that fucker didn't even flinch. He was as unhinged as all the rest of us. "Mia deserved a good night after weeks of being holed up in a place she doesn't feel like she fits in. You'd be wise to make her feel differently."

I shoved the barrel harder against his skull. "You want to give advice with a gun to your head?"

"Wouldn't be the first time." He rubbed at the blood trickling down his chin, but I wouldn't feel bad. He may have been loyal for years, but it didn't justify his behavior now. "I spent time with her, man. You're not going to win over that girl by blowing the head off of her friend. That's what I am to her . . . and nothing more. You and I both know it. You'd be wise to believe her if you want her."

An actual war ensued in my head, wrestling with the jealousy in me, with the adrenaline that pumped through my veins, with the rage I wanted to succumb to rather than the understanding I had to embrace.

As I lowered my weapon, he grumbled, "She's not a Diamond, and you're never going to win her over by acting like one."

I didn't kill him, but I might have broken his jaw when I whipped him across the face with the butt of my gun. "Fuck!" I raged and spun on everyone.

Hades rolled his eyes and said, "Guess it's better than a cleanup here tonight. Go send our girls out so you can get your ass chewed out by Mia."

The fact that I ground my teeth together and had nothing to say to him was how I knew I looked like a damn pussy-whipped ass. But I still stomped my ass out of the bathroom and over to the balcony and told everyone to leave.

"Except you, darling devil. You and I have unfinished business that needs attention."

She crossed her arms, displaying her cleavage as a damn distraction, I swear, as her curls whipped wildly in the wind. The moon lit her back, shining like a spotlight on the fucking suit jacket she was still wearing.

It wasn't hers.

It was his.

On my girl's shoulders. Keeping her warm when it should have been mine.

She was mine. Didn't she know that?

Her girlfriends left us, but not before Pink gave me a look. "*Adamantem infractum manet* only applies with the syndicate, dumbass. Not your heart. Remember that."

My men flanked the balcony entrance as the women walked back inside and left only Mia and me. I let the air cool me down as I stood there taking her in. She stood on top of this city like she had nothing to cower from, and maybe she didn't.

I owned this city, but it was clear she owned me.

I walked over to her and leaned on the railing, crossing one boot over the other as I stared her down. "You were dancing with my security."

The energy that rolled off her seemed to combust, and damn did I love watching her fury erupt. She tried to hold it back, I knew that, but her beauty came when she was unhinged. "I can't believe you!"

"Believe it. I'm taking you home."

"Oh, the hell you are. I intend to stay out until I'm done here."

"Done with what, exactly?" My tone held an edge.

"Dancing. Mingling. Maybe more." She threw her hands up. "I'll do what I want on my own time."

I swear she wanted to grate on every one of my nerves tonight. "You're done now."

"Why? Because you watched me on security cameras and raced over here like a Neanderthal when you saw me dancing with someone else?"

"Not someone else. My team."

"So you'd be fine if it were a random guy?"

"Mia, if a random guy tries to touch you after tonight, I'll deliver their hands to you personally."

"Get real."

"Real? I'd douse a man in acid for looking wrong at you."

"What?" She breathed out, probably trying to comprehend if I was serious.

I pinched the bridge of my nose. "They'd deserve it too, Mia. I swear to God."

"You're a real piece of work." She started to walk past me, like that was the end of the conversation. I grabbed her elbow, and she gasped at our contact, her chest moving with it.

Fuck if I wasn't going to look. That sweetheart neckline was where every man's eyes had been tonight. "Why fight me at every fucking turn, Mia?"

"Because it seems someone has to! You don't get to just interrupt girls' night because you can. We were just having a good time!" she screeched. Her composure was completely gone. She shook with the same level of emotion I'd felt on the way here. I'd pushed my bike to a hundred fifty on the highway in order to make it here in record time.

Now, her anger had skyrocketed to the same level as my jealousy.

"A good time, Mia? With his cock against your ass?"

"Well, if you want semantics, abso-fucking-lutely. And"—she leaned in, giving me a view right down her dress, moving her hands to her hips while she snarled—"since you're asking, I'll let you in on a secret: His cock was big enough to feel good against it too."

Her rage danced in my face, igniting my jealousy and fury to meet hers.

She wanted a fight, and I was more than happy to give it to her. She didn't think she had to be worried about how pissed off I got; she would soon learn. I rubbed a hand over the scruff of my jaw and told her, "You must be plastered to think talking to me that way is warranted."

"I could be stone-cold sober and not give a flying *fuck* how I talked to you after the way you acted in there." Her tone sounded like she wanted to tear me limb from fucking limb. "Don't you ever lay hands on my friends again."

"I'll do whatever the hell I want with my *team*." I pushed off the railing and moved toward her, willing her to back down.

"Not for me you won't." She stepped right up to my chest. "You think Archer wanted to dance with me? No. He did it to be nice, because I wasn't willing to dance with other guys but still wanted to have a good time. Because your ass didn't come out to dance with us, so I chose someone else. I'm *allowed* to have a good time. I fucking deserve it. And Archer doesn't deserve your anger. You owe him an apology."

An apology? Did she know who she was talking to? I saw red. No, I saw fucking black. She was going to make me lose every ounce of control I had left. She was sawing on the thread that was holding me together on purpose, I swear. "You're out of your damn mind."

"You can apologize to him, or I can go sleep at a hotel." She even pulled the phone out that I had bought her to start searching for accommodations.

I snatched it from her and launched it over the balcony. It shattered into a million pieces, but she didn't even flinch or look down. Most everyone shrank when I embraced my anger, most everyone knew they should fear it. Mia Darling? She stared at me like I were a child.

And then she followed up on that look with, "Having a tantrum like a five-year-old—like a literal student of mine—when you're an adult will get you nowhere. I'll just walk to a hotel and ask for a room."

"You stay at home, or you don't have a job, Darling," I growled, ready to fire her and hold her captive.

She laughed at my threat. Laughed! "Tell me, you have a handbook on my duties, *Mr. Knight*? Is there a page I should look at on sleeping arrangements? How about fraternization?"

I grabbed her by the neck and shoved her into the railing, but she didn't gasp in concern now. She clawed at my grip and tried to knee me in the balls even if she was practically hanging off the tenth story. "No rule book is going to be made for working within the syndicate. I could drop you off the side of this damn building and no one would say shit. You're *my* employee. *Mine*." Her eyes shifted with that word, but I was on a roll. "And so I do what I want with you. Not Archer. Not Hades. No one but me."

The city pulsed like it was alive as we stared at each other on that rooftop for a moment before she murmured, "Great. How lucky I am that I got you as a boss." Her tone was soft, almost too soft, as she bit her lip and then looked up at the stars. "A man who considers killing me or dropping me off this balcony without a second thought, while I only considered if I made him proud with taking care of his daughter today, or if he thinks of me at night like I do him."

That vulnerability. So fast it hit and scattered my emotions. So fast she dropped her guard that I didn't know what to do but take what I wanted from the real her before it was too late.

"Darling Mia" fell from my lips before I yanked her small neck toward me so I could devour her lips, so I could taste the sweet cherries that I craved, that I'd been fiending for since the last time I got access to them.

I scraped my teeth over her soft lips and her insecurities, I gripped her neck tighter to steal at her breath and anger toward me, and snaked my arm around her waist like it was her soul because I wanted to capture it and keep it for myself.

Her legs wrapped around me, and her body balanced on only that small railing as if she trusted me much more than she said she did.

She had to know I never considered actually getting rid of her.

She was fucking imprinted on me from the moment I saw her. My hand left her neck to bury into her curls and pull so I could tip her head up and get more of her. I wanted it all. Every part of her open to me. I stepped even closer, making her legs spread further apart, and then I kissed down her neck as I told her, "You're driving me mad. I told you I'd kill someone for looking at you."

She shook her head like I was ridiculous, but her hands were at my leather jacket, pulling me closer. "Not Archer. He's your security and my friend. That's silly, Jameson."

"He won't be anything if he dances with you again." It wasn't an exaggeration either as I smelled his jacket on her instead of her own scent. I kept hold of her waist as I pulled the switchblade I carried with me from my pocket. "His jacket on your shoulders should be a damn death sentence." I cut the buttoned area from her stomach. "Next time I'll use this on his neck and not his jacket if he touches you, Mia. I swear it. And you know why that is?"

"Why?"

"Because I think of you day and night. All the damn time. No matter how hard I try not to . . . because you're mine now . . . and everyone in this city knows not to touch what's mine."

I balled the suit jacket up enough behind her back that it slid from her shoulders, and we both watched as I threw the fabric over the edge and it landed in a pile on the road below.

Then, I slid the knife up to her neck and held it there, because I wanted her under my complete control for just a second, just a moment of her submitting to me rather than her controlling my every thought. "Say you understand."

She held my gaze in defiance, but her eyes had softened with my confession. She bit her lip and spread her legs further, so much that her dress bunched around her ass and I felt her wet panties soaking through my jeans. "Slit my throat and throw me over, fuck me, or let me go, Jameson. Your choice if I'm yours, right? But I will *not* be telling you I understand the reasoning behind you not trusting your men."

"You'd let me fuck you with a knife to your throat, Mia?"

Her eyes had turned hazy with lust, and she shook her head. "I shouldn't want you, but I can't stop thinking about how I do." She unzipped my black jeans and pulled my cock from them to stroke it. Her gaze was serious as she murmured, "Plus, if you wanted me dead, I would already be."

"You're drunk." Someone had to be the responsible one and stop how far this was going.

"Am I though? Three shots over three hours' time isn't enough to make my inhibitions disappear. You drink before you sped over here?" She kept her hand wrapped around my cock, stroking it to get all the answers from me she wanted.

"I could have been black-out wasted and I'd still have sped over here to stop you from dancing with another man. I told you not to make me come drag you home at midnight because you're too busy dancing with men you think are princes."

"I said I wanted a knight." She smirked at me. "Glad you could deliver on that."

"I'll deliver killing a man too, Mia. You're pushing me too far."

"Too far for an employee?" She lifted a brow.

"Fuck me." I groaned. "That's all you should be. But you're not. You're upending what I thought I should be for my daughter, what I thought I should be for a woman, and what I thought I should be for myself. I'm not a good man, Mia. I won't commit to you, won't treat you well, and will put a lot before you." I swallowed down the fear that I was starting to feel that she might not accept it.

"Who's saying I'm asking for that?"

"You should be asking for it all."

"Because I'm a 'darling teacher'? What if I told you I didn't want to be? What if I told you I just wanted this between us right now? I'm on birth control and get tested." She pumped my cock hard, and I growled at her words.

"You're tempting a man that isn't used to restraint."

"Show me, then."

"I'm not a good enough man to stop you, Mia."

"I'm not asking you to." She inched closer, and then she murmured that she just wanted the tip. "I just want to feel you. Nothing more."

"That's a dangerous game you're playing."

"Isn't that what we do? Play dangerous games and hope to win."

She nudged my cock into her entrance, and I let her. I wasn't proud of it, but it didn't matter. I was under her control, not mine anymore, even as I ground my teeth together and tried to hold back. "Only the tip, Darling," I told her.

A victorious smile whipped across her face as she played with the head of my cock for another few seconds before shifting forward to guide me into her entrance. The heat of her body on mine, the silk of her pussy sliding over me, and the feeling of her tight cunt enveloping the head of my cock was enough to push me over the edge. I groaned into her neck. "Fuck, baby. You're tight."

She wiggled to adjust and then moved down on my shaft fast, trying to take more of me. I hissed at her attempt to fuck me, to ride my cock the way I wanted her to, and it took everything for me to not grip her hips and roughly take her.

With another woman, I would have.

With anyone but the woman who owned me.

It was barely half of my cock inside her, but she gasped, and I saw how she realized that she hadn't taken nearly as much as she thought she had. I growled into her ear, "Just the tip, huh?"

She glanced up at me, and the blush on her cheeks made me want to see it everywhere. It took all I had to pull out of her, but I did. I needed the control back, needed my sanity intact too. I yanked her off the railing to whip her around, then I bent her over the iron and lifted her dress. "You're a terrible listener for a teacher, Ms. Darling."

She wiggled on the railing and looked back at me, whining, "It was still just the tip, Jameson. You're bigger than I've ever taken, so . . ."

"Just the tip or not, darling Mia, you've earned this punishment. Now, be a good little darling and take it."

She didn't have a thing to say to that. She moaned and rolled her hips into my hand as I massaged her ass cheek before I smacked it. Over and over. I loved hearing her gasp and then moan. Gasp and moan.

Her pussy was dripping, soaking, swelling just for me. She wanted my cock enough to whimper and beg for it. But first, Mia Darling had to understand who she could dance with, who she would listen to, and who would punish her. She was looking out at the city lights, but I needed her. "Everyone can see you up here getting spanked, Mia. They can see that I own you, and they don't care. You know why?"

She was panting as she turned to glance back at me, her eyes hazy with lust.

"Because I own this city and everyone in it, including you."

She shook her head as if she couldn't believe it, as if she refused.

Her thong was still pushed to the side, and I couldn't resist anymore. I slid my middle finger in and curled it enough that I hit the most sensitive spot right away. Fuck, her pussy was flawless. Immediately, she almost bucked over the railing, but my grip on her hips was firm.

I slid another finger in, wanting to feel her clench down around me. She whimpered at the pressure. And I groaned, "So tight. And so wet. You know how pretty and perfect this pussy looks right now, Mia? Like it was made for me. I should fuck you here, huh? Make you scream how much you love *only* me inside you."

She still tried to fight me with another shake of her head. "Only you now. I can have someone else later."

Fuck that. I gripped her hair so that her back arched and her ass was more on display before I leaned over her and told her, "I'll punish you until you understand that. And you won't even mind. You know why? You *like* getting punished . . . You like it all. Me watching you, me working this pussy over a railing, and me owning you. Not a good little darling at all, but fucking bad. Just the way I like it."

23

Mia

What in the actual hell was I doing? My crime syndicate boss had me bent over a tenth-story railing and was smacking my ass loud enough for all of Chicago to hear, and I wasn't protesting.

No. Instead, he was right. I did like it. I was begging for it. Literally pleading. And Jameson Knight wasn't just questionable. He was downright dangerous, murderous.

I wasn't even sure what he'd done to Archer after they left the balcony, and I should have asked, should have stopped what we were doing so that one of us could be sane.

Yet, I couldn't.

I was just a girl. Falling for a cold-blooded syndicate boss.

The thrill came from the power I had over him. He warned me off—threatened me, even, but that knife at my throat hadn't cut my skin enough to make blood trickle. He'd winced when I'd tried to take his cock, like he couldn't dare to hurt me.

He gave in to me . . . a man with so much power and control lost all of it when I was in front of him. He succumbed to me. I could look around and know that every city street was crawling with his men, his cameras, his authority. They feared him, but I didn't have to.

Every time he spanked my ass, he took his time massaging it

back to pleasure rather than pain, as if he couldn't handle delivering one without the other to me.

He didn't realize it was all arousing for me. I even heard how wet my pussy was when his aim moved to smack my folds.

And he talked me through it. "That's it. Can you handle another? Look how good you look bent over staring out at my city. Let me feel how wet you are."

There was no denying him anymore. I just cried out, "Yes. Please. I need this."

"That's right, baby. You need to realize no other man, not Archer or anyone else, can make you this wet, can make you want it this much."

He smacked me one last time and thrust his fingers in so I could ride him as I screamed into the night. White hot ecstasy seared through my body as I screamed his name in climax. Screamed that I needed him. Screamed that it was only him I wanted over and over again.

He let me ride his hand as the aftershocks made me weak, and then he held me against the railing murmuring, "You took it so good, baby. You did so good, darling." Then, he covered my ass back up and told me, "I need to take you home."

"But I thought we were going to—"

"I'm not fucking you on the railing of a nightclub tonight."

"Why not?" I harrumphed and wiggled to right my dress. We'd already gone this far. What did he have a problem with now?

He squinted his eyes at me before he rubbed his jaw. "I care about you more than I'd like to admit, Darling. You're not ready for the relationship we'd have if I—"

"You think you get to make the decision of whether I'm ready or not, Jameson?" I balled my fists. I hated being told I wasn't, that I couldn't move forward with what I wanted, that someone knew better than I did. "What about when I wasn't ready to take this job you tricked me into taking, huh?" I didn't care if it was to keep me safe, I just wanted him to feel the same frustration I did. "You practically tricked me into becoming a part of a damn crime syndicate, so don't act above it."

His eyes flared with an angry fire, and I knew I'd pushed him in a way he didn't want to be. His jaw clenched and his neck muscles tightened. "Tricked? You knew the second I offered you two mil what this was."

I practically growled, "Yeah, and even with that two mil, I can still make a decision to *fuck* who I want."

"Watch your mouth."

"No." I crossed my arms, furious that I could go from wanting him to despising him in two seconds flat. I needed to get a handle on my emotions. I breathed in deep and glanced out at the city lights. "You don't get to make me feel good and then retract back into being my boss immediately like I can't take anymore."

"I'm protecting you from—"

"I don't want to be protected! I want to be respected. Like every damn woman should be." I tilted my head and thought about what he'd told me, how he wasn't with women anymore, how his wife had left him before she'd been found dead. I knew I might be overstepping, but I had to say it. "I'm not your wife, Jameson. I wouldn't up and leave you or Franny without giving you a reason."

He reeled back as if I'd slapped him. But after a few blinks, it was like that slap instilled some sense into him. He frowned at me, and I saw turmoil in his eyes. He just nodded and quietly turned toward the door. "We should go home, Mia."

His tone was tired, defeated, and maybe held a bit of remorse. It sobered me up—from the alcohol and all the emotions running through me. I sighed and nodded as I walked past him. But I froze when I saw all the men still blocking the entrance. I turned to wince at Jameson. “Is Archer okay? You seriously do owe him a freaking apology, Jameson Knight.”

It was clear then.

I was going insane if I thought a crime boss would listen to me telling him to apologize.

But then his hand went to the small of my back as he walked me inside. “I don’t ever apologize, baby,” he murmured. “But for you, I will.”

24

Jameson

MIA SUBDUED THE MONSTER in me all the way down to the first floor, and I actually smiled at a few of the guys on the elevator before I heard it.

That faint popping sound.

Sharp. Precise. Deadly.

Mia heard it too. Her eyes widened and locked on mine. "What was that?"

"Stay behind me." I tucked her there as the music stuttered out, and I looked at one of my guys. "First priority is alerting everyone to secure my daughter."

He nodded and spoke into his earpiece, then the elevator doors opened to complete and utter chaos.

The club detonated into frenzied fear and mayhem. Screams echoed as people shoved one another to get out. The shoving turned to a stampede, their fear turned to survival. My men surged forward, organized and calculated. They scanned, looking for the culprits, and I immediately saw them.

O'Connor's men must have found out we were here, and they'd come for blood, no matter the cost. This wasn't just bad luck—it was a hit, and they'd pay in the form of me taking out their whole damn family after tonight.

Normally I would have embraced the rush. I enjoyed delivering a wound that a man couldn't come back from, relished in an enemy's life slowly bleeding out. But tonight wasn't normal.

Tonight, I had a woman by my side who was suddenly a weakness of mine, and I felt fear course through my veins and fog my judgment. I held her close with one arm and rushed forward, pulling out my Glock. Gunshots rang out around us as my men took O'Connor's out fast. Bodies dropped

Over and over again.

A damn army had been sent to take me out. And rightfully so. We all were good shots, and when I lifted my Glock to aim and fire, I didn't normally miss. One of O'Connor's men ran screaming toward me, bloodied from combat with one of my men, and I shot him in the center of his forehead.

We moved as a unit, fast and effective. When another man a whole damn head taller than me rounded the corner of the hallway we were exiting, I shielded Mia behind me for only a second so I could take my shot. I was faster than most with a weapon, and even though the guy aimed, he never got to pull the trigger. Instead, my bullet blew through his head and he dropped to his knees, dead.

I heard her whimper, but I yanked her around him and kept moving. Her safety was my only priority right then. Getting her back to Paradise, where she belonged, where she'd be protected, where *I* could protect her, was the only thing that mattered right then.

"Our SUV is up ahead," Hades yelled as he met us at the door. Normally I didn't operate this way. I didn't need to go out of the back alley and hide or drive off. Instead, I'd deliver all these fuckers to death's door for putting her life in danger. But her life was in danger, and that meant sacrificing my pride to get her out of here.

The fact that the Irish were bold enough to come for me on

our territory meant war. Not just for them. War for the Italians, for the Diamonds, for the cartels. For everyone.

Didn't they know who they were fucking with? Retaliation after I'd put one of their family members in the ground was warranted, but they were grossly outnumbered here.

"Franny?"

"Safe and sound at your mother's."

I nodded once as the ball of tension unraveled only to create a new one. "I want every one of them . . . every single Irish wiped out in the Midwest," I told Hades as our driver screeched out onto the road.

Mia looked at me with concern. "Jameson, some of them might be innocent."

"Every single one of them better be found, Hades," I told him.

"I wouldn't have it any other way," Hades said quietly. "Just the Irish?"

I knew what he was asking. They weren't operating alone, and it was only a matter of time before the East Coast got completely out of line if we didn't put them in their place now. "We start there and call a meeting for the rest."

And then Mia started to shake, the adrenaline leaving her body as shock took over.

Damn it. My darling was too sweet for the world I lived in. I shouldn't have tainted her by exposing her to it, but there was no way to extract her from it now. She was embedded in my soul, and I wanted to hold her at least until she was calm enough to yell at me rather than look at me with tears in her eyes.

"Not good enough. I want them all dead."

I pulled her into my lap and held her close. She twisted her head into my chest and clutched at my jacket. I didn't give a fuck what I lost with this war—someone was going to pay for making her cry.

The rest of the car ride was quiet, Hades texting off demands I knew would take effect sooner rather than later.

Once the SUV pulled up to my estate, I carried her to her room but didn't set her down on her bed. Instead, I went to her bathroom and set her down to carefully strip her of her clothes.

"I'm okay, Jameson. I really am. I can take my own shower." Her tone was quiet as if to soothe the tension she must have felt vibrating off me, and then she reached for my hand to look at the bloodied knuckles. "You got hurt more than I did. I can help you clean this up or—"

"You want to tend to me?" Her fingers brushed over the scratches on my hand, and even that touch had me wanting to pull her closer.

She met my gaze and nodded. "I don't want you hurt, Jameson."

She said it like it was normal, like she just wanted to take care of me after a shootout in the club. I growled at the thought, at how my dick liked the idea way too much. I spun her so I could unzip her dress. I let it fall before I slid her undergarments off too.

When I glanced up, I saw her reflection in the mirror, me standing behind her, her tiny body perfect in the way it was so small in front of mine. She bit her pink bottom lip, and I couldn't stop myself from letting my hand slide across her smooth, soft skin at her stomach. As I did, her nipples puckered and I saw how she gulped. I pulled her back to me and let a rumble leave my chest.

Then I moved my hand up so that I could brush my knuckles over her cheek as I told her, "You're so fucking precious, you know that?"

Her honey eyes met mine in the mirror. "Am I?"

"You're worried about a damn scratch instead of being pissed I let this happen to you."

"Jameson, I wanted to go out. If anything, this is my fault." She turned to look up at me directly. "I don't want anyone hurt because of me."

"Mia . . ." Jesus Christ, I was killing those men, and she wasn't going to stop me.

"If it's just about what happened tonight, I don't care."

"Then care that they put Rosy, Pink, and Olive in jeopardy too." I pushed her like I needed her to understand. I don't know why. I'd never had to justify my actions before.

"Fine." She breathed in deep before she sighed and walked over to the shower to test the water and get in.

I should have left her then, but her small voice stopped me when she asked, "Is it terrible that I agree with you? That I want someone to pay not for endangering my life but especially for endangering my friends'?"

I didn't answer her as I undressed, but when I stepped in there with her and pulled her naked body against mine gently, I told her, "Nothing about you is terrible, darling Mia. Not a damn thing."

We both watched the water droplets against the clear glass of her shower.

We got out, and she let me dress her in pink pajamas that had roses on them. I could see how spent she was, like the night had drained her of everything, and I picked her up to set her on bed before she murmured, "Ms. Prim and Mr. Bos have to be watered."

"Who?"

"My cape primrose there, and the azalea bonsai over there." She pointed at them.

"You named them, Mia?" It was ridiculous but a smile slipped from my lips.

"They started growing better when I did," she defended herself.

Her and these damn plants. I remembered how adamant she'd been about bringing them. I'd been perturbed before, but now I was intrigued. "Which is Ms. Prim, and which is Mr. Bos? I'll do it for you."

She leaned back on one of the plush pillows with heavy-lidded eyes and tried to cover a yawn as she nodded and pointed to a white pitcher of water she had beside the dresser. "Only use the water in there. It's filtered and at room temperature. I don't want to shock them right now because they're fragile after the move."

I listened carefully and frowned at her particular instructions, picking up the water and standing there with a towel wrapped around my waist.

"Water at the base into the soil for Ms. Prim. She's the pink flowered one. Just so the soil gets a bit damp, please." I did as I was told.

"Great. Now, Mr. Bos is the little tree, and you need to pick him up and just put water in the tray. After ten minutes, we'll dump the rest so we don't overwhelm his roots."

I did exactly as I was told, making note of how to handle it in the future. "How often do you do this?"

"Once a day for Ms. Prim and twice a week for Mr. Bos." She chuckled softly. "I don't know whether I should be scared or turned on with you listening and doing this right now."

"Both, probably," I told her.

"Yeah, I guess I should be scared of a lot that goes on around here." She glanced out the window and started rambling. "I know the risks. I always just feel like someone's watching. Which they probably are. You are who you are. So, I get it. But tonight, I felt . . . We could have died. And then Franny would have . . ." She hiccupped, and tears filled her eyes again. "She's okay, right?"

Her concern wasn't for her life, but for my daughter's.

My heart broke open with that knowledge, and I knew then I wasn't going to leave her alone in this room, no matter how emotionally tied to her I became. I set the pitcher down and commanded, "Move over, Darling."

"What for?"

"I'm lying beside you tonight. Just to hold you. Just to sleep."

"I don't know if that's a good—"

"You're right." I left the room and went to get some sweatpants. When I returned, she sat up in surprise.

"What are you doing?"

"Sleeping next to you."

"We just agreed that wasn't a good idea!"

"No, I agreed it wouldn't be good for me to sleep next to you . . . without clothes on."

"Speak for yourself." She crossed her arms. "I'm not going to do anything."

"Yeah, but I will, baby. No chance in hell I get in bed with you while I'm naked and fall asleep tonight. Now move over. It's either that, or I sit and watch you all night to make sure you're okay. Pick your poison."

"After I just said I feel watched?" she huffed. "Sleepover, it is. But don't think for a second you're getting lucky tonight."

I hummed and yanked her across the mattress so that her ass was right up against me. She gasped at the feeling of my body up against hers, but I didn't do much else other than whisper in her ear, "I'm already lucky, darling Mia, to have you by my side all night."

25

Jameson

I WOKE UP EARLY enough to watch the sunlight kiss the face of a woman I didn't know how to protect, though I wanted to with every fiber of my being. I had to shield her from my life, from danger, from me.

I should have been planning to let her go.

And yet, I knew as I stared at her dark curls against the white cotton sheets, the soft rise and fall of her pajamas, and the peace across her flawless face that I wasn't going to. I was keeping Mia Darling.

I went to greet Cal in the study and told him, "That was a direct attack on all of us last night. All the women we care about."

"I know," he said solemnly.

"They're done."

"They're working with someone else, Jameson. Most likely the cartels."

"I don't give a fuck."

"Paolo backs a lot of companies." Cal had moved the pieces into place, and he knew exactly where I was going with it.

"And we back more."

"Bane's not going to like it. Dimitri and Olive have a kid

now. So, you know they want to keep their hands clean with the HEAT empire too."

"Everyone gets dirty sometimes." I slammed my hand down on the desk.

"You've lashed out for Franny. And now again for a woman?"

"My daughter needs—"

"Don't start with the teacher bullshit." My brother gave me a look. Then he combed a hand through his hair and grumbled, "I need a damn drink."

"Me too."

"Dad would have—"

"Dad's not here. And you know why? Because his ass wasn't loyal to the family, to the syndicate, or to even you."

Pacing the room, Cal stopped to turn and look at me. "You think I don't know that, brother? You think I don't know what he did in the dark of the fucking night?"

His question held secrets, dancing in the shadows and mocking me because I couldn't uncover them all. "He won't ever do any of it again," I ground out, frustrated that somehow my father had tainted not only my life but my brother's too.

"*Adamantem infractum manet*," he grumbled almost like it was a curse rather than a show of power. "We need the syndicate to understand what you're doing, Jameson. Give them that so they don't question your leadership."

"They question my leadership, they shouldn't be a part of—"

"I know," he cut me off. "But lead with respect and transparency rather than fear, Jameson. You'll get further than our old man ever did."

I wanted to shout "no." I wanted to lash out and lean into the rage. But my brother was standing there asking me, and he was family. The syndicate was family too. "Call a night under Seymour Hall, then. But let me be clear: I'm lashing out for all of us. No one better mistake my leadership for emotion, Cal. They'll regret it."

He didn't say much else to me but raised his eyebrows. He knew there were lines even he shouldn't cross. Questioning me again and again was one of them.

I knew what I was doing.

I had everything under control. I made calls for a syndicate night before deciding that I needed a hearty breakfast. One I would make and carry up to Mia so we could eat together. I wasn't acting out of emotion. It was just a nice fucking gesture.

The screams I heard from her room when I was just down the hallway were bloodcurdling. I felt them in my soul, bone chilling and full of fear. Mia hadn't shared much with me, but I wasn't about to ignore this and afford her the privacy she probably deserved.

Archer ran down the hall from the opposite end to meet me as we both got to her door.

"What the hell is happening?" I asked him.

He pinched the bridge of his nose and winced because it was bruised from the punches I'd inflicted last night. Fucker. He should be happy he still had a job.

"She's having nightmares again." He had the damn audacity to step between me and her door.

"Again?" I knew my eyes held murder, but her screams had died down like the nightmare had passed. "Move, Archer."

"Wait a second, Jameson. *Fuck*. She didn't even want you knowing about them, and I realize you don't want me in the way, man, but you've got to see I'm there for her like you asked me to be. She's a friend."

"I slept in her goddamn bed last night. So, I think knowing about them is warranted."

He sighed. "I'm respecting her wishes."

"Over your boss's?"

"Yeah." One second passed, and then another. He held his damn place, knowing what it meant for our relationship. He was choosing her over me, and a part of me respected him for it. The other part I tried my best to suppress. "I just want her comfortable here. Usually, she has a nightmare, I knock, she stumbles to the door like a groggy mess, apologizes for her appearance, and then we eat."

"You eat breakfast with her?" I wanted to punch him again, but I knew Mia would be irate.

He cracked his knuckles, and then he met my stare head-on. "Why not?"

Because she wasn't there for his entertainment, for one. A lot of the staff ate together though. I didn't really have an excuse as to why he couldn't. Except for the fact that he knew as well as I did that she was off-limits.

He smiled at me then. "You got something to say, boss, say it." Now I knew he was goading me.

"Shut the fuck up," I told him, and then opened Mia's door. "You're dismissed."

Yet, Mia was frowning now as she woke up, groggy and rubbing her eyes. "Archer, Jameson?" She looked between us in question.

"Sorry, Mia. He heard them this time." Archer shrugged and looked sheepish.

She got a damn "sorry," but I didn't? He hadn't apologized for dancing with her, or anything from the night before. He was supposed to be dedicated to me, one of my guys.

It wasn't my first concern though. I rushed to her side to hold her face in my hands. "You okay?"

She frowned, "You heard?"

"I did. You were screaming like—"

"I was always a sleep talker. Any bad experience, I'd have nightmares. It's just my subconscious acting out about the shooting." She shook her head like it wasn't a big deal and patted my forearm before she stepped back and eyed me expectantly.

"Anyway, I'm happy you're both here, because Jameson has something to say."

"What?" I frowned in confusion. I didn't have anything to say while I considered what could make her bad dreams stop. I'd cuddle her. Tuck her in. Sit at her bedside all night. I was starting to sound obsessed even to myself, but I didn't care. "Mia, we need to talk about your nightmares—"

"No. I'm fine. They're getting better." She yawned as if this were just another day in the neighborhood for her and everything was completely ordinary. "I think it's a good time for you to tell Archer you're sorry."

"Me? Sorry? For what?" I was so genuinely confused, I took a step back.

"For his face." She motioned toward Archer's nose. "For how you acted last night."

"Mia, don't start," I growled.

She pursed her lips before getting up to check the soil of each of her plants, pushing one finger into the dirt like she was completely comfortable and at home as she repeated, "Tell him you're sorry, Jameson, or you won't be sleeping in my bed ever again."

"Are you fucking kidding me?" I didn't want to fight with her first thing in the morning.

"Do I look like I'm kidding?" She set down the pitcher and crossed her arms over those cartoon pajamas to stare me down.

Archer even shook his head "no" like she should stop. At least he realized what she was asking. "This is my damn house, darling devil. I'll sleep wherever the hell I want."

"Oh? Then I guess I'll be sleeping at Rosy's or even with Malek, right, buddy?" She sat and cooed at my dog, who had trotted in to lay his ferocious head on her bed. Then, she just gave me the look she'd give a toddler ready to have another tantrum.

Who did she think she was talking to?

Probably the man scared enough of upsetting her to listen.

26

Mia

IT MIGHT HAVE BEEN my day off, but I'd just survived a near-death experience and my friend had been punched in the face for dancing with me. So I did not care how the guy I was falling for was looking at me.

He could have been the leader of all the crime syndicates in the world and I still would have stared him down like he was a child.

He owed my friend an apology, or so help me God.

"I can go to a hotel, also. If you would like." I tilted my head at him. "I'll need a new phone, though, to call for accommodations."

Jameson's jaw did its normal dance of irritation before he pulled a brand-new phone from his pocket and set it on the dresser. "I already got one for you this morning."

"Great." I reached my hand out, palm up, and pointed. "I'd like it now to make that call."

He swiped the phone off the dresser like he was going to throw it again, but when I lifted an eyebrow, he growled and walked it over to me.

I started Googling hotels.

That's when Jameson pulled at his short dark hair and spun

to face Archer. "Sorry for punching your dumbass face. But if you dance with her again, I'll bury you."

Archer's smile was brighter than the sun before he laughed and said, "Have a good morning, you two."

I tsked as the door shut and looked up at Jameson. "That wasn't a very good apology."

"He appreciated it. Did you see the smile across his face?" Jameson said as he placed a plate of food down on the bed.

I chuckled and nodded. "You're all wild in your threats to each other, I guess. He means well."

"He means *too* well." He harrumphed.

"Don't be ridiculous. Eat and quit worrying on your day off."

"I don't get days off. This is *your* day off. Not mine."

"Fine. Enjoy the food with me, and then you can get right back to work." I looked down at the food, not wanting to make eye contact and blushing over the fact that I'd asked him to stay. I didn't want to eat alone, and I didn't know how to discuss what we'd done the night before or what was happening between us now.

I felt the mattress dip next to my legs and then his hand was on my chin, lifting my gaze to meet his inquisitive blue one. "You're hiding from me, darling Mia. What for?"

I shrugged. "A lot happened last night. We got . . ." How did I even broach this topic? Was there a name for hooking up with your boss on a rooftop before getting shot at? "Carried away on the rooftop."

"Carried away?" Was he holding back a smile?

"Yes, and obviously we shouldn't have done anything."

He frowned. "We shouldn't have?"

"No." I threw my hands up. "I'm just the summer-school teacher."

He hummed. "You're also the woman I can't stop thinking about. I think about your smile, your need to stand up to me constantly, your desire to always put my daughter first. I also think about that body of yours and about burying my dick into you twenty-four seven, Mia."

My stomach cartwheeled at his admission. "So, I guess we didn't nip that distraction of ours."

"No, but as long as you're here, we have all the time in the world to do that," he said casually, as if he'd made peace with it. And of course he would have. What did it matter if he screwed me and everyone else with no strings attached all the time?

I wasn't stupid enough to bring up knowing he slept with Valerie. I was actually considering if I cared. Maybe that would be the way to continue to distance myself, to break the emotional connection with him and not get caught up.

"Right. Do you happen to have an end-of-term date for me?" My heart stuttered at the thought of leaving, and a flash of hurt flew through me that I needed to get control of.

His grip tightened a bit on my chin. "When I say so."

This I knew how to do: argue with him and bicker. This felt comfortable now, easier than addressing the growing feelings between us. "And I have to accept that because I accepted the academy job, right?" I took one of the flaky biscuits on the tray and ripped it in half angrily before shoving a piece in my mouth. I shook my head at him. "You brought me to this place and kept me here where you know I'll never be able to leave and be the same." His hand dropped from my chin as he winced at my words. "I'll have to live like this from now on . . . Constantly seeing the blood of men when I close my eyes. Constantly worrying for Franny and you. Welcome to Paradise Grove, I guess."

"Not about me. I've told you before, I'm trying to distance myself from my daughter, and you shouldn't—"

"Don't tell me not to care, and don't act like you not caring is good at all for her. She's young. She needs you. And you know it."

He didn't agree out loud, but I saw the turmoil. Something like acceptance settled in his eyes before he murmured, "They aren't targeting you. They're targeting anyone close to me, which includes those women you were with yesterday."

"My friends," I clarified. "And Franny before."

He nodded.

Franny and my friends. I couldn't shake the feeling that I felt more at home with them and Jameson than I had with even my family for years.

And with Jameson too.

He accepted my outbursts, took note of my requests, and tried his best to respect my wishes. He'd solidified my place here in Paradise Grove and I found I didn't want to run from that.

I took two breaths, knowing that the words I was about to say weren't ones I should say, but I couldn't hold back anymore. "I want in. All the way. Because I can't have one toe in and one toe out."

He frowned at me. "In to what?"

"You said people work for the syndicate, partner with you all, marry into it too. Whatever. I'm working for you and by proxy for them. So, tell me everything. I want *in*." I shoved away the food and looked toward the ceiling. "I don't want secrets. I want to understand what I'm dealing with, what my friends and Franny deal with. I'm already invested in Franny. I've already made friends. Let me be a part of it. Work wise. Diamonds get in by working, right?"

"And by trust," he grumbled, like this was all a bad idea. "Your work is temporary."

He said it so flippantly, like I was so easily disposed of.

"Well, you *trust* me with your daughter. Plus, you said I needed to do this job without distractions. You know how distracted I can be when I don't know the whole story."

"The syndicate is now a distraction?" he asked, incredulous.

"Yes."

"Being a part of the syndicate is dangerous and—"

"Would it put me in any more danger than I was in last night?"

His jaw worked up and down as seconds ticked by.

"You told me people work for the syndicate and become a part of it all the time. It's an honor, and so why not me?"

"Because—"

"You don't trust me? Or anybody?" I lifted a brow at him.

"I trust you more than I trusted the woman I was *married* to," he retorted fast, his tone lethal.

Crossing my arms, I stared him down. "I don't even know if that's good or bad, Jameson."

He pulled at his hair like us talking about his trust issues was the most frustrating part of his day. "Jesus, I don't have time for this today."

"Well, when will you have time for discussing my future here with your daughter and my friends, huh?"

"Never, because you're not supposed to have a future with them!"

"Because I'm not a part of this here with all of you." I didn't ask it, but stated it.

"You're not supposed to get involved and get hurt, Mia! You're not supposed to be in danger because of me," he almost bellowed, but I ignored his outburst.

"So what? You're telling me no is your answer, then?"

He got up to swear again and again, cursing me and the life he lived, before he spun and walked over to put his hands on either side of me. "You want this?"

I didn't even stutter. "Yes."

"You think you're ready?" He watched me, looking for a weakness. I had a lot of them. Every part of me that was strong had come from the parts that were broken.

"Someone once told me I wasn't ready, and I hated him for it," I admitted.

"Who?" He seemed offended for me as his brows slammed down.

Chuckling, I pointed out, "You acted as if I wasn't ready to nanny Franny too and needed help, Jameson. Remember?"

He sighed before he backed off and sat down beside me instead. "Did you hate me for it?"

"No, because it was valid." I took a deep breath and looked out the window to murmur, "When my tennis coach in college told me that, though, I hated the statement. It meant no one would believe in me, and I'd have to believe in and trust myself over everyone else."

"Mia . . ." He took my hand in his as he said, "I want the whole story."

I nodded, realizing that I wanted to tell him it too, wanted him to understand that I was giving him all my trust and that he could do the same with me. "I started playing tennis young. And was good enough that my parents invested in my training through high school. We found this amazing coach. He came to family dinners, got close to all of us. And he was good, honestly."

Jameson frowned like he didn't know where the story was going but knew he wasn't going to like it. He rubbed his thumb over my knuckles and cautiously said, "Continue."

"I went to state in high school, they even thought I could potentially train for the Olympics . . . When I tore my MCL my freshman year in college, my parents were devastated. Family friends were in the tennis circles, we'd invested so much, and one bad move caused too many people to lose their faith and their hopes and their dreams. That coach, though . . ." I shook my head with a sad smile on my face. "He assured them. All pro bono, he'd be extra attentive, he knew all the tricks, he'd get me better than I was before. And I believed him. I trusted him. He'd coached me for years before he made a pass at me in the locker room with my cast still on."

My breath shook as I inhaled, watching the flare of fire and reaction in Jameson's eyes. "Mia." His voice was low, not full of empathy but rage. "Darling Mia, I want his name."

One tear rolled down my face. "You believe me so easily," I whispered with a laugh. This man had only known me for a month but took my word as gospel in the way my parents never had. "I wish I knew you back then."

"You know me now. Tell me his name." His voice was soft like he wanted to coax the answer out of me gently.

Wiping away the tear and sitting up straighter, I told him, "The name doesn't matter. The story does. My story." I made sure to emphasize that. "The first time he made a pass at me, I brushed it off and tried to tell myself it was a one-off. And truly he didn't try for a while again. But everything after, even his hand on the small of my back, felt wrong."

"All of his touches were wrong if they felt wrong, Mia." He said it so confidently, and his words acted like a balm to a wound.

"I know that now, but back then, I was confused. I wanted to trust him. He'd groomed me from a young age. When he tried again, touching me in places I knew I didn't want, I was so distraught that I confided in my mother, but her disbelief sent me spiraling." I shoved my curls and the thought of my former dark headspace away. "Looking back, I realize she did believe me. She bought me more conservative clothes and tried to stay by me more when he was around. I guess that was her way of protecting our reputation . . . and me."

Jameson got up to pace the room, his energy almost palpable. He was a man of action, and the past didn't allow him to be that here with me now. He sat down again, his blue eyes deep with rage as he looked at me. "What your mother did wasn't good enough," he growled. "She wasn't protecting you; she was protecting her pride and reputation. *I* want a damn name."

I patted his thigh, my heart cracking open and spilling more because I knew I could trust him to hear me, to believe me, to be there for me. "You would want a name, Jameson. But I don't need you to do anything, okay? I probably needed it back then, but my parents weren't people who rocked the boat, you know? My mother's pride and desire to not create waves was worth more than my sanity." I held up a hand to stop him from trying to comfort me, because I didn't need it anymore. "I got better and better, Jameson. Made it to our division conference . . . and then tore it again."

His eyes widened. "No."

I shrugged. "Bad luck, I guess. That time, he told me I wasn't ready after months of rehab. He said it over and over again. I wasn't ready. I wasn't ready and shouldn't listen to my gut. He knew best." I shuddered at the memory of his voice saying it. "And the day I told him I didn't care what he said, I was ready and I was going to listen to my gut, he tried to massage my thigh up, up, and up. And . . . I fired him on the spot." I winced at the thought of that memory. "I got up and tried to hobble to the locker room door. It was locked."

"The reason you hate being locked up . . ." He pinched the bridge of his nose as his jaw worked up and down like he was trying not to explode. "Jesus. I should have never cuffed you and—"

"Jameson . . ." I dragged a finger over his neck and to his chin to lift his face so he would meet my eyes. "You could tie me up as a hostage for days now and it wouldn't scare me at all."

I swear the blue in his eyes softened with my statement. "Your trust in me is devastating, Darling."

"I think it's warranted. I know you'd never hurt me."

He pulled me into his lap and twisted one of my curls in his hand. "I'm going to try my damn hardest not to."

I nodded. "And that's all I want. People around me who will try, you know? I thought that's who that coach was. He was a family friend. A pillar in our community . . . but he was a damn predator."

"And he should get what he deserves because of it. Give me a name and—"

"Jameson, it's not worth it. I was lucky that I stood my ground and screamed at him to let me out of the locker room. Another girl heard and banged on the door, and I got out before anything else happened."

"Enough already had happened," Jameson grumbled, and truly he was right. I was never the same after that.

"Maybe, but I found strength in walking away from him. Although, when I took on a lesser-known coach, it was like I spit in my parents' faces." I took a deep breath and told him the rest. "They stopped coming to matches. My community walked away from me and didn't watch me compete in the finals. When I won, only my sister was in the crowd. I quit after that. I was ready to win and then ready to be done. To this day, my parents tell everyone I would've been better had I waited and continued with my first coach. I'd be an Olympian. It's not true. I was ready. I *am* ready if I say I am, and I won't ever not listen to my gut again. I know my worth, and I stand by it."

"Darling Mia . . ." His tone slid over me like a security blanket and warmed my heart as he cupped my cheek softly in the palm of his hand. "Your worth is priceless, and so is the trust you have in yourself. Don't ever let a fool tell you different."

"You tried to when you hired me." I poked his shoulder.

"And I was a fucking fool." He leaned in, tilting his forehead against mine.

"I know." I chuckled and then admitted to him what a boss

probably never wants to hear out of an employee. "People can be absolute fools in this world. It's why I have a stupid complaint against me within the public school too. That same coach was hired by another parent in my town to help out this girl, Maisy. She confided in me about the coach, and I went off on her parents. Her dad said she and I must be lying. So, I might have lunged for him."

"Violence from you, Darling? Yeah, I believe it." He kissed down my neck and pulled me closer to his chest like he wanted to comfort me. "And I love to fucking see it."

I sighed. "I think I might like violence from you too sometimes. The way you ran me through that club was . . ."

"Amazing?" He looked up at me with mischief sparkling in those ocean blues.

"Highly dangerous, but somewhat attractive."

He hummed, and then he nodded once and then twice. "Are you ready to come to a Diamond gathering?" he murmured.

"Gut says I'm ready." I held his gaze, not wavering at all in my decision.

A rumble of approval vibrated through his chest. "I like the confidence. I guess I can't find out *everything* about you in a file," he murmured, staring at me with a newfound emotion I couldn't quite place.

"Nope. But I can tell you everything that's not in the file . . . if you want."

"Yeah, I'm starting to think I want a lot from you, Mia Darling."

He kissed me then, slowly and softly at first, letting his lips move over mine as if he were learning and memorizing them. I fell into it, holding onto his shirt as his tongue swept through my mouth and claimed every part of it. I moaned at how my body lit up for him, how his muscles felt against my chest, how his lips were soft but still commanded my every movement.

He ripped himself away, breathing heavily. "Or I might want *all* of you, Mia, and if I take all of you, you're not getting any of yourself back. So, we have to stop."

"Do we?" I tilted my head, and he growled at my question.

"I'll have dresses sent up for tonight. It's somewhat formal, but you can wear what you want."

"Plant pajamas?"

"If you want." He shrugged. "You'll still look better than the lot of them."

"They'll just accept my attending?"

"As my guest? Yes. And if you want in . . . Well, you know. Born in, marry in, or work for us in complete dedication."

"What if I want to be more than your guest?"

He dragged his teeth over his bottom lip, and I saw what looked like concern and fear in his eyes. "You might be ready, Mia. But give me some time to come to terms with you being in constant danger."

"If I'm a Diamond, you'd still be protecting me, Jameson."

"In the syndicate or not, Mia, I'm always going to protect you." He pecked my cheek and set me on the bed before he walked to the door. "We leave at seven. Be ready." And then he pointed at the food and said, "Now eat. I didn't make that for nothing."

"You made it? Why?"

"Because I thought you would be hungry when you woke up." So simple. So sweet. So not Jameson Knight.

I put a bite of food in my mouth and let him leave. Didn't ask what we'd be doing or where we'd be going or who would be there. It didn't matter.

I was ready.

27

Mia

Dresses and shoes with red bottoms and purses with a signature lock and keys were carted up to my room only hours later. All sorts of colors, all much more expensive than literally the whole wardrobe in my closet. The one dress that stood out to me was a deep pink, though, and he messaged me within ten minutes of me looking at them.

Daily report.

Franny's not even here for the weekend.

I need a daily report from you too.

Do you like any of the dresses?

I can send others.

He asked the questions so fast I couldn't respond, and I realized he might be nervous.

Or you can wear whatever you want.

I like the dresses. All of them.

What color are you wearing?

I sent him a picture of the one I had liked initially.

Damn. You look good in your favorite color, Darling. Now purse and shoes?

Still working on that. Do you realize whoever sent all this sent me ten of each?

And? Are the purses and shoes not your style? I'll get rid of them if you don't like any.

I like them all. They're ridiculously expensive.

If you like them all, keep them all. Remember, YOUR worth is priceless. The cost of a few shoes and purses doesn't mean a damn thing to me.

Was he sure about that? I Googled one of the purses and screenshotted him the price.

That one purse is worth more than a car, Jameson. I have ten cars' worth of shoes right now.

I'll send more if you don't pick one soon to wear tonight. You got fifteen minutes before I come to your room and then we're leaving.

Just to keep him on his toes, I knocked on his door ten minutes later. I felt different, more daring, riskier, more me. I didn't want to submit so easily to his demands anymore.

Not if I was going to be a part of this world. Not if I was going to make that choice for myself. I'd decided big things on my own before, and I'd do it again.

He frowned at me, and then after giving me a look, he nodded. Like he knew. Like he got me better than anyone else. "You look fucking divine, darling devil. Like I'm going to murder more men tonight."

"Please don't." I shook my head at him as he kissed my cheek.

On our way out, I stopped in front of the door that was off-limits.

"This stupid, beautiful, maddening door." I put my hands

on my hips and glared at it. "Such intricate lines and beautiful woodwork, and the keyhole is as old as time. How can you expect anyone not to want to go in there?"

"It's a window into the life I had before."

"A window you don't want me to see?"

"Mia, one step at a time . . . For me?"

I'd give him that. Just because I was ready for everything didn't mean he was. A relationship had to be give-and-take, trust and be trusted. I wanted that with him.

Well, I wanted that until he steered me through another side door, out to the garage, and I was shocked to see it led to another whole bay where there were more motorcycles and vehicles.

"Are we taking the SUV or—"

"Ducati."

"Oh, I don't— I have a dress on."

"That's short enough for this exact purpose." He eyed me up and down. "And other purposes."

I chose to ignore that as I stared at the bike. "I've never ridden a motorcycle before."

His smirk finally appeared with dimples. A genuine smile at my freaking fear. "I like knowing I'll be your first. Let's go for a ride."

"Jameson . . . I don't think so."

"Put your helmet on, Mia."

"It might be better for me to catch a ride with Archer, or Hades, or is your brother going? I'm happy to take an SUV with them. Could he pick me up?"

He positioned the sleek black helmet over my head and curls. Luckily, they were natural and wouldn't flatten completely even as he firmly slid it onto my skull. He hooked his arm around me and yanked me toward him, then so he was close enough to secure the buckle under my chin and test how snug it was on my head. "You'll be fine, baby. I got you."

That calmed my nerves a little, but I was still leery. It

may seem odd, but this might scare me more than what I'd been through the night before. Motorcycles were death traps. Everyone knew that. "I'd still feel better going with your brother in the SUV."

Jameson's eyes flashed as he walked over to that menacing-looking machine and threw his leg over it so fluidly that my mouth watered. Motorcycles might be death traps, but I might also be a simple woman. Him sitting there with his tats out and his helmet on, only his eyes glaring at me, did things to my ovaries.

"Get on the bike, Mia."

The command was delivered with enough authority that I knew I wasn't getting my way. I slid on to it slowly. I tried not to press my body up to him, but within a second, he'd gripped my wrists and placed them on his stomach before grabbing my thighs and pulling me close, so close I felt every one of his back muscles ripple against my chest.

Then he turned and murmured, "Hold on, baby."

The garage door lifted and he kickstarted the machine, revving the throttle before we launched into the evening sunset.

He didn't go fast or take any sharp turns. Instead, he cruised down his winding drive, letting the wind brush through my hair almost like a caress. I heard the chirping birds mixed with the rumble of his engine as we drove through the tree-lined streets of Paradise Grove. And the Ducati purred within the luxury of the town like it belonged, so smooth and sleek yet black and built like a threat, humming with power and silence and control.

Jameson was like the bike he owned. He didn't speak. Just rode. In silence, in control, in power.

All I could do was hold on to the man who wasn't supposed to mean anything. To the man driving straight into a syndicate meeting like he owned the damn night.

We cut to the main road, and that's where more rumbles of engines met us. More men. And we all headed toward what I knew to be the town hall. Where the government was supposed to uphold the law.

Yet, on the side of that building, a garage door raised and as it did, the floor inside opened too. Jameson revved his engine and drove right down into it, straight into a secret tunnel with brick roads that led to parking and sliding glass doors.

This must be where the laws were truly made.

We parked beside a matte black McLaren that had two men standing next to it, one of whom I knew was Callahan. They were smoking cigars while another woman almost half their size stood there glaring at them both.

Jameson killed the engine, and Callahan smiled over at us both. "Look who finally decided to bring her." His eyes danced with much more mirth than I usually saw in them as he looked toward me.

"So, she with you now?" the guy next to Callahan asked. His gaze was casual enough, but I saw how he assessed every movement I made.

"She's not *with* me. She's *mine*."

And just like that, the temperature changed. The air stilled and chilled me to the bone. The men stopped smirking.

We weren't there as a couple. I knew that. He hadn't promised me anything.

We were walking into a world where us screwing around didn't matter. My feelings for him didn't matter either . . . only his ownership of me did.

Ownership of everything was apparent throughout the event too. We walked through brick hallways, and I stayed quiet, taking it all in. Jameson didn't need to introduce me because everyone already knew who I was.

His.

28

Mia

Although we were underground, the ceilings were still high and the hallways were filled with art I was sure was expensive and original. A couple standing in front of one oak-framed portrait whispered something about Monet, confirming I was in the presence of elite society.

Cigars were being smoked, glasses clinked, and meetings were being had in rooms we passed.

The lower we went, the louder the music and hum of conversation became. Jameson held up his watch and then his palm for a scanner to allow access. Then, large double doors opened, and there before us was an extravagant ballroom lit with glimmering sconces and chandeliers that seemed to sparkle just as the Chicago city lights had. Carvings on the walls seemed to represent Paradise Grove with vines that grew up from them, giving it a historic feel.

Tables were set with linens and candles that flickered in the low lighting.

This wasn't just a meeting. It was a whole event, and even if Jameson was wearing his leather jacket and other men had helmets under their arms, they all dripped luxury.

Money.

Power.

Women and men milled about, but Jameson steered me to a center table where others gathered in suits, leather, and dresses that sparkled. Valerie was the first to beeline to Jameson, even with another man on her arm. As a waiter walked by, he pulled out my chair without a word. I sat down immediately, not wanting to eavesdrop on whatever she had to say.

Thankfully, Rosy, Olive, Pink, and their partners swarmed in around me. Callahan sat down right next to me. "Can't escape us now. Want champagne or whiskey?"

"We all want tequila," Pink grumbled as she plopped down on the other side of me. "I heard I missed the action last night."

"It's not fun action when bullets are involved, Bianca." Bane frowned at her.

"Oh, speak for yourself. We never see that type of good action anymore."

"You get enough action," he murmured as he gripped her neck, and the blush on her cheeks showed she did.

A raspy laugh came from Valerie, and she touched Jameson's chest before he nodded at her and the man she was with. Rosy put a hand on my shoulder as she bent toward me to whisper, "I'll get us two flutes of champagne . . . each."

Jameson grumbled at Pink to move over and then sat down next to me, but another man walked up and said, "Sorry to hear about last night. Won't happen again."

"Better not," was all my boss said.

But he wasn't just my boss. I found out he was *the* boss. Every billionaire, celebrity, and politician gravitated toward him. It was like there was a silent queue to speak with him, and every time one person stepped away, another one stepped up to take their place. They looked glamorous and like they were all having fun, but their smiles were thin and strategic, all while men in black suits and earpieces subtly kept their eyes on everything.

This wasn't a party. It was a syndicate event.

Even as our food was served, even as someone's voice was overheard welcoming everyone, nothing of importance was discussed. The real dealings happened in whispered conversations, in handshakes, and over dinner.

I didn't catch much of any of it. I only heard snippets of Jameson's conversations as I made note of how security was hidden, but it seemed ironclad—from the scanners allowing us in to the armed men to the cameras blinking in the light fixtures. And still, I felt most safe at his side, especially when I felt constant eyes on me even while Jameson's hand rubbed my thigh back and forth, back and forth.

That steady pressure of his large hand and how his palm dragged up further, closer and closer to my panty line, had me grounded even while I was surrounded by sharks and wolves. Men and women with this much power could sniff out blood, weakness, and opportunity in less than ten seconds. And maybe Jameson was the most dangerous one of all, because I didn't concentrate on anything but his touch, on the low hum of his voice, on how the heat of his body near mine warmed my skin.

I was hyperaware of how he drew circles on me, almost thoughtlessly, like we'd been together for years even though we weren't really together at all. But his touch was a test and a tease as his fingers grazed close to my panty line, like he was measuring how far he could go before I'd stop him.

All the way was the answer. I let him brush against the wet material and sipped my champagne when his eyes left the man talking to him to snare my gaze in his. He leaned in and whispered, "I'm fucking you tonight, Mia Darling. So don't drink another."

And then his hand left my thigh so he could stand. Another man, bulkier than most with blond shaggy hair, approached us on Valerie's arm. The man's smile was smarmy as he glanced our way. "Sorry to hear about the club."

"Are you?" Jameson asked, and I saw how his tone was measured, taking in the man's movements.

"Of course." He laughed, glancing around like he wanted to make sure he could make a quick exit if need be. "I think O'Connor's men just wanted to talk to Pink and Olive, but—"

Olive was quick to cut in from the table. "Trent, you want to talk to a Diamond, you make a meeting with us."

Trent's tone and posture changed as he stared down at her. "Well, you haven't taken a meeting with any of them as of late, Mrs. Hardy. Is it because your loyalties shifted to your husband rather than the Diamond legacy?"

Jameson rocked back on his heels. "Watch how you talk to her, Trent. She may afford you leeway because of how long you've been a Diamond, but I don't give a fuck."

Trent's composure was slipping. His face reddened, and he seemed to almost puff up in place as he growled, "Dalton and I deserve a little bit more respect, Jameson. I worked for your and Olive's father for years—"

"That doesn't afford you respect. It just makes me question your loyalties."

"Loyalty?" he blubbered. "To who? I've always wanted what's best for us. You think she does?" He pointed a thick finger at Olive, who just rolled her eyes like she didn't have time for his outburst.

Maybe this was something they dealt with all the time from him. Maybe the tension would dissipate, but when his finger whipped toward me and he practically snarled at me seated at the table, I felt the tension in the air thicken. "Or do you think this girl here is best for us?" The man sucked on his teeth before looking to me with irritation in his almost-black eyes. "She so precious that she was worth the body count of those at the club last night?"

More than a few people were looking our way now. Jameson breathed in once before he responded, "Trent, I'll tell you one time not to look at her."

He immediately looked away from me. "I'm just saying, it's obvious you lashed out because of her rather than letting O'Connor's men have a simple conversation with us."

Jameson didn't respond. Instead he stood there, raising an eyebrow, and let the man continue on.

"What? She that good to you?" The man's eyes held Jameson's. "Must not just be a nanny then." He shook his head like he knew he had an audience now, like he was gaining confidence in the way this was all going. He even elbowed the man next to him. "Dalton, can you imagine a woman so good we should give up chances at East Coast alliances? A diamond remains unbroken, and the East Coast will take care of the cracks."

Something in Jameson's stance changed then. The whole room felt it enough that the music even seemed to fade away. People whispered. Hades and Archer moved to stand behind him. Cal groaned.

Trent seemed to realize his mistake. He held up his hands. "You know, we can talk about this later. I get sometimes women can cause us to be emotional, right? She's pretty. I get it. Maybe I'll pay for her services after you're done with her." He chuckled timidly as he bumbled around his words, showing his teeth, yellowed like he'd had one too many cigars.

Trent was a stupid, stupid man to claim that Jameson was emotional. Most everyone in the room could have told him that. I knew then that this wouldn't end well, not when Jameson was already wound tight from the night before. He cracked his neck, and instantly the room shifted.

I stood to murmur to him, "It doesn't matter, Jameson. He's doing it to get a rise out of you, and who cares when it's just me. I *am* just the nanny. I don't really belong at your side here—"

"From now on, you always belong at my side, Mia." He slid his hand to my neck so he could rub his thumb over my cheek softly. "Don't ever say you're *just* my nanny again."

Then he turned and took one step forward. Both men backed up, but they couldn't go far. Other men were closing in and surrounding them as if they knew what was about to happen.

Everyone waited for Jameson, waited for a command, and I held my breath, not sure what was about to happen.

He leaned down and murmured to me, "Look away if it will give you nightmares, baby."

And then he told his men, "Veil and clean up."

The color drained from Trent's face, his brows slamming down in fear. "Now, hold on, Mr. Knight. Please."

"Jameson, tonight? Really?" Olive whined as men started to encircle both Jameson and Trent.

Pink whooped just as I saw Jameson pull a gun, and then the men blocked my view.

I heard one shot.

So loud.

So singular and potent, there was no mistaking what it was. Right after, a body dropped, and it only took them about ten seconds to disassemble the circle they'd made. Jameson used a handkerchief to wipe away some blood from his face, and the man was gone.

So clean.

So fast.

"Now"—Jameson's jaw worked before he turned to the man who'd come with Trent. This man stood there with wide eyes, his mouth opening and closing—"does anybody else want to say something about my date?"

No one said a single word.

He stared at the guy Trent called Dalton. "I'll give *you* five minutes, unless you'd like none like Trent?"

"Mr. Knight, I mean no disrespect like he did."

"Don't even look her way. You do, and you'll be bleeding out like him. Use your five minutes wisely. They'll determine whether you live or die after last night." He turned to me. "I'll be back soon. Darling, eat."

Should I admit that I could have actually eaten and enjoyed the meal? That what had happened in front of me was starting to feel normal, acceptable? That the crawling, gut reaction to that man who had stood before us just seconds ago was completely eliminated by the man I was falling for, and I relished in it rather than feared it?

I sighed as I watched him walk away and took a bite of the food in front of me. Steak and mashed potatoes that melted in your mouth. I wasn't hungry for food though.

"Well, the night's about to take a turn." Callahan sighed as he watched his brother go.

"Should we go talk with them?" Olive stood, like she was a bit concerned, and her husband stood with her.

"No. Because you know as well as I do that it's not going to end well."

She threw her napkin down. "Fine. Leave it to us women then." She glanced at Pink. "You're coming too."

"Should I—"

"You stay here," Callahan cut me off. "Enjoy yourself. You deserve it working for him lately. He's . . . unsettled right now."

I watched my friends hurry after Jameson, but I didn't follow. Callahan was the brother of the enigma of a man I was falling for, and that meant I was going to pry as much information from him as I could now. I was past professional niceties. "How so?"

"He's got you on that Ducati, right?" I nodded at his question. "And he only brings that out when he's feeling reckless."

"Not what I need to hear when I'm riding on the back of it." I glared at him.

He chuckled. "You can hitch a ride back in the SUV tonight if you want."

I hummed, knowing that Jameson would want me with him instead. "He feeling reckless because of what happened at the club and with Franny at the academy?"

Cal shrugged. "Maybe." He thought about it as we watched people mill about. "But also he likes you. A lot more than he normally likes people."

"Okay," I responded slowly, not sure where he was going with this.

"I think you're different from all this, Mia. And he always wanted something a little different. If not for himself, for Franny. His wife . . . fuck, she was diabolical, strategic. I think he thought that even though their marriage was arranged, he could make her see that too. But she definitely didn't give him different. She belonged among us."

Hearing his marriage was arranged had my heart twisting for him, for the love he didn't get, for the way his life must have been planned out. I sat there wondering for the first time if fitting in amongst the people in Paradise Grove mattered. I'd found I didn't fit in once or twice before and knew it was for the better. "And he didn't want that?"

"No. Because sometimes belonging and fitting right in doesn't balance out the damn group, right? Sometimes you need the opposite. Someone sweet. But also someone who's real and who's truthful. Someone who sees past the Diamond name, if you know what I mean . . . but now I think Jameson is probably considering whether or not he deserves that."

"Why wouldn't he?"

He smiled sadly. "He doesn't believe his hands are clean when it comes to his wife, Lex's disappearance, or my father's. Makes him just as bad as any Diamond in his eyes."

"Why?" I was taking the opportunity to pry. How could I not when I was thinking of the man all day at this point?

"You'll have to ask him, Mia." He shrugged. "Now, come on, let's dance before my brother comes back to act like your shadow again."

Callahan stood and offered his hand. Chewing my cheek, I hesitated. "He won't like it. Gave Archer a black eye for it already."

"Ms. Darling, I can handle my brother." He leaned closer. "Plus, if you stay here much longer, Valerie is bound to come bother you."

And that had me up and out of my seat, grabbing his hand. We moved between the tables and onto an empty dance floor, where the band continued the classical music. And then he spun me way faster than I anticipated, and I gasped before a burst of laughter flew from my lips as he dipped me low. "Callahan, what the hell?"

"What? I'm here to dance, not sway."

And we did dance for two or three more minutes, all around the floor, because Cal was so smooth with his lines I could barely keep up.

"You can waltz, teach, and survive a professional hit," he whispered in my ear. "Should I steal you from him?"

I couldn't help but smirk, but the joke between us died as I heard his voice behind me, cold, measured, and full of an edge. "You could try to steal her, brother, but I'd kill you for that."

Callahan didn't flinch or even look over my shoulder at his brother. He winked at me, his light-blue eyes dancing with mischief as he replied, "A death I might take chances on if she'd have me."

"She won't." Jameson stepped between us as Callahan let my hand fall. "Go dance with someone else. I'm cutting in."

"Jameson," I chastised.

Callahan conceded to his brother easily as he backed away and said, "Come find me if he pisses you off too much."

The low growl from Jameson's chest and his arm locking firmly around my waist signaled I wouldn't get much of a chance to do that. Not that I wanted to. I would have had to ignore the shift in my body, the tingle against my skin as his hand brushed over the small of my back, the tightening of every muscle in anticipation for being against him again.

"You're being rude to your brother."

"Am I? Wasn't he rude to me first?"

"How? He was a perfect gentleman. He sat with me, told me he'd even let me go back home in the SUV with him rather than on the bike. I'm starting to think I came here with the wrong brother—"

"Don't make me kill another man this weekend, Darling. Especially not my brother."

"Stop it, Jameson." How bad was it that I believed he might actually commit that crime for me, and it sent shivers down my spine? "He asked me to dance so I didn't have to sit there and be gawked at because I don't belong."

"You belong anywhere Franny and I are. He knows that. And he knows better than to touch what isn't his."

"Me?"

"Yes. You." The scruff of his five-o'clock shadow brushed against my cheek as he leaned close. "You're mine, Mia Darling. And I'll kill anyone who doesn't respect that."

"Your what, exactly?" I asked him. He hadn't clarified, hadn't told me this was exclusive, that he'd fuck only me, that he wanted only me. And from Valerie's display, I wondered if he even considered it. "Your daughter's teacher?"

"Among other things."

I looked down, trying to hide how that made me feel, the flutters in my chest, the blush that was rising to my face, and that's when I saw the blood on his shoes. Still wet. Still fresh. My eyes whipped up to meet his and explain. "It was just a dance with your brother. That's all. I'm sure you'll dance with other women too, and that's fine. We're not . . . Just because we had a moment of passion on the roof doesn't mean you owe me more than that." But I wanted him to owe me more. I wanted to dive into whatever this was with him and explore it. The thrill, the danger, the passion, all of it. I didn't want to hesitate.

Not when I was ready.

"Is that all it was? A moment of passion?"

I answered truthfully. "I'm not sure."

"And is it just moments of idle conversation you have with me through your day? At night? At the country club while you take care of Franny?"

"The country club is for your daughter. I'm on the job. That's time you spend with her."

"And the other moments?"

"It could be more if that's what we want, or it could be just employee-and-boss discussions."

"Well as your boss, and maybe more, darling devil, I don't want you dancing with anyone else. I thought I made that clear with Archer."

I sighed. "It's only dancing."

"And yet I'm dancing against you now and this feels like more than a dance. It feels like I feel your nipples against my chest, the heat of your pussy wanting my cock." My breath caught at his words, and I swallowed down the desire that was starting to overtake my rationale. "And now you're licking your lips like you want me to kiss you and claim you in front of everyone here."

I did. But he couldn't. We couldn't. We weren't official. We didn't know where it was going. We needed to think logically. At least, I needed to. For the sake of my family, for the sake of Franny, for the sake of myself.

But then Jameson's hand slid from the small of my back up to my neck, and he pulled me close. "Stop me if you aren't ready, Mia. But I am."

He gave me one moment. That's all. And I murmured, "I'm ready."

And then his lips were on mine, searing, possessive, ruthless in their claiming. He was unrestrained there in the middle of the dance floor, in front of the syndicate.

The line was drawn.

I was his for everyone to see, and every powerful person in Paradise Grove now knew it.

The question was whether or not he was mine and mine alone.

29

Jameson

HANDLING A SITUATION AND containing one were two different things in my syndicate. I handled business ventures, investments, day-to-day finances and dealings.

I contained explosions of passion, emotion, people acting out. The Diamond Syndicate didn't just exist in the Chicago suburbs and Paradise Grove—it was on the West and the East Coast and across the globe. I didn't have time for miniscule problems or weaknesses within my own syndicate. Or with my own allies.

For the man who had invited Trent, I gave two minutes of my time. Not five. And his argument had been an actual waste of those minutes.

The bullet in his head was a waste also. In med school, they told me every second counted. I felt the same with my business. It was a body I took the utmost care of, and when something infected it, every second counted in removing the virus.

"Get this piece of shit off the premises," I told one of my men. When Olive and Dimitri walked in with Bane and Pink, I pinched the bridge of my nose and informed them, "He was working with Paolo along with Trent."

Bane frowned. "You know for a fact?"

"He used the same phrase Paolo did. *The East Coast will take care of the cracks*. The same phrase Lex used to say about her company helping us Diamonds."

"You saying what I think you are?" Bane lifted a brow and I nodded before he grumbled, "Shit. Well, you wanted more action, Pink. Guess we get a little blood tonight, and might be time to get surveillance on all Paolo's properties. Doesn't seem they're going to stay quiet any longer."

I agreed, sliding my gun back into my belt holster. "Keep me updated," I told them, and then went to find Mia. *She* was my focus now tonight . . . or every night.

Trent was right about that. I *had* overreacted and killed a man or two at the club that I might not have had she not been there. Would it cause ripples amongst the East Coast? I didn't care now. The second Trent had said the same phrase Paolo Ruiz had, everything clicked into place. Val and Trent were close, and I had it on good authority she'd gone to him after I turned her away last night.

It meant he'd tipped off O'Connor's men and his loyalties were with them over us. For that alone, he deserved a knife in his heart. He got a bullet in front of everyone, though, because of how he'd talked to Mia.

No one got to disrespect that woman ever again. Not when they knew she was mine.

And when I saw her dancing with my brother, I had words with both of them, reminding her she was mine even though I couldn't clarify the rest. I just knew I was ready for more with her. Ready for everything.

I took her soft lips in mine now on the dance floor because they were my territory just as mine were hers. She'd learn over time what it meant to be faithful to me, that it meant not even my brother would be able to touch her. I wanted her home to ingrain it into her, so I pulled away to tell her, "We're leaving."

"But we should say bye to—"

"Blame me later." I gripped her hand and wove through the party. She'd see them all again in a month or so. Or maybe never, since I didn't want to share her with anyone. Not with the way men kept eyeballing her. Why had I sent short-ass dresses to her today, anyway?

But when I got her back on the Ducati, I knew why. Her exposed thighs against my clothed ones in the night wind heated my damn soul. I wanted her in a way I never wanted women.

To own her.

To punish her for letting my brother touch her.

To ravage her so she was wrecked for everyone else.

To rip her apart and then put her back together so she knew she was safe only with me.

The moonlight glowed on her skin, and her fingers gripped my abdomen every time I accelerated. She wasn't teasing me the way I had teased her under the table tonight. She didn't inch her hands down toward my cock or try to cop a feel the way I had.

But I fucking thought about her doing it, how it would feel for those hands to grip my dick instead of my stomach, for her legs to open wider for me on my bike so I could fuck her in the moonlight with the stars highlighting her pretty brown eyes.

I took the turns faster, the wind whipping past us, and blew through the lights, pushing the machine only a little. The Superleggera V4 was a damn beast, one of five hundred in the world, and mine wasn't stock. I'd custom dipped the carbon-fiber fairings in obsidian-infused paint, wrapped the handlebars in leather—the same Italian leather that I enjoyed in my Bugatti—and the exhaust was tuned to rumble lower and quieter. There wasn't any red on my brake calipers either. They gleamed of steel, and the dash flashed with an upgraded HEAT digital interface, the best in the industry.

My machine was made for me. Not the streets. And the

woman on that bike with me tonight was made for me too—how she held herself amongst my syndicate, quiet and almost apathetic to everything but my touch, her concern focused on my daughter, on me, and on her friends.

She didn't care about the power; she didn't care about the wealth or the prestige, and her heart made her too good for all of us. For me.

Yet, I was too selfish not to take it, couldn't have stopped myself if I tried. I hit the button on my dash to open the iron gates. Every second that idled by as the metal parted slowly was a second too long. The drive curved ahead, and I felt how she'd caught on to leaning with my body, but I leaned hard so that we were right on the edge of the drive, my estate in view with the darkened stone and glass glinting in the moonlight. I engaged the kickstand and looked back at her. She was breathless from the fast ride, her lips still swollen from my kiss were parted just slightly, and her dress bunched high on her thighs from being pressed tight against me.

I let the engine idle and the night air infect us. She didn't let go of my waist, her breath hot on the curve of my neck as I stared at her. I didn't move right away because I couldn't, not when every inch of her was molded to me like she belonged there.

"Ready to go home?" I asked her.

"Not ready," she murmured.

Good.

I wasn't either.

I unstrapped my helmet and yanked her thigh over my lap while gripping her waist so that her thighs straddled mine. I pulled her helmet from her head too, watching her curls tumble free, wild and soft in the night wind.

"Fuck, you're a vision on top of my bike, darling devil."

"This thing is dangerous," she said, but her hands were on

the tank as she wiggled her hips back and forth like the feel of the purr of that engine was the danger, not the actual ride.

"I think you like dangerous more than you originally let on."

She bit her lip, and I watched her pant at the feel of the vibration between her legs. "I was turned on the first time you grabbed me around the neck, Jameson. Have been turned on ever since." The blush that stained her cheeks was a sight I wanted to remember forever.

"How turned on are you now?" My gaze drifted to her pussy on my ride. "Spread your legs wider and show me, Mia."

My girl was ready to follow commands because there was no hesitation as my hands drifted up her thighs while she spread them further apart. When I pushed her dress up so that her panties shone in the moonlight, she gasped.

"Soaked through." I brushed my thumb over the silky material, rubbing her clit up and down, giving her the friction her body ached for. Her lips parted on a moan. "You still wanted me to touch you here even after the cleanup?"

"Probably more so after." She said it quietly and on a whimper.

I pinched her clit, but it wasn't enough. I wanted her saying it loud, and I wanted to feel her pussy when she did. I ripped the material from her body and plunged two fingers into her before I growled, "Say it again, Mia. Say you liked knowing what I'd do for you. Does that turn you on?"

"Yes," she moaned, arching into my hand.

"You like knowing you drive me so crazy that if a man looks at you wrong, he'll be on the floor bleeding out in seconds?"

"Yes." She almost cried, her eyes shut as I picked up the pace of my fingers pumping a sensitive spot within her. She was dripping onto my machine now, writhing for a release, but I wanted her crazy for one, as crazy as I was for her.

So I pulled my fingers out and slid the arousal over her clit. She gasped at the loss and tried to sit up, but I grabbed her neck and slammed her back down onto my ride. "You know your pussy doesn't deserve a damn orgasm after what I did for you tonight only to see you with my brother."

"It was a dance," she said, like that made it okay.

I smacked her pussy three times over so that it swelled and shined in the moonlight before I massaged it. Then I pulled her forward by her neck. "You won't dance with other men if I fuck you, Mia. You get that? I won't allow it."

"And what about you and other women?"

"Do you care if I do?" I wanted her to admit she did, admit she was as unhinged for me as I was for her.

She looked away as she said, "You let Valerie whisper in your ear, and a dozen other women touched you tonight. I can't dance with a man, but they can flirt with you?"

Her acknowledgment had my cock hardening to the point of pain, and I hummed before saying, "Turn around, baby, and put your knees right here." I pointed to the base of the tank and helped her maneuver so she was kneeling and facing away from me. Then, I took her hands and placed them on the handlebars. She was tiny enough that when she did, her ass raised in the air, just how I wanted it.

She looked over her shoulder at me and narrowed her eyes. "What are we doing, Jameson?"

"I'm giving you my apology, Darling. For letting another woman make you feel like they had any of my attention. It was you I thought of the whole night. You and this ass." I squeezed a globe. "This pussy." I spread her center open so I could watch it glisten in the moonlight. "And this pretty, tight hole."

I lowered my head to taste her arousal first. I let her rock her hips on my tongue, let her ride close to that orgasm I knew she needed, and then I licked my way up to the puckered hole that I could tell she was more hesitant about. She gasped when my tongue tasted it, when I worked it while my fingers slid into her center.

She told me immediately that no one had ever done this, that she was too close, that she was falling over the edge, and then her perfect holes tightened around my tongue and fingers as she cried out into the night.

I held her through her orgasm, memorizing how she spasmed, how she coiled up and arched and then came down from that high, slumping over my machine languidly, like she was spent.

I flipped her around so she was straddling me again, and she gave me a lazy smile. "I like your apologies, Jameson. Probably even as much as your jealous punishments."

I couldn't keep my hands off her as I massaged her thighs, my movements almost jerky with the pent-up need to have all of her.

"I like you sitting across me looking like that too. But it's time to get us home."

Her head shake was slow before she murmured, "I want all of you, not a tease."

"A tease, Mia?" I chuckled. "I think you got what you needed."

She almost growled, and then she lunged for my belt buckle, undoing it quickly enough that she could slide her hand into my pants and grip my cock to return the favor. "I need this."

Her hand pumped me once and I about lost all the control I had left. Gripping her wrist, I stopped her. Between gritted teeth I said, "Tell me you're not ready."

"But I am."

I was squeezing her neck with my other hand, so I let go of her wrist and gripped her thigh instead. I wasn't sure if it was to hold her back or to prepare to pull her forward. "I should have you in a bed first."

"I don't need romance, Jameson." She raised up and positioned me right at her entrance. "I only need you to have me where you want me and where I want you. Do you want me here?"

There was no need for the question. My arousal was shining in the damn moonlight at the tip of my cock, beading out in rivulets, dripping for her like she was for me. And I didn't give her any answer other than yanking her forward and slamming her pussy over my thick cock.

She gasped and I groaned, my voice feral as I said, "Damn I knew this pretty pussy was made just for me."

She rolled her hips and whimpered, "I needed this. Needed you."

"You got me, baby. And I got you," I told her before letting go of my control. I fucked her hard against my machine without any reservations.

I should have had some.

She was a weakness, an employee, and a person my daughter loved.

She was someone I couldn't lose, and that thought scared the shit out of me.

But the thrill and the fear made me drive into her harder, made me grip her hips enough that I'd leave bruises in the morning. I hadn't even considered that I was fucking her raw, that we didn't use protection, or that this could end badly.

Because I wouldn't let it. It wouldn't end.

I wouldn't let her go.

I'd keep her. Even if she didn't want to be kept.

I came into her hard on that thought.

30

Mia

When a person finally opens the door to their room of secrets, they aren't alone anymore. They shared their true self, the one they hide from everyone else, and you have to choose to accept who they are or not.

I chose Jameson that night.

I chose his fury, his rage, and his possessiveness along with his passion, thoughtfulness, and protectiveness. All of that created the enigma of a man that he was. He didn't leave my side the rest of the night, showering with me, fucking me in my bed again, sleeping beside me.

I chose him because I knew he chose me too. He stood up for me, asked me when I was ready, waited on me through the night, and held me tight enough that the nightmares I normally had ceased.

And the next morning, Franny coming home early solidified that decision.

He called me from the porch after he'd woken me up by being between my legs for breakfast and told me he had a surprise. No need to get dressed.

Standing there in my orchid pajamas felt less than formal when his mother and Franny pulled up in an SUV.

Yet, Franny jumped from the car and raced toward me with pigtails swinging, her binoculars around her neck, and a big smile on her face. That sweet baby girl hugged me first rather than Jameson. She whispered in my ear, "Daddy said he wanted me home now so we get to play all day." She squealed and ran out of my arms and into Jameson's, pulling him along saying that she wanted to play tag with Malek.

Jameson didn't disappoint. He ran after them both while I smiled at the scene before I realized it left me alone with Jameson's mother, who was standing by the car, eyeing me with newfound curiosity. "How was your night with the syndicate?"

"Different," I answered, not sure what else to say.

She nodded. "My son fancies you, it seems."

"Mostly, he knows I care about Franny." I tried to keep it professional and casual.

"Is that all, you think?" She stared at me with an older version of the blue eyes that could see into my soul.

"Anything more will have to wait and see." I met her gaze head-on and tried to hold my ground.

She hummed lightly and nodded before straightening her dress. "Well, Franny told me it was your idea to have tennis lessons every other day of the week?"

"Yes, I think it's good for her to get out of the house, and I played tennis back in the day. So, it's easy," I answered, wondering if it would be rude to run after Franny and Jameson and ask them if I could play too just to get out of this awkward moment.

"Do you think it's good for her to spend less time with her grandmother also?" she asked as a follow-up, and her tone held a bite to it.

I scrambled for an answer but frowned and bought myself time with a question. "I'm not sure what you mean?"

"Jameson said Franny will be spending more time at home on the weekends after having conversations with you and others.

I'm assuming that's mostly your doing, considering Valerie would never."

Of course she knew she had Valerie in the palm of her hand, and that alone had me standing a little taller. Franny's well-being was priority even at the detriment of every relationship I had here in Paradise Grove. That's how it should have been with Valerie too, but I wouldn't judge her. I got the allure of Jameson Knight. I just wouldn't succumb to it like others had.

"Franny enjoys having a close relationship with her father, and I think they should nurture it when Jameson has free time. A daughter needs her daddy, after all."

She let the silence build, and I heard Franny and Jameson chattering back and forth out near the forest trees. Then a laugh burst out of Franny so loud and genuine, I smiled and glanced their way. Mrs. Knight did too before she sighed and nodded. "I don't tend to defer to my son's employees, Mia. But I'm starting to see that's not all you are to Jameson or Franny. I hope you intend to stick around."

Her statement was respectful but much too inquisitive when I didn't even know the answer myself. I bit my bottom lip before I answered quietly, "For the summer. I'm not sure about after."

Thinking of how far in I was getting with this family, knowing there would be an end to it had my heart stuttering and my mind working overtime on how I could stop the inevitable heartbreak.

"Well, I am sure." She patted my shoulder. "I'm happy he's listening to you," she said. "And I'm pleased you put my granddaughter first. Don't stop."

That was all.

She folded into the SUV and waved goodbye as Franny ran through the grass to find a toy of Malek's. She threw it as Jameson walked back up to me. "My mother likes you."

"Does she now?" I peered up at his dazzling blues and immediately felt the butterflies in my stomach. I was so screwed.

"Of course. She doesn't stop and talk to anyone else."

"She seems to talk with most of your staff just fine." I didn't mention Valerie specifically.

"She talks *at* them. With you, she listened."

"She listens to you though. She said you told her Franny would be spending more time here. Your day clear up a little?"

"No," he answered, not offering more of an explanation.

Before I could pry further, though, Franny ran up with Malek, who stopped by my side for a pat on the head. "You're going to watch a movie with us tonight too, Ms. Darling? Rosy and Hades will too, right? And Archer maybe? It'll be movie night!"

"Movie night?" I raised an eyebrow at Jameson, wondering what this whole night might consist of. But also realizing I shouldn't be a part of it. This was father-daughter time. Not father-daughter-*teacher* time. I had to remind myself of my place even if Jameson and I had fun the night before. "Oh, Franny, I think I might have some plans, but—"

"What plans?" Jameson frowned.

"Is it a date?" Franny asked, like she knew all about boys and dating.

"How do you know what a date is?" Jameson looked doubly concerned now.

"Because, Dad. I'm not four. Of course I know what dating is, and Ms. Darling is pretty, isn't she? She probably has lots of guys wanting to go on dates with her."

I wish.

"I don't know, Fran Bran. Let's ask Mia." His gaze shifted to me, and he asked slowly, deliberately, "Do you have guys lining up to take you on a date tonight, Mia?"

My heart beat faster, and I licked my lips before answering him. "Not really your business, Mr. Knight."

He hummed and rocked on his heels before saying, "I think you should come to movie night, Mia. We'd *love* for you to be there. Nowhere else."

Crap. I'd need a break from that hungry, protective gaze if I stood a chance at not getting my heart broken when the time came for him to let me go. He hadn't said we were exclusively dating or anything of the sort. Instead, I had started contemplating if he'd make me leave, if I would be ready to by the end of the summer, and if he would care. I didn't get promises other than his kiss in front of other Diamonds, and I wasn't sure what that was . . . Didn't want to ask either. "I don't think that's a good idea."

Franny tsked. "Of course it is. Maybe we can dress up too. We'll watch a princess movie. We can dress up as princesses. Daddy, you'll be a prince?"

"Or a knight," he said, his gaze not leaving mine, reminding me of the night before and how I'd told him I needed even a knight, not a prince to dance with.

"Perfect!" Franny bounced up and down. "Maybe Daddy will let us put make up on. Oh, and we can bejewel things too! It will be a bedazzled party."

"Well, I . . ." Glancing at Jameson, I realized he would be of no help. That smirk on his face was practically diabolical. "I really do have plans."

I didn't.

"Cancel them then," Jameson pushed, no remorse in his eyes. Instead, those blue eyes shined bright as the sun with mirth, making me wish we could spend every moment out in the daylight.

"Sometimes canceling plans is rude." I glared at him.

"Saying no to a seven-year-old is ruder," he shot back.

"I can watch a little of the movie . . . I guess."

"Thatta girl," he murmured, and then he patted my ass as Franny ran past us to go invite everyone else.

He may have ordered hits on men and led the syndicate with a ruthless power that wasn't always met with forgiveness or understanding, but when it came to movie night with his daughter, he turned into a teddy bear that had me melting like the butter on popcorn.

It had only been a couple hours when Franny came to my room to ask, "Do you have any princess dresses?"

Compared to the one she was wearing, absolutely not. She'd forgone her normal attire for a dark-purple tulle that puffed out every which way. And the sparkles of the straps were intense. "Rosy and I made this months ago. She glued all the jewels on." Then she whipped her hands out from behind her. "And I just made these."

She was holding black shoes and a black belt. "I bedazzled them."

Yes, they were black . . . but with red and purple jewels lining the wingtips and the belt buckle.

"Franny," I gasped.

Her face fell almost immediately. "What? They don't look good?" She eyed me with scrutiny, and I knew right then I wasn't going to be the one to make her unhappy over a few male accessories.

Granted, I wasn't sure how much his belt or shoes cost.

"They look fantastic, was all I was going to say."

Her eyes widened in delight. "Oh good. I was nervous to show you this, but I think he'll like it too." Then she pulled a watch from the little side pocket of her dress.

"Oh. Oh my." That was for sure a Rolex.

I glanced at Archer, who'd escorted Franny to my room, and he was silently cracking up. "Archer, why don't you give these shoes and belt to Jameson. We can give him the watch together, right, Franny?"

"Good idea! Then, he'll be all dressed and ready right at seven."

And he was going to be really happy with the jewels decorating the band of it. "It looks magnificent. Like the best. Want to decorate my dress next?" I asked her.

My dresses were made to be destroyed anyway. I hadn't spent a ton on them, and they were all way too boring for a princess party.

Franny bounced over to my closet and chose the blackest one. It was short and loose and the perfect material to bedazzle. We spent a half an hour on that before she ran off to eat dinner and then came back to make sure I was all dressed. I followed her to the media room as she tried to contain her excitement.

It was infectious, though, and I found myself hot gluing more gems and crystals to Malek's collar while we waited for Jameson. The hot glue gun had become my friend, and I wasn't going to stop anytime soon. "We should decorate my plant pots, Franny."

"Oh, tomorrow?" she asked, concentrating on placing her next jewel. "I think Malek loves his collar, right?"

Stepping back, we both stared at it. The red and pink jewels might have been a bit much. "He's never going to want to take it off."

It was then that Rosy and Hades came down and I noticed the time.

Ten minutes late.

He told us seven. Seven ten wasn't a good sign.

It was actually an unacceptable sign for a seven-year-old who already had issues with her parents being absent. Didn't he know that?

Hades's face was grim enough that I immediately put my arm around Franny to brace her. "So, I think we should start that movie, huh, Fran Bran," he said.

"We're waiting for Daddy," Franny murmured, but her frown was evident, like she knew what Hades was going to say.

"He's going to try to make it, Fran Bran, but he got caught up in a meeting."

"Oh, well . . ." I spun and grabbed that watch that Franny had decorated. "Fran, why don't we add some jewels right across here?" I lined the hot glue right across the face of it.

She glanced at it and then at me, confused. "I think that's where Daddy tells the time."

I shrugged and grabbed a few jewels to do it myself. "We can tell him I did this. I think he'll like red and pink best."

One by one, I placed the sparkly diamond-shaped material to his watch face and pressed it on. When I looked at Rosy, she was laughing, while Hades looked like he might be sick as I asked, "Meeting in his office, right?" Now that the watch was ruined, I was already heading toward the door. Did this man not understand that Franny didn't need to be brought home from her grandma's only for him not to show up when he said he was going to? If he thought he was going to skip movie night, he had another thing coming.

"Yes, but—"

"Franny, have Hades make you a big bowl of popcorn while I go grab your dad, okay?"

I stomped past Hades without a second glance and kept stomping all the way to Jameson's office, making an extra ruckus when I swung open the door in my fluffy princess dress.

"Jameson Knight, you're not going to work while I sit with Fran after you promised her you'd be there. You've got to be kidding me," I said as I threw open that door. It bounced loudly against the wall while I stood there ready to tear him apart.

Yet he was dressed to the nines in a freaking dark-purple suit that looked like it matched Franny's dress. His hair was styled as if he'd spent time. And he had her bejeweled belt on along with the shoes. My heart twisted at seeing this man's effort for his daughter, but him being up here meant he wasn't exactly trying.

Then the scene registered—the look of pure concentration on his face as he maneuvered a long needle into his brother's arm. He murmured, "We're done here. Get out."

"Right," I whispered, my eyes on Callahan, glued to all the blood. "I . . . We can reschedule movie night." I was leaving, getting out of there, hoping to God he could save Callahan, hoping I hadn't made him lose concentration.

"Mia Darling, I have a movie with you tonight. Not them. They're all leaving. Now."

"Oh my God," I whispered and hurried over to his brother's side. He was losing so much blood. "No. What? He needs a hospital and more care, Jameson."

Callahan chuckled. "I'm fine, pretty girl. Just a scratch. No need to cancel movie night."

"That's not a scratch," I cried, looking at Jameson. "He needs to go to a hospital."

"Why, when I live just down the road? My brother is easier," Callahan stated.

"You're getting sewn up in his home office!"

Jameson shook his head and wrapped the wound, which seemed to cause more blood to gush out. "You need to stop instigating fights."

"Oh, you're one to talk." Callahan looked at me like I was in on the joke. "This man is about to start wars *for* you, but he wants to manage me."

"Not managing. Just telling you. Fighting with her enough that she stabs you isn't really constructive."

"Wait. *She*? Who's she, and when can I meet her?" I couldn't help but ask Cal.

"Mia, you're not meeting her," Jameson growled.

"I'm only wondering what happened." I pouted.

"Just know, it was warranted," Jameson answered for his brother, and the small smile on Callahan's face gave me all the information I needed. He was guilty as charged. "Now, I resigned from the hospital, so get the fuck out of my house before I tear those stitches out."

When his brother and then the men left, I stood there, looking up at him, not sure what to say. He leaned over the desk and grabbed a bouquet of flowers. He handed me ones with little fuchsia blossoms sprinkled in. "One for you. Other's for Fran. She okay? We gotta get down there." He moved so fast now, like he wasn't at all concerned about his brother who he'd had to sew up.

"Jameson . . . you sure you don't need a minute?"

He chuckled. "A little blood doesn't scare me anymore. And we're already late, Mia." He freaking winked at me. "Didn't you come in here to tell me that?"

"Right." I took a calming breath, then rolled my lips between my teeth before saying, "Maybe I need a minute. Do you and your brother always frustrate women?"

"I didn't mean to frustrate you." He dragged a finger over my cheek softly. "I meant to be on time." He massaged the back of my neck and pulled me close. "Come on, Darling. No one's hurt, everything's fine. Let's go enjoy the princess cartoon. So I can be your knight later."

"We'll see." I rolled my eyes, but we really wouldn't see. I wanted to jump his bones right then and there, but I held out for the greater good. When we got downstairs, Franny was beaming, ready to give her father his last bedazzled present.

Shit.

"I decorated the sides of it, Daddy, and Mia said because you were a little late, the jewels she glued to the face of it would make you be on time next time."

"Is that what she said?" Jameson glanced my way.

I gulped and twisted my hands. I needed to apologize. He was saving his brother's freaking life upstairs, and I'd had a silly tantrum about it.

But he just shrugged and took the watch to snap it on. "Serves me right for being late."

"But . . . No." That watch was well over six figures. I knew it. "That's a Rolex I just ruined."

"You didn't ruin it, Mia. I like the red jewels there!" Franny said.

"Yeah, darling Mia. We like the red jewels across the face of my watch. It'll help me be right on time for our next date."

"This isn't a date," I whisper-yelled at him.

"Of course it is. And I get that my girl might have a bit of an outburst when I don't show up on time."

"Don't be ridiculous. And I'm not your girl either. We haven't established any of that," I said because we *did* need to discuss it. I accepted who he was and would definitely be sleeping with him for the time being, but I had to be rational, I decided. I sat down on the opposite side of the couch, trying to not want to be close to him.

He snaked his arm around my waist, though, and yanked me over so that my leg was right against his as he murmured in my ear, "If you say so, darling devil."

Then we settled in for the movie, watching the princess defeat all rather than needing a prince or a knight. Or at least that's where I thought it was going, because I fell asleep against his shoulder and heard in my dreams Franny telling her dad, "She's our girl, Daddy. Even if she doesn't want to be."

His arm tightened around me as he murmured, "You're right, Fran Bran. You're right."

When I woke the next morning, I was in my bed, and Jameson was lying next to me. Like he belonged there. Like we belonged together.

I knew it wasn't true, but I couldn't help but play pretend for a moment and delude myself into enjoying him up against me.

I rocked my hips to feel his shaft rub against my ass and moaned when his hands gripped my waist.

"No nightmares, only sweet dreams this morning, then?"

31

Jameson

I'd lost control with her—succumbed to sleeping next to her, having feelings for her, exposing another weakness of mine.

And I didn't even regret it when she looked over her shoulder at me and murmured, "It's a good morning with you in my bed, I guess."

"You guess, Darling? What would make you sure of it?"

She rolled her hips again. "I'm pretty sure that would make it perfect, even though we shouldn't. It's Monday. We both need to get ready for the day."

I smiled at how groggy she still sounded, like waking up was a slow process that I wanted every part of. She rolled to face me, the haze of sleep from the night before still in her eyes. When she wiggled her hips, I gripped them immediately. "Darling, you're tempting me again. I'm finding I'm not good at restraint with you."

She chuckled but moved away and grabbed her pj's to slide back on. "Were you ever good at restraint, Jameson? I don't believe it."

She stood there in her panties and tank, hands on her hips, with the sun streaming in from the window, and I realized with her I'd never be good at control. With her, I'd probably lose it all the damn time. And I craved losing it with her, for her, and because of her. That revelation had me sharing more with her than I ever intended. "Most of the time I am. I need control as a Diamond. Much more control than I had at our event the other night."

She sat on the bed right next to me and folded her hands in her lap. "Why?"

"Because it's better to act with strategy than emotion. To plan and execute rather than lash out or get lost in an emotion you can't come back from."

She hummed. "Sometimes embracing what you really feel is the only way to move forward though."

"Maybe, but I *should* have more control with you. I enjoy you too much and don't want to consider that you might run off," I admitted, dragging a finger over her soft cheek.

She bit her lip and cautiously met my eyes to ask, "Might run off before our contract is up, you mean? Nervous you'll lose me and Franny's educational services early all because you aren't planning ten steps ahead without emotion involved?" Her question had my body tensing as if it wanted to refuse her words immediately.

We were past the contract. She had to know that by now. "You realize I am nervous to lose you, period, right?"

"Jameson . . ." She frowned, and I saw how the tension in her shoulders relaxed at my words. Then she reached out to weave our fingers together and whispered, "You won't lose me or anyone who matters for showing them who you are. And if you do, they weren't meant to have you in the first place."

I chuckle. "Mia Darling, how I wish that were true."

"You don't believe me?"

Looking toward the ceiling, I wasn't sure how to tell her, but the need to burned in my chest. "I married a woman who knew exactly who I was in the syndicate—all about me, Mia—and she abandoned us, walked away from her perfect daughter one sunny day when she was supposed to pick her up. My own wife left, and it's because I didn't give her what she wanted."

Her lips thinned, and then she jumped up to pace with her head down, her curls going back and forth as she shook her head. "Whatever a couple is going through, Jameson, you don't leave a child. That's on her. Not you." She froze and then winced like it caused her physical pain. "Did she betray you *and* the syndicate?"

I waited to see if she would ask the next question. The one I wanted her to ask. Did I kill her? She should have. She should believe that I would have. She needed to see I had that darkness in me, that it festered and grew and didn't make me a good man. "Don't you have another question to ask me?"

"No." She held my gaze. "I don't need to."

"Why not?"

"Because I know you wouldn't have done that to your daughter."

"So much blind faith in me, Darling."

"It isn't blind when I see how you love her every single day."

I breathed out a sigh of relief that this woman had more trust in me than most of the syndicate. My mother had asked about the accident. My brother and father too. Everyone who was close to me considered it, and I didn't blame them. But Mia's heart was something different.

Something too good.

Too trusting.

And then she asked a question I didn't expect. "Did you love her too? Your wife?" She looked away. "Cal told me it was an arranged marriage of sorts."

Of course Cal had. Rubbing my eyes, I nodded, not even sure where to begin. "We married for the syndicate. She had the right family that strengthened our partnerships on the East Coast. It was mutually beneficial."

"For you, or for the syndicate?"

"Well, we thought for everyone. She was beautiful, accommodating, and . . . strategic. I thought I loved her at first. Until I found out she loved power, money, and prestige much more than me. She wanted to save her family's company over everything, putting all of us at risk. I wouldn't allow it. She relished the game, and I learned that with her I had to play it."

"What does that mean?"

"It means I waited for her to tell me about the history of the scandal within her family's company. They'd been doing things wrong since their inception. She knew it, and all I needed was for her to be real with me. She wasn't. Instead, she tried to influence me to double down with her family, to risk the syndicate, to risk our family. When I wouldn't, she tried every type of manipulation. Looking back, I'm not even sure her desire for having Fran was genuine." I tried not to wince as I said it out loud, but the betrayal still hit like a steel pipe to the gut. I sat on the edge of the bed, smoothing the fine sheets to work out the wrinkles, to work out the flaws and the pain.

"Oh, God." Mia sounded sickened by what I was telling her. "Jameson, I'm sorry."

"Looking back, I see now how when Fran was born"—I let out a breath, heavy and jagged—"she barely would feed or hold her. She withheld love for my daughter when I withheld my influence for the sake of her family's company. And I hated her calculation and manipulation even as Franny loved her mother, because a daughter needs a mom. She played the game to win . . . so I did too."

"How?" Mia asked, her voice soft now as she sat down on the bed.

I looked at her then, at the way she tucked her knees under her, at how she folded her hands into her lap as if she'd be patient, waiting for me to make her understand.

"I didn't tell her plans for future partnerships or legislation. I let her go. So it seems I calculate and manipulate as much as her."

"But, Jameson, that's not true—"

"It is." I stood, my voice sharp as I paced a few steps before turning back to her. "Do you know what I wanted to do the second I found out she hadn't picked Franny up from preschool that day? I wanted to order to have her killed."

"But you didn't." She rose from the bed, eyes trained on me. "That's not on you."

My chest was tight as I admitted, "Had that woman come back, I may have tried to kill her."

I waited for her to recoil and flinch away. I wanted her to see the truth, wanted her to know there was a monster in me she'd have to accept if she stuck around. "I didn't care that she left me, but leaving Franny . . . My daughter won't ever know she left of her own will, and it's a betrayal I'll never forgive Lex for."

"What happened to her?"

I told her the line I'd been given about my wife for years, not sure I could overwhelm her with the rest. "She got the life she wanted. Ran with Paolo's cartels on the East Coast. He'd always wanted her, and she gave herself to him easily in hopes he could save her family's company. He didn't, though, and some of his partners lost a lot of money. Supposedly it was a car accident that killed her."

"Or an angry partner?" She'd pieced it together. Then she waved away her summary. "Either way, I'm so sorry."

"I'm not. I won't ever tell Franny her mom abandoned her. She'll only know she disappeared, and that will be on me in her eyes probably forever."

Mia's hand found my arm like she wanted to ground me, soothe me. "You? Why you?"

"Because I didn't keep our family together."

"*You* are *here*. You are her *father*. And a fantastic one at that. You smile when Fran ruins your freaking wingtips, for Christ's sake."

That earned the barest of a smile from me, but it was a sad one. "You had to tell me to be present."

"Just because you needed a reminder as a parent doesn't make you a bad one, Jameson. You didn't do anything wrong."

I let the silence grow between us as I wrapped a hand around the back of Mia's neck and pulled her to me so I could press my forehead to hers. "I don't deserve you or Franny."

"You don't get to decide that," she whispered. "Not anymore."

"I didn't give her mother what she wanted."

She reeled back. "Oh please. What's a mother?" She cleared her throat and tried to cover up her disgust. "Not someone who leaves their daughter for the prestige of a company, Jameson. Franny didn't deserve that. I get that she was your wife and you were in love with her once—"

"I loved her for being the mother to my child. But Lex and I . . . well, it's obvious we weren't healthy."

She put her hands on her hips. "Well, you've moved on to healthier things for you and Franny then . . . minus some small incidents from the other night." This woman was standing in the middle of my estate in panties and messy hair, discussing my darkest secrets without running. Without leaving. She was even trying to make light of it to make me feel better.

And the air in the room shifted to something brighter; my heart shifted along with it.

"What was so unhealthy?" I smirked, and she looked ready to stomp her foot.

She wrinkled her nose. "I was at that party or meeting or whatever you want to call it, Jameson. What you're all doing is a gray area at best. And you're all hiding in the dark of the night. You hide it like you're ashamed."

"We have legal and illegal dealings, Mia. Legal and illegal allies too. But let me be clear—I'm not ashamed of it. I might hide what I've done from the world because I'm not sure they're ready to handle it, but I'm not embarrassed. I'm fucking proud. And I'll share it one piece at a time and relish every time I do."

"You really don't care, do you? Not even about the fact that you've killed men?"

I smiled because I think she was trying to understand herself more than me. "Do you care? You've seen me take more than one life at this point. And you fucked me after on my Ducati. You care that I've killed men, Mia?"

"I . . . I don't know."

"If it helps, I've saved the ones worth saving too." I shrugged. "Those I've gotten rid of did enough bad to outweigh their good."

"Is that what happened to your father?" She brought her hands together and wrung them, asking the question quietly. "Callahan mentioned him last night."

I let the assumptions hang in the air as the silence stretched between us. It would be a deciding factor for her, to choose me or run from me. Cal would want her to make the decision on whether I was a monster or not before she was completely invested in us. I wanted to punch him for mentioning Lex and my dad but also hug his dumb ass, because his meddling meant well. He wanted Mia to know me. The real me.

"If I told you it was?"

"I would say you were playing God and it's a weight no one person should have to bear alone."

"Cal helps. So do Bane and Dimitri and Olive and Pink and all the others. We've all got our responsibilities."

"You lead as a team."

"A family. *Adamantem infractum manet.* If you bring corruption we haven't agreed upon, you bring death to yourself.

My father did. His dealings with the Irish were brought to the forefront after Lex died. We uncovered that he was stealing, trafficking, and going against everything we'd agreed upon. His life needed to end."

I knew that was the truth even as I saw the look on Cal's face when I did it, even when I had to tell my mother, even when I took his seat and moved on without so much as a speech.

The monster in me didn't feel bad. Didn't mourn his death, and didn't look back.

And Mia, for all her talk of moralities, didn't seem to care about the rules or about the fact that I was basically admitting to killing my own father. She came to sit beside me and grabbed my hand, wrapping it in both of hers and pulling it close to her lap. "A son shouldn't have to expose his own father."

"I put a bullet in his head, Mia. I'm not a son. I'm a monster. I realize that, and you should too."

"I think you did what had to be done to protect those you care about."

"Maybe. And maybe we're all monsters, because I think most of us would do the same for the people we care about too."

She sighed and rubbed her fingers over my knuckles. "I don't know about that. I've tried to live my life morally. Inside the rule book."

"Then why did you take this job?"

Her mouth opened and then shut. I wanted her secrets too, and she was hiding one I wanted to pry out. They were mocking me, hiding in the shadows of her mind when I wanted them out in the damn daylight. Yet, sitting in this room with her and letting her in showed me I needed to give her space to let me in too. Trust couldn't be forced, and I wanted her trust and loyalty more than ever before.

"Don't tell me until you're ready, Mia. But if you take a kaleidoscope to the world and turn it, you'll see it in a lot of different colors. Good and bad. There are reasons people do what they do in the world. Judging them in one or two colors won't really open you up to all of them."

She chewed her cheek. "I wanted the academy job for a summer, and for it to be professional. That was all. Pretty black-and-white. Do my job well and be done. Now, I'm here and I'm mixed up in all this."

"Nothing in this world is black-and-white." I got up to find my clothes, and she stared at my chest the whole time. "Our relationship doesn't seem to be that now either, does it?"

"We can make it that way." She sighed and shrugged. "We should. We should make rules and draw lines. I can even make us a PowerPoint if we need one. I'm a teacher, after all."

"Okay." I smirked at her because her ass wasn't getting just sex from me even if she thought she was. I'd let her think it, though, if that made her feel better. "Tell me how you want it to go, darling Mia. I'll indulge you."

"We'll just . . ." She cleared her throat and stopped staring at my naked body to meet my eyes. "Clear our distractions when we have them, and then go back to boss and teacher afterward."

I hummed. "That easy, huh? Tied up with a pretty pink bow, or is it fuchsia?"

"Right." She nodded like she'd figured it all out and stood up like we were going to be professional all of a sudden. "A fuchsia bow. Perfect."

I dragged a finger across her panty line and leaned in to whisper, "Let me know how it works out for you, darling Mia."

32

Mia

It was working out terribly. For two weeks, my daily reports to him got dirtier and dirtier as my need for him grew and grew. I couldn't help that he came to my bed every night and made me scream his name.

My mind told me this job was for the money—to go toward my goals and my sister—but my heart led me down a different path. One that was more dangerous and deeply entangled, but it felt so refreshingly authentic.

And I relished in that thought. This, here with Jameson, was real. He'd shared his secrets, let me into his world, and was waiting for me to confide in him mine. We were building a place here where I didn't have to hide what I really felt, and I cherished that after so many years of my parents wanting me to stay quiet, to fit into a mold, and to not cause waves even when I needed to.

A whole week passed in bliss. Sure, men filtered in and out to talk with Jameson. Sure, I never looked behind that door, but I was happy.

Franny was happy.

Jameson seemed happy too.

After a week had passed, we had settled into a routine.

On Monday, he asked for an update after Franny went to bed, and I invited him to my room rather than actually giving him a written one. We talked before we fucked, not that we should have. Our relationship was building into something I wasn't sure I could keep under control, but I told myself bosses could be friends with benefits and we could end things when we both thought it was the right time.

I told him how Franny was smiling more, how the tennis lessons were the highlight of her day, how she could read almost faster than me now.

It didn't escape my attention that Valerie didn't show that evening.

On Tuesday, Rosy winked at me and said, "Well, I think you're sticking, Mia. You rid us of Val finally, and Mrs. Knight complimented my breakfast!" Then she danced around her kitchen like she was celebrating.

On Wednesday, I called my sister again. She answered this time, sounding like sunshine and rainbows while Felix hovered in the background. She told me we could maybe wait on visits, and I read between the lines, knowing she was avoiding leaving him again.

I took solace in Jameson's arms that night, not mentioning my sister but instead letting him occupy my mind and body.

Every morning, the man woke up and watered my plants as I watched him.

On Friday morning, I murmured to him, "You need to stop tending to Ms. Prim and Mr. Bos."

"Why?"

"Because they'll get more used to you than me and want you watering them forever."

"Plants can't tell the difference." Did he smirk before he said it, though? And I could swear he had started whispering to them, like he wanted to imprint on them.

He wanted to imprint on me, make it so I'd never forget how perfect he was, I was sure of it. That day, Franny told me over schoolwork, "I think you should stay here forever. And you should get a pet too."

She patted Malek's head. The dog was lying between us, and his tail wagged at hearing his name. "You think I need one?"

"Of course. I think Malek would like a friend, don't you think?"

"I think that's a decision for your dad."

"Oh, he wouldn't mind you having a pet." She lifted her binoculars and scanned the room. "Want a dog? The pup's bed can go right there." The corner of our study had a reading rug, but of course that would be the perfect spot for *my* dog. It could then sit right next to Franny while we read.

"We'll see," I told her right as Jameson stopped into the study, glancing at his watch. A new one without jewels all over it.

I should probably find a way to get him a replacement, although I knew he wouldn't take it out of my salary.

"See about what?" he asked, leaning on the doorframe and smiling at both of us in his three-piece suit, so relaxed in the way he approached me now.

Franny ran over to my ear to whisper, "Repeat after me. 'I think another pet would be nice. A friend for Malek who can sleep by my bed.'"

I said exactly what Franny told me and tried not to laugh as Jameson's smile dropped off.

"You two have already commandeered the guard dog. He doesn't come near me anymore."

"Okay, but say you're lonely at night too!" Franny whisper-yelled so loud that Jameson could hear her, but he still waited for me to repeat it.

One side of his mouth curled up. "Go on, Mia. Say what Franny told you."

A blush rose to my cheeks as I said, "I'm lonely at night."

"Are you, now?" Jameson pushed off the doorway. "And a dog will help?"

Franny looked between us with narrowed eyes and whispered in my ear fast, "Say yes, Mia!"

"Yes. A dog would help."

"You want a *dog* keeping you company?" His hands were on his hips.

She grabbed my hand and put her other hand to her chin as if thinking. "Well, tell him I did a report on rabbits."

I smirked to myself, because she was such a good little negotiator. The truth had come out. A pet for her was necessary, not me.

She elbowed me, and I rolled my eyes, not thinking much of it as I repeated her words. "Franny's done a whole report on rabbits, and we think she's ready to take care of one."

Franny leaned in. "For company, and it'll teach her responsibility." She glared at me expectantly to repeat.

"It's to keep us company, Jameson. You understand? Plus, it will teach her responsibility." I batted my eyelashes at him.

Franny whispered, "And will be my best friend."

"And it will be *one* of her best friends, because of course I'm her best friend at the moment."

Franny snickered at that and then eyed her father as if calculating how much more work we had to do in order to get him to say yes. He was staring at me with those eyes and took a sip of coffee as Franny whispered in my ear, "We almost have him. Just say, 'Please, Daddy.'"

We were on a roll now, and I didn't even think as I blurted out, "Please, Daddy. We promise to . . ."

The words died on my lips as Jameson choked on the coffee he was drinking from his mug. He set it down so hard that some of the dark liquid sloshed over the rim of it. "I'll consider it," he grumbled.

A low whistle came from the doorway, and there stood Callahan. He must have seen the look in Jameson's eyes, because he called to Franny, "Let's go look around the house to see if there's a place to put a bunny cage while Ms. Darling and your dad discuss it, huh?"

"Uncle Cal, you really think I'm going to get one?!" Franny skipped out of the room while Jameson's eyes stayed glued to me, like I was all he could see, and he wanted to see everything.

"Jameson, I'm sorry. You don't really have to get her one—"

"Say it again."

"What?"

"Beg again, Ms. Darling, and you might get exactly what you want from me."

I chuckled but felt his command shoot directly to my core because I had no self-control. Still, I tried to make a joke of it because maybe that's all this was anyway. "Oh sure. Should I say *daddy* too?"

"I'm not opposed to it." His voice was full of gravel.

"Please, Daddy."

That must have pushed him over the edge, because he sucked on his teeth and slowly reached behind himself to remove the gun holstered at his back, placing it on the desk with a heavy thud that echoed through the room. Then his fingers went to his belt, and I watched how he loosened it with measured precision.

"Bend over the desk, Mia Darling. You've been a bad girl today."

"Bad enough that you're going to punish me?" I raised an eyebrow now, because I couldn't stop myself from being defiant with him. I grinned, planting my hands on my hips instead of obeying him outright. His eyes flared at my challenging him.

He was so used to being in charge and in control that I think he expected me to submit easily every time. Did he ever let go of the reins? Would he with me—just a little, so that I could worship the man he didn't let many see?

"Maybe I should get on my knees instead? Apologize for making you agree to a bunny or . . ." I stepped forward slowly, raising my dress a little as I did. "Maybe I should show you how thankful I am that you're the kind of father Franny deserves."

His jaw ticked, his hands curling at his sides, belt dangling in one. "I don't need you on your knees."

"Why not?" I stepped closer then and dropped to them in front of him. He sucked in a breath when I brushed my fingers over the expensive fabric of his slacks. "You don't like rewards when you've been a good boy?"

"Fuck." He swore, his voice hoarse as he stared down at me with a raw hunger in his eyes. He wanted this as much as I wanted to give it to him. "Mia . . ."

He said my name in warning, but my hands were already working on the zipper. When I wrapped my hands around his cock, he didn't protest, only groaned. I leaned forward to taste the precum that was already building at the tip, and his hand went into my hair immediately.

I dragged my lips over as much of him as I could fit in my mouth and squeezed the base of him while I listened to the way he hummed my name in a sort of reverence. I looked up at him and saw how his blue eyes had deepened, how he watched my every movement as he let me set the pace.

I only was able to taste him in the back of my throat three or four times before he gripped my hair and yanked me back. "I'll come down your throat if you don't stop."

"That's what I was aiming for, *Daddy*," I said, licking my bottom lip where I knew my spit would glisten over it.

He watched how my tongue darted out, and then he shook his head. "You're fucking trouble, Darling."

"Am I?" I smirked and—so fast—his hand went my throat

and maneuvered that belt around me. He wrapped it around my neck, pulling the leather through the buckle and tightening it so it was snug against my skin. His eyes were trained on me as if assessing whether what we were doing was okay.

With him and only him, I found it was. I trusted Jameson and knew he'd always keep me safe. Restraint with him brought pleasure, rather than fear.

"So much so that I should keep you leashed, baby. Seeing you on my cock has me wanting you with a damn collar for me to make sure you don't ever do that with another man."

"Hmmm. I don't think you could make this leash worth it." I tapped the leather and taunted him enough that his jaw ticked.

He yanked it a little, and I felt how it cinched on my neck, how he had full control now, how he could make me do just about anything he wanted. It should have scared me. I didn't like being restrained in any way.

Yet, with him, I felt a thrill and completely safe.

"I'll show you it's always worth it with me, Mia." He leaned close and whispered in my ear, "Now, slide your dress off."

I had a flowy white halter one on, and it was easy enough to untie and drop. I kept my eyes on him the whole time, watching how his gaze dragged all over my body. I shivered at the sensation, feeling it heat every part of me.

"Now, I want you to walk over to that desk, Darling. Nice and slow so I can watch." When I turned to do it, he stopped me with a yank. "Better yet, crawl."

Guess I had no other choice considering he had promised me a bunny.

33

Jameson

MOST EVERYONE PROBABLY WOULD tell me that I shouldn't have been fucking around with my daughter's teacher. It was reckless, but I didn't care anymore.

Mia was more than a teacher or a nanny to us. She was mine now. She'd given Franny a reason to smile every day, and she gave me a partner in the world.

And although she may have thought we were hiding the relationship, it was pretty clear to everyone in the household, I think even my daughter, that I wanted her in our lives for good. I wanted her to be mine *always*.

And I wanted to share every single part of the day with her, including the ones where I should have been working rather than cutting her teaching time short so that I could bend her over a desk for manipulating me into getting a damn bunny.

Fuck, she looked good in her lace thong and bra as she dropped to her knees without so much as one protest when I requested that she crawled.

Her ass was raised in the air and swayed with each movement she took toward the desk. I wanted to freeze that moment in time, wanted to fucking film it so I could rewatch it over and over again. The way her back arched and the way her hair fell over her bare back as I held my belt like a leash had me wanting to get on my knees too and take her right there on the floor. "I swear you're going to get anything you want from me any time you ask if you do this, darling devil. It's unfair."

She chuckled and stopped in front of the desk, not rising up yet as she looked over her shoulder. "Promise?"

I shook my head and tried my best to refrain from just giving in to what my dick wanted. "We'll see. Get on the desk, Mia. I still owe you your damn punishment."

She faked a pout before standing and then putting her hands onto the desk so she could bend forward. I moved close, letting my cock rub against her back and ass. "You feel what you do to me, right?"

"Jameson . . ." I yanked the belt tight, not wanting her to say a thing.

"You do this"—I rocked my cock against her—"every time you walk in a room, and when you call me daddy, I want to lose control." I stepped back then to test how wet her entrance was and chuckled at how it dripped over my fingers. "It seems you have the same problem, huh? We can't have that when others are around, though, can we? For that, you need to learn a lesson, right?"

She moaned as my fingers slid inside her and nodded. "I'm a teacher, after all, Jameson. I know when a lesson must be taught."

"Fuck, that's right, baby." I loved how she leaned into me punishing her. I shoved her down onto the desk so her ass was out and then I smacked it twice. The globe reddened immediately with my handprint, and when she yelped, I tightened my hold on the leash. "Be good girl, Mia. Take your punishment like you want. Moan for me or don't make a sound at all."

She moaned as I massaged her reddened cheek and then gasped out my name as I smacked it.

Again and again.

She even started to chant that she wanted more and more. "I want all of it, Jameson. All of you." I lost myself in her desire and my own desire for her. I slid my fingers from her pussy and lined my cock up at her entrance. "I need you, baby," I told her.

She begged for it, chanting "please" as I let the belt slide from her neck so that I could wind it around my hand.

I thrust my cock into her, not able to wait another second, just as I smacked her ass with my belt-wrapped hand.

"Oh, God. Jameson. It's too good."

"No. You've been bad, remember? So bad that you get it good, huh? So much of a darling that you're my devil." I pulled out and thrust in again and again. Smacking her each time. "Remember that you are *my* devil. That I fucking need you, Mia. Need this. Always."

Her pussy clenched around my cock then like she just might need me too.

34

Mia

I TRULY BELIEVE IF someone told Jameson Knight—the man who carried a pistol like it was an extra appendage and took care of men like Trent easily—that he'd be spending his Friday morning with us arguing over bunny necessities, he would have had them evaluated for head trauma.

"Why does it smell like a barn down this hall?" His voice carried into the study as I placed the water dispenser onto the side of the wired cage. My classroom space did sort of smell a bit like hay, but there was no way he was going to object when he saw Franny's face.

He stepped in, holding that steaming cup of espresso he always had, and wrinkled his nose. "Mia, I know I agreed to Archer taking you both to get this thing . . . but is it supposed to smell like that?"

Franny popped up from moving the shavings around. "Daddy, meet Wednesday!" She pointed excitedly toward the black bunny she'd picked out and beamed. "I think she likes her new home since she pooped three times already."

Jameson blinked twice and then looked at me. "The rodent smells."

I responded with a saccharine tone. “Your garage smells like oil and gasoline and is full of dirty metal bikes.”

“My Ducati isn’t just a bike.” He looked ready to fight. “And it doesn’t defecate in a room next to my cigars.”

“Your cigars in your office are just fine.” I held up a hand before he continued. “Don’t forget, you agreed to this.”

“I was emotionally blackmailed,” he grumbled, but Franny had picked up the bunny and walked over to her dad.

“Want to hold her, Dad?”

Before Jameson could say no, she was holding out the squirming ball of fur, so he had to take it. Nothing else could be done when Franny looked at him like that.

He sighed, muttering under his breath as he shot daggers my way before he set down his espresso and took the bunny. Never had I seen him look so uncomfortable. His posture was stiff, his brow furrowed, his arms outstretched. “She won’t stop wiggling.”

“Hold her bottom, Daddy. She’s a baby. She needs cuddles. Mia, hurry! We need a picture of Daddy and me with Wednesday.” She stood next to her dad and smiled big, pulling the rabbit close to Jameson’s stomach.

I grabbed my cell and snapped a picture just as Jameson’s eyes widened. “She just peed on me.”

“Really? I think that means she likes you!” Franny said, vibrating with excitement, swiping Wednesday back from her dad to go set her in the cage.

I walked up to Jameson and pecked him on the cheek as he told me, “Remind me again why we need a bunny.”

“According to Franny, I’m lonely in this house.”

“I’ll show you lonely in your bedroom tonight, Darling. You owe me.”

I patted his cheek. “Fine. You probably earned it by being such a good *daddy*.”

He groaned at my innuendo, but then his phone buzzed. He frowned when he read the text, and before even looking up, he stepped back and murmured, “It’ll be a late dinner for Franny and me. Valerie’s coming over.”

My world screeched to a halt. The record scratched, time stopped, and my bubble popped. “Everything okay?” How could I ask anything else? The words *Are you still going to sleep with her?* weren’t exactly appropriate considering he didn’t know I would listen to them before in the first place.

Plus, this was supposed to be casual considering there was a contract in place. I knew that. I’d told myself that time and time again, even though I was playing pretend that this was the perfect relationship half the time. “No worries. I’ll just eat here, or Archer and I can go grab—”

“Eat dinner here. I don’t see why he’s needed.” Of course he didn’t. His jealousy was warranted, but mine wouldn’t be.

So, I let him walk away and let the unease fester under my skin for the rest of the day. Franny and I took care of Wednesday, and I pretended my heart wasn’t in my throat while we had a tea party with the fluff ball.

When Rosy came to collect Franny, she eyed me warily and mouthed, “Talk later?”

She knew what I knew. Valerie was back.

As the sun dipped low in the sky, I sulked back to my bedroom and stared out at the trees. I’d have a life after this, one I could rebuild with my sister from a huge payday, but I wouldn’t have Franny. Or Jameson. Or whatever this imperfect life was.

And I hated myself for wanting it, for wanting something that was out of my reach. For wanting someone to want me the way I wanted them.

I’d wanted my parents to love me the way I loved them too. But that didn’t happen.

A sense of needing to belong hit me so strong that I found myself dialing my mother's number.

Two rings. It's as far as I always got before the call was ignored.

So easily, I was dismissed. So easily, I didn't fit into their life.

I needed that reminder, and a reminder from Jameson too.

I could have covered the vent. Or gone to shower, but I sat there listening after I'd told Archer I didn't need company and had eaten dinner by myself.

Sure enough, her laughter bubbled up through the vent, and she murmured his name affectionately. Immediately, my body tightened.

This was wrong. Completely and utterly wrong to be listening to them. I got up and stomped over to the bathroom to undress. I threw my clothes off angrily, frustrated that he was about to do what he always did with her. I could hear it in her tone, in how her laugh dropped low.

I shoved my panties down just as I heard his deep voice command something. I slammed the bathroom door because I knew that tone. Instead of turning the shower on, I snatched a towel to wrap around myself and headed back through that door so I could listen for just one more minute.

Maybe I'd hear something that would totally turn me off so I didn't have to think about him with other women anymore. Hopefully, he'd call her a terrible name and that'd be the end of it. Sitting on my bed, I leaned toward the vent on the back wall.

"I know it's been a while for us since you've been busy . . . but absence makes the heart grow fonder and all, right, Jameson?" She had that familiar rasp to her voice like she was ready for him to have his head between her legs, ready for him to take her roughly the way I was used to hearing.

"Does it, Val?" His tone sounded especially cruel tonight, probably because he'd missed having her like he always did. He seemed to enjoy commanding her in a way he never did me. "I'm not sure you missed me at all after I found out who you spent your time with a week and a half ago. After hearing that information, I'm quite sure I didn't miss you at all."

"Jameson, what do you mean?"

"You went to Trent's the night I turned you away. Did you not?"

"I . . . Oh, Jameson. I'm so sorry about Trent. Please. I shouldn't have ever talked with him. Just choke me, okay? Put your hands on my neck and shut me up if you don't want me to talk. Come on. I want it. Please. Want me over your desk again? I'll turn around. I'll be quiet."

There was silence, and it stretched so long that I imagined he might have been doing what she asked. I could only imagine if it were me, how he'd bend me over, how he'd stare at me, how he'd grab me right before he entered me.

But it wasn't me down there in that office.

It was another woman.

I ran to the bathroom and turned on the shower to scorch my skin, to try to gain control of the anger. If he wanted someone else, I didn't need him, I told myself.

Instead, I could get myself off. I plunged my fingers inside myself as pleasure but also jealousy coursed through me. I hissed at how easily my fingers slipped in. My emotions pumped adrenaline through my veins and unhinged some part of me that I couldn't control. I almost growled when my thumb moved over my clit in the same way he would have done for me, and then I moaned at the feeling of imagining his fingers instead of mine pumping into me.

I thought of him, and I couldn't stop. It was the mixture of emotions I'd been trying to avoid. I knew I shouldn't have any sort of feelings for him. He was supposed to just be my boss after all, but they were growing in me all the same. I pushed myself closer and closer to the edge, not able to think of anything but his piercing, blue-eyed stare.

I lost myself in the tornado of pleasure that was laced with a fear that I'd fallen too far with him already. But the white-hot euphoria that came with thinking his fingers were curling into me instead of my own caused an orgasm to lash through me so fast that I nearly blacked out.

With my breath coming much too fast and the water running cold over my body, I heard someone pound on my door.

35

Mia

"ONE SECOND." I SCRAMBLED out of the shower, grabbing a towel to wrap it around me. Only the briefest of moments had passed when I barreled out of the bathroom, but nothing could have shocked me more than watching as my bedroom door crashed open.

"Jameson! What on earth are you doing?"

"Who the fuck is in here with you?" He stormed in and immediately went to my bathroom to search it before he looked under my bed, then in my closet, and then strode over to my open window to look out it.

"What are you talking about?" I walked over to look out the window with him, clutching my towel. Did he think there was an intruder? Was someone really out in the forest like I'd thought days before? "Did someone break in?"

"Darling devil . . ." He turned to me, and his eyes were brimming with anger so dark that I couldn't even see where his pupils began. "Do not lie to me when I ask again. Who was with you? Archer? You had dinner with him. I'm going to fucking kill him."

"Why would he be in my bedroom?"

My confusion must have pushed him over the edge, because

one of those calloused hands went to my neck to shove me up against the wall. His grip was firm as he leaned in close. "I heard you through the fucking walls."

He must have heard me moaning in the shower through the vents.

"Oh God. I moaned that loud?" I said mostly to myself, but his grip on my neck tightened, and he leaned closer.

"And now I see your cheeks are flushed. You look like you've been properly fucked. And your lower lip is swollen like you've been biting it. So, where the fuck is Archer? Did you sleep with him?"

"Jameson, seriously? You have some audacity to mention him when you were down there with Valerie! I should be asking you if you slept with her . . . Again!"

"What?"

"I smell her perfume all over you, Jameson," I whispered, trying to explain away the fact that I'd heard them down there. How could I admit the rest? But then I knew I had to be honest, knew that if there was going to be something real between us, I didn't want it based on lies. He needed to know. I sighed and closed my eyes. "And I can hear most everything in this room if I'm listening. The vents connect, which is how you must have heard me."

Recognition registered in his eyes, and they hardened as he asked, "And exactly why were you listening?"

I looked away as shame burned on my cheeks. "Because you said Valerie was going to be here, and I wanted to know if you'd do the same as you've always done." I shrugged.

"Darling Mia. You've listened to us before." He sighed out as if he pitied me. I just nodded, not wanting to speak it out loud. A wave of emotions flickered over his face. "Most people would die before they admitted that to me."

"And do you think that's because you wouldn't let them live after eavesdropping?"

He hummed. "You aren't the least bit scared of me now, are you, Darling?"

At one point, I had been. Now, I trusted him with my life more than I did any other person. So I just whispered, "Should I be?"

"No." He pulled at his hair. "And it's fucking bad that I don't want you to be. You should realize I'm not a good man, realize that I'm asking you if you fucked Archer because I'm going to beat him within an inch of his life if you did."

"He's a friend of yours, Jameson. We've been over this," I reminded him.

He didn't even blink as he continued to stare at me. His icy blue eyes told me all I needed to know.

"*And* he takes care of Franny and this house when you're away. He's irreplaceable."

Jameson shook his head slowly. "No, Mia. *You're* irreplaceable. And it's a problem because normally I operate under the belief that any one of my staff can be replaced at any time."

"You need people that you care about and respect as your employees."

"No. I need hard workers. Not people who cause weakness."

His words were cruel. "You think I'm weak."

He growled. "You're not understanding. You're *my* weakness. You're now a person that any one of my enemies can target, and they could cause hell on earth quite literally if they hurt you." He took a deep breath. "You're also the person a friend of mine or even a trusted employee could look at wrong and I'd dispose of them."

"Jameson, that's—"

"The truth. Like I said, you're irreplaceable now. You're mine. Not just my daughter's teacher or my employee, darling Mia, but mine. And I won't share. Not with Archer or anyone else." He searched my eyes as he stepped forward, like he was looking for reassurance, but I wouldn't give it to him quite yet. "Tell me you understand."

"Are you mine, then, too?" I asked as Valerie's perfume wafted in the air between us. His hand skirted up my thigh past my towel to my pussy. The embarrassment of being soaked all over again was evidence enough that I needed to distance myself. Yet, I was too close to consider it now and couldn't stop from mewling out his name after how sensitive my body was from touching myself moments ago.

"Your pussy is still pulsing. Still wants more." He circled my clit with his thumb. I tried to move, but he had me firmly against that wall, going nowhere.

"I already got off," I said now that fury and jealousy were surfacing with the pleasure he was creating. "I'm sure you did too."

"What the fuck is that supposed to mean?" His eyes widened for a fraction of a second before he thrust a finger into me.

"I told you—I listened. I heard her beg you, Jameson."

"And . . ." he coaxed me, rolling this thumb over my arousal.

"And I didn't want to hear the rest. So, I went to the shower and got *myself* off."

"So let me get this straight." I heard the scrape of his five-o'clock shadow as he roughly dragged his hand over it. "You touched yourself thinking I was with another woman when I practically tore through the walls to get into this room thinking you were with another man?"

"Guess we handle our jealousy a bit differently within this convenient employer-employee arrangement we have." I tried for casual, hoping to remind us both that this was only supposed to ever last the rest of the summer.

"Convenient arrangement?" Jameson tore his hand away from me and then swore fluently over and over. "That's what you call this? A *convenient arrangement*, Mia? It's a fucking *obsession*. It's not fucking convenient that I can barely see straight thinking another man had you." His thumb swept up to my jaw and pushed my face to tilt toward his. He leaned down so that his lips were just a breath from mine.

He looked so wild and out of control that I knew he hated it. "Does that mean you want this between us to stop?"

"No. It means I want to give you whatever you want to make sure you don't look at another man other than me ever again," he rasped, his voice strained and almost primal. Like it took everything in him not to unleash whatever rage was underneath. And I didn't know if it was just the heat of the moment, but I wanted to believe him.

A part of me hoped he meant it.

And a part of me was scared that even if he did mean it, I'd never fit in enough to find my place here. "Then I want it rough."

"What?"

" . . . like you've done with her."

"Mia, you've had it rough from me already," he said as if to pacify me.

So I repeated, "Like you've done with her."

I wanted to feel like I belonged like she did, like I could fit into his world, like I could have all of him even if just for a moment.

His eyes locked on mine, sharp and searching, as if trying to make sense of my request. As if to make sure he heard me correctly. But then, a realization seemed to dawn. An understanding settled across his features before he motioned me toward the door. He gave me a single, measured nod. "Let's go to the office then."

I walked out of the room in just my towel, my head held high. I wasn't going to cower or hide my desires for a second longer. I'd done that enough and it got me here, to a place where the man I was falling for was sleeping with another woman.

But right before I passed him in the doorway, he leaned in and murmured, “I’m going to fuck you just like I have her, darling devil, and still, you’re going to learn it will be completely different because it’s *you*, Mia. You’re the one that belongs by my side. No one else.”

36

Jameson

HER DARK CURLS DRIPPED water onto her shoulders as she stood before me in my office, her cheeks flushed, her lips apart in anticipation, and her skin pebbling with goose bumps. She stood there unsure, as if another woman could take her place. As if I didn't think about her all fucking day.

As if I'd let Valerie come between us. I'd ended our arrangement the day I'd had relations with Mia. The only reason she was brought to my house was for me to question her on her ties with Trent. I'd had my men drag her away after.

It was then I heard Mia's soft moans, though through a vent, no less. And I lost all control. "My darling devil." I said it to her every now and then to coax a little of the sass from her and as a term of endearment to remind her that she was as bad as she was good. Sometimes I think she hated that last name of hers. Sometimes she wanted to lash out, and with me, she could.

But what she didn't realize was I used it as a reminder for myself too. A devil resided beside the darling that she was. It slumbered peacefully because she patted the devil's head and kept it docile.

Yet, when my sweet darling was provoked, was hit on, was in

any sort of jeopardy, the devil beside her awoke. And that devil was *me.*

Vicious. Unapologetic. And barely contained lately.

When it came to her, I was unhinged. I knew it. My men knew it. Soon, I was going to make sure the whole world knew it. "You know the mafia has a name for the women they deem theirs. Untouchables. And our syndicate has a name for them too. The Sanctums. Do you think I gave Valerie that title?"

"I don't know," she murmured, shrugging her shoulders. "Did you?"

"It's fucking coveted, Mia. So much so that not even Lex had that from me. Franny does. It's why I've ripped apart the Irish and am ripping apart a cartel for coming for her. Olive is a Sanctum from her own birthright, Pink from Bane."

"And why not Valerie?"

"Because she was a means to an end. Nothing more."

"You took her every other day, right in this room."

"I did. Just like you want me to take you, right?" She had to understand that she was nothing like Valerie was to me.

She dragged her teeth across her bottom lip before nodding. "Do you want me to turn around?"

Fuck. She wasn't going to let this go, and so I had to indulge her. "You listened to us." I raised an eyebrow. "You tell me."

"You told her to turn every single time, like it was your favorite position, and then . . ."

"And then what, Mia? I fucked her rough enough for you to hear?"

She leaned against the desk I'd taken another woman on and stared at me with hunger in her eyes rather than jealousy. "Loud enough to know you don't fuck me like that."

"Goddamn it, Mia." I combed a hand through my hair and pulled on it in frustration. "Do you want me to hold nothing back from you ever?"

Her answer was fast. “Yes.”

I growled not just at her response but at how quick my dick hardened at her giving me free rein.

“I want you to take me like you’re holding nothing back, like there’s no hidden agenda.”

“You think I have that with you?”

“You’re not reserved with Valerie. Almost as if she knows who you are and you give that to her without apology. I want Jameson Knight without restraint tonight.”

Giving her what she wanted was not what either of us needed right now. Valerie’s negligence had caused more betrayal. It had infuriated me right before I’d thought Mia was with Archer. My composure was gone for the night. I wanted to hurt someone, not make them feel good. I wanted to get out the pent-up aggression inside me, not give Mia the love she actually deserved.

I pulled my Glock from my waistband, ready to wind down for the night and send her back to her room alone. I was about to set it on the table and pour myself three fingers of whiskey, but her eyes widened and flared with desire at seeing the weapon in my hand.

I chuckled in disbelief that a woman with such innocence seemed to have a kink for such violence and danger. “You look at my weapon like it might turn you on, darling devil.”

She didn’t deny it. “I’ve seen what they can do as of late. They’re tools that can hurt, but they’re also tools that can protect. Women seem to need that more than I ever thought.”

I hummed, remembering how she’d confided in me about the coach I was looking into. She hadn’t given me his name, but I was going to find it. And I was going to exact what I thought necessary, knowing he took advantage of her. I turned my gun in my hand, back and forth. “You think it’s the weapon or the person who hurts or protects?”

"Both," she murmured.

I stared at her and saw vulnerability there that I wanted to take advantage of but also wanted to erase so that she could be stronger than anyone around her, so that I could protect her from even myself.

Holding her gaze, I told her, "This is a bad idea."

"You think I've got the bad ideas even though you just fucked another woman down here?" Her question was meant to cut sharp and quick, to piss me off, and she knew it. "Was she a better idea, then?"

She had to be kidding me. I stalked toward her, Glock at my side. "What the fuck would make you think that?"

"It's either that, or you just can't go again with me." She even lifted her chin as if she wanted to taunt me. "And in that case, I should find someone else."

"Careful, Mia."

"Or what? You'll put me in my place?" Her eyes flicked toward the gun, and her hands tightened on the side of the desk, gripping it in either fear or anticipation. I hoped it was both.

When my chest touched hers, I leaned down and whispered, "You and I both know, against you, the Glock in my hand has all the danger of a Bible because I'd never hurt you with it."

She licked her lips as I walked over and put the barrel to her chin before dragging it down toward her cleavage, pushing the towel apart so that it fell to the floor. She didn't move to cover herself. Instead, she sat on my desk like she belonged there, naked and on display just for me. And when I dragged the metal over her nipples, they pebbled as she gasped. Her eyes fluttered closed and she arched into it.

My will to stop was long gone. My hand acted on its own accord, sliding the gun across her stomach, her hips, and down her outer thigh only to inch back up her inner thigh and watch how she shivered. "Even now, Mia, you don't look at all concerned. Tell me . . . what's more dangerous here between us? My hand that holds the trigger, the gun between your legs, or the pussy that brings me to my knees time and time again?"

I knelt to watch the barrel encircle her clit, just for a moment, just so I could see the goddess that Mia was. She rode the metal, bringing her hands up to comb through her hair as she murmured that it felt so good, so different, so right between her legs.

Could a man be jealous of his own gun? I pulled it away and set it on the desk so I could put my mouth on her instead. She tasted of metal and sweetness. Just how I wanted her to.

But she yanked at my hair and shook her head at me. "No, I want you. Not your mouth." She wanted what I'd given Valerie, and she pushed me back to ask pointedly again, "Do you want me to turn around?"

I stood and looked down at her. "Mia, fucking you like I did her isn't—"

She cut me off. "Tell me to turn around."

"Turn around, then, and be quiet," I ground out, unbuckling my belt.

"Yes," she murmured as she bent over the desk. I got to see her flawless skin glimmer in the low lights of my study and her ass swell as she bent over my desk. She glanced over her shoulder at me. "That's what I heard every time you took her."

I gripped her curls and balled them in a fist to lean over her. "You're not her, Mia."

"It's fine, Jameson." She gave me a small smile, as if I needed reassurance. "I liked listening to you, liked imagining I was her, that you'd touch me the same way. And I touched myself every time. It was wrong, but—"

"It *was* wrong." Didn't she realize I barely even pictured Val when I had been fucking her? We were both getting off, but it was nothing more. With Mia, I wanted to freeze time and take in every damn movement she made, every facial expression, every sound, every touch. I wanted to memorize all of it.

I pulled my cock from my trousers and lined myself up to her entrance. I didn't give her time to adjust but instead slammed into her hard, rough. Raw.

Her walls pulsed tightly around me as she gasped, but I didn't stop. I thrust in again and again. "Utterly. Fucking. Wrong."

"Jameson, oh, God," she cried out. "I'm sorry. You're right. You're right."

I grabbed one of her hips and tightened my hold in her hair, burying myself deeper and deeper with each thrust. I hated her apologies. I didn't want them. I wanted her to realize the difference between her and every woman I'd had before her. That none of them mattered. That only she did. But I was too lost to explain and maybe too damn scared she didn't feel the same. "Shut that mouth or I'll gag you."

And I buried myself deep in her again, beyond what I did with anyone else, beyond what most women could endure. Yet Mia met my thrusts by ramming her pussy back onto me.

Over and over again.

Our skin slapped together, our breath heaved together, and our bodies felt like they molded together.

I came deep into her center and didn't pull back at all as I did. I wanted to mark her and own her in every way I could.

We were slumped over the desk, both breathing hard as I murmured into her ear, "I fuck other women without an agenda, Mia, because with them I have *nothing* to lose." I loosened my grip on her hair and combed my fingertips through it softly. "But with you, I'm scared to lose *everything*. Scared to lose you . . . My darling Mia. My darling devil. My darling everything. *My* Sanctum."

I'd informed the Diamonds after having her on the motorcycle. All but Mia knew it. And I wasn't even sure she heard me say it as I flipped her on the desk then and kissed that mouth hard enough that she had to know I owned it and she owned me.

She'd be protected always now.

I feathered kisses down her neck and collarbone and all the way down her stomach before I pulled her to the edge of the desk and knelt before her where she told me, "I don't think I can take more."

She started to sit up, but my hand went to her neck, pushing her back down on my desk as I told her, "I don't think so, pretty girl. Tap my wrist if you can't take it, but otherwise, in here, I say when this ends." My hand clamped down hard enough that I knew her ability to breathe was gone.

Her eyes widened, but I don't think it was from panic but rather from pleasure. She didn't tap my wrist, just held it as I hooked her leg over my shoulder and thrust my tongue into her, working her swollen clit with my thumb as I did.

I tasted my arousal with hers, my damn seed on her walls, and my cock hardened all over again.

I lapped and licked at her center, humming out my approval so it could vibrate through her before I rose up to hover over her. Her breathing was shallow, and her lips parted just a sliver. "Open wider, baby."

She listened with her legs and her mouth, and I slid back into her slowly, inch by inch, as I spit down into her mouth, watching our mixture fall in. I pinched her clit and pulled out to ram into her this time as I let her breathe, swallow, and taste us.

I memorized her: how her eyes dilated, how the blush crept to her face, and how her pussy felt on my cock.

37

Mia

I GASPED FOR OXYGEN, for life, for relief, but searing, knee-buckling, soul-shattering ecstasy flew through my veins instead. Tears filled my eyes as I cried out, and Jameson let more swears fly as he pinched my clit and pushed me over the edge again.

I convulsed around him, my body putting its last bit of energy into trying to keep him in me. Instead, he scooped me up and carried me to my room. "Shhh, now, darling Mia. I've got you."

I turned into him. "I feel too much for you, Jameson. Way too much."

"And still I want you to feel more."

I fell into the blue of his eyes, into the emotion that was there, where I felt safe now. Where I felt like I could belong and be whole. "I feel everything already." I didn't say I loved him aloud, but I knew I did.

"I know, baby. I know. I got you. You're mine now. Only mine." He didn't say he loved me either, but I wanted to believe that's what he meant.

And when he laid me down and tucked the blankets around me, he hovered over me, one hand on each side of my face on the pillow. "I didn't touch Val tonight, Mia. But she was here only because I found out she betrayed me almost as badly as Lex."

His voice held pain, and I didn't know how to react. The woman had been close to him. My words were measured as I asked, "What do you mean?"

"She put her jealousy before Fran and ran to Trent to tell him about you women here the other night."

"No," I whispered.

"It may have been unintentional like she claims, but I don't care. She jeopardized your safety and the other women. And it's shown me once again that she could jeopardize Franny's. I had her taken away." There was pain in his voice, and I understood it. He wanted his daughter protected at all costs and felt like he'd been betrayed time and time again. "Just promise me you'll always put Franny first. Even before me." His words held weight and foreboding, but I didn't care.

I knew what I'd do for Franny always. "I wouldn't have it any other way."

He shook his head as if he were working through some sort of turmoil. "I'm telling you now. We should stop this. If you fall for me and something happens to you . . . This isn't the life for you. Don't fall for me, Mia."

My heart stuttered at his words. I rejected them immediately, but I didn't say it out loud. Instead, I just told him, "Probably not something you should worry about, Jameson." My fingers ghosted over his chest and his heart. "I do what I want, when I want, when I'm ready. Got it?"

He kissed me then, softly, slowly, caringly. And then he sank into bed next to me to kiss my shoulders, my hair, my cheeks, and my neck before he tucked me up against him so he could hold me through the night. I didn't ask him any more questions because I didn't need to know any of them right then.

Maybe I was lost in my love for him or blinded by it.

For five more days, we acted like things hadn't changed.

He took us to the country club and invited me to meals that I ate with Franny and him. His mother even came to one, but she mostly made small talk with me while Jameson sat quietly. He worked all other parts of the day, men filtering in and out of his office. Some were dragged to the basement, and they never seemed to come out.

Rosy and Archer told me that Val's betrayal ran deep and that they didn't want to talk about it either. Jameson didn't accompany me to the range for shooting, so Archer went with me instead.

We acted like nothing had changed. Although it had.

He was quieter. Lost in his thoughts.

I was too.

I'd fallen in love with him, and I was scared he knew it, scared he couldn't fall back in love with me.

Another woman had betrayed him, and I think it proved to him that I couldn't be trusted no matter how much he wanted to believe that I could be. He slept with me, but his guard was up. I felt him building walls and growing his distance even as he smiled with me and Franny throughout the day.

After five days, he went to attend a meeting outside the house, and I sat there in the evening wondering what I was doing. I needed to make plans, needed to face reality that this position was going to come to an end, and I wouldn't be in Paradise any longer.

Nothing was real if Jameson couldn't be real with me, and I needed that more than anything to stay.

I was sulking in the hall when Franny rounded the corner, squealing at me. "My momma was here today . . . in her room."

"What?" I glanced around immediately, that feeling of being watched from the forest back with force, but I tried to be rational. "Honey, what room?"

"The room next to Daddy's, silly. It's my momma's room. In case she ever comes home, Daddy said."

"But, baby . . . your momma being home . . . that's not possible." I got down on one knee with my heart racing, my pulse thumping at the idea that Franny thought she was seeing her mother when I knew the truth. Jameson hadn't told her about her mother passing, and I'd have to be the one to do so if he didn't do so soon enough.

"Of course it is. She's as pretty as she always was, Mia." Her smile was so happy, so genuine, that I started to get concerned.

"Is your mommy still here?"

"Yep. In her room."

And then Archer rounded the corner, and his face said it all. It looked as if he'd seen a ghost. "Archer?"

"Jameson is on his way. He said for you to stay here."

But then Lex Knight appeared just down the hall.

And I lost my breath.

My whole world tilted, throwing me off it.

She was freaking stunning. In every way I wasn't. Long blonde hair that had a perfect wave, which framed her angular face. So symmetrical, with high cheekbones and full lips that were painted bloodred to match the red dress she wore. I saw where Franny got her nose, her cheeks, her body frame.

She was perfect, but in a vicious way.

"Mia Darling, come have a drink with me." She said my name like Satan might have said Eve's name. With a lure of sweetness laced with the risk of death.

"Archer, take Franny to play outside," I told him. Lex may be Franny's mother, but that girl had my heart, and I wouldn't let anyone, even her mom, hurt her if I could help it.

"Mia," he warned, but when I looked at him, he knew I meant it. And I hoped he saw the concern in my eyes, saw that we protected Franny at all costs.

"Please." In that moment, I saw Archer choose between his boss and me. He held out his hand to Franny, and she took it to skip away with him.

"Be careful. Xavier's there, but . . . be careful."

I breathed a sigh of relief as I watched them retreat down the hallway.

"She's growing up so quickly, isn't she?" Lex said as if she'd been with her daughter every single day since she was born, like she hadn't left at all. "Shall we?" She raised a brow at me and then turned on her red-bottom heels to walk toward that room, toward the one door he'd never opened for me.

And so I walked, one step at a time—my heart beating, my knees shaking, my world crumbling—to that room.

She didn't wait for me but left the door cracked open. And still I froze there, my heart pounding as my eyes caught on the intricate carvings swirling like vines around the knob, coiling toward the keyhole like they'd been guarding this secret.

My fingers trembled as I pushed the door open, and the smell of patchouli and jasmine with a hint of citrus hit me. It was the type of perfume that lingered, stuck, and embedded on a place and never let go.

It smelled of her and not at all of me.

I stepped in, slow and deliberate, and her dark eyes met mine from across the room. She sat at a window seat, an oak table next to her with another empty chair across from that, waiting for me. The window was open, a breeze billowing through the white curtain as if to distract me from the dread that had slithered up my spine.

I heard Franny giggling outside, and Lex pointed to the chair. "Come and sit. Do you like tea?"

I glanced around to see if Xavier was anywhere to be found, but I didn't see him. "I don't bite, Mia," she informed me as if my waiting in the doorway was rude.

Either way, I wouldn't let her see that I feared her, so I moved to sit down and took the tea from the saucer. She smiled, and her eyes shifted to the garden below. "Did my daughter inform you that her mother was home?"

"She did. She seems excited."

She nodded, a small smile playing on her red lips. "I found out that Jameson never told her I was dead." I wanted to ask her how she'd found that out, but she tilted her head at me and asked, "It seems sort of like fate, doesn't it?"

Was she telling me that Jameson protecting his daughter from the pain of thinking she was dead was actually a blessing for them? She had to be kidding. "I'm not sure I understand, Ms. Kni—"

"Missus," she corrected. "And don't you? For a woman who's been sleeping with my husband, I'm guessing you know quite a lot about the situation." She may not have meant for the husband part to cut through my heart, but it did. She said it like it was completely normal, like they were still together.

And maybe they were. My mind was reeling, reconsidering, questioning everything.

"Jameson must think you're very good with her. My business . . . our business and the responsibilities of our family have kept me away." She fixed a piece of her blonde hair as she looked in the mirror before turning to me.

"I don't understand."

"Did he tell you I was dead?" Her smile was slow as the words dropped one by one like a ton of bricks on my heart. "He's had to have suspected for a while that I wasn't. Jameson was always smarter than most men. Then again, I did quite well orchestrating all this, if I do say so myself. Don't you agree?"

I didn't need to answer her. The way I pulled in air as if it were scarce and the world was disintegrating before my very eyes allowed her to draw her own conclusions.

She dragged a finger over the table. "He made this room for me when they moved in, you know? He had all my stuff packed up and brought in here. And I think he keeps every part of it immaculate not because he wants to preserve the memory of me. No, it's got to be because he believed I might come home one day . . . and here I am."

"I . . . don't understand." It was all I could say as I leaned back in my chair for support.

"Catch up, Mia. He'll be here soon, and I know he's going to be irate." She chuckled and rolled her eyes. "God, that man can get mad. He'll say this is calculated and manipulative, and of course it is, but honestly, who isn't? The man's been just as strategic as I have. Maybe more so."

I shook my head, wishing her away, wishing this whole stupid room away. "I wouldn't use the word *strategic* to describe him." If he'd known she was alive . . . that wouldn't be the word I'd use. Deceptive. Cruel. Ruthless. "Not strategic," I whispered again.

"Whatever." She shrugged. "He's made this completely and utterly way too complicated with the security he's implemented everywhere. He had to know my coming back was inevitable. I'm sure he actually wants that after how he pushed my family's company into a corner."

"I don't understand," I whispered. My mind scrambled to grasp what she was saying, but my heart was breaking at the same time.

"For a woman who's spread her legs so willingly, I'd expect you to know a bit more, Mia. Then again, you're sleeping with your boss after he drugged and kidnapped you." She sighed with the summary she painted, and I tried not to flinch at her words.

"That's not what is happening here."

"Isn't it?" She tilted her head. "You're sleeping with my *husband*."

"I didn't think he was a husband." The words bubbled out of me fast and almost hysterical. "I thought he was a widower."

"And instead you became a mistress." Her attack was snake-like, as if she'd been coiled up and ready to strike. Her bite was filled with poison, leaching all the trust I had in Jameson.

"It's not what I wanted." I knew that much even if the whole summer now seemed like more of a lie than any part of my life now. I'd tried to be so true to myself here and instead got pushed into being within a façade all over again.

"No matter. I'm okay with the little dalliances he may have with you and others, as you realize I'm Franny's mother and his wife." She gave me an almost sad smile, like she felt sorry for me, like I was now the secret they'd hide behind closed doors.

"For now, I think it's best I stay in this part of the house. Once Jameson and I work things out and talk through all this, I hope that will help you both." Although her words were meant to be kind, they were laced with condescension. I was playing checkers and she was playing chess, a hundred moves ahead and in a position to take my king before I even realized the game we were playing.

It wasn't a fair fight. She'd come with weapons and armor and ambushed me. I stood and started to back away toward the door. I needed to call Jameson, to check on Franny. I needed to pull apart the truth from the lies, separate my emotions from the reality of the situation.

I needed out of Paradise Grove.

Even as I backed away, she kept on. "Mia, marriages have ups and downs, right?" She sounded almost dejected now, and her lip poked out.

"Well, of course, but—"

"Did he tell you about me when you first moved in here?" Her eyes were laser sharp, focused on me now, searching for answers.

"I think it's best that you and Jameson discuss that." I tried to make sure my voice didn't shake as I walked toward the door. I was getting the hell away from her and from him. Away from this place where I'd been deceived and made to believe I was given a whole truth when I only got half of one. "I don't think I'll be here much longer."

And that's when I heard the low voice of the man I loved, but it was filled with an anger I didn't recognize. "Why the *fuck* are you in here?"

38

Mia

Of course Jameson was mad that I ventured into this room with her, that a truth had been uncovered that he didn't want me to know. He'd deceived me, had lied and twisted facts, but his only concern was where I was in his house?

I could have killed him.

I wanted to. I wanted him to understand and feel my pain, but I let the silence stretch instead. Let him see the wife he had behind me and watched how his face changed.

The fury growing in his eyes brought me a sliver of satisfaction and relief, but not much. He didn't gasp like he'd seen a ghost or even look at all surprised to see her. I hated that I'd been hoping all she said wasn't true, that I wanted to justify the connection we had with each other. It only took me looking at him to know she wasn't lying.

Jameson had kept all this from me.

"I think it's best I leave," I murmured, knowing they needed to talk more than I wanted to admit. Jameson and I would be done in the end anyway.

There was no repairing this.

"No." He stepped in front of me, his brow wrinkled like he was concerned now. "You're definitely not leaving this room,

Darling." Then he opened the door wide and looked at his wife. "*She* can and will."

"Jameson," Lex gasped, but a slow smile crossed her face as she stood. "You're not even going to welcome me into my own home."

"Get *out* of this room and wait downstairs to talk with me."

"My love, you don't have to do that. Mia understands." She folded her thin, manicured fingers together and looked at me. "Right, Mia? We spoke about the fact that we're still married."

Jameson's jaw moved, but he didn't deny it. He stood there and let his wife tell me that he was hers. Not mine.

Never had he been mine.

My heart froze, cracked, and shattered in front of both of them. It took all I had not to break down and cry. To grab at all the tiny pieces of myself I saw crumbling apart. But neither of them deserved my tears. I'll forever be happy that I was able to mutter, "Yes, I understand everything she said."

"Alexandra, get out of here or so help me God, I'll have you dragged out." Jameson's threat was quiet, but it echoed in the room with finality.

She tsked and smiled at me as she made her way to the door. "Told you he'd be mad. I know my husband so well." She patted his chest once, and he winced at her touch before she left us alone.

The word *husband* lingered in the air, ricocheting around my heart so loudly that I couldn't contemplate his reaction to her.

"What do you mean you *understand*, Mia Darling?" His words were measured as we stood there, facing off with each other.

He had the audacity to look hurt, to look like he was broken, like he had any right to feel anything at all.

"I understand that you're married," I stated, and was happy

that my voice didn't shake. "That you have a life with a kid and a *wife*."

That word choked me, and my hand flew to my mouth to hold back the sob. When he stepped forward, though, I jumped back, and his hands flew up like he wouldn't dare come near me if I didn't want him to. "Now, Mia . . ."

Oh God, I couldn't listen to an explanation. Not one word. I wanted no appeasements or rationalizations. I wanted to say my piece and leave. I deserved that at the very least. "You know, I thought maybe you'd get there. Start to share your life with me a little, and then *maybe* this room. But you weren't going to do any of that, were you?"

He frowned at me. "That's what you think?"

"It's what I *know*. You've never had the ability to trust me, or maybe you didn't care to, since you knew. You've known about her this whole time, haven't you? And you're just going to keep up this fucking power trip you all are on without thinking of the turmoil and destruction it causes. This syndicate isn't about protecting someone like me. I don't belong. You protect what's yours. *Adamantem infractum manet*."

"You think you're not mine." It wasn't a question but a statement that he said almost to himself as he rubbed his jaw. And then he stood there shaking his head over and over. He wanted to disagree with me, but then it was like recognition dawned, like reality set in. Maybe he finally got over the shock of actually seeing his wife return and he realized he could have the perfect home with all the partnerships and everything he wanted.

"Jameson, let's be honest with one another for once. This was never going to work because you couldn't trust me enough to make me yours."

"And you just expected that trust?"

"I told you everything! I was sleeping with you and—"

"And what? You thought I should tell you everything in return because we were sharing a bed?" His tone was cold as ice, pushing me away.

Good. I wanted his fury and his hate.

"Oh no, Jameson. I know you fuck every girl you want to in this house. I'm not special because of that. Quite the contrary, it seems." I lashed out at him like he did at me. We were both hurt, both swimming in our pain and trying to drag the other person down too.

"So quick to assume that, huh?"

"Well, you know I heard you and Valerie. Thank God I didn't have to hear you and your wife."

"Jesus fucking Christ." He shut his eyes and growled up to the ceiling like he couldn't bear any of this. "Darling Mia," he murmured, looking down at me with tears in his eyes. "I can't do it . . . can't even try to push you away. I don't want to hurt you. Don't want to fight with you either."

Of course he didn't. I wasn't meant to stay here and work this out with him. He and his wife needed to work things out, not us. I crossed my arms and murmured, "Well, we don't have to fight. No use fighting anyway."

He nodded and looked away. "I don't want this life for you. Didn't want you to fall for me because I knew what it would bring." His voice softened like suddenly now he had a conscience.

And it probably would have been better to just walk away, but I had to know, was ready for the closure that would destroy me. "How did you know what it would bring?"

"What are you asking me?"

He knew damn well. "I'm asking if you love her! If you knew you were still in love with her when you made love to me. Because you've kept a shrine for your wife in this house the whole time, Jameson."

"She's not my—"

"She *is*," I hissed, slamming my hand down on the dresser. "She's alive. And you didn't get a divorce, Jameson. So, she's yours. And I'm not."

"That's where you're wrong. You'll always be mine," he growled back immediately.

I scoffed and then locked eyes with him. "Did you know?"

"Know what?"

"Did you know that you were making me a mistress? Did you know she was alive?"

"Mia—" He was going to console me, but I didn't want any of it.

"Did. You. Know?" His answer was all that mattered to me now. "Yes or no?"

39

Jameson

I KNEW I'D LOST her the second I saw her standing in that doorway, the door open to the part of my life I didn't want her to see. And then she asked that question, the words slicing through me like a damn blade, lethal and aimed to gut me.

Her shoulders were squared, her jaw tight with emotion, but her honey eyes normally filled with such warmth had already left me. They were hollowed out from something worse than rage. Heartbreak and betrayal filled them now. I'd thought I could push her away by acting like what we had was a damn affair, but seeing her pain was too much.

Her gaze held mine, her arms crossed over her like a shield against me as she waited for an answer.

Yes or no?

We let the silence stretch, let my decision hang in the air.

I wanted to lie, to tell her I'd just figured it out too, to shield her from the woman that Lex was, from the man that I had to be, from the life that came from being a Diamond.

It was filled with power struggles, deception, and vicious strategy.

Mia wasn't like that.

She put love and joy first, unflinchingly, over power and prestige. She was honest even when it was hard, real even when it was uncomfortable to be.

I loved that about her. That was the damn problem.

I was in love with her, so in love that I couldn't lie, that I had to tell the truth and let her walk away from it. From me.

Did you know? Yes or no?

"I suspected that she was still alive. Yes." That one-word affirmation had me wincing and shutting my eyes tight, like it hit us both in the gut with its finality. I knew what it meant. I knew she'd never forgive me as I opened my eyes to tell her, "Fuck, I told you not to fall in love with me, baby."

She smiled softly, but it was so sad as one tear slid down her cheek. "And I told you not to worry, Jameson. Didn't I? But I didn't mean it, because I fell so in love with you that I'm still standing here, in your wife's room, hoping you have a damn explanation."

What could I say? She couldn't want this. She shouldn't have wanted any of this, and I'd kept her here long enough. "I don't have a good enough explanation for you, Darling."

"Will you even try to give me one?" Her eyes pleaded with me.

Fuck. It took all I had not to give her what she wanted. What I wanted too. "I can't, baby. I just can't."

Her chin wobbled before she straightened and took a deep breath. "Then tell me for how long."

"I always suspected. Didn't know for sure until after the Diamond event."

"How did you know?"

"Val admitted she told Trent, another one of her lovers, about your going to the club. He's the only one who could have leaked that to O'Connor's men." I sucked on my teeth, still furious with myself that I hadn't bagged Trent earlier. I'd known he'd flipped for some time, but we hadn't seen him as a threat. And he probably really hadn't been except for the fact that O'Connor's men didn't have smart leadership now.

They floundered and killed themselves off by approaching our Sanctum.

"We dug and got actual footage of Lex that night." It was footage I hadn't wanted or pursued until then. It put the decision to kill her on me once and for all. Without footage, I could have let her just drown in her decisions to save her family company with Paolo. Now, I had to consider if killing my daughter's mother was necessary.

She'd made the move now after we sent Val to Paolo to deal with.

The word was out that we knew, that it didn't matter if Lex was in hiding anymore because we wouldn't partner with Paolo's cartel or Wilshire either way.

She could have taken the high road and fled, but Lex consistently chose the low one. She'd come to my home for a final showdown.

"So you knew when you told me to put Franny first?" The tears filled her eyes then, and I took a step toward her, but she backed up, not wanting me to touch her.

Lex had been planning for years, but her plans never were perfectly laid out. She hid in the shadows of another man's bed, thinking she could make it all work out in the end.

That woman never thought of anyone but herself.

Lex knew the damage she caused. It's why I told Archer not to have her anywhere near Mia. I swallowed it down, my throat tightening around the deception. I wanted to protect her and shield her from what I'd suspected. She didn't deserve to be chained to this world I'd been born into, one where a woman would abandon her family for a partnership and bring it back like a prize.

"I couldn't be sure, and it's not your job to be burdened with the situation unless I'm absolutely certain that it's going to affect or devastate Franny."

"My *job*?" she asked, her voice almost shrill. "If this is just about my job, then I think our little girl will be fine so long as her mother and her father don't have ulterior motives."

Our little girl.

Not just mine. Because that's who Franny was to us both now. Even if Mia didn't see that.

I frowned. "That's it? You're not going to ask about how her mother being home might affect her or—"

"Is that really my place here if it's just a job? Or better yet, is it my place when her mother's home, Jameson?"

"Your *place*? You do it all the time either way, Mia," I bellowed, even though I knew that wasn't the thing I wanted to argue about. I wanted to argue that it was her place, that she was more of a mother than Lex would ever be, that she didn't just have a job here, she had a fucking family. She was my damn family, and still I saw her slipping through my fingertips so fast I couldn't catch her.

"Maybe I questioned how things would affect Franny, Jameson, because I thought you trusted me to do that," she threw back. "But now I see you didn't really trust me with anything at all. You weighed this whole scenario in your mind without ever bringing it to my attention. You freaking hid it, actually. So, I'm not a partner or a trusted nanny. I'm a pawn. And I won't be that. Especially not now, considering the *threat* has been neutralized, has it not?"

That was the real blow. We both knew it. I reeled back like she'd smacked me, and tears welled in her eyes. "Are you quitting on me, Mia?"

"In order to quit a job, you have to have one in the first place. This wasn't a job. This was witness protection with benefits, I guess. And I'm done with it. But if that's the way you want to spin it, I *am* quitting. Consider this my resignation effective immediately."

"Mia, you can't— Just give me some time. Let me talk to . . ."

"Your wife?" She raised an eyebrow at me.

I took a deep breath. "Please let me work this out."

"Do what you have to, Jameson. I'm sure I won't be able to leave here until you tell them I can anyway. But just know I want to, that you gave me a reason to when you withheld all this from me." She walked toward the door. "And know that when I told you not to worry about me falling in love with you, I meant it. Because, quite frankly, falling out of love with you today was as easy as me swinging open this door."

With that, she walked out of the room, and I roared in anger, ripping it apart. She didn't come to check on me. I knew she wouldn't. She had no reason to.

40

Mia

I HEARD THEIR VOICES on the other side of the wall as I pulled my duffel from the closet. He may have told me to stay, but I wasn't listening to anyone anymore.

Instead, I was just listening to their damn conversation in his office.

He must not have cared at all if I heard. He had to know I could, and yet they argued viciously with a passion that only two people who loved each other could have.

"Did he make you do this, or did you come up with it yourself?" Jameson asked her like he was spitting vitriol.

"Jealousy doesn't suit you, Jameson." Her words slithered through me and sliced at my heart.

"Jealous?" Forget the vent, his bellow could be heard through the walls. "Do you even hear yourself? You think I'm jealous after years of you acting *dead*?"

"Don't be dramatic. I did what I had to do, Jameson. You pushed me to it."

"Pushed you? Had you asked, Lex, you would have known the plan all along was to build ties with the FDA and that import checks were inevitable. Instead, you packed up and left your daughter and your husband for a better partner."

"My duty tied me to it. Think of *my* turmoil."

"You left."

"Yes, because you wouldn't help Wilshire, Jameson! God, you sat there like a doormat while I was pregnant, and I had to conjure up the plan myself. I *had* to leave you and Franny for my parents' company. I put in years of planning, and it would have worked if you hadn't—"

"It never would have worked because your family's business was embedded in a scandal so big they couldn't get clean. They still aren't."

"So, help me. Help us. Paolo is willing to give you a cut. Think of the money you'll make. Think of how happy we could all be." My stomach rolled with her logic, with the idea she could get her family back so easily after leaving them for so long.

"You think I sat like a doormat? I fucking restrained myself from putting us in the line of fire by being a parent and dedicating myself to making the Diamonds what they are today."

"Had I known this was your plan all along—"

"You didn't, because you never confided in me about your fucking company, Lex. You never wanted a real relationship."

"Well, I could now. That's what I want now anyway. If this is what you were aiming for, Paolo and I—"

"Do you think I give a flying fuck about Paolo and you?"

"Fine. Act like you don't, my love. It doesn't change the fact that I'm back. That we're married. That Franny *needs* her mother, right? I'll be a good wife, and if you want me to stop seeing Paolo, I will. Just let them have a warehouse or two a month. It would make the Diamonds stronger and save my family's company. It's really the only way at this point." She sounded defeated.

"Why did you fake your own death, Lex? You thought if you were gone I'd partner with Paolo?"

Even I could hear that she shouldn't have answered that

question but she did, as if she were proud of it. "Well, of course. I knew you were mad at me. I knew we'd gained a lot of enemies. What better way to lose them than to get rid of myself? It afforded Paolo the perfect opportunity to ask for help from you . . . but you wouldn't even meet with him. Not until the academy incident."

"What the fuck are you saying?"

"Oh, Jameson. Don't make me spell it out. I'll come back to you if that's what it takes. I could be so good to you and Franny. You understand?"

"I don't want you fucking back after you ran to Paolo, Lex. I will never want you back."

I heard her scoff as my stomach rolled. "Oh stop with the jealousy, Jameson."

His growl of frustration had me leaning in closer to hear what he would respond with. "I don't care about you and another man, Lex. I've said it time and time again." His visceral anger was loud.

"And yet you're yelling like you do." She was right. I thought the same, thought that his anger was much too palpable for a man who didn't care, who was apathetic.

"Because you can't understand the concept that this isn't about you or him."

"No. It's about us," she told him. "I realize now that Paolo shouldn't have sent those men to the academy to get Franny to prompt a meeting, Jameson, okay? I am sorry about that. We'll make it up to you."

My body ran cold at her admission, that the man she loved had actually been the one who'd orchestrated that shootout.

I heard a scuffle and then Jameson growl, "I should fucking kill you."

"A gun to my head, Jameson?" She laughed. "Really? Go on then . . . Shoot the woman you know you love."

And I waited to hear what he'd do, what he'd say, if he'd act.

"I can't." I heard his voice break, and something in me broke too.

I didn't want him to pull the trigger, but she was right. He still loved her, and that thought made me sick, so sick I couldn't stay another second. I ran from my room with my packed bag, even leaving my plants behind. Yet, I halted in front of Franny's door. It crushed me to consider not saying goodbye to her. How could I when we'd been through so much already? When it was me and her against her dad, trying to get to the country club or trying to get a bunny? When it was her and me in a crawlspace hiding, or her and me standing our ground after gluing jewels on her dad's Rolex?

My hand reached for the knob, trembling.

But I didn't touch it.

I couldn't.

Franny came first. Always. And telling her I was leaving would have broken her. I touched the wood of the door and murmured, "I'm so sorry, Fran."

But her door opened quietly and there she stood. A stoic frown on her face. "Are you leaving, Mia Darling?"

I knelt down beside her and pulled her in for a hug. "I have to for a little, okay? I need to think, but I promise I'll come back, Fran."

She sighed and pulled away from me before she pouted. "Somehow I know this is daddy's fault. So, heart-in-pinkie promise, okay? You have to let him figure it out."

I tried my best not to start crying then, gulping back the sobs building in my throat. I held out my pinkie and locked it in hers. "Heart-in pinkie-promise, Fran. Now, back to your room until morning, okay?"

She nodded and gave me another hug before she turned on her heel. I closed her door behind her, not wanting her to see my tears fall as I hurried down the hall to Archer's post. "I need to leave, Archer. And you need to take me. Please. Take me somewhere he won't find me."

"Mia—" He was about to object.

"Please." The sob that ripped through me was guttural, tangible, and so raw that I covered my mouth to try to muffle it. "Just for a few days. I need to get away from here and think."

He exhaled like it hurt and warned me, "Only a few days."

I nodded, tears streaming now as I patted Malek, who was whining next to me with his body pressed close. He knew as much as I did that something was very wrong.

That I didn't belong for another second at the Knight Estate.

Archer had Xavier pull a car around, and then we disappeared into the night without a trace.

41

Mia

ONLY AN HOUR OR so had passed when the first call came in on my phone. Archer made sure to disengage whatever tracking device was embedded in it, and I turned off the location for good measure.

"He's going to find us one way or another." Archer sighed inside my room at the hotel we were staying at.

"I know." I nodded, my voice sounding so stupidly weak that I hated even talking. "I just need time."

Archer grunted as my phone beeped with a text.

Darling Mia, you left without a word. You expect me to accept that?

Yes. We both know we need time apart.

Give me one good reason why I'd allow that.

Your wife who is very alive is the perfect reason. You should have told me.

He called again and I ignored it again, scoffing at him for trying.

"He's going to keep calling."

"And I'm going to keep not answering," I informed him, clinging to the anger in me so I didn't break down.

Jesus, baby. Answer.

She's not a reason. I told her we're getting a divorce immediately. No reasons are going to keep me from you. I walked into your room and knew it immediately. You belong here. So, I don't want a reason. I want you back.

I need time . . . to myself. I thought I had your trust.

You do. I'm sorry, baby. I am. I was trying to protect you.

Fuck, Mia. Turn on your location. Where are you?

Don't come looking for me. You won't find me.

I'll scour the world for you until I do.

I don't want to be found.

Too bad. I'm not going to spend another second without you.

You can and you will, because I can't be there with you and your wife.

Another call. Another ignore.

If you'd pick up your phone, I could tell you that she's gone.

It doesn't matter. Just make sure Franny is okay and that you feed my plants until I'm ready to come back and get them.

I won't feed them. The dirt is going to dry. They'll die.

How dare he? He knew how much I cared about them. Two seconds later, he followed up with:

Damn it. You know I'm going to feed them. But they'll miss you. I don't talk to them the way you do. And the dog and that bunny you let Franny get miss you already too. They'll all be moping around the house tomorrow with Franny.

How is Franny?

She's asleep, but tomorrow she'll be confused, Mia. Our house isn't a home without you, and we want you back here.

You'll find a new nanny for her. She'll be okay. I'm just the teacher she'll miss for a little.

No.

You're not just the teacher.

You're just everything to us. You're everything, and I'm not letting you go. Tell me where you are and we can talk in person.

No. Stop texting now. We are about to have dinner.

Who is we?

My phone rang again, and I contemplated if I should block him. Then Archer's phone rang, and it was clear that Jameson had figured out the accomplice in my escape.

Tell me where the hell you are right now, Mia. Or when I find you, I will dismantle that man from head to toe and wrap each piece of him up in a damn box for you as a keepsake.

Archer was looking over my shoulder. "That's definitely not happening. I'll be fine."

He said you won't.

He knows I will, Mia. I never lie.

"Okay, he probably will, but don't worry about it." Archer chuckled. But his eyes grew serious. "He *is* starting wars for you, Mia. The whole cartel back East that Paolo manages might end up completely wiped out now that he knows who orchestrated the school shooting and Trent coming to our event the other night. Crime wars always end in a hell of a showdown. If you want him to calm down, you should let him see you."

"He doesn't deserve to, Archer," I almost screamed, and then I shut my eyes to stop from breaking down. "I love him. You get that? I trusted him to trust me too. I told him I was ready for all this, and he was supposed to believe it. He was supposed to be ready with me being ready. Does that make sense?"

Archer rubbed at his jaw. "He doesn't trust easily, Mia. You can see why now. Lex fucked with him for years and years."

"I know." I sighed and pushed the food away that Xavier had brought us. "But he's let his past bleed out and drown the future he could have had with anyone else. I . . . maybe him and Lex are better together. Maybe they can rebuild their family and—"

"No." Archer stopped me and glared. "Think about Franny. Think about that house. Think about him and you. *Adamantem infractum manet* means that diamonds remain unbroken, but that's because they don't fold under pressure. They don't break, even when the world wants them to."

"I'm not a Diamond."

"Of course you are. He made you a Sanctum, Mia. Don't you know?"

His words sliced at my heart and brought tears to my eyes. "Why though? Why me, when he can't trust me? His wife wasn't even—"

"His wife wasn't you." I hadn't known if Jameson's words were true just a few nights ago, if he meant I was his and he was mine, but hearing he'd claimed me as a Sanctum solidified it.

I sat there in silence, not saying a word to Archer . . . but I felt my place with them all, felt my heart settle where it should, beside them.

I was different from my parents and the town I grew up in. I wouldn't stay silent when I knew things were wrong. I wouldn't be quiet when I was ready to be loud. And Jameson accepted that. He wanted that from me. And I wanted it from him too. I wanted all of this. Him. Franny. The Diamonds.

"Do you think he'll learn to? Learn to trust me?"

"I think he already does, he just has to *realize* that he does. I also think he's blindly in love with you, and men like him do desperate things when they're in love. He didn't know for sure about Lex. He was a damn wreck, Mia, on what to do. You know that."

"He still should have confided in me."

"I think this is going to be his lesson on what happens if he doesn't in the future."

I sighed and tried not to cry, tried not to feel betrayed.

"I'm going to go take a call from Hades, which is going to equate to getting my ass reamed out, so take some time to think about it while I'm on the phone, please. Because I'd like to have a less torturous death than the one they're planning for me at the moment. If not for me or him, for Franny," he said, patting my shoulder. And then he murmured, "And forgive me for letting these women bombard you here, but they couldn't be stopped."

And he opened the door to let Rosy, Pink, and Olive in.

I cried then.

42

Jameson

"WHERE THE FUCK IS my darling?" I yelled, launching everything off my desk while Hades and Cal sat there like this was normal behavior.

"You *know* where she is. In good hands," Cal taunted. I whirled and stormed toward him, but Hades was up to step between me and my brother.

"Archer's got her, and she is safe. You need to handle this shitstorm instead."

The shitstorm meant nothing if Mia left, because I knew I wouldn't recover. I wouldn't be able to be the man I needed to be for Franny or anyone else without that woman in my life. "I'll never forgive Lex for this." I shook my head and shut my eyes to try to block out her betrayal.

"I know, Jameson. We all know." Cal sighed and removed his wingtips from my table without me having to tell him or shove them off.

I sat down beside him, letting go of my anger and instead feeling the weight of the world bear down on my shoulders. "And if Mia doesn't forgive me . . ."

"We know what happens in that case too."

"What?"

"Even if Mia *does* forgive you, the East Coast need a . . ." Cal cracked his knuckles. " . . . reorganization. You also need to figure out what you'd personally like to do with Lex and Paolo. Sooner rather than later. I realize Mia's your priority, but—"

He was focused on the nation and our connections, but I was only focused on my family. That's who Mia was to me and Franny now. I had to make her see that. "She's not understanding what I did. It wasn't about her trust." I pulled at my hair and slouched inward, disappointed in myself that I hadn't done the one thing she wanted. She wanted me to be real with her, to not hide a damn thing. And why wouldn't she have wanted that when her parents had hid her turmoil from everyone?

Fuck. I wanted to tear them apart too. Everyone who'd hurt her needed to pay.

Including myself. She was making sure I suffered by not letting me see her, though.

"Are you listening to me?" my brother asked.

"I just need her to know that I'm fucking sorry, but it was for her own—"

"Good? Safety?" He leaned back and put his feet back up, all relaxed without a damn care in the world. "Mia doesn't care. She wanted your trust and love rather than your protection. Relationships 101, don't hide your very alive wife from your girlfriend, you dumbass."

"Shut the fuck up." I shoved his feet off hard.

Nothing fazed my good-for-nothing brother, though, because he went on irritating me. "Fine. I don't want to deal with you anyway. Just give me a decision on what we're doing with Lex and Paolo. Especially Lex, since the senator's holding her."

Killing the mother of my child wasn't something I could do. I knew it and so did she, though a bullet in her head was what she deserved. Instead, she'd been thrown in a holding cell after a call to the senator.

"Or I'll never give you a decision on her. She can fucking rot in there." Her lies and deceit were worth a death sentence, and she knew it.

Lex's plan fell through over and over. She'd left me, hoping Paolo would help, but when that fell through, her only hope was removing herself from the picture. I wasn't going to partner with Paolo while she was alive, and she knew it.

Yet her pivoting and faking her own death in hopes Paolo could sway me then didn't work either. And she was so wholly committed to saving her family's legacy that she willingly yanked half her teeth out to disguise another burn victim as her.

All with the help of Paolo, who she'd strung along since high school. His love for her would be his demise. Paolo was never good at hiding a damn thing, and his fear of losing her and the remnants of his cartel caused him to fumble and slip up in his meeting with me with just that line.

Had they stayed quiet, I would have left them to their own downfall and devices. Now, I only cared about getting her out of my life and out of Fran's.

She had been here, had talked with Franny, had upended everything I'd built for my daughter and myself in the last few years while showing no remorse at all except when she thought it would sway me.

"Look, the senator wants us to figure out a solution with her and Paolo." Cal smirked at me as he asked, "Sure you don't want to take your wife back and just smooth out all the waters?"

"Fuck. You."

Cal shrugged. "Figured. Start a war for Mia, then?"

"She's worth it. I'd burn down the damn nation and all our ties too if it meant keeping her, Cal. I love her."

He nodded and let the words sink in. He glanced over at me and smiled. "Happy for you, bro. Don't keep messing it up with her then. Be real and be honest. Mia needs that." Then, he clapped his hands together. "Enough of this emotional shit now. Paolo's done, and Lex should be too. We're going to have an issue with the whole East Coast by the time you're done." Cal was considering the fallout. "And international trade. The Ruiz family has ties even now."

"You think I should care?" My eyes were closed as I asked the question, but I opened them just to take in my brother.

The smile across his face was now diabolical. "I think I'm going to enjoy watching them be destroyed. I intend to go East to rub it in their face too."

"What happened to diplomacy?"

"I lost it back somewhere between a knife being thrown at me and Fran thinking that Lex has any place near her in Paradise Grove."

I winced at the reminder. "Fran thinks her mom is home." I fisted my hands on my thigh. "How the fuck am I going to explain that?"

Cal walked over to me and pulled a stress ball from his pocket to hold out for me. "Take it. You're going to need it this next month, because you're going to have to tell Fran her mom died. And we're going to have to deliver on that."

For three days, they held me back from going to see her. Olive, Pink, Rosy, Archer. All of them.

Or she did.

I'd tracked them down to one of the Hardy hotels but had been informed that Olive would make her husband lock it down if I tried to enter.

I did anyway.

And Dimitri caught me. That fucker.

He claimed he was protecting my own Sanctum from me, and not one damn person argued with him.

"Daddy, you seem mad that Ms. Darling is gone," Franny told me the next night.

Rosy had been doing most of the nannying with my mother throughout the day. She glared at me every time she could though. Even my mom scolded me: "Make it better, Jameson, or so help me God I won't forgive you—and I forgave you for even your own father's passing."

Great.

She'd turned my mother against me.

"I'm not mad, Fran Bran. Just anxious for her to come home."

"Then you should probably send more flowers, because she wouldn't have left me and our bunny unless you made her *really* mad."

That night, I sent not just hundreds, I sent thousands of flowers. Every type of flower in that dark-pink color she liked. Then I called and called, but she ignored every one of them.

Stop sending flowers.

Come home and talk to me then. Or let me into that hotel.

I need time.

Time is about to be up. I am going to break into that hotel.

Dimitri said you already did and he stopped you.

You've turned all my friends against me.

My mother even.

And my daughter.

Franny would never turn against you.

She already has. She's suggested I send you a pink car, and I will tomorrow.

Don't you dare.

I did anyway. The car arrived the very next day.

She threatened to never speak to me again if I didn't give her a little more time, and I was scared enough that I held back.

I held back seeing her, but held nothing else back.

I even told her Franny missed her and sent her damn pictures of that stupid bunny.

And I killed Paolo.

And tortured him. Didn't send her pictures of that, though.

The man begged for his life, saying that he never meant

my daughter or my lover harm. He hadn't known she was a Sanctum.

"You knew my daughter was, though. For that, you'll suffer."

"I can pay you billions, give you hundreds of women and daughters if you spare me—"

"The revenge I'm seeking isn't worth billions. My revenge is fucking priceless because you threatened them. My woman. My daughter. My Sanctum. You get that, right? No Untouchable and no Sanctum should ever be threatened. *Adamantem infractum manet*, Paolo."

"It wasn't me. It wasn't me." He cried and cried, but I didn't care. My men brought in the acid and my knives.

I stopped listening to him and got to work.

43

Mia

After cars and flowers and sorrys I didn't care about, Jameson texted me the one question I knew I couldn't ignore.

I love you. You know that, right? I wanted to say it in person. In bed. With you wrapped around me, Darling. But I need you to know that.

Please tell me . . . Are you ready?

Was I? Could I be? Could I forgive him? Could I forgive myself for not building his trust in me enough?

I may not have had my parents or my hometown anymore, but I had something better here. Archer had practically risked his life to be here, and I knew Olive and Dimitri were barricading Jameson out on the daily. Rosy stocked the hotel fridge, and Pink threatened bodily harm to anyone who hurt me further.

Sometimes family wasn't the people who gave you life, but the people who chose to be in yours and support you through the best and worst times. Their love was intentional, their support a choice, and their acceptance the reassurance I so desperately needed.

They were the people that chose me, and I chose them. And I wanted him to choose me too. Maybe that's what hurt most. He'd chosen not to confide in me when all I wanted was for him to feel safe doing so.

"It's probably time for me to talk to him, huh?" I asked Xavier. Archer had gone to get us food, and Xavier normally sat at the table reading.

He frowned at me, and the color had seemed to drain from his face. "Now?"

I sat a little straighter at the oak table where I was fiddling with my water glass. "Probably sooner rather than later, right? Are you okay?" I studied how beads of sweat were starting to form on his forehead.

He shrugged like he wasn't sure what to say, but his eyes darted to the door in a way that had my eyes darting there too, and my mind going on high alert. Xavier was always reserved with me, but I blamed it on his unequivocal veneration for Jameson, nothing more.

He patted my shoulder as he stood, and then I felt the weight of something heavy fall into my lap before he walked past me to go to the door, open it, and then turn and say, "Sorry, Mia."

And there stood Lex. Her face was tight with tension, with bags under her eyes, and the red dress she'd worn days ago was still on her. Her hair was messier, and I wondered if she'd been locked away all this time. Even if she had, she stood tall and rolled her eyes at Xavier's apology. "Go do something else, Xavier. You're going soft."

He hung his head and walked right out of the hotel, leaving me even as I called after him.

When Lex turned to slam the door, I slithered my hand down quickly to feel the metal of what he'd dropped in my lap.

A Glock.

A weapon of defense against the woman he knew I would have to face down.

She turned to take me in, and I steadied my breath as I sat there, hiding what might be my lifeline against her in my hand but sliding my finger onto the trigger.

Her blue eyes were glassy, wide, and glued to me. "Happy Xavier could give us some time alone. Thankfully, his watch gave me access, and I had a few guys the senator lined up to get me out of that stupid holding cell. So, now it's just me and you again to discuss a few more things."

"He shouldn't have," I blurted out. "I'm sure he's calling Jameson right now."

She rolled her eyes and took a few steps into the room. My hand tightened its grip.

I had to be ready.

She touched the bedsheets and then the TV, taking in my living arrangements. "Xav won't do a damn thing. I've been paying him for his girlfriend's handbags so he can get fucked for three years now."

"Okay," I said slowly, and then, "Why are you here?" Archer had told me earlier this week she was unhinged and they had her locked up. So, I glanced behind me and considered how far I could fall out of this window. Would I survive a four-story drop just to get away from her?

"Jameson needs to see reason, and I guess you're the only one who can talk him into that. God knows he's not talking to me." She gestured at her dress like he was the one who'd betrayed her by locking her away.

"He put me in jail, can you believe that?" A shrill laugh tumbled from her lips.

"I don't know how I can help you, Lex."

"My name is Alexandra Wilshire to you," she spat, pointing a bony finger at me. "I'm an heiress to a billion-dollar pharmaceutical company. A woman no man should turn down. Especially not Jameson. The partnerships I secure for my family will make us the equivalent of world *royalty*. He should want that for us. For Franny."

"Okay," I murmured, not sure what she was trying to prove. I didn't care about any of that. I cared about getting away from her and making sure the people I cared about were safe from her too. "I'm sure you'll be happy with those partnerships—"

"I won't!" She slammed a hand down on the granite TV stand and took another step toward me. "You did this, you know? *Ruined* my family . . . And you're going to fix it. For *my* family. You understand?"

"I don't know how I could—"

She set her purse down on my bed and pulled a gun from it to hold by her side. "He thinks you two love each other, and you can be perfect, but what's perfect, Mia? Do you really want this life?"

That ringing in my ears started. The feeling of being trapped flew in and pumped through my veins.

I squeezed the metal on my lap tighter but didn't point the weapon. I ran through the scenarios in my head. If I aimed the gun, I knew it had to be with the intent to kill. Would Xavier have left me a loaded gun? Did I have trust that his loyalty truly did lie with me secretly? Was this the family that I thought it was? "The life I built with Jameson and Franny would be—"

"No." She raised her gun. Her hand was steady, not shaking at all like mine would have. "You don't have a life with them. That was my family before, and it will be again now. He's going to help my business. He has to, Mia. Do you understand?"

"They're yours now? As opposed to a few years ago?" I couldn't help but say it, because she'd left Franny. I knew the pain she'd caused, and it was all for greed. For power.

"A year ago, I was solidifying a partnership that will help to make sure that Franny is always taken care of. I'm her mother, after all." She was talking fast and staring off, her brow sweating. I wasn't sure if she was even focused on me at this point. "Paolo promised me he'd be good to her too, and we'd get even better leverage with her."

"Paolo? Leverage with Franny?" I questioned, not understanding what she meant, not comprehending that she could possibly be insinuating what she was.

"He's the head of the cartel, and they have ties to men all over the world that would love to partner with him if he had a young heiress to offer too, Mia. Franny could help us expand."

"You're trying to offer Franny to another man? Your *daughter*?" Even with a gun pointed at me, I couldn't hide my disgust.

She continued, "Franny will be fine giving it up in a few years. Don't be ridiculous. Arranged marriages are—"

"She's *seven*."

"And so what?" Her voice was shrill. "She'll do what needs to be done for this family."

"You can't honestly think it's worth trading your daughter for a partnership."

"Of course she's worth it!" She tilted her head. "Everyone is expendable. I would have overturned that whole damn school to get to her."

"School?" The pieces fell into place slowly but surely. "That was *you*, not Paolo, who came after her at the school?"

"Paolo was a great scapegoat, though, don't you think?" She threw her head back and laughed and laughed. The moment she took her eyes off me, I raised that gun, ready now to meet her on equal ground as I stood too.

She didn't cower from my aim or from the gun in my hand. Instead, the smile across her face held nothing but condescending amusement. "Oh, Mia Darling. You realize you're pointing a gun at a woman who's been threatened time and time again. I'll even admit to you that it was me who planned the school shooting, me who had made sure that it looked like the Irish doing our dirty work, me who wanted you dead in the club too. It's me. Surprise." She singsonged. "Who else would it have been? Franny's Sanctum. Not one person was going to do what needed to be done against Jameson but *me*. So, I did the hard work, and now you're going to tell him to hand over our daughter while he gets over his puppy love for you. You'll do the right thing."

"Right for who?"

She set her hands on her hips, letting her gun tilt over them. "Everyone. You know it too. This is the right thing. You can't pull that trigger because you *know* my daughter belongs with her mother. And her father." She took a step closer, and I raised the gun higher. She didn't back away, just kept walking until we were only a foot apart. "*That's* a family."

"Sometimes that's true. Sometimes it's not," I whispered. Sometimes a family, sometimes a mother and a father, could break a child so far down that they never found their way out. I knew it because I'd experienced it. I knew what a family was supposed to be, and it wasn't her. "A family is the people who show up even when it costs them something. They show up and they stay, not because of a blood obligation but because it's their choice."

I knew that now more than ever.

"God, you're naïve. My parents instilled from a very young age that families are there to uphold the businesses, Mia. And I *have*."

"I'm sorry that's all they taught you."

"I'm not. Because I can do it. I will do it. For them and for me. So, go ahead if you want. Pull the trigger if you think you can." She held her thin arms out with her palms up.

I shook my head back and forth as I swallowed the fear that

was bubbling up inside me. My hands were shaking, but my gaze remained steady on her. "I think you should go."

Her laugh turned into a cackle. She even set down her gun to hold her stomach and laugh a full belly laugh.

"You're so fucking *weak*. I can't believe he fell for you, of all people. A woman who would never be ready to stand by his side. Or to be a mother to Franny. You'd never ever be ready for that or shooting me, you stupid little *darling* bitch."

"Just go." The ringing in my ears was getting louder. I didn't want to do it, didn't want to take her life.

"No. You're not ready, Mia. But I am. I always have been. I can be ready to fuck my husband and another man in one night for the good of my life. Mine." She barred her teeth aggressively now. "And I'll be ready to hand my child over too." She grabbed her gun. "I'm ready to hand her over and kill you, because I don't give a fuck if she's my daughter or"—she began to lift her arm to point the gun at me—"you're the love of my husband's life—"

I pulled the trigger. One shot. Loud. Lethal.

The gun had been loaded. Ready for me too.

"You're wrong, Alexandra. I'm more than ready to protect my family."

The ringing stopped. And so did that woman's heart.

I sat there with that gun in my hand for seconds. Minutes. Maybe hours.

Her blood spread across the marble flooring, turning it red where it used to be white.

I heard his voice from what felt like a mile away.

Jameson Knight had finally been let into the hotel, it seemed.

When I looked up at him, he appeared concerned, his five-o'clock shadow much darker, the shadows under his eyes more pronounced. My enigma of a man looked like he'd been put through hell since I'd last seen him.

Better than me, though, seeing as how I was soaked in blood in plant pajamas. "It was her," I told him, but my voice didn't really carry. It echoed around me over and over. "It was her, it was her. I swear it was her. Your wife . . . she's the one who came after us at the academy."

Jameson almost flinched at the conclusion, but then he said cautiously, "Darling Mia, I'm sorry, baby. I'm so sorry."

He did sound sorry, but I wasn't sure what for at the moment. I lifted the gun and turned it in my hands. "Sorry for what?"

"For not getting here faster." His breath seemed to be shaking. "For her getting out and to you. For her planning a damn shooting at the school you worked at. For you thinking I didn't trust you—"

"Don't be." I shook my head. "You know, I didn't know if this thing would work. If I would do it right. But I shot her straight in the heart just fine. She maybe wasn't even going to shoot me. I really don't know."

"She would have. She was . . . She killed a cop already today. It's okay," he said again, like that would make it all better. "You can put the gun down, Mia."

It shook in my hand as I stared at the black metal. "I shot her, and I'd do it again."

"Mia." He breathed my name, and hearing his voice alone consoled me. It shouldn't have. Not like this. Not here, kneeling in blood.

I closed my eyes and let one tear fall. "Can you save her?"

"Oh, baby, even if I could, I wouldn't." He took one step closer. "It's going to be okay, Darling. I promise."

"Heart-in-pinkie promise?" I whispered to him what his daughter would normally ask me.

He murmured, "Heart-in-pinkie promise."

"How can I believe you?" I touched the red liquid and then smeared it back and forth over my fingertips. "I'm worse than you. I killed her *mother*. Franny's mom."

"Goddamn it." He moved to come to me, but I raised the gun at him. His men standing behind him raised theirs at me.

He didn't even defend himself but rather turned to them and said, "You harm her in any way, I will not only kill you but your whole fucking family."

Weapons were lowered and holstered. All but mine. "You warn them for me, but don't warn me for yourself?"

"Darling Mia. Remember when you said you believed me. That you knew I wouldn't do anything to hurt Franny. I believe the same for *you*. You're our darling. My darling. My daughter's darling, baby. You didn't kill her mother because that woman wasn't a mother to her. You were. You are. You always have been."

"How will you tell her . . ." I choked on the idea.

"*We* will figure that out together. Let them clean this up and come home. You've done the job you needed to do."

The second tear fell then. "I killed her. She threatened to sell her, Jameson. She wanted more partnerships for her company, and I couldn't . . . I didn't know what else to do."

"Sometimes doing what's right feels like the hardest thing to do. You did what I couldn't, love. You did what had to be done."

"Why aren't you screaming and turning me into the authorities?"

"Because you're a Diamond now, Mia. We do what has to be done, and it might be behind closed doors, but we're proud. Be proud you saved our girl."

"I only work for—"

"You're about to marry into that role. They won't lock you up. You're my Sanctum too. Completely and utterly untouchable."

"Why would you make me that?"

"Because even if you weren't ready to love me, I was ready to love you enough for the both of us."

With that, he wrapped me in his arms and carried me to the SUV.

He carried me back to Paradise Grove.

He carried me home.

EPILOGUE

Mia

Adamantem infractum manet.

I knew what it meant now, because I didn't break after he carried me home. I didn't break when he washed the blood from me, and I didn't break the next day when I listened to him tell Franny that her mother was gone again.

Instead, I held that little girl while she cried in my arms and knew I'd done the right thing. You did what you had to for your family, and I knew they were mine.

Jameson only had to hold me through the night and whisper sorry again and again for me to forgive him now. I knew he meant it, knew he'd kept Lex from me to protect me. "Your world is mine now. Don't ever keep it from me again. Not if you want me to stay."

"It's all I fucking want. You're staying now even if I have to cuff you to the bed again, darling. I won't let you go."

"You want me here past the contract then?" I chuckled in his arms the next night.

"I want you here forever and ever."

I sighed with my head against his chest, thinking of all we'd been through. "Even knowing what I've done?" Because my heart wasn't completely over the fact that I'd taken another woman's life. Not because she'd be missed, but because Franny would miss the idea of her.

"Mia Darling, *especially* after knowing what you've done. Know why?"

"Why?"

"Because I don't want a perfect person, baby, or a perfect happily ever after. That's not what a marriage between us will ever be."

"A marriage?" I scoffed. "Getting a bit ahead of yourself, no?"

"No, because you're marrying me, darling Mia, even if I have to ask you every day for the rest of your life."

"Don't know if I want that when you're claiming I won't get my perfect happily ever after."

"You won't, but you don't want that either. You want the real parts, baby. Just like I do. And I'm going to enjoy those real parts the most, all the imperfect ones like when you and Franny are laughing at that stupid bunny for messing up my study, or when you're ignoring me because my daughter has all your attention, when you tell me you're not ready for something and you choose to lean on me instead. When you look at me with those pretty brown eyes and insist I water your plants, or when my men choose to protect you instead of me. I'm going to enjoy it . . . You know why?"

"Why?" I asked him with tears in my eyes now.

"Because the real you was made for me and no one else. I love you, darling Mia."

And since that night, he didn't keep a thing from me. He probably overshared every meeting and invited me even to the ones that were so boring I had to find a way out of them. Olive, Pink, and Rosy helped by excusing us all any time they could.

It took getting used to, being a part of a community I felt I belonged in. But Jameson embraced every part of me. He didn't ask me to play nice or to pretend things were fine if I was uncomfortable. He didn't keep doors closed or shut me out either. Not only did I have a seat at any table he sat at now, he was the one to pull out the chair for me and wait until I was seated to begin . . . always.

After Lex and what happened in that hotel room, I knew my life would change, but it changed for the better with him carrying me out of that place and carrying me home.

Fran had been waiting with a big smile and the bunny in her hands when we arrived. "Finally, daddy did something right," she told me and then turned to her daddy. "Mia might need another puppy after how you made her feel so bad she had to leave. A dog would make her feel better."

Jameson frowned but didn't dare ruin the moment by telling her no.

Instead, he asked if I did want a dog the very next day. Franny whispered in my ear to say yes and I chuckled before I told her we needed to wait a bit.

"Heart-in-pinkie promise we can talk more about it in a few weeks?" She made sure her dad was listening.

"*I* even heart-in-pinkie promise." Jameson held up his own pinkie and that had both Franny and me giggling.

It seemed that became Jameson's goal after that, to make sure we giggled and laughed every single day, to make sure I felt like I belonged there too. Even now, as he stood in his office, pouring himself two fingers of bourbon after putting Fran to bed, he asked, "Want anything, Darling?"

I was curled up on the chaise lounge, wearing one of his navy button-downs as I smiled softly at him. "Nope. Seems we have a clear schedule for the rest of the night."

He turned to come sit next to me, his sleeves rolled up to showcase those tattoos I loved so much. "You know better than I do. I hate checking that calendar."

He'd given me access to his personal schedule, all his bank

accounts, asset reports, and probably twenty other things I didn't need.

"By the way, did you happen to look at the contract with the Hardy Brothers and the new report we have for the East Coast?"

I blinked. "Um . . . yes?"

He bent down and brushed my cheek with the backs of his fingertips as he smirked. "I give you access to everything in my life and you find it boring, darling devil."

"It's just a lot of reading," I whined, but as I did, my phone lit up on the side table, and I saw Marian's name pop up. It was way too late for her to call. I sat up straighter and frowned. "My sister is calling."

Jameson moved me closer to him as if he knew I might need the support. "Answer it, baby."

"Marian?" I said her name quietly.

The breath she let out was all I needed to hear to look at Jameson with fear in my eyes. "I know it's late, but if you could . . . I . . . Can I take you up on that offer to fly me out of here now, Mia? I lost the baby, and he's . . . the weather is really bad. Really, really bad. He's so mad, Mia." She broke down then.

She didn't have to say the words. I stood without realizing it, gripping my phone. "I'll be there as soon as I can. Go to the airport. Now."

I ended the call, and Jameson was already up and pulling out his phone to command to someone, "Have the jet prepped within the hour. I want wheels up before midnight."

It only took me ten minutes to pack, and another ten to let Rosy know to care for Franny just for the night. Cal and Archer were in the SUV by the time we were ready and whipped open the door as we walked out. "What are you guys doing?" I frowned as Jameson held the door open for me to climb in.

"Jameson said we might be needed."

As he got in, I frowned at him. "We're not killing Felix,"

I told him, and then I looked at Archer and Cal. "You all understand?"

"I didn't say I was going to." Archer glanced out the window as the SUV started down the driveway. "We're coming along just in case."

"Right. Plus, I got to go to the East Coast anyway." Cal shrugged, rolling up his sleeves. "Jasmina's pitching a fit about her damn uncle." I knew now she was the one who stabbed him and who'd lost her uncle, Paolo, to Jameson's wrath.

"Well, she's in mourning."

"Like hell she is. She hated that fucker, and we all know it. She just wants to make a damn point. So I'm going to make one back."

Jameson rolled his eyes. "So much for handling the East Coast."

"I am going to handle it and her," Cal retorted, and then he looked at me. "You holding up okay? We're going to get you to your sister fast. We'll make sure she's all right."

I nodded and stared out the window. I let them talk business and was quiet most of the way there. We landed just after midnight in Asheville. Jameson had arranged to have men get her to the tarmac. She stood there in cutoff jean shorts and a white tank with the mountains winking behind her in the distance, a mess of a dark ponytail piled high on her head and heavy makeup over her cheeks.

It still didn't hide the bruises.

I ran down the stairs in my black maxi dress as quickly as I could but knew my guys followed. Archer, Cal, and Jameson stood beside us as I hugged her. She glanced at them as she pulled away from me and said, "You have a lot to explain, Mia."

"So do you, Mar," I told her before brushing my fingers softly over her cheek. "I missed you, sis."

Her eyes watered then, and I shook my head to stop her from

crying. "Weather was shit before, but I promise it's gonna get better, okay?"

She looked up to the sky and nodded twice before following us to the plane. Archer offered to help her up the steps.

"It's fine. I don't need the help," she told him.

But he told her back, "I know, but you'll take it anyway, huh?" And she let him help her.

Once we were all settled, I asked her, "Want to talk about it?"

"Not tonight." She stared straight ahead at all of the guys sitting a couple rows up. "Instead, you can talk about who you're with here and why they own a jet."

I sighed. "It's a very long story."

"Well, seems I'm going to have all the time in the world. So, you can start with the fact that your old coach is missing."

"What?" I frowned.

"Yep." She turned to me, and her hazel eyes sparkled with a bit of joy. "No one can find that man, and I'm guessing those men had something to do with it."

"Jameson Knight," I barked out his name, and he jumped in front of me before turning around with those blue puppy eyes.

"What'd I do?" he asked.

"What in God's name did you do to Coach Butkin?"

He didn't even attempt to hide it. "I asked you for a name, Mia. You know no one gets away with hurting my Sanctum."

"Jameson," I groaned, but what could I do other than chuckle?

Tonight, my sister was safe, my Franny was home, and my man was here with me, taking care of all of it.

The life I had with him wasn't normal or clean.

. . . but it was real, just how I had always wanted.

For a bonus scene of Jameson and Mia, just sign up for my newsletter here!

https://shainrose.com/newsletter/

And are you ready for more?! Callahan and Jasmina are on their way. Make sure to join Shain's Facebook Group to be the first to see the sneak peek: https://www.facebook.com/groups/shainroseslovers